AFTER HOURS

A. R. THOMAS

First Edition.
Editing: Claire Allmendinger at BNW Editing
Cover Designs: Lou J Stock
Formatting: A R Thomas
Proofreading: Katie Salt

DEDICATION

Because rules are meant to be broken.
Especially when they are over six feet tall, have bright blue eyes, and call
you pretty girl.

PLAYLIST

Dressed in White ~ TS Graye
Often ~ The Weekend
Dirty Mind ~ Boy Epic
Desert Rose ~ Lolo Zouai
Don't Play ~ OZZIE, THEMXXNLIGHT
Pain & Pleasure ~ Black Atlas
I Need ~ Maverick Sabre
Midas ~ Maribou State, Holly Walker
Tonic Water – Dazy Remix ~ Moglii, Novaa, dazy
Codeine ~ Solv
The Morning ~ The Weekend
Make Me Feel ~ Elvis Drew
The Best I ever Had ~ Limi
Best Mistake ~ Ariana Grande, Big Sean
Away From Me ~ CHINAH
Another Love ~ Tom Odell
Train Wreck ~ James Arthur
Blame ~ Grace Carter, Jacob Banks
Wildfires ~ SAULT
Strong ~ London Grammar
Falling Up ~ Dean Lewis

Swimming Pools (Drank) ~ Kendrick Lamar
After Hours ~ Maths Time Joy, Flores
Whatever You Want ~ Vasser
Had Some Drinks ~ Two Feet
Can't Pretend ~ Tom Odell
I Forget Where We Were ~ Ben Howard

CHAPTER 1

Lauren

"I've got to go. I don't want to be late." I slam my locker, leaving Amberley, my co-worker, in the staffroom, and hurry down the corridor towards the main reception as two women from housekeeping whip past, their voices low but abuzz with excitement. Turning, I stare at their retreating backs, perplexed by the stir our boss's presence has caused. It's all anyone has spoken about this week. How *The* Cain Carson-Ivory is visiting the hotel and staying to oversee its opening for the next few months. I've worked at the hotel for a month, and he is a hot topic. Luckily, I wasn't here when Carson-Ivory Hotels and Resorts took over, but I remember there was a similar energy when I started and how my colleagues gushed about working for Cain Carson-Ivory. I'd never heard of the man. I don't understand the hype, and meeting him is low on my list of priorities. If the gossip mill is true, then he is as rich as he is harsh. Many of the employees were let go. Some chose to leave, not wanting to work for a larger chain company, and one or two employees were frog-marched out of the main doors due to discrepancies that we mere front desk employees aren't allowed to know about.

The hotel was shut whilst it was redesigned with state-of-the-art technology, along with a new spa and swimming facilities. A team of designers had transformed the suites into luxury accommodation. It is the glittering crown of London's hospitality sector, boasting Michelin restaurants and a guest list that mocks the BAFTAs. It's the sweet shop of A-listers where my friend Amberley is concerned.

We hit it off on my first day, both fairly new to the hotel and eager to impress. I may not know of the owner, but landing a job at such a prestigious hotel demands nothing but the best. I'm a devoted member of staff and have adjusted to catering for London's elite, but Felicity, my line manager, is quite frankly a bitch in heels. If she can find anything, even the smallest detail, she is standing in wait, ruler in hand, ready to write us up and demean us. The woman is a drain on my sanity—haughty, rude and, unfortunately, my boss. I know my feelings about the woman are widely shared throughout the hotel.

As I approach the doors that bring me to the conference rooms and reception, I stare down at my pencil skirt and smooth it out, making sure I look presentable, conscious not to draw her attention my way, when the ornate wood bursts apart, smacking me full pelt in the face. The nauseating crack splinters throughout the corridor and resides in my teeth.

I cry out and stagger back until I knock into the wall, sliding down as I fall to my knees with a painful thud. "Fuck," I whine. Pain swells, seeping outwards and dragging against my nerve endings. It throbs until my head feels like it's ready to crack. My eyes pulse and each painful sensation has my stomach unravelling and threatening to spill from my lips. The ground sways, mocking my very gravity as I clumsily drop forward, clutching at my stomach. Being on all fours only sends more blood rushing to the one place that truly does hurt, my forehead. On a soft shake, I kneel up, touching the sore spot under my fringe. "Double fuck," I whimper at the egg-sized bump forming. It feels too big, tight, and achy underneath the light brush of my hair. "Oh god." Shakily I pull my fingers away, checking for blood. I expect my fingers to be laced with it, but my hands are clean. Sagging into the wall, I suck in slow but deep breaths to ease the nausea crippling me.

Hands tilt my chin. Another swipes my fringe as I blink in neatly suited legs and shiny expensive shoes. "Double fuck for sure," a deep voice sympathises. My eyes pull up to find concerned brown eyes, kind eyes. But he doesn't have my attention for long. No, it's the bristling man behind with an arrogant stance, looking down at me with disregard, that has my attention. He is ridiculously tall—or maybe he seems so because I'm plastered to the floor in an unattractive heap— with long legs and a wide chest that is inflating with increasing annoyance. His jaw is smooth but darkened. His lips are stretched into a grimace as he stares down a beautifully portioned nose and bolts me to the marble floor with a look lost in pity and irritation. The cool marble seeps into my bottom and cools my clammy palms. "Are you okay? Do you feel sick or lightheaded?" brown eyes asks, tilting my head as he inspects the growing bump. I frown, biting my lip, trying to take mental stock of my injury. My fingers find that same bump, my skin tightening uncomfortably. "It's some egg," he comments. I grumble and chance a look at the disinterested-looking man with his hands stuffed impatiently in his trousers, working his jaw as his blueish-grey eyes bore into mine with complete disregard. He sways, blotting in and out of focus in a kaleidoscopic twist. The light detail in the marble flooring swirls and ebbs as serene as open water, and both men bob along with it, inflicting me with a sense of seasickness.

"Sorry," I say, trying to stand, "I keep forgetting it's a

swing door." I chuckle, but it turns sour. "I feel a bit sick," I murmur, clutching at my stomach. I frown worriedly, because everything in my line of sight has lost all sensory control.

"You might be concussed." Gentle hands keep me steady. I lean into the wall and close my eyes, trying to dispel the horrible sensation swirling in my stomach. "You're pretty pale," he comments.

"That seems an unfortunate genetic, as so are her legs," arrogant ass drawls. My eyes spring apart as quickly as the door did. I may be concussed, but I'm sure I heard him right. My mouth drops open, and my eyes narrow.

"Excuse me!" I snap. How dare he. Who the hell does this guy think he is? I push off from the wall on a little wobble and stick my finger in his face. "There is nothing more unattractive than an egotistical man putting a woman down. Especially after he just knocked her over, you prick!" I shout. "You didn't even say sor—" I don't finish my sentence as a stomach full of vomit shoots out of my mouth and decorates his trousers and shoes. Slapping a hand across my mouth, I gulp loudly as I cough and wheeze amidst the strain of being violently sick, but it only bursts free from the flimsy prison of my fingers. I heave again, and he steps back just in time to miss another spray.

Amberley swans through and takes in the scene with a look of horror on her face as he, the moody one, leans down and breathes roughly, "You're fired!"

What? No!

I shake my head in disbelief—fingertips pressed to my parted lips.

His only response is to mockingly nod a 'yes.' His eyes spark. He's enjoying this.

"Cain, just take a breather. Have Justine send something," brown eyes placates. But the moment won't leave. It's here, in technicolour and ridiculing me in an expensive suit.

Cain? I stare at the man who just fired me. Cain Carson-

Ivory. He sneers, and I blink furiously to dispel the hot tears rushing to the surface.

"Fired?" I whisper, my voice cracking. "But I just started. I love this job. I *need* this job," I say to brown eyes as Cain, my boss, the owner, storms out, crashing through the same set of doors that caused this debacle. The loud bang has me flinching. I step to follow my boss, an apology hanging heavy on my tongue, but brown eyes cuffs my arm and holds me back. I twist around, blinking numbly, as I try to form words to express my regret. He wrinkles his nose, and I cover my mouth. "Sorry." My eyes fill quickly, the tears dripping down my cheeks in big fat hot blobs.

"You need a hospital. Come on."

I need a time machine. I want the world to swallow up the last few minutes and dispose of them somewhere undetected. Away from my boss.

"But my job." I puked on my boss. This is terrible. I lost my job. Panic surfaces and sinks its claws right into my heart, squeezing it at an unnaturally fast pace. I try to gain control of my breathing, try to breathe just a little deeper, but the claws unsheathe extraordinarily long nails that pierce and remind me that no amount of controlled breathing is going to make this any better. "I can't lose my job. I just can't." I used all my savings to secure my flat and furnish it. I left my hometown with two suitcases and a ton of heartache—not heartache, I conclude, humiliation and worry. I have no intention of returning home so soon. He'd never allow it.

My poky flat may be a far cry from the life I was led to believe would be mine, but I will take second-hand homeware over a deceitful partner any day. Or his corrupt father.

"Don't fret. I will sort it." He rubs my back as more tears run after the last lot.

"You will?" I whip my head up, but the motion sends me dizzy. "Oh god, I feel sick again."

"Sure thing." Brown eyes shrugs, unfazed by my boss's

temperament. "You really need to be checked over," he imparts sympathetically.

"Lauren. Are you okay?" Amberley rushes over and rubs my arm. "What happened?"

I lift my fringe. "Double fuck." She gapes.

"Yeah, double fucks all around." Brown eyes chuckles. "I'm Perry," he introduces himself, then resumes checking my pupils as he walks me back through the staff quarters and out into the private car park. I bite my lip to stop crying, and I throw my friend a panicked look, but she is too busy gawping at Perry.

"Do you want me to come with you?" Amberley says, as her eyes flash to the sports car we are headed to.

"No point in losing pay. I can take her. Can you inform her manager she is unwell?" Perry says, and my friend nods robotically as she watches in fascination. I can tell by the excitement leaking into her concerned eyes that this Perry guy is just as well known as our boss. He walks us the last few steps to the sleek car, helps me in and hangs over the door frame. "If you're sick in his car, he will literally never forgive you," he says, shutting me in. My friend waves sheepishly at me through the windshield as I stare back in confusion.

Perry joins me and closes us in.

"Maybe we should book an Uber?"

My suggestion is met by a blank stare. "Absolutely not. I've wanted to drive this thing for months. You're doing me a favour." He flashes me a bright smile.

The drive is uneventful, and by the time we arrive at the hospital, I'm feeling a little better. Perry escorts me inside, and we are seated after a brief chat with the nurse.

"I'm going to lose my job, aren't I?" I wring my hands and keep my face averted as Perry leans on his knees. I don't want to witness the pity on his face. It was already evident when my boss fired me back at the hotel—twice I caught his eye and saw him looking at me with the same kind of defeat one might view a vulnerable and cornered animal about to be eaten by a predator.

"Cain can be too quick to react. I mean, you did puke on his shoes." He chuckles deeply.

"He...you...I was knocked down. Look at my face!" I gape, pointing at my deformed forehead.

"I am. You're gorgeous, alien lump and all." He winks.

"Is it really that bad?" I ignore his compliment and slouch back on the uncomfortable waiting chair. I start messing with my fringe, suddenly conscious of the bump.

"I mean, you've got an impressive lump on your head, but your fringe covers it."

"What about the word idiot written there for calling my boss a prick?" I say, embarrassed. That particular moment has become stuck on repeat in my mind: the words as I angrily uttered them, the hostile shock on his face when he heard them, and the moment my stomach lost all control. It keeps playing over and over. How those few words had cut through his vacant interest and set it on a knife's edge. He went stiff, stood taller and broader as though he was carrying the entire hotel on his back, ready to launch at me, his face contorted in sharp rage. His teeth had snapped together before he ended it all with his parting shot. He'd been large and authoritative, with his deep and rich tone angled to wreak havoc at a moment's notice.

Perry laughs, loud and impressed. "I've got to admit, I've never witnessed anyone call my friend a prick before." He kicks back, hooks his ankles together, and knits his fingers behind his head. "I mean, other than myself." He snorts out a laugh.

"Please don't laugh. I need this job. I've not long moved here. It was hard enough securing my position when the hotel was taken over. Shit." I sigh, rubbing my temples.

"You know, you have a pretty vulgar mouth for front-of-house." That timbre—the slow, deep rumble has me stiffening. I slowly look up as my boss lowers into the chair opposite mine. He straightens his suit at his wrists and the bright hospital light glints off his watch and cufflinks. His feet are placed firmly apart. He's in steel grey from head to toe. Gone is the black suit from before. I swallow a blush. "You finally have some colour back in your face," he observes, his nostrils flaring with annoyance. His sudden appearance had led me to believe he was regretful of his behaviour back at the hotel, that some small part had niggled at him in my absence and resulted in him driving here to rectify the situation. However, his posture, the low but crisp way in which he speaks, suggests otherwise. His brow has left the soft curve of his face and is arched high in question. His lips have since twisted into a brutal sneer—add that to his well-built frame, and he is unnervingly intimidating.

"Shame that my legs don't meet your standards," I mutter.

"They're nicely bruised," he quips. I frown and look down. Lifting my skirt enough to see my knees are, in fact, scuffed and bruised. I look at Perry, who is giving him, Cain, a hard stare.

"No thanks to you two." I can't quite bring my eyes to meet my boss again. Perry, who is far more relaxed and easy-going, slings an arm around my neck and grins at me.

"Ah, don't be like that. You'd never have met me if I hadn't knocked you on your arse."

"Oh, so it was you!" I laugh shortly. My boss shifts in his seat and glares my way, nailing me to the chair. I go rigid and unhook myself from Perry's grasp, muttering about how long we will have to wait. I go from staring at my fingernails to picking at the seam on my skirt, but every now and then, I lift my gaze to find my boss's burning right back. The hairs on my neck pucker and stand to attention. My heart is still perfecting a scattered pulse, and when our eyes lock, my lungs collapse quicker than a punctured balloon.

"Miss Lauren Lindel?" I startle in my chair.

"That's you, alien head." Perry nudges me, and I giggle nervously. My boss is still staring at me. Eyes hard. Knuckles white as he works his hands against one another, cracking one of two fingers in the process. Why is he here? It's painfully obvious he would rather be somewhere else. His agitation overlaps his beauty and has those around him faltering upon inspection. I get up and move away, but stop and look back at both men. Suited, lounging, almost model-like in the waiting room. I hate to admit it, but I agree with Amberley. He's hot. It's all she has said since we started—how hot our boss is. Both of them are, in their own right. Perry is cheeky and roguish, Cain athletic, brooding and intimidating. I scan a look around and see women eyeing them up.

"I appreciate you bringing me, but I can probably make my own way home." I clear my throat and give them a small smile of thanks, hoping to God my boss takes pity on me and allows me to keep my job. He doesn't speak, even though his lips twitch to deliver words I'm sure I'm not ready to hear, and his jaw flexes in a way I know will only cause more upset. When his shoulders rise in agitation, I begin to step away. A shiver sweeps down my spine, and my eyes widen in concern that he may stand and humiliate me once more in front of these people. However, those large hands knit together between widely spread thighs, and he drops his head, watching me with thinly veiled dislike. I'm already walking away when I stop for a second time and look back at Cain—or Mr Carson-Ivory. "I'm sorry about." I point to his clothes, my cheeks burning hotly. I want him to like me. I need him to feel an ounce of sympathy for my predicament. Desperation burns brightly in my gut and has my insides squirming in fear. I need this job. I have an apartment, bills, and a loan to pay off. I can't return home. "The grey looks better." I hold my compliment in two loosely clasped hands and deliver it with a shameful gleam of hope in my eyes. I even grin when Perry laughs loudly and find myself flicking a look between them to try and ascertain my boss's mood. No words are spoken in response. His grimace doesn't falter, and those eyes that I know will have left many women melting and men baulking are an unwavering dagger to my chest. Sighing, I follow the nurse across the waiting room and through a set of locked doors, where she escorts me to another bay to wait for more tests.

CHAPTER 2

Lauren

It's a long wait from one room to another. When I'm finally given the all-clear, I'm shocked to find Perry is still waiting for me in the main accident and emergency room. "Oh, I didn't think you'd stay. It's been hours." I blush.

Perry jumps up and walks to me. "So, what's the verdict? ET on his way for you?"

"Haha. Mild concussion. Just got to take it steady. I feel a lot better minus the headache," I inform him, scanning the room for my boss, but I can't see him anywhere. I refrain from asking the only thing that has been on my mind since I left both men—do I get to keep my job?

"Let's get you home." Perry holds out his elbow for me to take. Tentatively, I slip my fingers through the small crook and tilt to look up at him, trying to gauge some sort of answer in his disposition alone.

"I can go back to work. I need some bits from my locker

anyway." I have no intention of going home. I need to make up the hours I've lost today. I angle for an answer, assuming that he and Mr Carson-Ivory have already spoken about my job, but his answer is as elusive as my boss's mood.

"You're one of those, huh?" He wants to know.

"One of what?" I slip my coat on and take his arm. He leans to unfold my collar and lifts my hair out of the way. I decide there and then I like Perry.

"Admit it, if your brain was hanging out, you'd still ask me to take you back to work." He sniggers, leading us outside.

I wrinkle my nose and remind myself I no longer feel sick.

Laughing lightly, he steers me down a ramp towards the car park. "I can't take you back to work," Perry informs me. His tone, the low bite to his words, and the soft but noticeable way he tightens his hold are heard loud and clear. I no longer have a job.

"He said no then?" Stopping, I turn to look at him, silently pleading for him to help me somehow. I can already picture my future employment asking why I left my previous job. I drop my head because he has no intention of answering. His eyes say it all. "Dammit."

"Cain's right. You have a filthy mouth." He chuckles and nudges me with his shoulder. "You don't look the type," he muses and purses his lips. "Your friend, on the other hand." He widens his eyes playfully.

I don't feel so playful. In fact, I want to cry until my throat feels bruised and my eyes are swollen. The need to flee is overwhelming. "Perry, I really appreciate you bringing me to the hospital, but I think I'm just going to make my own way home." My voice wobbles, and Perry winces. I start to walk away, desperate to put some space between us before I blub like a baby.

"Lauren!" he calls.

I spin around. "Good luck with the hotel. It's really

gorgeous." I throw him my brightest smile and half jog to the taxi bank. I can't believe I've lost my job.

—

I push my way into the apartment and throw my bag down, thoroughly pissed off with today. I'm noting it down on my calendar as the day of double fucks. I screw my face up and write underneath: Cain is a prick. Yes, he is! I even go as far as doodling a little cactus for good measure. I twist and stare at the small apartment I'm renting and purse my lips. I doubt someone like Cain-bloody-Carson-Ivory would ever be seen dead in a place like this. The small room comprises a small kitchenette and my sofa bed. It's a far cry from the luxury we deliver at the hotel.

Head throbbing, I go to my bathroom and find some painkillers, clutching them in my fist tightly as the pain ebbs and pulses. The distinct sound of *'I'm a hustler, baby'* rings through the apartment. Rolling my eyes at the ringtone Amberley set for herself, I take myself to my phone.

"Hi!" I chirp. I don't want to crack on the phone. So far, I've managed to keep it together.

"Are you okay?" Amberley's worried voice has me closing my eyes and biting my lip as tears, hot and angry, swell behind my eyelids and push their way past the weak defence to bead on my cheeks.

"Mmm hmm." Salty paths glide down my face, and I drop my head in shame as despair clings like a nasty form of bacteria to my tongue.

"I'm coming over," she declares, and the line goes dead before I can protest. I could do with the moral support. I decide to jump in the shower, dose myself on meds, and ice my bump before she arrives. When she does, she is carrying a bunch of flowers and has a sympathetic pout. "Oh shit." She grimaces at my head. Seeing her now has me tearing up so much so that I cover my face and sniff behind my hands. "Oh, hun. It's going to be okay." Flowers press into my hair as she pulls me in for a tight hug.

"I threw up on his shoes." I wince and strangely find myself laughing. Amberley's dark chuckle accompanies mine. "Everything is such a mess," I mutter.

"He didn't come back to the office after you left," she says flippantly and turns, looking for a vase.

"He turned up at the hospital," I blurt, still stunned at finding him sitting in the accident and emergency room in his designer suit, sporting one hell of a cold stare.

"What?"

"I know. He made another odd remark about my complexion, and when I came out, he was gone." I walk to the kettle, but Amberley shoos me away.

"Let me do this. You go and chill." I smile in thanks and pull a vase out from under the sink. "Perfect." She takes it from me. "Now go and sit down." I plop myself on my sofa and rest my chin on the back as I watch my friend moving about. "So, what did he say?" she asks, tip-toeing to reach the mugs.

"That I'm pale." I roll my eyes. I am pale, but that is beside the point. "Said I had unfortunate genetics," I grumble, still smarting.

"Fuck off!" Amberley's horrified face meets mine, and I nod slowly. I'm still mad about that.

"Yep, and then he said my knees were nicely bruised. What even is with that?" I scoff, getting comfy as she walks over with two mugs.

"He can't say that. He's your boss," Amberley snaps, glaring into her cup.

"Technically, the bruised bit was said after I was fired." I shrug and puff out my cheeks, sighing loudly.

"And before?" she argues.

"Well, I did call him a prick for saying I was pale." I eye her with a wince.

"Lauren!" Amberley cackles.

"I didn't know he was our boss," I whine.

"Oh!" she says, abruptly remembering something. "Felicity was knocked down a peg or two. Mr Carson-Ivory did this," she clicks in my face, making me jump, "and told her to wind her neck in." Her head tilts back as she laughs.

"Can he even talk to her like that?" I frown, thinking he sounds more and more like a prick as the day goes on.

"Who cares? She's a bitch," Amberley scoffs. "Lauren, I wish you could have seen it. Her face was a picture."

"I bet!" I grin, but my smile drops away when it causes my head to throb.

"You're going to challenge your dismissal, right?" She holds my gaze with interest, blowing into her cup.

Sucking in a breath, I give her a half smile. "I know I should, but I need to find another job in case it's refused, and that thought alone makes me feel exhausted." I doubt anyone who goes up against Cain Carson-Ivory walks away unscathed. "Would you dare take him on?" I can't battle the ego of two men born of money: my ex, Martin, and his father are more than enough.

Amberley shakes her head and relaxes back into the sofa. "No," she says quietly. "Meet me for lunch tomorrow, and I can help you pick your bits up unless you want me to grab them for you?"

"I'll come and get them. He's not scared me that much. Lunch sounds perfect, but you're paying. I'm jobless." I laugh.

"It's a date." Amberley twists, facing me. "I'm going to miss your face." She pouts, and I rest my head on her shoulder.

"I know. I loved working with you."

"Let's watch a film," she suggests, kicking her shoes off.

"Put a comedy on. You need a good laugh." I tuck my feet under me, and Amberley orders us a takeaway. We settle in for the night and giggle until our cheeks ache and my gut ceases to feel tight with worry. Even my headache passes.

I'm glad I was sick on his shoes. I hope I ruined them.

CHAPTER 3

Cain

"What the hell is that smell?" Justine, my assistant, coughs as I stalk into my office, my trouser leg cemented to my skin as vomit seeps past the barrier and slides into my shoe. I work my neck, as the tension in my shoulders has them rising at ninety degrees.

"Vomit," I bark, staring down in disgust at the remnants of some woman's stomach as it soaks into my Italian loafers. Crossing the room, I kick them off and dump them in the bin.

"You're not leaving those there. They stink!" Justine exclaims, standing up from behind the desk as I undo my suit trousers and rid myself of those also. "Okay…woah!" she splutters, averting her eyes.

I am leaving them and anything else that will remind me of the events that have occurred in the last ten minutes, including the uncouth woman whose pale and innocent face has plagued me on the short walk up here. My patience was already hanging by a thread when Perry injured the woman.

Slight, angelic, and shockingly rude, I'd taken in her petite frame with something akin to greedy surprise. Delicate fingers and narrow shoulders, her back dipped in a way that accentuated the curve of her arse, and her endless creamy legs that were fucking biblical: toned, smooth, and tarnished from her fall.

"I need you to get me a clean suit," I growl, shrugging the jacket off. I throw my phone on the sofa and stuff the jacket and my shirt in the bin. Where are my keys? The scent of sick wafts upwards, attacking my nostrils fiercer than any door. Curling my lip, I pull the bin bag over the clothes and tie it in a tight knot. "This is fucking ridiculous." I walk to the sofa and drop down in my boxers, cursing under my breath. Royce fucking Ivory, and now this. I was a hair's width from taking the one thing from him that kept him afloat, bar my mother. His business. It was so close to being mine I could almost taste the victory—until the vomit. The day was shaping up to be anything but successful.

Justine eyes me across the open space and quips her brow. Her mouth pinched tightly. "What?" I snap.

"I do hope you're not going to continue the rest of your meetings with your boxers hugging your cock like a pole dancer."

Chuckling softly, I lean forward and rest my elbows on my knees. "Justine."

"Boss?"

"Why are you looking at my cock?"

Eyeing me with distaste, she stands abruptly. "Oh, for heaven's sake, Cain, grow up." She purses her mouth and glares at me across the room. Her greying hair is cut into a short and stylish do, her long skirt is fitted, and the blouse she has on is tucked neatly away, making her look as formidable as me. "You have a suit across the hall, cock friendly." She strides to the door, disgruntled. "You're a prick," she declares over her shoulder.

"So, I've been told," I retort, unimpressed.

She really did call me a prick—right before she decorated my favourite shoes with puke. I lean into my hand and rub at the headache threatening to take hold. Pinching the bridge of my nose, I feel it begin to ease under the small amount of pressure I'm applying. I can't complain, not when one of my employees is probably in a considerable amount of pain after Perry barrelled through the door, knocking her off her feet.

She looked too damn good on her knees. Her skin was porcelain pale, the kind that flushes too brightly with the right amount of attention. The kind that blemishes if held too hard. The kind of skin that I could leave my mark on.

My phone pings with a text from Perry.

Patient looks pale. Might need some sexual healing. I stole your car. P

My heart lurches. It hadn't occurred to me that Perry would be attracted to her too. "Justine!" I yell, standing and stalking across the hall to my suite. "Cancel my meetings and drop me at the hospital."

The clinical essence circles me like heavy smoke. It clings to my skin and embeds into my suit, burrowing too deeply to allow me to win the war currently being waged on my mind. Stuffing my hands into my trousers, I stand on the threshold and draw in a deep breath. All I manage to achieve is to suck in everything I despise about these places. The atmosphere is alive with pain and impatience, the burning tinge of frustration that makes your hair stand on edge, and the continual wail of someone's cries. I hate it. I hate these places and the despair they bring. The gaping wound they leave when you entrust someone's life, only for them to return with tainted hands and unwelcome news—news too sour for any stomach to handle.

My stomach revolts at the memories whirring into motion and the unsteady stream of distorted images rolling across my mind's eye.

I find Perry almost immediately. But it takes me another moment or two before I make my way across the accident and emergency waiting room. His face sags into shock as I sit down. Guilt shatters his composure. I shake my head in warning. I am barely keeping it together. Coming here has cost me. He knows how I feel about hospitals. The turmoil I'm suffering by just being here will be insufferable for us both. And yet I have no explanation as to why I came.

The light and pained feminine voice cracks through my internal struggle. "Please don't laugh. I need this job. I've not long moved here." My chest pangs with regret at dismissing her so quickly. I finally look away from my friend and stare openly at the woman sitting beside him: professional, demure, and, I'm loath to admit, innocently beautiful. I thought it back at the hotel when she dropped to her knees. Delicate and disorientated. A real damsel in distress. The thought had made me sneer, but it all dropped away when she stuck her finger in my face, and I stared, caught completely off guard, into her hurt and fucking gorgeous face. I had wanted to protect and praise her all at once. At least until she decided to Picasso the fuck out of my shoes. "Shit." She breathes in steadily, rubbing at her temples, and her hair moves, revealing a large bump protruding from her forehead. I shift, uneasy and concerned that she hasn't been seen yet.

"You know, you have a pretty vulgar mouth for front-of-house." I announce my arrival as I adjust my suit and eat up her blush with vigour. "You finally have some colour back in your face." I observe.

"Shame that my legs don't meet your standards." Her lips flatten. It was easy to insult her back at the hotel, to put a leash on my attraction by ensuring she finds me rude and, in turn, less appealing.

Now, not so much. I'm too perturbed by the discomfort of the memories my subconscious is handing me. "They're nicely bruised." Another observation of mine. Her skin really is the perfect mix of porcelain and silk. Curious, she inspects her knees, her skirt lifted enough that I want to stand, cross her legs, and drape my jacket over her bare skin because I hate the thought of anyone else glimpsing to look at her creamy thighs. Perry glares at me, and I simply raise a brow. This isn't the first time he has taken one of my cars, but it is the first time that I have come after him to retrieve it. He stares intensely at me, trying to gauge my mood. If he is expecting me to unravel the inner workings of my mind, he can join the fucking queue. I have no idea what I am doing here. Or why I chose today to come here when we both know I would rather walk through fire. I was already in a bad mood. Royce fucking Ivory had seen to that. The day I rid the world of that man can't come soon enough. My eyes slip back to the woman playing with the chain of her watch, and I suck in a perplexed breath. Her fringe hangs forward, hiding the large bump, and her soft mouth is turned down in a miserable frown.

"No thanks to you two," she scoffs and glowers at Perry, her fingers instinctively reaching for the injury. My friend grins and leans in, wrapping his arm around her neck. Muscles all over my body tense, ache, and strain to move with the conscious effort of suppressing the desire to rip his limb clean from her.

"Ah, don't be like that. You'd never have met me if I hadn't knocked you on your arse." Their display of familiarity stings my equilibrium. I've always envied Perry's ability to make friends. The man has no doubt concussed this woman, and yet she is welcoming his hug. If it tells me anything, it is that she is far too forgiving and too nice for the likes of us. And that I hate my friend's hands on her.

"Oh, so it was you!" She laughs shortly. Her light and lyrical chuckle rings out like a mating call, and every fucking man in a ten-foot vicinity perks up. I shift and glare at a man eyeing her up with a small smile on his face. My eyes drop to her, and she goes stiff as a board, removing Perry's arm and finding any inanimate object to occupy herself with. Every so often, she lifts her big almond eyes to find me watching her with something akin to obsession. Little does she know, I too need something to focus my mind on to keep from spiralling into a place darker than the innocent shine in her endless eyes. She's become the object of my fascination. A living, breathing specimen that my mind refuses to detach from, in fear of losing itself to the horror and memories this place is assaulting me with.

"Miss Lauren Lindel?" She startles in her chair.

Lauren. It suits her, not too flimsy nor too strong. Feminine.

"That's you, alien head." Perry elbows her softly. What small thread of control I had over my rattling emotions cracks like a rotting tooth. The pain slams into my chest, and every reason for coming here mocks me in the face of my shaken resolve. I work my hands, cracking and snapping my knuckles to keep myself from breaking out in a sweat.

"I appreciate you bringing me, but I can probably make my own way home," she mentions, smiling uncertainly as she flicks a cautious look my way. "Erm, I'm sorry about—" Dainty fingers point at my clean attire. "The grey looks better." Lauren grins awkwardly, and it hits my solar plexus like an arrow seeking out its target. She edges away, and I stare after her petite legs until she is out of my eye line.

"I need to get out of here," I choke under my breath. Perry stands fluidly and follows me out of the hospital as I eat the floor up with wide, fast strides. "My keys," I bark.

"Cain. Why the hell did you come?"

"I don't fucking know." It's just a building. Brick, mortar, and glass. No different than the many hotels I own or my own home. "I want updates," I demand sharply, a tactic to keep my mind busy. I click my keys and see my car's lights flash a few rows over in the car park.

Perry grips my shoulder. "Hey, take a breath, man," he murmurs while jogging alongside to keep up with me. "I don't want to have to admit you too." His eyes crinkle at the corners, but I have no patience for his humour now, and shrugging him off, I stalk ahead. "I saw the way you looked at her," he adds, voice low but curious. I drop my head, refusing to acknowledge his comment. My chest is caving in on itself.

I clear my throat and try to draw in more air, sucking in another lung full and feeling more constricted for it. *Fuck.* I yank at my shirt, undoing the top few buttons and hauling air down my throat—the crisp, cool oxygen pours into my body like lit petrol.

"Cain, just take a minute." I drop my head further. I need to get the fuck away from here. "She's going to want to know if she still has her job!" he calls behind me.

I cross the street and turn back to face him. "I think firing her was answer enough," I drawl, but it comes out in a strained huff of air. Perry shakes his head in disappointment. Firing her is not an option, but I'm too angry to make rational decisions. I'm impulsive when I'm worked up like this. He knows it. I know it. Right now, I refuse to have this discussion. I should have stayed at the hotel.

—

I cross town, my foot heavy on the accelerator and my head dizzy with anger. It was a mistake to go to the hospital. I've taken extreme lengths to keep from entering a hospital again.

My first experience was one too many, and I don't plan to revisit the tragic events of that night. I'm not sure what it is about her that compelled me to follow them to the hospital, but standing in the building, haunted by my father's traumatic death and the devastation that followed, has left me feeling bereft and angrier than ever. Yet the person I chose to blame is the only blameless person out of us all.

Lauren Lindel.

She doesn't deserve my anger. She deserves her job back, but I can't think or feel past the horrors rushing around my mind since entering the hospital.

Before I set off, I text Justine, asking for a full report on her. I know she works front-of-house; her uniform told me as much, but I don't want her professional background. I want the grit and dirt. The things she folds away, protected and secure from even her closest friends. I want to part her fringe and capture a look into her mind, just so I can hold it in my hand and bend her to my will when she finally loses the look of disgust. I'm not a likeable person, and yet people pursue the possibility of befriending me—desire to leave some kind of impression. But Lauren seemed as indifferent to me as I do most women, and it pissed me off.

By the time I pull up in the underground parking of Perry's gym, Magnitude, I've decided I want Justine to have her details on my desk first thing. Retrieving my gym bag from my boot, I text my assistant and double-check for any updates before I take the elevator up and stalk down the corridor to the private changing facilities.

Mikael, one of the personal trainers, is working out in one of the studios as I pass by but collects up his things when he sees me, stern-faced and on edge. I suspect Perry has called ahead. "Need a partner?"

"Perry call you?"

"He said you might need to blow off some steam."

"I'm not here to fuck around or build up a light sweat," I warn.

"I hear you." He grins. "Studio four is free. I'll meet you there." He nods towards the studio as I step back into the changing room. I change out of my suit and hang it up. I don't bother with a t-shirt and replace my shoes with trainers and put on my shorts. The door creaks, and I turn to find Faye from reception slipping inside, her lip caught up in her teeth and an easy shine in her eyes. My gaze drops to my bag in fury. Now, had it been another woman sporting a fringe and fine bone structure, I'd have smirked and sauntered her way.

"Faye, get out."

"You look a little tense," she whispers. For fuck's sake, did Perry put her up to this?

"I could get you fired for this," I grunt, stuffing my phone into my bag and zipping it up.

"I doubt it." The light brush of her fingertip rims my shorts. It trails round to my front, where she applies just enough pressure to dip the tip below the elastic.

I grab her hand and spin, yanking her to my front, and surprised brown eyes pop with unease. "The only workout I need requires something a little more challenging," I snarl. Why the fuck would he send a woman my way when I feel as unhinged as I fucking do? I'm already close to one lawsuit with Lauren for unfairly dismissing her. I don't fancy adding Faye to the pile.

"You'd be surprised what I can—"

Scoffing, I cut her off, giving her a steady push back and putting her at arm's length. "I'm not interested. The only woman I'm in the mood to fuck is concus—" I halt when her expression twitches to curiosity. Instead, I shove my bag in a locker and draw in a deep breath through my nose.

"Cain—"

"Faye, fuck off," I snap and stalk out, heading straight for the far door at the end of the corridor. As soon as I cross the threshold, I snap sideways, dodging a fist. I jab once, twice, then a third time, and Mikael blocks each attack as seamlessly as I strike. I don't want to dance around the mat and spar. I want to brawl. I want blood. I want to execute every memory I have raining down on me until I'm too exhausted to stand. I want to sweat blood and go to war with my own mind—to punish anyone in my way. Because the real cause of my internal battle is sitting a couple of miles away, in a home that doesn't belong to him, with a life he stole, and until I can extract the kind of revenge he deserves, my only choice is patience—calculated patience and the soul-deep rush of satisfaction from dismantling the life he stole from beneath his very nose. Those that fall victim to my fury in the meantime should be only grateful they're not my true target.

Lauren's pained expression flickers in my mind as Mikael steps in for a right hook that I only just manage to duck away from. She could appeal her dismissal and would have every right to. It is unfair, after all. The hotel doesn't need that kind of publicity. And as pretty as she is, she's not worth me losing sight of my end game. I barrel at Mikael and jab successfully to his jaw. His head snaps back, and he flips round to face me, eyes narrowed, working his lower jaw before he lifts his arms and moves in a circle around the mat, orbiting my movements.

"Fucking hit me!" I roar at him.

Experienced feet dance across the mat towards me as Mikael ducks, spins, and glides round with his foot out. The kick knocks me backwards with a pained grunt, my chest vibrating at the direct impact to my ribs. The pain is liberating. I groan in appreciation and advance, striking him with precision and the weight of my anger flying through my fist.

We fight until my muscles are screaming for a reprieve, and Mikael is cupping his jaw and hissing in pain. I, too, can feel the tender burn of bruises forming beneath my skin. Bruises like those on Miss Lindel's pretty little legs.

"Remind me never to piss you off," Mikael grunts. Sweat drips off his brow, gliding down his neck to soak into his vest.

"Remind me to spar with you more often," I pant, dabbing my neck dry. He gives me a light smile as we grab water, and I sit against the cold wall, sliding down. I rest my head against the cool brick, bringing my temperature down.

I sit for a while after Mikael has gone until the door opens and a stream of adolescents arrive for a class. Taking that as my cue to leave, I wander through the gym and back into the changing rooms to grab a quick shower. Only once I'm dressed do I check my phone.

Verdict is in, one mildly concussed and miserable ex-employee. If you're going to fire her, at least fuck her happy first ;)

Sure, because that will go in my favour if she ever decides to file a complaint. Fired and sexually harassed. How this man runs his own business is beyond me. I take little satisfaction in knowing he hasn't suggested he fuck her.

Why would I need to fuck her when Faye is on tap?

My mobile rings almost immediately. "Tell me you did not fuck my receptionist?" he demands as soon as I answer the call.

"Hey, you sent her my way," I scoff and chug back half the water.

"To see if you wanted a deep tissue massage with Dawson!" Perry snaps.

"I think she wanted to massage my dick," I mutter.

"Fuck... that sneaky bugger. Maybe I can offer Lauren her job? I know the gym will double in business if she works reception." Over my dead body!

"Lauren is staying at The Carson Ivory. She'll be in tomorrow to collect her things, no doubt. I will speak to her then."

"So, I just broke her heart for no reason?"

"Would appear so. Justine is on standby for you."

"Cheers. Cain, she deserves her job back."

"I know."

"You sure you are going to be able to cope, knowing she works for you, all pale and petite? I think the universe is trying to test you." He sniggers.

"I think I can manage."

"It's almost comical that you think you have this under control." Perry laughs and hangs up before I can retort. Arsehole.

My phone pings with another notification, only it's my assistant again.

Congratulations, you are now the majority shareholder of Ivory Corp!

The elation I hoped for is subtler than I expected, and the keen sense of pride I thought I would feel isn't there. I stare at my phone and read over the words that bring me closer to my end goal, and I feel nothing but the same biting anger. The violent burn of revenge that has followed me from my youth to my adulthood.

Royce Ivory will be a ghost to this world.

Just like my father is.

CHAPTER 4

Lauren

P ain is the first thing I feel when I wake. The pressure between my eyes ripples across my face, reminding me what a terrible day yesterday was. It hurts a great deal more now. I trail my fingers over the bridge of my nose and flinch. Pushing free of the quilt, I walk quickly into the bathroom and pull back, horrified at the mess that is my face. "What the hell?" I'm sporting two black eyes, and my bump is a deep shade of purple. "No!" I cry, touching the area. This is just bloody great. I drop, sitting on the edge of the bath, and sigh. I begin to frown, but the swelling forbids it. I barely woke during the night. The painkillers had been strong enough to ease me under, and Amberley had stayed over to keep an eye on me but had to leave early for work.

I flick on the kettle and rummage in the freezer for a cold compress, biting back a moan as dizziness washes over me. Hesitantly, I hold the icy block to my face, then dose up on pain relief. I take time with my makeup, determined not to waste the day. I'm going to spend the morning looking for jobs before I meet Amberley for lunch. It takes longer than expected to cover the bruising, as my face is swollen, and even with pain relief, I'm still hurting. I took one hell of a bash to the face. If I ever see Perry again, he owes me big time.

After a productive morning, I've managed to secure an interview this afternoon at a competitor hotel, and I'm expecting a call back later for a waitressing role should all else fail. Quite frankly, I will take anything to tide me over until I can secure myself something more permanent. I make the rash decision to put my favourite dress on before I meet Amberley. If I'm going to turn up to collect my belongings, it will be with my pride intact and a killer dress as a silent fuck you to my boss. I may be pale, but I look damn good in this dress. I drag a deep red lipstick over my full lips and smirk back at my porcelain profile. I've always been one to keep my head down and work hard, but something about Cain Carson-Ivory has made me want to have the last word. Even if that's me holding my head high and rocking the shit out of my power dress as I stride out of his hotel. My usual coat is at work, so I pull down a more formal cream one and pair it with nude heels. I look sexy but, more importantly, professional. Amberley has text telling me to meet her at Porto, so I book an Uber and leave my house feeling heaps better.

I find her sitting at the back with a coffee already in her hands. "Hey!" I smile, taking the seat opposite her.

"Jesus!" She gawps. "You look hot."

"Well, I have two black eyes and feel like an alien, so this is my way of making myself feel better." I grin. It's half true.

"Oh no, really?" She frowns at my face. I pull out my phone and find the image I took before I covered it up with a ton of makeup. "Ouch!"

"Even talking hurts." I moan and pick up the menu, having a quick scan as the waitress comes over, and I order a coffee.

"I might just have a salad as I ate a huge breakfast." Amberley rubs her stomach.

"I'm still full from our takeaway." I laugh, then wince. Not only do I look like an idiot, I can barely enjoy myself because I'm in so much pain.

"Does it hurt a lot?"

"I've had some painkillers." I shrug, trying not to let it bother me. "But yes." Each time the skin around my nose and eyes tightens, it sends a sharp stab of pain across my face and my eyes water. "I think I'll have a salad, too."

"Their avocado one is nice," she says absently, still searching for something to eat.

"I have an interview this afternoon and a callback," I tell her and smile at the waitress as she brings over my coffee.

"Wow, that's amazing."

"Are you ready to order?"

"I'm just going to have the chicken and avocado salad," Amberley responds, holding the menu out for the waitress to take.

"I'll have the same, thank you." The waitress leaves us, and I load my coffee with sugar because the pressure around my nose is making me feel sluggish. I'm feeling a little light-headed, but I refrain from admitting that to my friend.

"Where's your interview?" Amberley asks, checking her phone.

"At The Grande Morvelo." I give her an awkward smile, and she looks up slowly from her phone.

"You sneaky bugger." She spits. "Do they know you worked for CI?"

"I think that's why they agreed to the interview." I laugh.

"He's in the office today, by the way," she informs me.

Good.

Shrugging, I lift my coffee and take a sip. I'm glad he is. I just hope I get to see him before I walk out of there, and I hope I get the job at The Grande, because that really would piss him off. No employer wants to lose someone to their competitor.

Our salads arrive, and Amberley and I make plans to go out this weekend—that's if I'm not rotated into work should I get the job. It's a short walk back to the hotel, and when we arrive, Amberley comes through the main entrance with me and not through the service entrance like usual. The lobby is a two-storey high extravagance. Its Olympic-length and gleaming marble floors glint underneath dripping chandeliers. No expense has been spared, and the hotel is brimming with the richest people in the world. Its owner included. Felicity, Beryl, and Marcus are all behind the reception desk, and as soon as Felicity spots me, she comes walking quickly towards me, her legs restricted in her pencil skirt.

"Lauren, a word, please?" She purses her mouth, and my friend gives me a sympathetic look over her shoulder as she heads towards the staff area.

"Of course." I smile. "As soon as I've collected my belongings." I walk past her and hear her tut in annoyance.

Amberley is in the staff room and pokes her head around her locker. "What did she want?"

"Don't know," I shrug, "told her I was getting my things first."

She laughs. Neither of us likes Felicity. She's hard work and is more than happy to tread on any one of us to achieve a higher status. The door bumps open, and she walks in, her nose thrust upward and her mouth stuck in her usual pout.

"I won't be a minute," I say and look back at Amberley, rolling my eyes.

"Actually, I was asked by Mr Carson-Ivory to send you straight up to his office when you arrived."

"Okay. Thanks." I turn my back on her, and Amberley swallows a laugh. Her head is shoved deep into her locker to stop herself from giggling.

"Shut up," I mutter, and she wheezes. She's crying with

laughter. When I look back, Felicity is gone, and I sigh grate-fully. "She's gone."

"Lauren, you bitch!" She spits, full of laughter. "I thought she was going to have a fit when you turned your back on her. Her eyes twitched!"

"Well, she has always been so rude to me. Wish me luck." I widen my eyes and clip the lock shut.

"He's going to need it more than you." Amberley gives me a once-over, and I grin. "Oh my god, you dressed like that on purpose! Lauren, you're a bloody dark horse. You're always so quiet," she muses, surprised.

My cheeks heat, but I don't avert my gaze. "I just refuse to be this worthless speck to him. If I'm leaving, it will be with my head high."

"I think someone else's head will be high too." Amberley chortles, pointing to her groin area, and I gasp loudly, knocking her hands away.

"Give over. Anyway, I'll call you later and let you know how my interview goes." She pecks my cheek, and I leave her to straighten up. I walk back past the main desk, and a busi-nessman walking towards me does a double take and gives me a sexy grin. Okay, so maybe I do look super hot in this dress. I smile back, feeling full of confidence. Too pale, my ass. I take the elevator up with an older couple and assist them to their room before I double back and go in the direction of Cain's office. He can bloody well wait.

It's located below the penthouse suite and, from what I'm told, has an incredible view over London. I give the door a loud rap and stand back to wait for it to open. A poised woman with greying blond hair in a grey skirt suit opens the door. "Miss Lindel?" she asks, giving me a once over. I'm tempted to lift my fringe as proof of identity.

"Lauren's fine." I smile and breeze in.

"That'll be all, Justine." The sound of Cain's voice brings my head up, so I affix my front-of-house smile in place. He is wearing another three-piece suit in dark blue. I can't deny how good he looks, but I do prefer the charcoal grey. It really sets off the silver in his eye colour. They're bright blue, crisp and cool, silvery in certain lights. Those eyes drop down the length of me, and he shifts in his chair. "Have a seat." He points with his hand to the low-back leather chair.

"I don't mind standing," I respond quickly.

Cain opens his mouth to say something when someone barrels in the door behind me, and I spin around to find Perry. Oh, so bursting through doors is a speciality of his. "Hi, sorry to bother you," he looks at his friend, then double-takes, "Lauren?" he says, shocked.

"Hello, Perry." I smile and lift my chin.

"Wow." He walks over and pulls me in for a quick and unexpected hug. "How are you?"

"Black eyes and a mountain head won't stop me." I laugh, and his face blanches.

"Fuck, black eyes. I'm so sorry." He dips to look at my face, and I grin, touching my nose. He looks up from when he has bent down and offers me an apologetic look. "I really am sorry."

"Honestly, it's fine. These things happen," I tell him brightly. I do forgive him. He is hard not to like.

"Are you two quite finished?" Cain snaps.

Perry rolls his eyes and looks at me. "I don't know, are we?" he asks playfully. I really want to laugh, but I shake my head at him instead.

"If I'm honest, I do need to go. I have an interview in forty minutes, and I want to make sure I'm there in time," I clip, checking the small watch on my wrist.

"Already?" Perry blurts, surprised.

"Yes," I snap, affronted. "Despite the little hiccup yesterday, I have a glowing resume," I tell him with a bite in my tone. Nausea ripples in my stomach, and I press my hand to my navel, hoping to quell the sensation, suddenly feeling dizzy again.

"I was just surprised. I know you do," he responds softly.

"That's why I called you up here," Cain interrupts, and I turn, swallowing a smug smile. I'm not one to gloat, but I can tell by the tension in his shoulders that he isn't used to sucking his pride up and admitting when he is in the wrong. Perry moves farther into the room, and Cain lifts what I presume is my resume. His eyes flit between that and me. I refuse to shift under his gaze and square my jaw, meeting him head-on. I don't speak but simply wait for him to address the huge elephant in the room—his shitty attitude.

After a beat, he still says nothing, and I almost turn and walk out, but he lays the paper out flat and frowns at me. "I may have been too harsh yesterday." I offer a smile out of politeness but don't acknowledge him verbally. "You can keep your job." Perry groans lightly behind me.

Is that it?

Not even a 'please accept my apology'. Nothing. I lift my brow, thoroughly disappointed. I absolutely love working here, but I'm not sure I can work for him. With my interviews as added insurance, I find myself glaring at him. He can stuff his job!

"Mr Carson-Ivory," I begin. Perry winces and drops his head, moving to pick up some files beside mine. "I take ownership of my own fault in yesterday's incident." I wasn't looking where I was going. "However, when I was knocked to the ground," I slant a look at Perry, and he presses his lips together, "you insulted me." I don't let him get a word in, but I can tell by the way he shifts his arms that he is about to stand up. I hold out my hand. "Don't bother. I'm leaving. Although I appreciate the transport to the hospital, the manner in which you dealt with the matter was enough to put me off working for you. Keep your job and shove your attitude." I smile insincerely, walk to the door, yank it open and step through, letting it bang shut. My body droops when all the tension I am holding falls away. Shit, I didn't mean to add that last part. My cheeks burn.

"Fuck me. She is hot!" I hear Perry through the door. "Cain, she chewed you up, mate. Fuck, that dress wa—"

"Was her trying to be something she's not," Cain mutters darkly.

"I can hear you. Asshole!" I snap, outraged by his disgusting personality. I stomp down the hall, all too happy to get away from him. That arrogant, cold, miserable prick!

The door opens and closes behind me, and heavy, sure footsteps match mine. Someone's coming after me, probably Perry, to try and make light of the situation again. He takes my wrist, and I turn around quickly to tell him to leave me alone when I come face to face with my boss. Dizziness washes over me, and I blink. "Lauren?" he whispers, concerned, before everything goes black.

⌒

I wake with a start and sit up, panicked. "Woah!" Perry laughs, pressing me back into the low sofa. I recognise the office. Cain's. "You blacked out," he tells me. What?

"Lauren, lay down," Cain demands, hovering over me with a deep frown.

"Oh my god, my interview!" I cry, scrambling to look for my phone to check the time. With a quick tap, Perry is sent away, and Cain takes my hand in his much larger one and drops to a crouch in front of me.

"You're going to miss it. The onsite doctor is on his way to check you over," he says calmly.

I don't feel calm. "No, I can still make it," I argue, trying to stand, but I feel woozy again.

"Sit down!" Cain barks, and I jolt in the seat, blinking up

at him even though he has dropped down to my level. "Forget the interview. I want you here." I scowl at him, but he lifts his brow, and I sense he knows he has the upper hand and will use it to work in his favour. "You have a job here," he repeats coolly.

"I think I should go home," I reply, looking away.

He laughs sharply, and I sneak a look at Perry, who is grinning over at me from the other side of the office. I roll my eyes at him, and Cain grabs my chin, bringing my attention back to him. "No. You just fainted, Lauren. The doctor is coming to check you over. Please just stay seated," he replies, losing patience.

"I bet he tells you I have a concussion," I muse sarcastically, and Perry coughs out a laugh. Cain grates his teeth together, and I relax back on the sofa. I'll wait for the doctor, then I'm going home. Maybe if I call The Grande on the way, I can explain and reschedule. I chew my thumb, worrying about my future again. Strong fingers pull my hand away from my mouth. "Don't," he chastises.

Rolling my eyes, I drop my hand and scoff. Bossy twat.

A light tap at the doors allows me a moment of mental clarity as Cain stalks to open it and welcomes the doctor in, a very hot doctor.

"Hello," I say brightly and lift my hair. "I had an accident yesterday, which will explain my little wobble," I inform him, throwing Cain a narrowed scowl. His jaw locks as he shoves his hands forcefully into his trouser pockets, pulling them taut.

"I'd still like to check you over." The doctor smiles. He's tanned and tall. Gorgeous.

I scowl into my lap and check my phone. I still have twenty minutes. Maybe I can get the tube? "I have an intervi—"

"Fuck the interview!" Cain roars. I jump, and so does the doctor, for that matter.

"Dr?" I smile at him, and he gives me a patient smile back.

"DeLuca." He introduces himself.

"Got any sedatives for Mr grumpy over here." I thumb-point towards Cain, who shoots a look of horror at me. He growls, and I worry my lip. Shit. I seriously need to learn the art of shutting up!

Perry and the doctor laugh loudly. DeLuca turns to my boss. "She seems okay to me, Cain." So, they're familiar then?

"Check her," he snaps and storms out, making the door crash loudly.

"Phew!" I chuckle. Dr DeLuca smirks at me with deep brown eyes, and I stare back. Wait, I recognise him. I blink and recall it was the man in the lobby who smiled at me early. Recognition flares in my eyes and his teeth show when he gives me a full smile.

"Do you want to tell me what happened?" DeLuca asks, picking a few instruments out of his bag, and he clears his throat when I lean to see what else he has hidden in there.

His head lifts, and our faces almost brush. "Oh," I chuckle. "Perry knocked me over with the door. I threw up on Cain's shoes, and I have a concussion," I tell him stoically. "So, you see, a minor blip." I plant my hands on my knees and then decide to scoop my fringe up and show him.

"Wow." He pulls back when he sees the bump. "Any bruising?"

"Yes," I twist for my phone, "one second." I unlock it and bring up the photo. "Here." Perry stalks forward and stares apologetically at me.

"You've done well to cover that up," the doctor appraises and shines a light in my eyes. "Pain?"

"Mild headache. My face is sore. Achy," I admit.

"What was happening when you fainted?"

"I don't know. I had fainted," I point out slowly, trying not to smirk. DeLuca throws his head back, laughing robustly. "I'm joking, sorry. We had words, and then I left. Cain." I flick my eyes up as the door opens, and the man himself steps inside with his phone pressed to his ear. "Mr Carson-Ivory," I correct, "took hold of my wrist loosely, and I spun round. Probably too fast, and then—" I use my hands to imitate my face planting.

Gentle fingers brush my hair aside. "How are you feeling now?" DeLuca leans in, and I side-eye him when he feels around the base of my neck, pressing softly to assess my pain reflex.

"Well, that feels nice," I confess, and he shakes his head, hiding a laugh.

"Are you always such a flirt?" Cain growls.

"I beg your pardon?" I spit. I blink at the doctor, embarrassed, but not because I was flirting. I wasn't. I was just being polite. Maybe I do feel a little woozy, and everything I think in my head is coming out of my mouth, I concede reluctantly, but I wasn't flirting.

Cain bares his teeth, and I pull out of the doctor's touch. "Thanks, but I'm fine," I tell him and use the back of the sofa to stand.

"You really should be at home resting, Miss Lindel," DeLuca berates, replacing his things in his bag. "What pain relief are you taking?" he asks, but I move around him and collect my bag up from the sideboard. "Do you have transport to get home?"

I nod and pull up The Grande's number, calling them. I ignore the men hovering around me and wait for it to connect. "Oh, hello. I'm supposed to be having an interview. However, I've had a little accident," I explain apologetically. "I know it's rude of me to ask, but can we reschedule? I can assure you I'm usually always punctual," I plead softly.

My mobile phone is ripped from my hand. "She has a job. Cancel the interview," he snaps and disconnects the call.

"What on earth!" I cry, looking to the other two men for backup. "You can't do that!" I snap at Cain, then wobble to the side. Dr DeLuca rushes at me, but Cain scoops me up.

"Leave her," he growls, and the doctor holds his hands up. "Perry, please arrange a room for Miss Lindel so she can get some rest."

"Please put me down." I lay rigid in his arms. He is all muscle. Bloody hell. Cain walks me over to the sofa and sits me down. The burn of heat from the short space of contact fires along my arm and throbs like an iron fist holding me still.

"Don't move," he grumbles and walks to talk with the doctor for a moment. Perry is on the phone and, after a few minutes, puts the receiver down.

"Managed to get one across the hall," he says.

"Perry, quit fucking around."

"There is a room across the hall," Perry reiterates slowly, a mocking gleam in his eye.

CHAPTER 5

Cain

She's weightless, a slip of a woman, seemingly dead in my arms if it wasn't for the warm breath teasing my jawline. "Perry!" I snap as I scoop her up and stalk back to my office. He pokes his head out of the door.

"Shit, what did you do?" Accusation rings in his tone. He moves back, peering past, to look at Lauren as she hangs limply in my arms.

"Nothing," I scoff impatiently, "she fainted. Call Matteo."

"Why, so you can both fight over who gets her first?"

Stopping short of the sofa, I turn to glare at him, Lauren still hanging in my arms. "She needs checking over. I don't trust anyone else," I grate loudly.

Holding his hands high, he grins. "Is this going to be like that time in New York?"

"Perry, call Matt." Agitated, I wait for him to reach for his phone before I place Lauren down on the sofa. This is nothing like New York. Sabrina wasn't an employee, and I had no idea about the engagement. Perry comes to stand beside me, staring down at Lauren. She looks peaceful, calm, and for once, she isn't pinning me to the floor with angry eyes. "Better keep your cool around DeLuca, or he will use your little outpatient as a way to get at you for fucking his fiancée." I grind my teeth loud enough for him to hear. I can deal with DeLuca. I was more concerned that Perry had a soft spot for the girl.

"I did him a favour," I scoff. "I never would have fucked her if I had known who she was," I spit, and Perry begins to chuckle. "You're not funny." I sigh. Usually, his antics and constant digs would have me chuckling, but I feel thread-fuck-ing-bare.

"This chick has you so worked up. You're fucked. Seri-ously fucked. Should I plan your funeral now?"

"Plan away. I'll bury you with me."

"Can you play The Sun Ain't Gonna Shine Anymore?" He sways on the spot, singing the lyrics.

"Fuck me, you're annoying," I grumble.

Lauren groans, and we both lean over her as her eyes dance wildly behind her eyelids. They spring open, disorien-tated and panicked. She sits upright, almost head-butting us both as she tries to stand.

"Oh my god, my interview!" she cries, horrified, scram-bling to look for her belongings. There is no fucking way I'm letting her leave for that interview. Concussed or otherwise. I drop down to her level. Something about putting us at the same height teases at my resolve. Her breath catches, her eyes slant suspiciously, and despite the dislike rolling off her in waves of animosity, I still want to kiss her senseless, press her back into the sofa, and remove that frown completely.

"You're going to miss it. The onsite doctor is on his way to check you over." What kind of establishment secures an inter-view in such a short space of time? Either one that is facing difficulties or a fucking competitor!

"No, I can still make it." She attempts to stand, but her steps are uneven.

"Sit down!" I snap. "Forget the interview. I want you here." Fuck me, I want her here, in this office, on the sofa. Now. It's eclipsing the sense of worry I have for her health. Perry snorts, and I grind my teeth. Lauren scowls. Working for me is no longer of interest to her. I'm not surprised—I spoke to her like shit, but I'm not losing her to a competitor, and I'm almost certain that's who this interview is with. "You have a job here," I remind her.

"I think I should go home." Jesus, this woman is infuriating.

I laugh sharply, and her eyes slip away to my friend behind me. Taking her chin in my hand, I pull her face my way, and again, I find myself lost in the temptation of her mouth and imagine crushing my lips to hers. I've wanted to kiss her since she pointed her finger in my face. "No. You just fainted, Lauren. The doctor is coming to check you over. Please just stay seated," I growl, irritated by my lack of control.

"I bet he tells you I have a concussion," she remarks with a small smile playing on her mouth. My brows rise, and I fight another laugh. I wonder if she is just as prickly in the bedroom. I bet those full lips have an answer for everything. I bet she'd sing like a canary if I tanned her arse bright pink and crushed my mouth against the raw flesh.

Her thumb gets shoved into her mouth as she chews on the soft flesh. I take her hand, enjoying the way it feels small and fragile on my own. "Don't," I mutter. I could easily pull her finger and slip it into my mouth. Give her another reason to faint.

She's an employee. Off limits.

Our eyes latch, and I'm ready to yank her by the ankle and have my way with her, but Perry murmurs behind me, and I remember we're not alone.

When DeLuca arrives, I find myself on edge. We have

been friends for many years, but we have an annoying habit of being drawn to the same kind of woman. Only Lauren isn't like the women we are used to. She doesn't scream money. Her confidence isn't held with a sense of arrogance, and she is prim, bright, and witty. She has no game plan. She just is. What you see is what you get. She's fucking stunning, from her lengthy lashes hidden beneath a delicate fringe to her smart mouth and intelligent eyes.

Matteo eyes me curiously when I move to say something, but I step away just as quickly, the warning lost on my tongue. His attention is soon pulled towards the injured woman resting on the sofa. His eyes widen slightly, and his lips twitch.

He walks straight to Lauren, places his bag down, and crouches before her. Unlike me, he gets her hotel face. "Hello," she chirps, lifting her hair for him to inspect. "I had an accident yesterday, which will explain my little wobble." She narrows her eyes at me, and I stuff my hands in my pockets and grip them tightly. Oh, how I would love for her to narrow those big almond eyes if we were alone. I wonder if she'd feel so confident on her knees.

"I'd still like to check you over," my friend coaxes.

Lauren pouts and pulls out her phone. "I have an intervi—"

"Fuck the interview!" I snarl. I don't hear the next few words spoken between them because my blood is rushing through my ears and sending my heart into a furious frenzy. I seriously need to get my shit together. The good doctor will be working on me if I don't calm my temper.

"Got any sedatives for Mr grumpy over here?" Lauren thumb-points at me. I'm so fucking close to storming across the room and shutting her up indefinitely with my mouth that I step forward.

Laughing, Matteo looks back at me. "She seems okay to me, Cain."

"Check her," I bite back and storm out, stalking up and

down the corridor, trying to calm down as I call Justine. "I'm doing it," she answers.

"I said first thing, Justine. It's nearing mid-afternoon, and I have one concussed employee plastered to my fucking sofa."

"What?" she blurts.

"Get the file!" I seethe.

"Right away," she promises before I cut the call. I allow myself a few more moments before I centre my temper and push back inside my office.

Apologetic pretty eyes meet mine when I re-enter. "How are you feeling now?" DeLuca leans in too closely and moves some of her hair aside. I want to throttle the bastard. Perry eyes me, and I drop my head. I need to fire this woman and fuck her or forget her altogether.

"Well, that feels nice." My head swings up.

"Are you always such a flirt?" I growl, still working through my feelings as if this little woman has managed to leak her way into my fucking head.

"I beg your pardon?" she chokes, completely shocked. Her cheeks flame bright red, and I sneer as Matteo holds her hair in his fingers. The small smirk he is wearing tells me he knows what the fuck he is doing.

Lauren moves away, seemingly embarrassed, and stands. "You really should be at home resting. What pain relief are you taking?" Matt questions and I step forward to listen, but Lauren is already gathering her things up. "Do you have transport to get home?"

She nods and puts her phone to her ear. Is she calling a lift? "Oh, hello. I'm supposed to be having an interview. However, I've had a little accident," she rushes to explain. I see red. I power across the room and snatch the phone, telling them to stick their fucking job before I disconnect the call.

"What on earth!" she snaps and looks to Perry for help. "You can't do that!" She stomps towards me but wobbles, her balance as fickle as my temper.

DeLuca rushes to her aid, but I manage to get there first and scoop her up. "Leave her." My friend holds his hands up in defeat, a small smile pulling at the corner of his mouth. "Perry, please arrange a room for Miss Lindel so she can get some rest."

"Please put me down," she garbles stiffly. I do as she asks, but only because I know if I don't, I will do something stupid, like kissing her.

"Don't move," I mutter and stalk towards Perry and Matt.

"I'm confused. Is she a guest or your lover?" Matt muses.

"She's none of your fucking business," I warn.

"Managed to get one across the hall," Perry says. That's my suite. Is he trying to make me lose my fucking willpower?

"Perry, quit fucking around," I growl.

"There is a room across the hall," Perry reiterates slowly and nods to a pale-looking Lauren at my back. I suck in a deep breath and incline my head in acceptance. At least this way, I can keep an eye on her, even if she is going to be sleeping in the room I keep here.

Perry offers to get her settled. Matteo leaves with him, and I take a seat and simmer in quiet. I'm nursing a glass of brandy when they finally reappear.

"That's one hell of a lump," Matt remarks, looking at Perry.

"I already feel like shit about it, but thanks for reminding me," he mutters and helps himself to a drink. "Matt?"

"No, I'm good, thanks. I will hang about for a bit to keep an eye on her."

"Do you think she needs to go back to the hospital?"

"No. She is over the worst, but she will be tired on and off for a while. The dizziness will subside soon. I'm more concerned about the pain she is in. A lot of the bruising has come out. She needs rest and lots of it."

"Is it safe for her to be sleeping?"

"How did she sleep last night?" He looks directly at me, the nosy fucker.

"I don't know. She was at home."

"Alone?"

"I would assume so." I shrug.

"With a concussion? Smart," DeLuca mutters sarcastically.

"You just said she is fine," I retort snidely.

Matt shakes his head. "Given that she passed out today and is still woozy, it's best you try to rouse her every so often. I'm due at the hospital in a few hours, so I need to head home and grab a couple of hours' sleep before my shift." I level my friend with a hard stare, and he sighs, frustrated. "I can keep an eye on her for a bit, but one of you should pop in and check on her after I'm gone. Every hour or two, tops," Matteo offers, his tone hard.

"Okay." I sip the last of my drink and stare at the remnants coating the glass.

"How do you know her?"

"She works here," Perry pipes up when I glare at Matt from my seat.

He takes a chair opposite me. "And she's in on her day off?"

"Yes." I hiss. The room quietens, but the tension builds.

—

Matteo and I have spent the last few hours slipping in to check on Lauren. He's gone now, and I stand at the door, trying to psych myself up to go in alone. It feels wrong, and I know I should wait for Perry to return, but some part of me wants to be alone with her, even if she is asleep. I grip the handle and quietly let myself in. It's dark inside. The distinct sound of nightlife rushes up to meet the gap in the window but gets lost and carried away on the wind, where it filters out until it's an echo in the sky. That's not the sound I want to hear. The soft, steady snore I've grown accustomed to these last few hours reaches my ears. Matteo seems to think it's down to the swelling. I just think she snores, and I oddly like how comforting the noise is.

Her silhouette is laughable in comparison to the bed. Her small frame is lost amongst the quilt. Her dark locks are a stark contrast against the white sheets, yet her porcelain skin merges with the bedding. I move farther into the room, closer to her, where I see her face tilted upward and her lips parted slightly. "Lauren?" I whisper, trying to rouse her slightly, enough to gain movement but not to wake her. "Lauren?" I say louder, my voice deeper. She shifts and hooks her arm over the duvet. A light pink bra strap sits against her skin as she hugs the pillow and presses her face into it and murmurs. I stand still and watch her for a moment. She's relaxed and seemingly content in her sleep. Slowly, I sit on the edge of bed and gently move her hair out of the way, revealing her delicate features, "You're causing me all kinds of trouble, pretty girl," I murmur. Her nose wrinkles, her lashes a silky curve against her cheeks. She grimaces in her sleep. She's been doing that a lot. "I really want to fire you," I admit lightly. "I really want to do an awful lot more." My finger twists up a soft strand of hair, and I watch as she breathes, completely unaware of the turmoil she is causing me.

The door clicks open, and I stand abruptly and move away as Perry peers around the frame. "Is she okay?"

I eat up the carpet quickly as I move away from the woman in my bed. "I fucking hate you right now."

"You wanted her in your bed, and now you have her. You're welcome." He grins and follows me into my office.

"I would prefer her to be conscious and less antagonistic," I drawl.

"Then stop pissing her off!" He laughs, taking my office chair and kicking his feet up.

"Why do you care?" It's not often that I insult a woman, if ever, but it seemed the only option with Lauren, given that she works for me. It's easier if she doesn't like me—easier to manage my attraction to her. She's not the kind of woman I ever pictured myself with, intimately or otherwise. But she's the only woman on my mind.

"I like her, okay? You can bend the rules just once." I can't, not since the fiasco in Paris where an employee and client were caught up in an affair. I know that relationships will be formed on hotel grounds. I also know they will develop further when employees clock off, but if I can minimise that, ensure that fraternisation on hotel property is strictly forbidden, I will have less drama to deal with. Not to mention that I'm the boss, and starting an intimate relationship with an employee is a piss poor way to set the curve.

"Would you fuck one of your staff?"

"Yes."

"I'm not joking."

"Neither am I. I can hardly say no when for the last two weeks, I've been fucking Farah in accounts."

"You're a fucking liability." I sigh.

He grins and hooks his hands behind his head. "Tell me you haven't considered fucking her, and I'll leave it alone."

I tilt my head enough to lock eyes with him. "She's an employee," I state, coldly.

"So?" He shrugs. "Rewrite your policies—problem solved." I drop my head and groan. "Why don't you get some sleep?" He nods towards the sofa. "I can check on her for the next few hours. She'll probably wake up soon anyway."

I prefer her when she is asleep and not glaring at me.

I prefer her a hell of a lot more than I do any other of my employees.

CHAPTER 6

Lauren

A stream of crisp morning light pours in through the windows, rousing me awake. I blink in my surroundings, mildly confused but equally as comfy, and I allow my mind to succumb to the soft pleasure sliding over my limbs. Rolling over, I stretch out in the big bed and burrow into the plump cushions because I don't have this kind of luxury at home—miles of mattress greet me, and I sigh blissfully. I've slept solidly for hours if the sunlight is anything to go by. Checking my phone, I find it's coming up to half past seven. I've had nearly fifteen hours of sleep. I do feel better. I lay still for a moment, allowing my mind to catch up, and I groan with embarrassment when I recall fainting like an idiot at my boss's feet. The arrogant ass is probably used to it. Throwing the quilt back, I take my time sitting up. Nausea is still an unwelcome friend, and so it takes me several minutes to allow the sensation to pass as my abused forehead aches dully. I need a shower to erase the lethargy.

It's not often I get to enjoy the benefits of the hotel, so I decide to make the most of it and use the en-suite, which makes a mockery of my out-of-date bathroom. The shower is huge. Grinning, I strip out of my underwear and get in, turning the water onto full power. The powerful stream catches me off guard, choking me. "Bloody hell!" I splutter, staggering out from under the spray. These things need a health warning. "Luxury, my ass," I grouse, pressing at my bruised face. Dammit, that hurts. After a few minutes, I manage to find where best to stand and let the water pound my body. It's heaven, pure, delicious heaven. Groaning, I tilt my neck as aches and pains that have been deep-rooted ease away.

My face is going to look a mess, and I have no makeup to cover it up. Maybe I can call Amberley to bring some to work with her? I stay under the spray for an age and finally get out, wrapping myself in the fluffy arrangement of towels on offer. I did notice a coffee machine in the room when Perry first escorted me in last night. I'm going to have a drink and then meet Amberley before I leave.

I'm browsing the different coffees when the door clicks open, and Cain saunters in uninvited. I'm about to tell him to get out when his eyes widen, but I soon realise it's because of my face and not my attire. "Fuck," he hisses and strides to me, tilting my chin up. His fingers are smooth and large against my petite face. He's wearing another crisp suit. However, he is yet to complete the look with a tie, and the top few buttons of his shirt are undone. My eyes zero in on his tan flesh, the smattering of hair visible. He knocks my chin up, and I blush deeply like a naughty child caught peeking at a wrapped present. I swallow as his lips twitch.

Embarrassed, I furrow my brow and square my jaw. "Good morning to you, too." I flick my brow up and wait for him to acknowledge me in a polite manner. I'm still angry about his attitude, and for all the grandeur of his hotel and his sparkling reputation, his personality is abysmal. He frowns as he inspects my face, tilting my chin just so. I dip and look away because I'm a mess, but his grip tightens, and he turns my face back. He steps in, and my eyes pop as those azure irises browse my face with irritated concern.

"Good morning, Lauren," he muses, a telltale smirk playing at the corners of his full mouth. "I hadn't realised how bad your face was," he says, his hands leveraging my chin.

"Another unfortunate genetic," I say dryly. His eyes snap to mine, and I wait for him to apologise. He has to, surely? I've given him the perfect opportunity to address it. His thumb traces the bruises, and my breath skates over his arm before dancing back over my skin.

"Perry has arranged for breakfast to be sent to your room." The pig-headed tosser. Clenching my jaw, I tug my face free and turn away from him. I think I'm actually starting to hate him.

"Okay." My response leaves little room for further conversation. I select a coffee capsule and load it into the machine. It whirrs and hisses and the rich scent of coffee fills the room. I'm surprised I can smell it with the amount of swelling around my eyes and nose.

"You can have the rest of the week off to recoup. Should you feel well enough, you can return to work as normal on Monday," he informs me coolly. I stare at my coffee and close my eyes. After he demanded The Grande cancel my interview, and I further missed my call back for the waitressing job, I'm not looking too good as a prospective employee. Financially, I'm not in the position to throw away a job when there is one for the taking. One I love. Going home is not an option. I would be stupid and immature to refuse his offer.

"Thank you." My voice is quiet. I don't want to be thanking someone who can't apologise for their terrible behaviour. Silence bats between us as I focus on my drink, but my eyes betray me and lift to the window where they pin onto the reflection of my boss standing with his hands tucked in his trousers, watching me quietly. My boss, who looks like he is ready to rock the runway and give any photographer heart palpitations. His eyes burn back at me, and I suck in a whisper-quiet breath as he shifts on the spot. He's far closer than I realised.

"Morning!" The door crashes open, and Perry bulldozes his way in. I jump and rip my gaze away from the heated stare of my boss. He really hates me—the intensity burning off him, the fierce lines slashed on either side of his face as he locks his jaw. I collect up my mug and hold it tightly in both hands to disguise the tremor.

"You know there is a way to open a door without ripping it off its hinges," I mutter, turning to rest my bum against the cabinet. He sniggers and wheels over a breakfast cart.

"Hey, alien." He gives me a cheeky grin, and I catch Cain gritting his teeth. Perry squeezes his way in between us both and pops his own coffee capsule in. "You look like shit," he says without thought. "Well rested shit," he blurts when I snap back, offended.

"Oh, because that's so much better!" Scoffing, I take my coffee and move to the laid-out dining table. I hadn't really taken full stock of the room when I was escorted in here last night. It is, in fact, a suite. I stop and look around slowly, taking it all in. It's very masculine, with rich dark colours and ample seating. Come to think of it, the toiletries aren't supplied by the hotel but are personal. I sniff a tendril of hair discreetly and smell the distinct tones of sandalwood.

"Ta-da!" Perry whips the lid off the trolley.

It's packed high with a variety of breakfast options: pancakes, fruit, pastries, bacon and eggs. "I can't eat all that!" I stare at Cain, shocked.

"It's a good job it's not just for you then," he drawls and pulls out a chair for himself, Perry transfers it all to the table, and I watch in horror as they both take their seats, expecting me to sit with them. I blink at Perry, and he gives a subtle incline of his head, encouraging me to sit.

"Don't be a grump. It's the least you can do after you stole Cain's room." He smirks, pointing a knife in Cain's direction —my boss's room?

"What?" But he called downstairs to arrange the room. I may have been a bit out of it last night, but I remember that much. "But you…" I stutter. "This is your room?" I shrink under my boss's cool gaze.

"You're welcome," he grumbles, loading his plate with food. I sink into my chair between them and stare blankly at the food. I am never going to live this down. When I don't pick anything to eat, they both begin moving things in front of me, and I give them a weak smile. Amberley is going to pester me stupid about all of this. What a nightmare. "You're being unusually quiet. Something the matter?" Cain's deep rumble brings my head up and around slowly. I blink at him and shake my head. Yes! I slept in his bed. If anyone gets wind of this downstairs, my work life will be hell. Felicity will make sure of that. I open my mouth to say something, apologise even, when Cain's eyes slip past mine, over my shoulder, landing on his bed. He clears his throat and resumes eating, leaving me tongue-tied and red-faced.

We eat in silence. Or at least I do. Both Cain and Perry are chatting over me about work matters. They must not care that I'm privy to such information, but the truth is, I've shut off. My mind is a chaotic blur of anxiety. People will know I never left yesterday after I was sent upstairs to Cain's office. I frown into my coffee, obsessing over what to say when my phone chimes. Abandoning my drink, I jump up, check it, and sigh in relief when I see it's Amberley.

Where are you? Beryl said you didn't come down after your meeting. What's going on? X

• • •

I look up, and Cain is watching me, so I turn my back. I quickly type a response.

I passed out. Long story. I need makeup! x

My phone rings almost instantly. "Hi," I breathe.

"Fucking hell, Lauren. Where are you?" she exclaims loudly.

"In one of the rooms. The doctor came to check on me and," I give a long sigh, "I still look like I took a round with Tyson. Can you bring me some makeup?"

"Sure, what room?"

"Oh, I don't actually know. One sec," I twist to my boss, "What room is this? My friend is going to bring me some makeup," I whisper, my cheeks burning red as I see his face darken.

"Sure, let's all have a fucking meeting whilst we're at it," he spits.

"Whoo hoo, gang bang!" Perry cheers.

"Amberley, I'll meet you downstairs," I say in a rush and disconnect the call. Glaring at my boss, I stomp towards his bathroom and grab my clothes off his chair. Prick. Prick. Prick, I chant with each footstep. His constant aversion to me grates heavily as I tug my dress on. I use my finger to give my teeth a freshen up with his toothpaste, and I shove my knickers into my bag. With a determined sigh, I open the bathroom door and walk through the room.

"Where are you going?" my boss asks.

"To meet my friend."

"You've hardly eaten anything."

"I can't afford to eat any of this," I mutter. "Deduct my

stay from my wages." My cheeks flame, and I hurry toward the door.

"The doctor is on his way to see you. Sit down," Cain demands, rising from his seat.

"He can check me downstairs," I squeak and bolt from the room.

"For fuck's sake!" Cain curses loudly as the door clicks shut. I hear Perry laugh deeply and another 'fuck off' before I get out of range.

I reach the elevator bank and press the button frantically. The doors whoosh open, and Dr DeLuca smiles. "Lauren!"

"Hello," I croak, slipping inside.

"I was on my way to check you over." He frowns, taking in my crumpled state.

"Oh, yes, sorry. Maybe you can do it here or downstairs?" I suggest. My eyes plead with him to agree, and he must notice because he nods slowly.

"Sure, how are you feeling?" he enquires as we begin to descend.

"Better. I slept really well."

"I know," he chuckles, "you were snoring. It's probably the swelling." He motions to my face. Snoring. When? My eyes widen—I'm mortified. DeLuca laughs. "Cain was adamant I check on you throughout the night," he explains.

I pale on the spot. "What?"

"It's okay. It's my job." He rubs my arm reassuringly. "Don't worry. We were never alone. He supervised," he adds, assuming I'm thinking the worst. I wasn't. My boss. Supervised?

I pull back, feeling sick. If this gets out—if my colleagues find out—I can kiss my job goodbye. "I'm sorry." I press my palm into my stomach and give him an apologetic smile. I didn't even wake. Something about Cain coming into the room whilst I sleep sends an odd shiver down my spine.

"Are you okay?"

"Yes, sorry. I just didn't know." Clearing my throat, I offer him a smile as the elevator comes to a stop. I try to hide my face as the doors ping open.

"I'll cover you." DeLuca smiles, and I bite my lip. He holds his arm out, and I hesitantly move toward him.

"Thanks." Hooking my arm through his, I drop my head, and we walk quickly through the foyer and towards the staff area.

"Lauren!" Felicity's voice grates.

I groan, and he chuckles. "Not right now, Miss," he replies, escorting me away from prying eyes and to the locker room. I can hear how busy it is from out here. Whimpering, I look around for somewhere else to go, and seeing that the meeting room door is ajar, I walk on and push inside. DeLuca follows me in. "Perfect." He smiles, looking around. He places his bag on the table and pulls a chair out for me. "Take a seat."

"I really appreciate you doing this," I say quietly. He gives me a thorough check-over and even goes as far as to check my blood pressure and oxygen levels. He lifts my face to inspect the swelling, and his thumb rubs down my cheek in a caring gesture. My eyes bounce to his.

"You know, even with all this bruising, you are an incredibly beautiful woman," he imparts gently. His Italian accent is very light, but it catches on the word beautiful.

"Oh." I blush, adding more colour to my already bruised face.

"What is going on!" Cain barks, making me jump guiltily in my seat.

"Nothing!" I blurt.

DeLuca is far more relaxed. He stands slowly and turns to my boss, unfazed. "All her vitals are okay, and the swelling is looking a little less prominent." He turns to me. "Your bruising will fade. It may take some time. Any concerns go straight to A&E."

"Okay. Thanks, Dr DeLuca."

"Matteo." He smiles, and I press my lips together to stop from grinning like a damn schoolgirl. He is far easier to handle than my boss.

"That'll be all," Cain growls. DeLuca's jaw flexes, and I sit quietly as he packs his things away. I give him a little wave as he exits the room, leaving me with my grumpy boss.

"You know, you're kind of miserable," I inform him coldly when I find he is glaring down at me. He buttons his jacket and shoves a hand in his trousers, fighting a smirk.

"Thank you for your observation."

"I felt it was only fair, as you seem hell-bent on pointing out my pitfalls," I retort. "Why are you here?" I ask suddenly. Why does he keep following me?

"I came for the verdict."

"Still pale," I snap, and he laughs deeply. Cain leans back against the wall, and I get a full frontal of his long, athletic body. His jaw is angular, and his lips are full. His hair is a light brown blonde, and his eyes are as bright and cold as a winter morning. Predominantly frosty. I shiver under this steady gaze.

"I pushed a nerve, I see."

Is that what he wants? To better me? Well, he can go to hell. "Nope." I throw a wan smile and stand. "I need to meet my friend. Excuse me,"

"Excused," he murmurs, as I slip past and leave him in the room.

Amberley rushes out of the locker room and barrels towards me, pulling me into a hug. "I want all the details," she whispers in my ear.

"I'm kind of still reeling," I whisper back.

The meeting room door opens, and Cain appears. With us in the way, he squeezes past, cupping my hip as he does. "See you Monday, Lauren." He gives Amberley a polite but impersonal smile, and I stare after him. My hip feels the sting of his touch. A physical reminder imprinted into my flesh as if the bruising to my face wasn't enough. Amberley frowns at me in question, but I shake my head, pretending everything is fine.

"Come in here," I tell her, heading back into the small meeting space. "Look at my face," I whine.

"It's pretty shocking," she admits, unloading the makeup on the table. "Details now," she demands, grinning. I spend the next half hour giving her a complete rundown with her sitting gobsmacked and, more concerningly, silent. "It's just a huge mess. Do you think I should still look for another job?"

"No, you love it here. I love having you here." She holds up a compact mirror, and I check my reflection.

"Thanks."

"So, it was his suite?" I nod. "Like you actually slept in our boss's bed?"

"Apparently." I groan.

"Where did he sleep then?" she asks quizzically.

"I don't know. I didn't ask," I whisper. "Probably in another room."

"If there was another room, why not put you in it? Why put you in his room?" she quizzes.

"I don't know." I blanche.

"I bet he's sniffing his bed right now." Her laugh is dirty as sin.

"Amberley!" I scold.

"Oh, come on. He looks like the dirty type. He's probably wanking off as we speak." She chortles.

"Gross." My cheeks flame, but the image she has evoked has my pantyless thighs clenching. Clearing my throat, I stand up and collect my bag. "I need to get home. Thanks for helping me out." A change of topic is definitely needed.

"Sure thing. So, you're back in on Monday?" Amberley checks her own reflection and applies her lipstick.

"Yes."

"I doubt we can hit the town this weekend. How about we have dinner instead?" It sounds perfect.

"I'll let you know how I feel. We might be able to have a few cocktails after all." I wink.

"Yes, girl!" She holds her hand up for a high five, and I shake my head. Rolling her eyes, she stands and slaps her own hand after I leave her hanging.

I laugh loudly and leave the room. She follows me out, and I decide to avoid Felicity and exit through the service entrance. "Speak later," I say.

"Naturally."

I leave the hotel and head towards the street. It's busy already, and I get pulled into the throng of people rushing about on their way to work. I'm barely a few metres down the pavement when a car horn sounds, and Perry pulls up beside the kerb. "Alien!" he shouts, making me groan.

"Go away." I laugh.

"Who me, Perry Tyson?" he jokes, and I burst out laughing.

"Yes, you. You door-bashing idiot." I grin.

"Get in. I'll drop you home." What? I blink, unsure what to do. I've never been ashamed of where I live, but he is sitting in an expensive sports car, and his clothes are, without a doubt, designer. His friend is a hotel mogul with an arsenal of money large enough to secure every member of staff's future. They leave footprints in a world I own no shoes for. I'm suddenly conscious of my home.

"It's okay." I wave him off, suspecting he is feeling guilty.

"Get in the car!" he bellows out of the window, drawing attention. I scurry to the door and hop in. "Knew that would work." He laughs. I elbow him playfully, and he sighs happily. I'm not one hundred percent sure what his job role is at the hotel, but I probably shouldn't be elbowing him. I try to relax in his car after nervously rattling off my address.

We drive in relative silence until we pull up at my apartment block. "This is me," I say, somewhat awkwardly. He must think I live in a complete dive. Perry peers up through the windscreen, worry evident on his face as he takes in the sketchy-looking block of flats. Yep, a dive! I can see Deeks, one of my neighbours, across the car park. "Thanks!" I chirp and push free.

"You're not even going to invite me in for a drink?" he complains.

"Not unless you want out-of-date milk and shit tea bags?" I say honestly. Perry wrinkles his nose, and I laugh self-consciously. I frown, embarrassed, then turn, walking away quickly. That bump on my head has really muddled my brain-to-mouth connectivity.

CHAPTER 7

Lauren

"Lauren, I really wish you had called us," my mother's worried voice berates down the line. Even at this distance, I find comfort in it—despite her tone. I miss her and my father.

"I know. I'm sorry, but I'm okay. The doctor said the swelling and bruising would subside soon," I say, upbeat. I knew they would get into a panic, and with my father's high blood pressure, I would hate to think I added to that stress.

"I do hope you're not at work?"

"No, I'm due back on Monday, all being well," I reply, lifting a dress to my front and assessing it in the mirror.

"Don't push yourself. I hope you're getting plenty of rest!"

My deceitful eyes flash in the mirror. "I am." I worry my lip and move to the sofa, sitting down. "Amberley is coming over to keep me company," I tell her, hoping it pacifies her and she and my father don't drive to London in a fit of worry.

When Martin, my ex-fiancé, and Kristy's relationship

came to light, my parents demanded I stay home, assured me that it would all blow over and running would mean they had won. Of course, I was humiliated. She had been my friend. We'd braided each other's hair, shared secrets, and swapped clothes. Apparently, she had felt that extended to sleeping with my partner. They hadn't won. I wanted nothing to do with them. Henrik, my potential father-in-law, had won. He'd made sure of that, threatening me before I could even digest the betrayal. He had an image to uphold, and if it meant tainting mine further to keep his clean, then so be it. He made it impossible for me to stay.

"She's a good friend," my mother hums. I know that she is thinking that Kristy isn't, and she'd be right. Catching them together had me suddenly questioning my self-worth, distrusting my ability to make decisions and believe others. Before I could even come to terms with the deceit, Henrik had happened. Martin's pleas of forgiveness had been lost on me, and his father had intervened. Corrupt and callous, he'd made the situation go away the only way he knew how—bribing me into silence with the threat of hurting my family. Whatever information he had on my family was still unknown. At times, I wondered if it was just a ploy, but seeing this side of him scared me. It wasn't worth risking my family's safety. He had money and connections, and I'd seen him ruin other people, so I'd done his bidding and left.

Left my family, my life, and a job I loved. It had all gone in less than a second.

"Yes, she is. I'll call you in the week, okay?"

"Not Thursday evening. We're having dinner with the Lewis's."

"Okay. Say hello to dad for me. Love you."

"You too, dear." I hang up and blow out a huff. I feel awful for lying, but I wasn't entirely untruthful. I do feel better, and the swelling and bruising have improved. I've barely had a headache for the past forty-eight hours. I know I should probably give drinking a miss, but after this week, I sorely need to let my hair down. One small drink can't hurt.

~

"I love this song!" Amberley shouts over the music.

"I know. This club is amazing!" I shout back. We're at BANK, a club that has risen in popularity in the past few weeks. Amberley knows the bouncer, and he was able to get us in. It's nothing like any other club I have been to before. There's an elegance about the place. The music is classy and sexy, and not many people are dancing, and those that are, aren't thrashing about compared to the other places we have frequented in the past. It's refined and full of the rich—no wonder Amberley wanted to come here. She loves rubbing shoulders with celebrities. I feel underdressed in my high-street dress and bargain heels. Colour stains my cheeks, but Amberley couldn't give two shits as she sways to the music and sips on her expensive cocktail.

"Stop fretting," she admonishes and takes my empty glass. "Let me get you another drink." She shimmies her shoulders.

"I don't know. I was going to stick to one."

"I can get you something weak, like a spritzer?" she coaxes, and I relent, smiling. She leaves me at the high table we're occupying. I look around, self-consciously pulling at my dress and fiddling with my hair, but everyone is preoccupied and pays me no attention. I take in the décor as I nibble at my lower lip. The dance floor is a metallic gleam beneath a lake of glass. Booths in a deep, dark velvet green circle the main floor, and where there aren't booths, there are high tables. Either end of the room is backed by two huge bars, and above one, a gleaming VIP area sits proudly, the low seating railed off by gold metal and tray-bearing staff. Pendant lights give my hair a faint red shine. I check my reflection in one of the ornate mirrors, grateful I still look okay, and the bruising isn't showing. I take in my simple black dress, and my mouth turns down—everyone looks runway ready.

"What the fuck are you doing here?" Cain's angry voice slices through the club, and eyes that weren't on me, now are. I snap back, offended, and glare as he stalks the short way to me. He's wearing another open-neck shirt, and under the neon lights, his eyes and white shirt stand out against the dark interior.

"Excuse me?" I splutter. Of course, he is in a place like this. My desire to be inconspicuous has shrivelled and died an embarrassing death. No thanks to this man.

He rakes his gaze down me, and his lip curls. "You've got a concussion," he reminds me icily. "You're leaving!" Taking my wrist, he tugs me down from the stool. I move on a clumsy stubble and trip into his chest. "What the fuck, Lauren," he growls, and I choke, utterly staggered by his behaviour. What the hell is wrong with him?

My eyes bounce off our audience before I attempt to yank out of his hold, but he keeps my wrist firmly gripped in his large hand. "Get off me. If it weren't for your mate, I wouldn't have a concussion, and I feel fine!" I snap, getting in his face. "I've only had one drink, anyway," I scoff, prising my wrist free. What is his deal?

"Lauren, do not fucking test me," Cain warns, stepping in to leer over me. His hands take up residence on my bare shoulder, and he starts steering me toward the exit. I struggle, digging my heels in, but the floor is smooth, and my heels ski along it, splaying my legs out like a newborn foal. The bastard laughs.

I manage to put some space between us. "What is wrong with you? You're acting like a crazy man!" When I attempt to sidestep, he crowds me, walking me backwards until the deep walls of an alcove close in around us. "I would give anything right now to be someone other than your boss. *Anything*," he rasps, his knee slotting thickly between my thighs. "You're lucky you have a contract separating us." What on earth is that supposed to mean? The contract doesn't seem to prevent him from treating me as he does. When I don't move, his hand lands beside my head, and I stare wordlessly as his bright blue eyes spit fire back at me. "You need to leave, Lauren. Please fucking go." Something close to desperation flickers in his cobalt gaze.

"Amberley is still here," I growl, shrugging him away, stumbling to remain upright. "You may be my boss, but we are out of work hours, so fuck off!" I surprise myself by saying and stab him in the chest with my manicured nail. "This is so embarrassing," I choke quietly, my neck warming as people watch all around.

His face contorts, and he yanks me to him. "Boss or not, I'm about to tan your pale arse bright red," he seethes. I gasp and pull away, disgusted, but he tugs me back. "Then you'll be fucking embarrassed."

"You can't speak to me like that." I shriek, outraged. "You're my boss. It's highly inappro—"

"Whoa, hey!" Perry rushes at us. "Hey, alien." He smiles awkwardly at me, but I don't reciprocate. "Cain, people are staring. What's going on?"

"Apparently, I'm leaving!" I snap, crossing my arms and narrowing my gaze at my boss. *Tan my arse.* My chest is swelling with each angry intake of breath. Cold eyes hold mine, and I stiffen as his threat plays on my mind for all the wrong reasons.

"Why?" Perry frowns, confused.

"Ask him." I nudge my chin towards Cain, and I catch sight of Amberley cautiously making her way over.

"She has a concussion," Cain states simply.

"Yeah, and she's back at work in less than forty hours. I think she's fine," Perry mutters. "Cain, what did I fucking tell you? You can't hack it." Perry grabs his friend's shoulder, speaking directly into his ear. My boss mutters something about not being able to have a moment's peace from work.

"Hello," Amberley says, giving me a tense smile. I roll my eyes and take the drink she has in her hand.

"Don't you fucking dare!" Cain snaps at me. His eyes are blazing, and both Amberley and Perry look around, astonished at his attitude towards me. I lift the drink slowly, and Cain takes a step towards me. The glass touches my lip. "Lauren," he warns. I take a decent-sized sip, and his face twists in anger. He moves, gripping my cheeks gently, my lips pursing, and the cold liquid seeps free, dribbling down his fingers. He towers over me and leans in. His eyes go dark, blazing fire back at me before they drop to his fist, soaked in alcohol. When they slowly raise back to me, my gut clenches nervously. Perry places a calming hand on his shoulder.

"Stop it," I choke.

"The drink, Lauren. Give it to me," he punctuates slowly.

I shove the glass into his hand, my eyes pricking with embarrassment, then stride away. Arsehole. My chest heaves, my gut heats, and I blink away the image of him staring hotly at me.

"What the hell was that about?" Amberley chases after me. "I can't believe he made you spit the drink out!"

"I can't stand him. I'm definitely going to look for another job," I admit with a soft shrug. Eyeing me with sympathy, she gives me a quick hug as Perry comes over. Can she really blame me?

"I hate to say it, but he really doesn't seem to like you." she muses, sipping through a straw.

"Hey, ladies," Perry pecks my cheek but keeps formality with Amberley.

"Hi," I mutter.

"Lauren, sorry that happened. He's had a bad day." I want to declare that I don't care, but Amberley speaks up first.

"What brings you here?" Amberley flutters her lashes at Perry, who laughs at how brazen she is.

"Well, I own the place, for starters." He laughs, frowning.

"Oh, we didn't know that." Amberley grins. I chance a look over Perry's shoulder to find Cain standing watching from afar, my drink at his mouth. He lifts the glass in a show of thanks. God, I truly hate him.

"Let's go," I say quickly.

Perry stares at my friend. "Are you sure you girls don't want to stay for a drink? Amberley, right?" Perry smirks at my friend.

"Would love to, but we need our jobs more." Amberley snorts.

"Another time, maybe," I answer sullenly.

"Ignore him, stay," Perry offers.

"Thanks, but I'm ready to call it a night," I croak, pulling her along.

"See you around, alien." Perry grins. I don't know why, but I look back at Cain, only to find he is standing with a group of people. Sensing he has an audience, his eyes lift to mine, and his gaze narrows—even from across the room, I can taste his dislike. It lances my stomach and leaves me feeling inferior. Scoffing, I look away and feel my shoulder droop with sadness. Why the hell does he loathe me so much, and why did he have to speak to me like that just now? I'm mortified. I can't wait to leave and rush from the club, hailing a taxi to take me home.

"Morning!" Beryl smiles. "Is everything okay?" Her narrow brows pull together when she turns to me in concern.

"I'm fine," I assure her. "I became unwell and had to go home," I lie.

"Someone said you slept here?" She laughs, shooting a look between Amberley and me.

"I wish!" I laugh.

"Me too. Beats my apartment any day!" Amberley murmurs.

"Odd." Beryl blinks, her lips pinch, and she shuffles the mouse, bringing her screen back up. "I could have sworn I saw you the following morning," she pries further.

"Maybe I have a doppelgänger." Amberley looks at me, and I roll my eyes. These women are the noisiest bunch I have ever encountered. I clock Felicity striding our way and quickly intercept a guest before Beryl can get up. "Good morning, welcome to the Carson-Ivory. How can I help?" I smile brightly and studiously ignore Beryl's tut.

"I've made a reservation, Mr Carmichael," the man drawls, checking his watch, a sure sign he is in a hurry. Giving him a polite smile, I put his name into the computer and pull up his details.

"Mr Carmichael. You're in our executive suite——" I begin.

"Yes. Yes. I stay there regularly." He huffs, holding his hand out for the key card.

"Of course." I smile. "It's lovely to have you back with us," I add, pretending I recognise him.

"Mr Carmichael," Felicity greets, giving me a suspicious look. "All checked in, I see."

"Yes, yes," he mutters and strides off in the direction of the elevators. Clearly, he's not a morning person. I fight a smirk as he almost trips in his haste to get away.

"Enjoy your respite?" Felicity questions, watching me with shrewd eyes. I take in her thin but pretty face and severe blonde bun. Her cheekbones are sharp enough to pierce skin. I wonder how her own skin is still intact as she barely smiles. What I want to know is why I'm on a late shift this week when I'm contracted to work the day shift, but I know better than to argue when she is already suspicious.

She watches me expectantly. "Yes, thank you," I reply chirpily. Amberley snickers, ducking her head to fight a laugh we both wish to expel at high speed from our throats.

"Must be special to be placed in one of the rooms," she spits quietly and turns her back on me when another guest approaches the main desk.

Gritting my teeth, I twist away and widen my eyes for effect at my friend, who is already shaking her head in despair at me. Beryl tuts at us both and shoos us away. I'm more than happy to go. In fact, I can see a guest looking a little lost, so I walk across the foyer and approach her. She's an elderly woman with a neck of jewellery and a bag bigger than her own frail torso. "Hello, can I help you, Ma'am?" I bend down a little to meet her eye level.

"I've… I can't seem to find my key card," she mumbles, looking around and lifting her bag to search. "It was just here." Giving me a quizzical look, she twists around, sighing impatiently.

"Let me have a look. Where were you sitting?" I smile, holding my hand out, encouraging her to take a seat.

"Thank you, dear." I escort her to a seat. "I was sitting right here, and I know I had it." Her wrist jingles with more jewels, dazzling diamonds that are as bright as the chandeliers overhead.

"Okay, well, not to worry. Sorry, I didn't catch your name?"

"Mrs Grantham-Heath." I recognise that name. Her family owns a jewellery empire.

I give her a poised smile and crouch down to look on the floor, looking for her card. "It's such a smooth surface. It could have slid along the marble," I voice.

"Yes, I suppose," she replies distractedly. I crawl along the floor, glancing under the ornate chairs and tables. Where the hell is it? Pressure begins to dig into my knees, sending a deep ache to stab down to the bone. Humming against the pain, I bend lower, trying to look under a low table, when I see the outline of the card. "Got it!" I call back lightly and reach to retrieve it. I twist around and find two wide-placed legs and shiny shoes in my way. "Excuse me, sorry." I blush, embarrassed, and push to a stand, where Cain's stark and bright eyes stare blankly at me.

"What are you doing?" he rasps quietly.

"Mrs Grantham-Heath dropped her card," I explain, holding it up.

"Oh, you found it!" her wispy voice sounds to my right. She stands slowly.

I smile widely at her. "It was under the table," I tell her and hand it over.

"You are kind. Thank you, dear."

"Of course. Can I help with anything else?" I ask silently, praying she says yes because Cain's bristling body is in my peripheral vision. I want nothing more than to get away from him and his shitty attitude.

"Oh no, you've done more than enough. Thank you." She pats my hands, then turns to my boss. "Your staff are a credit to you," she informs him, hitching her bag on her shoulder, and I beam at the compliment. I watch as she walks away, mumbling to herself.

"Now I understand why you forever have bruises on your knees," Cain drawls, sending my cheeks bright pink. I chance a look up, only to find a few of my colleagues are watching the exchange.

"Excuse me. I need to return to work." I say quietly. Why is he making it his personal mission to draw attention to me?

"In future, issue a new card. I expect more from my employees than scrambling around on their knees," he imparts hotly and leaves me standing open-mouthed as he strides across the foyer with the confidence of a man who has buckets of money and exits out of the main doors, adjusting his suit jacket as he goes. I really wish I could put him in his place, but

I need this job. I plan to keep looking—long-term, this isn't going to work for me. Cain and I don't gel. When I finally turn back to reception, I find Felicity smirking at me. Another person I don't gel with. Maybe it's me, I concede, heading back to reception grumpily.

The remainder of my shift, thankfully, goes by uneventfully. Cain doesn't reappear, and we are too busy for anyone else to make any passing comments. I leave work irritated and dejected about my career at Carson-Ivory. Whilst the hotel was being taken over, everyone was too preoccupied with ensuring the place ran smoothly during the transition, the pressure of a new owner and management forcing us to each keep a low profile. We'd been terrified to lose our jobs, yet I slipped through unnoticed and found an easy rhythm at work. I was building up a good rapport with the clients and woke up geared for the day, but now I can't wait to get home. I'm no stranger to hard work or difficult people. Felicity is one of them, but having my boss openly dislike me hits on a deeper level. I leave through the staff entrance, make my way to the street and hit the path, moving quickly amongst everyone. I keep my head down and breathe a sigh of relief, glad to be going home. I'm not in the mood to cook, so I decide to double back towards the tube and go across town to my favourite Thai restaurant for a takeaway. I can pick up some wine, watch a chick flick, and put on a facemask.

I'm passing the hotel when Perry beeps his horn at me. Assuming he is simply saying hello, I give him a wave and carry on my way. "Hey, Lauren!" he shouts after me, abandoning his car and hopping out to jog down the street to me. "Hey, hold up!"

"Everything okay?" I say, looking around to make sure my boss isn't in the vicinity.

"Yeah, what are you up to?"

"Nothing." I frown, then laugh. "Heading to grab some dinner, then home," I tell him. "I'll see you soon." With Cain being so dismissive, I'd rather keep my distance from Perry, too.

"Hey, you're not mad at me, too, are you?" he laughs, taking hold of my hand and stopping me.

"No," I murmur, but he crosses his arms, dissatisfied. "Perry, I just want to do my job and go home, you know." My shoulders lift, defeated. "Cain," I sigh, "we didn't get off to a good start, and I could do without the hassle." I rub my forehead and smile, hoping he will be understanding and leave me be.

"Well, I'm not Cain," he points out. "So, dinner, where are we going?" He grins, dimple and all.

CHAPTER 8

Cain

Lawrence Danvers sits opposite me in the restaurant where we agreed to meet for lunch. He is ten years my senior and one of the few people I trust. He is also one of the select few who know about Royce and my plan to dismantle his life. "I know Justine mentioned it in passing at our last meeting, but I think she might be onto something. If Royce forged your father's signature on the will, then it is void, and Carson Court is yours, not to mention any other property. That's if the entire document isn't fake. You're already a majority shareholder. His company is as good as yours." Danvers clicks his tongue after taking a sip of his whiskey. "I think it would be prudent to have a specialist examine the document."

"Let's do it," I agree. A low hum of excited energy ruptures in my gut and glides through me. If we can prove this, then Royce is ruined.

"It would be perfect if we could find the original will. The more I think on it, the more I believe Royce would have doctored a new document to secure his place as head of your family." I don't correct Lawrence, but the mention of him being family sends a sickly sweep of anger down my spine.

"I'll see if I can gain access to the house—if not me, then Perry."

"Whoever drew up the original will needs to be investigated, as it's likely Royce blackmailed them, coercing them to forge it for him."

"Do some digging," I mutter.

My phone pings and I find Justine has finally sent the file. A paper copy will be on my desk tomorrow morning.

"New investment?" Lawrence leans back in his chair, interested.

"Something like that." I swipe my thumb over the screen and click the attached document. The first page is a profile of Lauren smiling on a terrace overlooking a large lake and golf course. I skim a few pages of family photographs and her with a female friend until I find her standing with a man. He's thin and tall with blonde hair and narrow eyes. They beam into the camera. My chest seizes, but I shut the sensation down, refusing further emotion to take hold. Below gives me a brief rundown of her connection to him. His name, age, and occupation.

Martin Johansson. Ex-partner. Affair. Country Club heir. I recognise him. That name. Skimming further, I find a name that has me sneering. Henrik Johansson.

"What do you know of Henrik and Martin Johansson?" I ask, thumbing through for further images. I've met Henrik in passing once or twice, and the snowy-haired fool is nothing but a brown noser. I knew Lauren worked at a prestigious golf club on the outskirts of Oxfordshire before, but I hadn't considered she was involved intimately with anyone there, let alone the owner's son. I frown down at her picture. She is young, content even. Nothing like the guarded woman I know.

The affair between her friend Kristy and Martin is briefly summarised. I can't tolerate cheaters. Her friend is an angular woman with poker-straight blonde hair and large teeth. Personally, I think Martin is an idiot. Kristy is certainly no Lauren, that's for sure.

"Very little. They golf with my brother. Eric always liked the country lifestyle. They own several country clubs and golf courses. Small-time real estate." He means in comparison to me.

I hum as I stare at another image of Lauren laughing into the camera. My mouth tilts up. Her neck is exposed, and her eyes dazzle. She is exquisite.

Our waiter approaches and places the bill down. I note the figure and close the leather pouch as they take their leave.

"Why?" Danvers interrupts my train of thought. I pocket my phone before I get carried away staring at her. I'll read through it tonight.

"An employee used to work for them. Got me thinking it's a possible opportunity for me to explore."

"You'd hate Henrik. He's a smarmy prick."

"I've met him. I already hate him." I hook my arm over the back of the chair and glance across the dining room. "But I don't need to like him to do business." I shrug.

"Does this employee have anything to do with the incident that occurred at the hotel?" My eyes slowly roll back to him, where he views me across the table, a small twitch playing at the corner of his mouth. I'd called Danvers to anticipate the claim of unfair dismissal. He knows little, but enough to know that I was in the wrong.

"Maybe, although as I mentioned, she has accepted an offer to continue her employment, so no harm done."

"Yet." Danvers never misses a beat—it's what I like about him.

"Yet," I drawl.

"Do you need me to amend any policies?" He holds my blank stare. Clever bastard.

"We'll see."

His smile provokes a pang of irritation to flare in my chest. Raising my brow, I collect my phone and stand, buttoning my suit jacket. "Always a pleasure, Danvers," I droll out.

"Get that employee to loosen you up." He stands too, and I throw money down on the table. "I can have the paperwork on your desk first thing," he teases.

"I'll be in touch." I depart and head out of the restaurant. My car circles the small half-moon drive, and the valet slides out and drops my keys in my hands, bidding me farewell.

Something about the possibility of Royce's fraud overflowing and tainting my father's dying wish has me driving to the cemetery. Shoving my hand in my trouser pocket, I stalk down the maintained gravestones. When I hit my first million, relocating my father's grave was my only priority. Visiting his dilapidated resting place had always enraged me. The stone had long discoloured and started to crack, and the grass was overgrown and forgotten. He'd been forgotten.

Nicholas Carson was a man of complete honour, a well-respected name in the business world, and a regular feature in society. He didn't deserve to be buried amongst the bark of a rotting tree. He deserved a fucking landmark. Emotion pummels my throat, and I tug at the top button of my shirt and stare ahead at the mausoleum.

The whitewashed walls are as clean as the elements allow. I step instead and tap the stone wall. "Anyone home?" My lips twist painfully. It's what he always said when he returned home, briefcase in hand, a tired strain in his eyes, but he always wore a genuine smile. He loved my mother and me with a ferocity that had made him complacent. He'd won it all. The picture-perfect family, a home other people envied, success, and respect, and it was all blown away with the squeeze of a trigger and the evil greed of another.

My eyes slam shut.

I feel like a twelve-year-old boy again, only this time I'm swamped in a man's suit, but the feelings are the same: suffocating. My head drops, and my shoulders curve in on themselves as the vision of my father sitting broken on a chair torments me—his trousers dirty, shirt a crumpled mess. His face was hollow, his skin gaunt and covered in greying hair. Hair that had been as rich as my own. The heavy metal object perched in between his cracked lips. His hold had been resolute, tight. His finger pressed with a fatal intention on the trigger. He hadn't shaken. His eyes were hard with determination to see his suicide through.

He had given up on himself. On me.

I drop to lean my head against the cold stone. Lost to a memory I can't escape, even in my sleep. Lost to it even now in the cold light of day.

"Dad?" I'd trembled.

He turned, surprised, guilt rippling his features, and squeezed.

The bullet had ripped through his neck, blood spraying like a careening wave decorating the walls. It continued to spurt from the open wound. Shock, pain, and regret had screamed at me from his wide eyes as he gripped at the hole, spluttering and gurgling on his blood.

"No!" Remembering my broken choke has me shaking on the spot, even now. I stand tall and pull myself out of the past.

Dragging in an emotional breath, I stare at the neatly carved lettering. "I've nearly got him." My words echo around the pristine chamber. "Nothing to say?" I continue, my forehead furrowing deeply. "Everything you worked for, all of it. It's going to be ours again."

Silence greets me.

Stone-cold and empty.

"You always were a man of very few words." I frown, adjusting my stance and staring at the ceiling. "I visited a hospital for the first time since—"

The last time I'd entered a hospital, I'd been drenched in blood as paramedics had frantically tried to stem the bleeding. My father's pale, lifeless body lay on the gurney. My mother and Royce were uncontactable. In fact, I'd been handed over to the care of social services for twenty-four hours before they had come to collect me. "I still fucking hate the places." I rest against the cold interior wall. "This is the part where you ask her name," I whisper, not wanting to admit it even to myself.

Lauren Lindel had me fucked up enough to face entering a place that I've hated as much as the man who requested I call him dad in lieu of my actual father.

"You're right. It's probably best if I leave her alone." My gruff voice has me rubbing my forehead tiredly. "Why'd you do it?" I ask suddenly. My eyes bore angrily into his name carved in the grave. "You left me to him." I open my mouth to sling an insult that clings to my vocal cords but choose to slam my mouth shut.

I know my father had left me long before he chose to take his life.

"Same time next week?" I ask the empty air. "Great, can't wait." I laugh shortly and stride back to my car, a black cloud hanging over my head.

I could really do with punching or fucking someone.

Lauren's startled face flits across my vision, and I drop my head against my headrest, groaning.

I should leave her alone, but I know I'm not going to.

I'm in too deep. Hell, I wanted to kiss her whilst she was sleeping in my bed. Injured and vulnerable, but I wanted her all the same.

Shame worms its way into my chest.

Being this close to my father and thinking these things punctures my lungs. He'd be appalled. He loved us with a quiet reverence that I don't possess. No, I like to claim things. Collect them like trophies, own them so very completely that there is no doubt in my mind that they are mine. I want to own Lauren, even if for a short while. I ache to take ownership of the look of adoration on her face. To win all her thoughts and keep them so that even when we go our separate ways, I'm a constant feature in her mind.

For once, I want to own something that no one can take away.

Even the memory of me can't be forgotten. I won't let her forget.

I'm going to own every part of her until I forget my own fucking name, and she has to remind me of it. I want to hear her cry my name in every decibel her throat can muster.

—

I drive straight home and hit my home gym, working all my frustration out. My feet race against the treadmill, sweat dripping down my face and back. My mind, though, is in the gutter, fantasising about a woman with glossy hair and a trim waist knelt on the hard marble of my hotel foyer. Gritting my teeth, I sneer at how easily she enters my mind. How easily she distracts me from ruining Royce.

The shame I felt earlier is working against my need to approach Lauren in a non-professional capacity. She doesn't deserve my attention. Fuck, my head is a mess.

Danvers could easily draw up a new policy, allowing me the luxury of acting on my attraction, and there would be no repercussions—just the endless oblivion of no-strings sex. I hit to increase the speed and begin sprinting. My lungs scream for a break, but I grunt and fight the pain, snapping the invisible band around my chest and letting the pain-free void enter my mind.

Only then do I blank out and run until my legs are weak. I shower, dress, and call Perry. I'm in the mood to hit BANK and play gentleman to whichever woman takes my fancy.

He answers on the second ring. "Are you ready to head over to the club?" We had already discussed possibly going later.

"I can't right now." Of course he can. He owns the place.

"Why, where are you?"

"Some Thai place. Lauren, what is it called?" Surprise jolts through me. Whilst I've been sprinting her out of my mind, he's been cosying up to her!

I catch the tail end of her voice as she mutters the restaurant's name. I've never heard of it. "Why are you pushing this?" I seethe.

"It's just dinner!" Perry snaps defensively, but I cut him off and stare at my phone. I could head to BANK and continue with my evening as planned or go to the restaurant.

Mind made up, I grab my keys and leave the penthouse.

Chapter 9

Lauren

Perry puts some food on my dish and then selects some rice and pops it in his mouth. "This place is amazing."

"I know. I love it here," I say. "I found it during my first week in London,"

"Where did you live before?" he asks, lifting his hand to gain the attention of the waiter. I watch him with a light smile on my face. He is easy company, funny, and generally a nice guy.

"Not too far away, a village just outside of Oxford." I tuck my hair behind my ear as a waiter approaches us.

"Two more, please." He points to our glasses.

"Spicy, huh?" I laugh.

"A little. I feel like I've been cheated in other restaurants after this meal." He sniggers and blows out a stream of air. The food here makes my breath catch. Perry has got a sweat on, but I don't want to tell him. I'm enjoying watching him try to keep up.

"Do you own any other clubs or just BANK?" I ask, picking up some chicken and dipping it into the spicy sauce.

"BANK is a new venture. I own a string of gyms," he tells me, leaning back as the waiter places our drinks down. I know the gym at the hotel has been revamped. Maybe his and Cain's friendship is as new as Amberley's and mine.

"You paired with Cain to revamp the gym at CI?"

"CI?" he frowns.

"Carson-Ivory. That's what we refer to it as—not in front of guests, obviously." I grin and pick up some rice next.

"Yeah, it was in dire need of new equipment." Perry's phone rings and my heart fluctuates in my chest. Dropping my gaze, I try to hide my unease. Is that my boss? "I can't right now." Perry flicks a look at me, and I smile, feigning indifference. "Some Thai place. Lauren, what is it called?"

"Erm," I blush and rattle the name off. Shit, that's Cain. I can hear the low hum of his deep voice.

"It's just dinner!" Perry snaps defensively, then sighs. He pockets his phone and gives me a small smile.

"Everything okay?" That's code for, is that my miserable arse of a boss?

"Yeah, all good." I don't want to bring Cain up if he's not going to mention him, so I keep any further conversation neutral and chat mainly about family. I find out Perry is a trust fund baby and take the mickey out of him for it. "Trust me, I'm aware of the privileges presented to me, but I took my money and made it count."

"I know. I'm only winding you up." I chuckle. "If my parents hadn't supported me, I couldn't have moved here." I lie easily. They do support me, but everything I have now is because of grit and determination to survive the malicious intention of another.

"Why did you?" he asks, wiping his hands on a napkin.

I was being blackmailed. My fiancé cheated on me. The truth hangs like a sickly disease around my neck, making it difficult to swallow.

"I love the city, the lights, sounds. The town I grew up in was fairly small, and not much went on there," I say, wrinkling my nose. "It was either work for my brother or stand on my own two feet." I couldn't think of anything worse than working for James. I'd hate to mix family and business, not to mention the scrutiny of Martin's betrayal—or how it led to his father blackmailing me to stay quiet. I couldn't walk two feet without one of his polo-shirt-wearing minions feeding back my whereabouts. I'm not about to admit that to Perry, though.

"Why hospitality?"

"Why all the questions?" I joke. "I like people," I begin—apart from Martin and Kristy—they can suck rotten eggs for all I care. His father, Henrik, can join them too, for good measure. What makes it all so much worse, other than my childhood best friend hooking up with my long-term boyfriend, is that I was being blackmailed into silence for something my brother is hiding. James and I aren't close, yet whilst his life is no different, I have had to make multiple sacrifices.

I could cause a lot of damage to your family.

I'm not doing this for James, but for my parents.

"Apart from Cain." He sniggers, making me chew my lip. Oh, and him. My face flames.

"We can't get on with everyone, right?" I shrug apologetically. It is his friend, after all. "I plan to keep my distance," I tell him cautiously. I don't want word getting back to my boss that I don't like him. "You two seem very different," I comment.

"We're actually very similar. He's just more bull-headed." Perry shrugs. "Ah, speak of the devil." He waves to someone over my shoulder.

"What?" I choke on my rice. I manage to right myself before my boss appears, and I twist around, finding Cain weaving his way through the tables. Looking back, I glare at Perry. "Thanks a bunch," I mutter.

"Now, now," he laughs. "Hey, man!" Perry stands and claps Cain on the shoulder. Cain's eyes burn down as I sit awkwardly in my seat. Why did he have to come?

"Miss Lindel." Cain offers me an insincere smile as I stand quickly.

"I was actually just going, so feel free to take my seat." I offer it out to my boss and pull my coat on. Perry smirks at me, and I debate picking up my chopstick and throwing it at him. He is most definitely a shit-stirrer. However, as annoying as his actions are, I can't help but like him.

"Bullshit, we were going to order dessert," Perry calls me on my lie. I go bright red.

"I've got an early shift," I say, my voice slipping into a whisper. I find my purse and take some notes out. "That should cover my half," I croak.

"How are your knees?" Cain stands face to face with me, and I blink up at him. My knees? Oh, right, the key card.

"Fine." I swallow.

"I heard you were on your hands and knees earlier, you filthy chick," Perry adds, laughing, relaxing me slightly.

My lips tug up. "You wish." I deadpan him, and he throws his head back, laughing. Was Cain talking about me? I frown at him in question.

"You're really leaving?" Perry pouts. "What about all this food?" I stare longingly down at the dishes we ordered and cup the back of my neck, feeling stupidly insecure around Cain.

I look at him now, hoping to see anything other than disdain, but nope, it's still there, nailing me to the middle of the restaurant. Perfect. "You have it," I say huskily. "Night, Perry, Mr Carson-Ivory," I whisper.

"Could you brood any harder?" Perry comments dryly at my boss as I walk away. I fight a smirk. I like that Perry challenges Cain. I just wish I didn't feel so rattled by him. I push free from the restaurant and leave both men behind. As I walk past the window, I peek in and find myself struck by how handsome Cain is. His profile is strong, his jaw and cheeks sharp. His light brown hair and deep, blizzard-cool eyes really pop against his tan skin. I drop my head before they look up and wrap my coat around myself.

I really wanted that spicy beef dish, and I flick my eyes back at the table, annoyed. Although, I'm more annoyed at myself for hightailing it out of there. Why couldn't I just dig my heels in and force myself to get through the rest of the evening with Cain in attendance? After witnessing him quite happily take my seat and food, I have come to the very obvious conclusion that he isn't a gentleman in the slightest. Frowning, I quicken my strides, desperate to put space between us. I wish I had stood my ground with him, at the very least. When I'd bumped my head, it was second nature to snipe back at him, but perhaps that's because I wasn't feeling myself.

"Alien!" Perry's voice sings songs beside me. I jump with a yelp, too lost in thought to hear him pull up. Laughing, I stick my tongue out at him when his deep chuckle carries through the streets, then I stop when I catch sight of my boss in the passenger seat. "Get in." Perry nods to the back. With Cain inside—no thanks.

"It's okay. I don't mind walking," I reply, staring straight at Cain, conveying my own dislike. Like I'd want to get in the car with him? Is Perry mad?

"You're not walking!" Cain's deeper and less patient voice whips out.

"Excuse me?" I splutter.

"We have your food. At least let me drop you off so you can eat," Perry suggests. "Come on. It'll take fifteen minutes, tops. Then you'll be home." I eye them both, and Cain's head drops back in annoyance. My gut twists at his obvious irritation. Everyone likes me—why not him—what did I do? I mean, apart from the puked-on shoes and calling him a prick? I hesitate and look down the street as it begins to drizzle. To save further argument or embarrassment, I agree to get in.

"Do you remember my address?" I ask.

"Why would he?" Cain asks slowly, turning to Perry.

"He gave me a lift the other day," I say quietly, my voice drifting off when Cain's cruel stare pins me to the back seat.

"All in a day's work." Perry winks at Cain, who grunts ogre-like up front. Why is he so miserable all the time? I keep quiet for the remainder of the journey. Both men are chatting, and with the music and their low rumbles, I can't make out what they are saying, so I don't bother joining in. "Here we are," Perry says, bringing my head up.

"Thanks." Cain leans to check out the building, and his lip curls. Snob. When they don't mention my food, I opt to leave it and cross the road towards my flat, but the doors clunk shut and both men walk towards me. "What's going on?" I ask Perry, knowing I won't get an answer from my boss.

"We're coming up. Dinner." Perry widens his eyes and lifts the cartons.

"No," I blurt.

"What do you mean, no?" Cain snaps, lifting his brow and towering over me.

"I just mean, I'd rather you didn't," I squeak, my eyes bouncing between both of them.

"Tough. We're hungry, and we're coming up," Perry argues in a more reasonable manner. Cain, on the other hand, looks like he is ready to put his fist through the nearest windscreen.

"There isn't much room," I explain. Shit, did I put my pyjamas away this morning? I rack my brain, trying to remember where I put them. Please say I did—they are my ugliest ones.

"I gave you a lift. We're coming up," Perry tells me forcefully and heads towards my apartment, with Cain's taller frame following closely behind him. I get a waft of aftershave and bite my lip. I watch his wide shoulders and lean body walk with confidence towards my dingy place. Why can't he be unattractive?

"People will talk," I say, hoping they will leave.

"So," Cain laughs.

"I've already had comments about staying in the hotel overnight," I say quietly. "I don't want to add to the gossip."

"It's not gossip. It's true," Perry comments on a laugh and pushes his way in as I grumble at the back. "Lead the way. I'm starving," he sings. Groaning, I walk ahead, and we take the four flights up to my flat. I'm grateful that the less savoury occupants don't make themselves known.

"What's wrong with the elevator?" Perry pants. Not so fit, Mr I-own-a-string-of-gyms. I smirk at his shallow gasps.

Shrugging, I suck in a lungful of air, feeling a little out of breath too. "It's not worked since I moved in," I tell him over my shoulder and see Cain staring around the place in disgust. I stop at the top step and wait for him to look up, and when he does, his lips flatten. "If this place isn't to your liking, feel free to leave," I say, pointing back the way he came.

"Or you could let us in so we can eat our dinner," he says snarkily. Perry chews his lip, and his eyes twinkle at me. He enjoys watching Cain and me butt heads. Gritting my teeth, I inhale deeply, praying to some higher being to give me strength.

I look at Perry. "You're not off the hook," I mutter and unlock the door, letting us in.

"Yeah, yeah." He pecks my cheek, shocking me, and my eyes fly to Cain, who bares his teeth and looks around the room with a sharp and disdainful sweep.

"You weren't kidding when you said there was no room," he murmurs dryly, slipping his coat off to reveal a crisp white shirt rolled up to his forearms. I glance away and then begin rushing about, sorting room for us to sit. I stuff my pyjamas in the small sideboard I have and throw most of the cushions on the floor for me to sit on, and motion for them to sit on the sofa. God, this is awkward.

"I'll grab some plates," I breathe. They fill the small two-seat sofa, and I refrain from laughing when Cain grumbles. Ha! I hope he is uncomfortable. With any luck, he'll get the TV remote wedged up his arse. Hopefully, it will dislodge the stick stuck up there. "Here we go," I hand out plates, and Perry starts distributing food for us all.

"Where's your dining table?" Cain questions, looking around the small room. His brow is furrowed, and his lips are flat.

I point over his shoulder. "I usually eat at the breakfast bar," I explain. I feel ridiculously self-conscious about my place now. Usually, when Amberley turns up, I feel relaxed and cosy, but with him, not so much. I can guarantee his furnishings aren't from bargain buckets.

Frowning even further, so much so his face contorts as he cranes his neck and looks into the bathroom, "So where's your bedroom?" he murmurs, painfully confused.

"You can't ask that!" Perry barks out a laugh, and my cheeks flame hotly. Cain's do too. I'm glad Perry picked him up for prying. It's nice to see him looking uncomfortable for once.

"You're sitting in it," I reply dryly and shove a mouthful of cool rice in my mouth. No more questions, please.

"What?" Cain and Perry say at once.

"Well, you're sitting on it." I point to the sofa. "It's a pull-out." I shrug and drop my head, hating the look of shock on Cain's face. Is he so silver-spoon-fed that he doesn't realise how us mere mortals live? Welcome to the real world, moneybags.

"Babe, we need to get you in better digs," Perry mutters.

"Why? Don't you like slumming it?" I grin. My face,

however, is glowing like hot glass. I knew they'd hate it. I did try to warn them. I avoid Cain's gaze. I don't wish to witness the pity pouring off of him. I'm sure all of this only lowers his opinion of me further.

"I don't mean to offend you, but wouldn't you prefer having a separate bedroom?" Perry wonders, picking some food up and biting into it heartily.

"I haven't really thought about it," I confess, flicking a look at Cain, who is watching me quietly. Oh god, he thinks I'm a pitiful mess.

"Why not?"

"Can't afford it, so there's no point," I admit with a shrug. "Anyway," I say chirpily, hoping to change the conversation. My damn eyes keep flicking to the athletic frame spread out on my sofa, so I look quickly at Perry. "Tell me about this new venture. Are you planning to open more clubs, or is BANK it for now?" I wriggle, getting comfy, cross my legs and dig my chopsticks in the carton to get some beef out.

"BANK for now, but I plan to open more in the future," he tells me. Cain chews his food, soberly watching me over the short space between us. I have to admit, I never quite imagined seeing him in my little apartment—*The* Cain Carson-Ivory—mogul extraordinaire with his knees almost up to his ears, eating cold Thai in my poky London flat. I can't help the grin.

"Something funny?" His deep command rips my head up from where it was choosing a piece of beef. Widening my eyes, I look at Perry for help, but he is grinning too—maybe he knew what I was thinking.

"Not really. Not for you two anyway," I muse.

Cain opens his mouth to retort, but his phone rings. He stands quickly, nearly dropping Thai all over the floor. "Fuck sake," he spits and yanks his phone, dropping it in the process. It slides across the floor to me, flashing wildly, ringing like a gong through the quiet shell that is my flat. The name Kat dances on the screen. Leaning forward, I pick it up and hold it out, but to my surprise, he snatches it and shoots Perry an aggravated look. He really didn't want to come here tonight— that much was obvious. At least Perry will get the brunt of some of his anger, and not just me.

"I'll swing by shortly," he says, checking his gold watch. "Soon, Kat. You'll know when I'm there," he delivers hotly. He's staring at me. Staring with eyes that are deepening to a cobalt blue. A tinkle of a laugh on the other end makes my teeth grind. So, he can be accommodating, then? Why not with me? Unexplainable hurt lances my chest. Knowing he dislikes me bothers me to no end. He disconnects and lowers the phone, and I lift my brow. "What?" he snaps.

"I was just wondering why I get Miserable Cain and others get a more placid version." I nod at his phone, and Perry snorts. Cain snaps a look at him, and he shovels a load of rice in his mouth and grins. He's such a child at times. I laugh inwardly until Cain replies.

"There is nothing placid about me," Cain drawls.

"Well, from what I get to experience, there's nothing nice either," I say candidly.

"You remember I'm your boss, right?" he growls ominously.

"You remember you're in my house, right?" I snap back.

"Okaaay. Let's take a breather," Perry interrupts. "Well, that was a new record." He cheers. "I think you managed at least half an hour before you started to argue," he informs us.

"Shut up." I huff, eyeing Cain, who is leaning back on my sofa, glaring at me with a clenched jaw, whilst Perry mutters something unintelligible about us being like a married couple and unbearable sexual tension. Cain pales, and I bare my teeth at Perry. This has absolutely gone too far. They need to leave. Or Cain does. "Whilst this has been fun. I'm ready to pull out my shit couch, in my shit flat, so if you don't mind." I sigh, giving them both a pointed look. Cain's face splits into a wide smile, and I gasp inaudibly, sucker punched by how completely approachable he looks—how stupidly attractive he is with a smile on his face. On a light shake of my shocked head, I drop my gaze and close up my food carton.

"For someone who works in hospitality, you're a poor host," Cain muses, tugging his shirt back up the short way it has slid down his forearms. I stare at him, wanting to say something equally cutting back, but I haven't got the energy to fight with him.

"Okay," I murmur, neither agreeing nor disagreeing with him. He frowns at me, and I get up, picking up the few empty cartons Perry placed on the coffee table and taking them to the bin. I hold up Cain's suit jacket. "Goodnight." I offer my most insincere smile. I really don't like myself when I'm around him. I get claws.

Cain's jaw flexes, and he yanks the coat out of my hand and strides towards the door, leaving Perry behind. "That went well," my new friend muses. "Night, alien."

Cain stops and looks around my place, waiting for Perry. His gaze falls to my calendar, and my eyes widen as he leans in and reads some of the notes. With an angry frown, he looks back at me, and I just know he has read the 'Cain is a prick' note I jotted after my accident.

"Let's go!" Cain snaps. I try to apologise, but he is already storming out of the door.

"Like I said, it's best we keep our distance." I huff to Perry as I let him out and shut the door, glad to be free from Cain's constant disregard. I pick up the pen and scribble over the comment on my calendar.

Shit. If my work life wasn't already bad enough, he would make it unbearable now.

CHAPTER 10

Cain

As soon as I exit the apartment, I'm brimming with anger. She noted me on her fucking calendar. My phone rings, and I answer it when I see it's my half-sister Kat again.

"It's rude to disconnect before the conversation is over!" she mutters petulantly.

"I said you'd know when I get there," I grunt.

"Why? Are you planning to douse the place in gasoline and drop a lit match on it?" she laughs sarcastically. "He's not the only one you're burning, Cain." She's referring to her father, Royce.

"Not my problem." I end the call again and take the stairs two at a time.

"Are we practising for the marathon?" Perry huffs behind me as he follows me down the stairwell.

"What apartment block doesn't have a working lift?" I growl in response.

"This shit hole." Perry steps in beside me as we leave the block of flats. "Imagine sleeping on your sofa every fucking night."

"I'd rather not," I reply, heading straight for his car. I send Justine a text and drop my location.

I want all the information on this building.

"She looked embarrassed," Perry says, pulling away. I find myself looking back at the building and shift in my seat. She did, and I dislike that I put that emotion there.

"Her choice of accommodation isn't our concern," I lie breezily. I wasn't in the right frame of mind to face her tonight.

"Cain, you could have her out of that flat by morning and in new digs before she could pull that shit sofa out." Perry gives me his best puppy dog eyes, but he forgets I'm not some eager woman trying to please him.

"I could," I drawl. I could, but I won't. She'd hate me even more than she does now.

"You're an arsehole."

My hands fist until they crack. "I'm aware." We drive mostly in silence, and every now and then, Perry glances at me in annoyance. He's too fucking nice.

"Why are you getting so close to her? You don't like any of my other employees?"

"I didn't give any of them concussions." He grins at me, then shrugs. "She's different. I like her. She isn't out for herself or eager to get in your good graces because it poses an opportunity. She didn't even know who you were."

"I don't like it," I mutter.

"Then why come to the restaurant? Why go to the hospital?" We drive for a few more minutes, and he pulls up outside a large residence. "You want her, Cain, and for once, I can actually see why. She isn't the kind of woman you can fuck around with. Don't hurt her," he says sternly before exiting the car and waiting for me to meet him on the pavement. We're deep into the richer side of London. I grew up here and spent most of my youth and teenage years behind the large metal gates of Carson Court—gates that will soon belong to me once again.

"Are they home?" Perry asks. They, meaning my spoiled bitch of a mother and her waste-of-space husband. Her husband, who cheated my father out of his business, weaselled his way in and slowly began chipping away at my father's fortune while plucking his wife from beneath his very nose. He ripped everything my father had built away from him in a blink of an eye: his businesses, his home, and his wife. Me. I became a tool for them to use, and my proud and respected father had wilted before my very eyes. It became too much, too great a loss. He could have lived without the business and our family home, but losing my mother had destroyed him. The last time I had set foot in this house was to clear out my belongings, years after my father had killed himself, and I was no longer trapped in their care.

Shaking my head, I walk over and key the code in. "They left for St. Lucia a few days ago." The gates click, and I push my way in.

"Do they know you've already acquired that property?"

"They will. I signed the paperwork this morning." That, along with the deeds to this place. Royce may own the building, but I own the land because, while he has become complacent in his own smugness, I've been working to rip it all from him. He thinks his business is at risk, so his focus is there and not on how everything else is unravelling around him. He'll fight me tooth and nail, of course, and that's what I want—for him to use all of his money fighting me every which way he can because he will lose every penny battling me, fighting to keep something that was never his in the first place. And when I finally take ownership of his businesses, he will be as penniless as my father, as broken and destroyed as he left us.

"What about Kat?"

"I'd never hurt her, but if she chooses him." I shrug. "Well, that's on her." My friend chews his lip thoughtfully.

Kat opens the door before we reach it. "Happy with yourself?" she spits, brow arched high as she leans against the doorframe.

"Nice to see you too," I comment, keeping the smile off my face. I don't wish to antagonise her further. I drop to kiss her cheek, and she turns away before my lips connect. I sigh and carry on into the house.

Perry pecks her cheek. "Hey, chick, did you get your haircut?"

Kat fingers the tips and ducks her head away. "Hi, Perry."

"You got anything to drink in this place?" he asks, walking into the main foyer. I stare at Kat. Her cheeks are pink as she watches Perry. When she finally looks back at me, I raise my brow, and she rolls her eyes.

"Yes, the bar is through there." She struts past and refuses to meet my eye again. "What's your poison?" she says, moving past Perry and heading through the parlour to the far side where my father's bar is still installed. I grit my teeth, angered that even after all these years, the house is still in its original glory.

"Pretty little blondes." He grins, sitting on a bar stool, as Kat moves about behind the bar and crosses her arms. "Your breasts look phenomenal when you do that," he observes, and she drops her arms almost immediately. My friend chuckles, but I clip him up the back of the head. He knows Kat has had a crush on him since they met. He loves to poke fun at her, and she loves to see him. I sometimes think he is what keeps Kat and me together. He is our glue because if it weren't for his playful manner, the shoulder for her to cry on, she would have cut me off a long time ago.

I drop into a seat and check my phone.

"What's his issue?" Kat asks Perry.

"Stop prying," I grumble. "I'll have a beer." She is frowning at me, so I level her with a hard stare. "I'd love to say I like what you've done with the place, but I'm almost certain little has changed since my father owned this house." She has the decency to look embarrassed.

My friend intercepts and tries to ease the tension building. "He wants to fuck an employee, but,"—Perry pulls a face— "when one makes the rules, one must abide." He sighs dramatically and holds his hand out for the bottle of beer that Kat holds out. She's just shy of twenty-one. I was fifteen when our mother had her, and despite the hatred I feel for her father and our mother, I feel only love for Kat. When she reached out a few years ago, I couldn't turn her away. She was as spoiled as I was at her age. I know she doesn't understand all of this, but she's old enough now to truly know what kind of man her father is, learn the hard way who our mother is, and why they can't be trusted. This is the first time it has affected or will affect her. I'm taking her home, the financial security her father manipulates her with.

"You cock-blocked yourself. Oh, the shame." She smirks, placing my beer down and sliding it toward me.

"What do you want?"

"You know if you buy Carson Court, I will be homeless too." She throws down the letter, my lawyer's logo staring back up at me. Her eyes fill, and I hate that I'm hurting her. Like me, this house is all she knows.

"No, you won't. I wouldn't see you out on the street." I swig my beer and look away when she drops her gaze and fights the tears burning hotly in her eyes.

"But our parents can live out of bin bags?" Kat scoffs.

"Your parents." I tip my beer her way. "Not my problem."

"Cain, this has to stop." Her hands slap against the glass surface. "I'm sorry for what my father did," she says passionately.

"You know nothing, Kat, just the bullshit you've been placated with. Your father is a cancer, and I'm his fucking cure." I slam my beer down, and she flinches from the loud crack. I don't check the glass like she does. I know it's reinforced.

"Cures aren't supposed to hurt." Her lip trembles.

"This one does," I growl. "That letter was for your father. You should never have opened it," I admonish.

"I recognised your lawyer's name," she whispers. "Where the fuck am I supposed to go? You're making him sick." Her words catch, and she swallows.

"Good!" I roar, making her jump. My chest heaves as I glower at her across the glass top. Perry places a hand on my back and tells me to calm down. I suck in a deep breath, but she is teetering on the edge, too.

"You're a cancer, too!" she cries, her tears spilling over. My heart lurches painfully, my hands go lax, and I stare at her in shock.

"Kat," I murmur softly, holding my hand out, but she wraps her arms around her waist and leans against the back bar, causing the bottles to clink and rattle, tears running down her face.

Perry's chair scrapes back, and he moves around the bar to pull her into a hug. She sniffles, and his eyes bore into me over her shoulder. Fuck.

"Kat, I'm sorry you find this hard."

"Lots of people cheat," she hiccups. "I know it's not okay, but they loved each other. I'm sorry that they hurt your father."

I laugh shortly. I'm over this bullshit she is being fed. Perry shakes his head at me, pleading with me to go easy on her. She needs to know the truth. If she still chooses her father afterwards, then she is on her own.

"Your father was my father's closest friend," I remind her, "his business partner."

Her brows narrow into a frown. "They fell in love!" she wails dramatically.

"He stole from my father. Bought his company right from under his nose, with his own fucking money!" I bellow.

Her face falls, and she searches my eyes, then pulls back and looks at Perry, who gives her a sympathetic smile. "This is deeper than you realise, Kat," Perry says softly.

"No." Her head shakes. "He wouldn't."

"He did." I huff a short, disgusted laugh. "My father trusted him, and he stole from him like it was nothing. He tore my family apart, moved into this place, and inserted himself into our lives." My father was already established, respected, and he let Royce in on that too, and the bastard bit the hand that fed him. Hard.

"They fell in love." She wipes her cheek dry.

"Olivia loves the money," I say scathingly. Our mother was accustomed to a life she was not about to leave because of her husband's inability to see that his friend was a thief. "As soon as my father lost the businesses, she lost interest, and your father made his next move. Hell, it wouldn't surprise me if she was in on it from the start."

"Cain, I know they hurt you, but you can't help who you love. I know they feel guilty."

"Kat, it's embarrassing that you believe that." I step away, too angry to listen to the lies they've told her.

"They never meant to hurt anyone. They mourned him when he passed away." She tries to placate, but it only angers me further. Passed away? The fucking audacity. More lies they have rammed down her naïve throat.

I growl, fury rattling me to the core.

"Cain, don't," Perry warns, pointing his finger at me. It's

like a trigger, like someone finally pulled the firing pin, and the only bullet being shot is the truth. If it kills Kat, then her parents only have themselves to blame.

"He killed himself, Kat. Put a gun in his mouth and killed himself. Your father stole everything that he worked for, everything he adored and prided himself on, and then he took the only thing he had left: me. Their lies alone give me enough reason to ruin them. I love you, but I won't spare you." My words come out in a shaken rush. "If you keep defending them, keep believing the lies they spout, you're no better than them. Wake the fuck up, Kat."

"They said he had a heart attack," she chokes, "they said—"

"IT'S ALL FUCKING LIES!" I roar.

"Cain, take a minute. Go and get some fresh air," Perry mutters.

"Keys," I demand. Perry throws his keys at me, and I stalk out, the sound of Kat's sobs coating the blood rushing through my ears.

I'm starting the engine several minutes later when Perry jogs out to meet me. He hops in and buckles up, and I peel off from the kerb and put my foot to the floor. "She's in shock. I'll check in with her tomorrow."

"No need. I will reach out to her."

"Cain Cancer Carson. It's got a ring to it," he jokes.

"Fuck off." My palms shake against the leather of the wheel.

"Just got to get rid of his name. Ivory isn't really your colour," Perry adds.

"Passed away! They fucking sicken me. He stole from me, so I will steal everything from him: his name, his reputation, his home. Anything he touches, I will take and exploit."

"The Midas touch."

"Perry, I'm not in the mood for your jokes, and quit playing games with Lauren," I spit angrily.

"No can do. Maybe you can gift her the house. She needs a better place to stay," he remarks, smirking. It propels my anger to thrum through the car.

"You didn't tell me you had taken her home the other night." My fists clench around the wheel.

"Would you prefer she walk the streets at night?"

"You don't Uber the rest of my employees home."

"Yeah, well, you don't want to fuck them." I glare at him, but he holds it just as fiercely. "You're welcome." He smirks. "I say you sleep with her. At least then you will be in a better mood to deal with all this shit with Royce."

It's not a good idea, but it's the only one I know that will work.

CHAPTER 11

Lauren

Amberley skips towards me as I smooth down my skirt. I've double-checked that I look my absolute best should Cain appear. I refuse to allow him room to pass judgement on my attire or work. I can't shift the deep burrowing sense he is purposely needling me. Besides, after he read my calendar, I want to avoid further mishaps. His eye is always too critical, too invested in finding something, and although I know he is a businessman who demands high-quality service and dedication from his employees, with me, there is something more, a compulsion to pick at me. Slowly. Peeling back the smallest of skin to expose me and make me vulnerable. What's more, he is good at it. Even after a good night's sleep, I've woken irritated and on edge. Even in sleep, I can't escape him, it would seem. I don't recall having any dreams, but I have this foreboding feeling that he was there. Standing over me. A shadow, playing with my emotions.

Shuddering, I shake it off. "Morning!" I smile, adjusting

my name badge. I need to forget about Cain. In fact, from now on, I will only address him as Mr Carson-Ivory, both verbally and mentally.

"Hey, girl." Amberley grins. "I had the most chill night ever, bubble bath, face mask, wine. It was divine."

"Sounds like it." I wish my evening could have been as relaxing as hers. Instead, I was landed with our miserable boss and his pain in the arse sidekick. "Do I look okay?" I ask, twisting to face her head on. I stand with my arms slightly held out and lift my chin to give her a good view.

"Erm... Yes. Why?" She frowns, completely confused by my unusual need for assurance about my appearance. I'm not one to overthink my looks. I know I'm not unattractive. I don't play it up or down. I just am, and I like that.

"I thought I looked creased," I lie.

"Nope." Amberley twirls and hooks her arm with me. "In fact, you are creaseless. You could give Feli-shit-y a run for her money," she mutters under her breath. I scoff, squeezing her arm in mine, and we make our way down to reception.

I spend most of the day dealing with emails, bookings, and checking guests in and out. It's an easy day, and it goes by without a hitch. Felicity is too busy doing her own thing to pay me much mind, and our picky boss hasn't shown his face.

"Lauren, can you give me a hand? I can't get into the luggage storage." Beryl huffs red-faced. She holds up the key. "I've been wiggling this thing about for ages, and it just won't budge." She blows her hair out of her face and sighs.

"Yes, sure. Let me just shut this down." I close the window I have open on the computer and leave Felicity for a few moments whilst I follow Beryl to the storeroom.

She puts the key in and twists it about, but nothing happens. "See, it's jammed," she vents, shaking the handle.

"Let me have a go," I say, and she harrumphs, passing me the key. I insert it but can feel the lack of movement in the lock. "It's barely shifting," I mutter, wiggling it about, much like she did. For god's sake!

"Should I call maintenance?"

"Just a moment," I say and push my weight into the door. I twist the key, and it turns without a problem. "There we go." I smile and pull the door open. "Do you want a hand with the luggage too?"

"Please." She wanders in and points out the cases for me to pull down. They are heavy, and I nearly drop one as I pull it towards me.

"Jesus!" I curse, stumbling into her and the other cases.

"Oh, my word!" Beryl cries, then begins to titter with laughter.

I giggle too. "Sorry! I think this one has a ton of bricks in it!"

"Must do. Thank you." She adjusts the handles and wheels them towards the door.

"I'm going to go speak with maintenance about the door. Are you sure you're okay with the suitcases?"

"Yes, dear." We exit the store cupboard, and I insist on helping her until we reach the reception again. The deep rumble of a man's voice has my feet slowing. I tilt my head, trying to listen, but one of the wheels is squeaking, and Beryl is panting up a storm. I really hope that's a guest and not Mr Carson-I've-got-a-huge-stick-up-my-arse!

"Good Afternoon, Mr Carson-Ivory." Beryl smiles. Great! I let the suitcase roll to a stop behind Beryl and offer a bright smile as he comes into view. His eyes flare, and my heart gives a tight squeeze. Something about knowing this man has been inside my home, shared a meal with me, has my stomach liquifying.

I'm all too happy to give him a wide berth, him and his unflinching cobalt eyes. The hair on my neck prickles, so I know I'm being scrutinised. "Lauren," he calls, stopping me in my tracks. I twist with the same beam I affixed to my face moments ago.

"Yes?" Beryl and Felicity are glued to our interaction.

"I expect you to look presentable always." His eyes drop to my chest. It heaves, and his eyes tighten. "Fix your badge," he mutters and knocks his knuckle on the marble top. "Goodnight," he bids both women farewell before turning his back on me and striding off. Gritting my teeth until they almost crack, I twist around and strop off towards maintenance, adjusting my badge when all I really want to do is throw the fucking thing at him!

"Look presentable always," I mutter under my breath. I'd love to see him lug a hefty suitcase about in heels and a pencil skirt, the snobby twat. I never wish ill on anyone, but I really want his day to be shit, maybe a flat tyre or for him to wake with a fat spot on his perfect face. And yes, he has a perfect face, I admit begrudgingly. His lips are not too wide, but full and tempting. His jaw is strong, as is his nose. He is stupidly handsome, stupidly rich, and successful, and his overwhelming sense of self-importance makes me sick with the need to be liked by him, even though I can't say I like him back, his personality at least. That sucks.

"That is what I said." His clipped tone makes me shriek, and I spin around and crash into the wall. Shit!

"It's just that I was collecting luggage, so that's why my badge was askew," I say in a panic. Slowly, I right myself and smooth out my shirt. Will I forever put my foot in it with this man?

My boss adjusts his stance, and he looks even more formidable with his legs planted firmly apart and his chin angled just so. I blink at the level of authority rolling off him. His eyes dim, reflecting an emotion I don't recognise, but it makes me shrink and heat all at once.

"I assisted Beryl," I explain. "I'm on my way to maintenance as the door is jammed." Wait—I thought he was going.

What is he doing back here? "I thought you had left," I say softly.

"That would suit you, wouldn't it?" His gaze narrows. I keep my chin up and suck in a deep breath through my nose. My stomach churns, butterflies exploding from out of nowhere and fluttering frantically to escape the intensity of his gaze.

"Mr Carson-Ivory, I know we got off on the wrong foot," I begin.

"Vomit will do that." He wrinkles his nose, and I laugh awkwardly. Yes, I suppose that is true. "I'm a little disappointed, Lauren. After agreeing to continue your employment, I felt you'd be grateful for the opportunity, and we'd see evidence of your glowing resume in your work," he scorns, lightly adjusting his cufflink, all the while looking me dead in the eye.

"I am," I whisper. Grateful and working to the standards CI expects. I've read their policies, my contract, and the employee handbook enough times to quote it word for damn word.

"My main concern is *that*." He points at my face, and I automatically touch my diminishing bump. "No. That look," he elaborates.

"My attire and makeup are within company policy," I choke, shocked by his accusation.

His eyes do a lengthy sweep on me, and he nods his head ever so slightly. "It is. However, the look in your eyes isn't something we require at The Carson-Ivory,"

"Excuse me?" Thoroughly perplexed, I gawp at him, looking over every inch of his inflated ego. He's needling—taking a sliver of my professionalism and pocketing it for his own gain. What the hell does this man want, or expect of me?

"If you can't disguise your dislike for me, your own boss," he raises his brow, and I swallow audibly, "how can I expect you to be front-of-house and deal with difficult guests?" he murmurs. "Did I make a mistake in continuing your employment here?"

This is punishment for last night.

"No, Mr Carson-Ivory." I offer him my best smile. It feels strained, and my cheeks are heating with every passing second. He watches, absorbs my discomfort and the bastard revels in it. "I apologise," I croak. I'm not sorry that I don't like him. The man is a power-hungry prick with a lack of tact. Apparently, he hasn't yet realised that about himself, despite being able to pick up my flaws, pale skin and all.

His smile dips into a smirk, and the placid smile I'm fighting to keep on my face weakens. "You can go." He speaks abruptly, and I flinch. Go, as in fired? I blink up at him. "To maintenance—" He nods down the corridor.

With a small nod, I rush off, gulping in air. I trail my hand along the wall, needing to feel the comfort of a hard surface. My legs are jelly, and my stomach is twisted up in knots. I really underestimated him. I honestly believe had I not puked on him, he would still dislike me as much as he does.

I make it to maintenance, tap on the door and push my way in. I could have easily called them from the front desk, but coming down here was a way to put space between my boss. I never expected that he would follow me to torment me in private.

"Hello." I'm breathless, and it doesn't go unnoticed by the few men sitting drinking tea.

"You okay?" One stands. I think his name is Albert. He's an old chap, and I really like him.

"Yes, sorry." I waft him off and take a seat. "I could have called, but I wanted the exercise," I fib. "The luggage door is sticking. It will only open if I put my weight on it," I explain.

"Why don't you sit for a few moments, then we can go take a look," Albert offers, picking up his cup and taking a swig. "I believe a new door is on order," he tells me. Oh, it is?

"That's good," I reply and allow myself to catch my

breath. I sit with the guys for a few minutes, then Albert and I leave with the others sniggering about Albert and his wandering eye.

"Ignore them," he mutters. "My eyes are fine," he tells me, and I laugh. However, as we near reception, he begins preening, and I press my lips together.

"Ah, Beryl, how are you?" He beams, and I see the older woman's cheeks flush slightly. "Felicity." He inclines his head.

"Oh, hello, Albert. Have you come to sort the door?" Beryl queries.

"That I have, lead the way!" He holds out his hand, talking to her directly. I watch them with a smile on my face. Did they set this up? Beryl fluffs her hair and Albert comments on her pearl necklace. The sneaky pair! Fraternisation is strictly off-limits. It was one of the first policies I signed. I doubt they are going for a quick smooch in the luggage room, but a little flirtation can't hurt.

"What's that look for?" Felicity spits.

"Oh, just,"—I point after Beryl—"that was kinda cute?"

"They're old." My manager drawls, disgusted. "And it's against policy."

So what? Age is just a number! "Well, I think it's sweet," I say, taking Beryl's seat and ignoring the snooty woman beside me. If she shoves her nose any higher into the air, guests will see right up her nostrils!

The last half hour of my shift goes well. I keep telling myself not to let my boss get to me, that tomorrow is a new day, and everything will work out. I need to ensure, going forward, that I carry myself in the appropriate manner. It is true that I have become a little too familiar with my boss, and I should show him more respect, even if I keep my job. I leave after giving Amberley a quick hug and hit the tube.

My phone dings with a notification, and a message from my ex, Martin, flashes on the screen.

. . .

Please talk to me. I'm sorry. I still love you, Lauren. We were friends first. I want us to be friends again. x

I lock my phone and close my eyes, but it only allows the image of Martin thrusting into Kristy to pop into my mind once again. Humiliation engulfs me as new as it felt the day I caught them together. My lips turn down, and I swallow the achy ball of pain in my throat. Some days I feel her betrayal more than his. We had been friends since we could tie our own laces.

My thoughts are consumed with the pain of their betrayal and my work situation—how am I going to win my boss back over? I don't even realise I've passed my stop until I look up and find the train empty. I jump up in a panic and get off as it slows. I hate the tube. I forever feel claustrophobic as the muggy walls press in. It's a few minutes before I reach ground level and come out onto the street, clutching my bag to my side, short of breath, unsure where I am. I'm not used to this part of London, so I stand, uncertain on the path, looking around, trying to gather my bearings. Fresh, cool air swirls around me, and I feel my lungs chasing the worry away as I suck it in. This is a bloody nightmare. Martin calls my phone, but I reject him. I don't think this day could get any worse!

"Lauren?" The deep timber calling my name has my back tightening, and dread hits my stomach at lightning speed. Why, just why? Eyes wide, I slowly twist around to find Cain, a few feet away, staring at me from the entrance of a restaurant. Dr DeLuca follows him out shortly after, and he greets me with a wide and genuine smile. I chew over silent words and finally give an awkward smile.

"A little far out," my boss murmurs. Is that code for too expensive? I sweep my gaze down the wide street lined with expensive cars, vine-covered buildings and more pedestrians donned in designer clothes. Unlike me in my dowdy coat, hugging my rumpled bag like a nitwit.

My jaw works, and I try to suck back the retort working its way quickly up my throat. "I missed my stop," I say shortly. I look back over my shoulder at the tube. "I actually need to get home." I don't want to go back down. I was going to call an Uber. I'm flustered, and seeing him has only made me less put together. Why is he everywhere? He's like a bad smell, only hotter, and he doesn't actually smell. Well, he does, but it's some faintly rich and woody scent that hits low in the stomach.

"Something on your mind?" My boss queries, his tone is light, and when I brave meeting his gaze, his blue eyes are sparkling with a fire I know too well. He's poking fun at me.

Grinding my teeth, I give them both a smile. The one I direct at DeLuca is far kinder. "Not at all. Excuse me," I mutter. *I love my job. I love my job*, I repeat over and over as I walk away.

"Lauren!" That's not my boss. Matteo catches me up and flashes me an easy smile. "I'm leaving myself. Can I give you a lift?" he offers. My eyes meet Cain's over the doctor's shoulder to find his irritating smirk has dropped into his shiny shoes. Ha, victory!

My boss makes extra quick work of joining us—his hands shoved deep in his trouser pockets. He looks distinguished and pissed off. "I don't think that will be necessary, Matt. I can get you home, Lauren," he intervenes.

"Oh, no need. I can go home with Matteo." I tilt my head and smile up at the hot doctor. He's not really my type, but I like the way he looks at me, and after Martin's little reminder via text, I want to feel wanted. My boss grits his teeth, and I celebrate on the inside. Up yours, you miserable twat! "Lead the way, doctor." I grin.

DeLuca winks, and I flush. Is he hitting on me? I hope so. I sorely need a confidence boost after Martin and Mr Grouch breathing down my neck. Matteo walks to a car on the kerb-side, and I take a step forward, but Cain yanks me back until my back collides with a jolt to his front.

His lips hit my ear. "Lauren," he warns, his hand fisting around my wrist. "I would say getting into the nice doctor's car isn't entirely appropriate, given that he is a guest at the hotel." This close, I can smell the rich musk of his aftershave. It's divine, alluring, masculine, *and my boss!* My brain chimes in.

I rip my arm free. "Hmm, it's a shame my boss didn't get that memo when he invited himself into my apartment," I shoot back and put some distance between us as Matteo looks up from the other side of the car.

"Ready?"

I look back and debate refusing. If he is trying to hit on me, leading him on is unfair. But when he smiles genuinely, I relent. "Sure am." I sigh, forcing my nerves aside.

"Don't." Cain's deep voice catches me off guard. His tone is low and only loud enough for me to hear, but that's not what causes me to rethink my decision to leave now. It's the note of pleading it carries. Don't go with DeLuca?

I spin around and purse my lips. "Am I going to get fired?" I ask quietly.

Cain frowns and shakes his head lightly. "No, of course not." He swallows and lifts his head, squaring his jaw. Gone is the moment of hesitation in him.

"In that case, see you tomorrow," I reply and leave him standing on the path when I get in Matteo's car.

"Goodnight." Matteo lifts his hand in that way only men do before he zips up my window, blocking Cain out. The car manoeuvres us out into the road, and my eyes latch onto the wing mirror where my tall, formidable, and gorgeously angry boss stands immobile as we drive away. "Finally, I get you to myself." Matteo clicks his tongue and gives me a wink. So the hot doctor does want in my pants?

I grin over at him. "I hadn't realised you'd been trying." He's been trying? This is insane. Amberley is going to faint when I tell her!

"Only since you walked into The Carson-Ivory," he admits with a deep sigh.

I gawp over at him. "Oh." Maybe I should come clean now and keep things professional.

"I have to say I was mildly pleased you'd hurt yourself." He winces, but I laugh.

I give him my address and smooth down my skirt when he drops his gaze to my bare knees.

Matteo clears his throat. "Are you going to invite me up?"

"To mine? Definitely not," I stutter. I'm never taking a man up there again after the last disaster. His eyes dim with disappointment. I'm attracted to him. It's nothing that catches me off guard or has me lost in thought, but I know an attractive man when I see one. There's no harm in a bit of fun, right? People do it all the time. I bite my lip and look over his face and his long frame stretched out in his car. He is hot. Besides, I'm not likely to see him around too much. "But I could come to yours?" I voice slowly.

CHAPTER 12

Lauren

It's another fifteen minutes before we pull up outside an elegant white brick house in Mayfair.

Does this make me cheap? Probably. Oh god.

Matteo has kept my mind busy the entire drive, chatting about work and asking me how I've been feeling. "I can take you home?" he suggests when he cuts the engine. I'm staring up at his big house, worrying my lip as I contemplate what will happen beyond that door.

I shake my head softly. There is absolutely nothing stopping me from enjoying a night with this man. It's not my usual style. I like to date a little first before I become intimate, but I've quickly learned that London is nothing like home and one-night-stands are pretty common. "I want to come in." What's bothering me is Mr Carson-Ivory's request. He didn't want me to leave with Matteo, and that small plea had me secretly wishing he had fought to drive me home himself. "However, you're a guest at the hotel and——"

"Not entirely." He laughs. "Your boss and I go way back. As you can see, I live fairly close to the hotel. I can't say I haven't crashed at one of his hotels every now and then. He called a favour in with you." He's referring to when he came to check me over when I fainted.

"Okay. I'm not really sure why. He and I don't really see eye to eye."

Matteo gives a deep laugh, and I smirk. "Honestly, if you worked under me, I'd be pretty pissed off too," he muses, his eyes twinkling.

"Why?" I pull back, perturbed.

Matteo reaches over the console and tucks my hair around his finger. His eyes are full of heat, and it makes my stomach knot with excitement. "Excuse me for being so blunt here, but you're fucking gorgeous." His eyes then drop to my legs, and his hand follows—his finger draws a dainty circle on my knee. "You've got incredible legs," he hums, "and they look particularly good in heels, and it'd piss me off having to work around someone I couldn't have." I'm not even sure I understand where he is going with this. Is he saying he wishes he was in Cain's position? Swallowing, I stare at him, trying to read between his words. He's got narrow lips, and I quickly compare them to my boss's fuller ones before shaking the thought away. Cain Carson-Ivory needs to get out of my head. "Lauren, nothing will happen that you don't want to do. We can just share a drink and get to know one another." He's facing me fully in his seat, and I blink a look up at him, nod, and he unclips my belt, freeing me up. "Last chance. Do you want me to take you home?"

I shake my head, and DeLuca's face splits into a wide smile. I grin back as he exits the car, and I meet him out on the side of the road before walking to his door. My heart picks up, and I look around, feeling a little self-conscious in such a well-to-do area. This is nothing like where I live. I can't see a scrap of rubbish on the road, and even the path seems somehow cleaner. My eyes zero in on a sleek car near the end of the road. Is that? It can't be. Surely lots of people have that car. My gut begins to twist up in knots. I narrow my eyes, trying to focus and gauge whether the silhouette behind the wheel is, in fact, my boss or someone else, when Matteo's hand lands on my lower back. Cain's roughly spoken 'Don't' rings through my skull, and I almost ask that Matt take me home. Being here feels wrong. Not because I don't feel safe, but because I want it to be someone else's hand on my back.

The things Matteo mentioned in the car start filtering in and slot into place. Cain is attracted to me. That's why he is giving me such a hard time and why he is always so short-tempered around me. That's what DeLuca was alluding to, wasn't it? Matteo walks us in, and I'm too dumbfounded by this revelation to initially acknowledge the interior of his home. He takes my hand, drawing me farther into the house. It's a modern and elegant townhouse. Original features are smoothened into the decor by contemporary art and furnishings.

"Your home is beautiful," I say, trailing my hand along a sideboard.

"And now I have one more beautiful thing in my home," he murmurs behind me.

"I'm a thing now, am I?" I smile.

"You're a thing that's been on my mind a lot."

"I see." Who would have thought this gorgeous doctor would be attracted to me? I always felt I was pretty, but plain. Not someone to make you look twice, but enough to look at. I've had boyfriends before, but Matteo is very much a man—a hot man—but he is no Cain.

Cain is something else entirely. I should leave.

"Would you like a drink, Lauren?"

I chew my lip, and when I look up, he is staring at me expectantly and kindly. "Please."

Matteo walks us down to a stunning kitchen. I watch his

back retreat, mentally at war with myself. Nothing can ever happen with my boss, not to mention I signed a document adhering to his non-fraternisation policy. His friend may have alluded to Cain finding me attractive, but I've learnt that can be a fickle thing. At least for a little while, here with Matteo, I can enjoy his flirtation.

"Oh wow, this is—" I look around, trying to find the right word. "I love it." The units are a deep, dark midnight blue, with brass fixtures and chandeliers.

"I recently updated it."

"Well, your taste is spot on," I hum.

"Glad you think so." Matteo moves around his kitchen, pulling down two glasses and selecting a wine from the well-stocked fridge. "White okay for you?" I hope he isn't banking on my being as sophisticated as him. I'm beginning to feel a little overwhelmed in his big house.

"That's great, thanks." I take the glass and a healthy gulp.

"You seem nervous," he observes.

"A little. I was on my way home not half an hour ago, and now I'm here." I laugh and silently plead with a look that he will be patient with me. It's been a while since I was approached by anyone, and I can't say I'm overly experienced. My last relationship was more than three months ago, and although things weren't perfect, I was happy, and we were looking to buy a house. We were engaged. Until her. Being cheated on with your best friend is a sure way to make you doubt yourself and wreck a three-year relationship.

"Lauren. Nothing has to happen, nothing you're not ready for." Matteo takes my hand and lifts it to kiss my palm. "Come with me." Nervousness fizzes in my stomach and muddles my brain, but it's someone else's face in my mind.

"Is that on the list for later, or can we schedule that in for another time?" I garble.

DeLuca throws his head back, laughing. "I'll take what I can get and nothing more."

"Okay," I squeak. I was full of such confidence not long ago, but a lot has been said. Things I didn't know now are swirling around my mind. Matteo is beautiful, and honestly, the whole sexy accent has me flustered, but Cain—there is something unorthodox about that man. An edge I can't help but want to meet. Knowing he is attracted to me, as Matteo suggests, gives me the kind of butterflies I've yet to experience with DeLuca. Butterflies that have been fluttering in my stomach from the moment I laid eyes on my boss. We move into the living room, and it's like something out of a magazine, clean, crisp and aesthetically pleasing.

"How are you feeling? I know concussions can take a little while to recover from," Matteo asks, taking a seat at one end of the sofa. I find a place at the other end.

"Good, thanks. Honestly, I don't even feel like it ever happened anymore." I bring my drink to my lips and inwardly slap myself because I'm terrible at this. Flirting has never been natural to me. I'm clumsy and awkward under a man's attention. Except Cain, who makes me mad enough not to even second-guess myself. "Did you always want to be a doctor?"

DeLuca laughs. "No, I was meant to take over the family business. I had been trained for it my whole life."

"So why didn't you—what changed?"

"I was following a car with a young family inside. It was icy, and they crashed. It was late, and there was very little traffic on the road. I called for an ambulance, but for a while, it was just me and all these bloodied bodies."

"That's terrible."

He nods. "I felt very helpless. The father died on impact. The mother was unconscious with a severe head wound." He shakes his head. "The smallest of the children was screaming, and the other was knocked out and bleeding. Glass had,"—he points to his neck—"nicked his artery."

"Did he die?"

"No, I kept pressure on, and the ambulance arrived and

took over. I've never felt more proud of myself, and the next day, I quit the family business and went to med school."

"I take it your family wasn't pleased." I can sympathise. My parents both pushed me to join James and have security being in a family business, but I wanted something else for myself. Sometimes I'm not even sure what it is.

"No. They still hope I will return to Italy."

"Do you think you ever will?"

"No." He smiles at me, and then the blare of a phone breaks the moment. "That's my work phone," he mutters.

"I hope it's not an emergency,"

"You and me both. Don't move." He leaves me on the sofa as he strides off in search of his phone. It's a good few tense minutes before he returns, and when he does, he is holding his medical bag. "Lauren, I'm sorry. Perry has got himself into a mess."

"Perry?" I jump up and adjust my clothes quickly. "Is he okay? What happened?"

"A misunderstanding, by all accounts. I do want to check him over, however."

"Of course. Can I come with you?" I ask, concerned. When he nods, I gather up my bits and follow him out of the house to his car. We drive for about twenty minutes until we pull into an underground car park. "I hope he's okay."

"Perry is used to getting himself into scrapes," DeLuca enlightens me.

"You're all good friends, I take it?" I mean Cain also.

"We have a fair bit in common," he muses, getting out. I frown at his response and follow him through the car park to the elevator bank. I can't help watching his expression in the glass box we ride in. Gone is the carefree man. He has his doctor's head on, and by the intense shine in his eyes, knowing it is a friend who is hurt is bothering him. "Stop," he mutters and twists to smirk at me.

"You look so intense." I press my lips together.

The elevator bumps to a soft stop, and Matteo exits, walking directly past the main desk. "He's expecting me, Reggie." I eye the old man standing behind the desk.

"Good evening, doctor." The greying man smiles at me and takes a seat, looking at the multiple security cameras. We get in another elevator, and Matteo mutters about how inconvenient they are.

"Now, now." I giggle.

We come to a stop and step out. We're on the top floor, and our walk is a short one to the double dark wooden doors halfway down the corridor. Matteo gives a series of loud knocks, and a few minutes later, the door swings open, and I come face-to-face with my boss.

"What the hell is she doing here?" He bares his teeth, then looks directly at me. "What are you doing here, Lauren?"

"I came with Matteo to check on Perry," I whisper, stunned at his animosity.

"Where is he?" Matteo responds, ignoring Cain's aggression. DeLuca slips past, and I quickly try to slip by, but my boss grabs my wrist and pulls me back.

He cups my face and stares at me long and hard. "I can't say I'm not disappointed," he hisses before letting me go and walking into the apartment.

I follow his bristling frame inside, shame heavy in my gut. I wanted my boss to learn to like me, and all I've achieved is to piss him off further. It's an open-plan apartment, but Matteo is too busy rummaging in his bag to notice. I'm glad. What would he have done if he had seen Cain touch me like that? Perry is propped up in the kitchen, sporting a fat lip. Ouch.

"What happened?" I rush over, and Perry's face snaps up, shocked to find me here. His eyes go from Matteo to me, then Matteo to Cain.

"I just wanted to look like you so badly." He grins, then winces as fresh blood seeps out of his cut.

"Ha ha," I mutter as Matteo checks his eyes.

"It's deep," Matteo finally says. "Who did you piss off this time?"

Perry side-eyes until he is looking at me. "Best we don't have this conversation now."

"Oh. Sorry, do you want me to go back into the corridor?" I flush. I never suspected that Perry wouldn't want me here. I just assumed after our encounters, we were as good as friends. He's always inviting himself into my life.

"No." Perry shakes his head. "How've you been, alien?"

My eyes slip to Matteo, and I quickly look away. "Good." I croak. "So, now that you look like me. Happy?"

Matteo and Perry laugh, but Cain walks around us all and glares down at me. I swallow my unease, refusing to meet his eye. "I've reached true happiness. Is E.T on his way for me?" Perry jokes. Rolling my eyes, I fight a grin, but Matteo smirks at me, and my smile intensifies. Cain growls and circles back so he is standing behind me.

"So you two, huh?" Perry asks, and his gaze briefly centres on Cain.

"Well." I clear my throat. "We're. We... I."

"Just go home with men, willy-nilly," Cain growls.

"Did you just say willy-nilly?" Perry shudders.

"I beg your pardon!" I turn to face my boss. Matteo stands tall slowly at my side, and I lift my chin, happy to have his support. "I didn't just meet him an hour ago. In fact, I'm pretty certain this man has watched me sleep under your instruction," I remind him of what he thinks I don't know. Cain's eyes harden, and he looks at his doctor friend.

"Carson," Matteo begins, but Cain lifts his hand, uninterested in his friend's opinion.

DeLuca growls, and I slap Cain's hand away. "What are you, a Jedi?" I scoff, and Perry bursts out laughing.

"Ow, fuck." Perry cups his torn lip.

"Who I go home with is none of your business. What is your problem? You've done nothing but needle me since we met!" I want the truth from his mouth, not some passing remark made by his friend. I want to hear him admit this is all because he can't have me.

"No problem," Cain delivers coldly.

"No?" Matteo questions. "It doesn't take a genius to know what is going on here. You were too slow, Carson." I peek a look at Cain, but his eyes are centred on his friend. They glare, and the set of Matteo's shoulders suggests there is more to this than just me.

"Let's give these two space to measure their dicks. We'll be in the bar," Perry mutters, steering me away.

CHAPTER 13

Cain

M atteo doesn't look at me as he drives off with Lauren —something akin to jealousy hangs low in my gut, weighing in on my mind.

I've never begged a woman like that before. I laugh at the absurdity of it as I run my hand through my hair and shake my head in shock.

"Don't."

Pathetic. I watch as the tail light disappears around the corner, and I cross the street to get in my own car. For the first time in a long time, I come to terms with the reality of rejection. A shocked laugh bursts from my mouth.

So, this is what losing feels like. I swallow the sickly bitter taste of my own medicine. This is no doubt how Matteo felt when I bragged about bedding some stranger, only to come face to face with her at dinner the following night when Matteo introduced me to his fiancée properly.

I'd confessed on the spot and watched as his future spiralled out of control.

I suppose it's only fair he subjects me to the same treatment.

I'll let him believe he has a chance. The abrupt realisation that he has Lauren alone and could easily take her home has me driving after them. I don't believe for a moment she will invite him up to hers. She was embarrassed when Perry and I entered her apartment. If anything, they will go to his. I drive directly there, hoping I'm wrong, but when I park up, I locate his car in the distance as Perry calls me. I answer over the hands-free.

"Where the fuck are you? I thought you said you were on your way?"

"I am," I growl.

"Ooh, moody, looking forward to seeing you," Perry teases. I stab the button to cut him off and turn the engine over as Matteo walks Lauren into his.

Fuck!

That lucky bastard.

I can't quite pinpoint if I'm more disappointed in myself or her.

I drive to Perry's, angry and dejected. I've never felt jealous of another man, let alone my fucking friend. Any decent man would concede he has lost, but this only propels me to challenge the attraction between us further. Lauren is going to have a choice to make because I don't fucking share.

Perry is waiting at the kerb, chatting idly with the doorman. He springs my way, and when I notice a break in the traffic, I lean to swing the passenger door open as he bends down to say something through the open window. The door bounces off his face with a loud thud.

Perry roars, rearing back and cupping his mouth. "Cain! You twat!"

Laughing, I hop out as he walks to the pavement, blood

dripping out of his bust lip. "Now you know how Lauren felt," I muse.

"Fuck," he hisses, leaning to check his reflection in the wing mirror. "You arsehole."

"I reckon the girls will dig it." I shrug as more blood seeps out. "You need to get it checked out."

"Call Matt," Perry says as we head into his building.

"He's with Lauren." My friend spins with a look of shock on his face.

"Even more reason to call him," Perry replies, calculated. Grinning, I dial his work phone, and we take the lift up to his place.

"You might need stitches or glue. It looks deep," I observe as he keys his way in.

"Feels it," he grumbles.

Matt answers, and I give him a brief rundown, feigning an emergency. Perry pouts, and I cut the call, dropping down onto his sofa. "He took her home," I impart and Perry whistles, or at least attempts to, but it produces a bloody bubble instead. I grimace, and he huffs, grabbing some paper towels to hold to his face.

"Why are you so indecisive with her? You want to fuck her, and I'm pretty certain the feeling is mutual."

"Like you said, she's nice. If things turn sour, it could come back to bite me on the ass, and I don't need anything to fuck up my plans for Royce."

"So, Matteo. How's that feel?" Perry eyes me with a twinkle in his eyes. I don't find him funny.

"Like I want to punch him clean in the face."

"I mean, if it's any help, and I'm talking from experience —" he begins, and I shift to look at him. "I think a punch isn't substantial enough. Why not advance to a car door," he drawls, and I bark out a laugh. "Seriously, you need to make a move. If what you said about Lauren's ex is true, she won't want to dip between mates."

"I know." I sigh as the door knocks.

"That was quick," Perry murmurs, standing.

Too fucking quick. I hoped Matt would take Lauren home first—either he has left her back at his or she is with him, and I don't like the possibility of either of those outcomes.

I swing the door to find my friend, accompanied by the only woman to have ever caught my attention. Unfiltered jealousy roars through me, and my hand fists the door. Fuck, I want to hit him so badly. His mouth twitches, but it's soon schooled by a serious look.

"What the hell is she doing here?" I sneer and then turn my attention to Lauren, wanting to shake sense into her. "What are you doing here, Lauren?"

"I came to check on Perry." Concern laces her voice, and I feel a pinch of guilt for being such a colossal prick to her.

Ignoring me, Matt slips inside. Lauren tries to sneak in, but I snatch her wrist and hold her back. Desperation, jealousy, and annoyance rattle around my head.

I cup her face, looking for any sign of intimacy between them, but I can't be sure with how much she is chewing her lip. "I can't say I'm not disappointed," I bite before dropping her face and walking into the apartment.

Matt is already pulling things out of his bag as he speaks quietly to our friend sitting at the breakfast bar. Perry's face snaps up, and his eyes sweep between us all before landing on me with discomfort. It's awkward as fuck, and I can feel the tension seeping from the carpet and locking us all in place.

Matteo finally says, "Who did you piss off this time?" I smirk at that because Perry is a natural at provoking people with his incessant need to wind them up.

Perry side-eyes until he is looking past me at Lauren. "Best we don't have this conversation now." I frown, unsure why he is being evasive.

"Oh. Sorry. Do you want me to go back to the corridor?" Lauren's cheeks flare brightly.

"No." Perry shakes his head. "How've you been, alien?"

My fist tightens when her eyes slip to Matteo's and not mine like they used to. "Good," she mumbles. "So now that you look like me. Happy?"

Matteo and Perry laugh, but I can't find an ounce of humour in the current situation. I pace the kitchen and come to stand behind Lauren, vibrating with pent-up anger.

"So you two, huh?" Perry directs the question to Matteo before he looks at me, and I grit my teeth.

"Well." Lauren garbles, embarrassed. "We're. We... I."

No, that's right, pretty girl. You're mine.

"Just go home with men, willy-nilly." I find myself saying as I glare at Matteo dabbing at our friend's lip.

"Did you just say willy-nilly?" Perry shudders.

"I beg your pardon!" She steps forward, glaring at me. Matteo stands slowly, and I raise a brow at my friend. Is he seriously squaring up to me? "I didn't just meet him an hour ago. In fact, I'm pretty certain this man has watched me sleep under your instruction." I hold Matt's stare with my own hard one. Heat works its way up my neck, but I refuse to cower. Yes, I did instruct that because I was looking out for her. I raise my hand in a calming gesture.

Matt is brimming with as much anger as I am. Lauren's soft hand knocks mine away, but I want to grip it and pull her in for a hot kiss—to put her and my friend in their fucking place. "What are you, a Jedi?" She scorns.

Perry laughs. "Ow fuck." Cupping his mouth, he turns to Matt, who holds up some gauze.

"Who I go home with is none of your business. What is your problem? You've done nothing but needle me since we met?" Lauren continues, her chin tilted, and her eyes shooting daggers at me. She is beautiful.

"No problem," I lie. The problem is five feet of pale petiteness that I'm addicted to watching on the work cameras. I swallow that admission.

"No?" Matteo questions. "It doesn't take a genius to know what is going on here. You were too slow, Carson." My attention slowly returns to my doctor friend, where I fight the urge to show him just how slow my fist isn't. It's no more than he did to me when I slept with Sabrina. I may not have known who she was, but he still felt the sting to his pride.

"Let's give these two space to measure their dicks. We'll be in the bar," Perry mutters, hopping down and shooing Lauren out of the room.

I turn to Matt with a calm expression on my face, but he is smirking at me. "Like I said, too slow." He shrugs.

"You think I haven't already?" I scoff, enjoying the way his smirk falters. "She was mine the day you came to check on her. You've had your fun—now back the fuck off, Matt."

"You obviously didn't make a good enough impre—"

"Matteo, back off." I level him with a stare. My chest heaves, and he stares, perplexed. "Leave her alone."

He pulls back, bemused. "You're being serious?" he muses slowly, his stance softening in realisation. "Cain, mate. I didn't think you were *that* serious."

We've had many run-ins about women—both being attracted to petite brunettes—it was bound to happen. I'm aware that he has slept with women I have, and it's never caused my gut to burn with jealousy as it does now.

Turns out I am serious, very. I refuse to share Lauren. "I am." I clear my throat as his hand falls to squeeze my shoulder.

"You were going to hit me." He laughs lightly, packing his things away.

"I wanted to."

"I'd have hit you back,"

"I'd expect nothing less."

"For the record,"—disgust is the only emotion I can hear in Lauren's voice, and we swing to look at her as she holds her little finger up—"major turn off. Go find someone else to sword fight your pencil dicks over." She stalks out, the door slamming.

Matt might have a pencil dick, but I fucking don't. I wiggle my finger in his face. "She was talking about you, mate." I snigger, and Matt shakes his head.

"The only thing big about your dick is your balls." He grunts, unimpressed.

"Wait, you didn't sleep with her, did you?" I demand, my face twisted in anger.

"I don't kiss and tell." Matt smirks. I can't work out whether he is ribbing me or trying to maintain our friendship by not admitting the truth.

"Not much to tell if all you did was kiss."

CHAPTER 14

Lauren

It's been a few days since I've seen my boss, and for that, I'm grateful. Doing a week of late shifts couldn't have come at a better time. I doubt he will be loitering around the hotel during the evening. I've not seen or heard from Matteo since being at Perry's apartment, and even if I had, I would ensure we kept things professional.

The loud trill of my phone wakes me before my alarm. On a loud, exaggerated groan, I twist over and reach for it. "Hello, Mum," I say groggily.

"Lauren, surely you're not in bed already!" she reprimands loudly, making me flinch at her shrill tone.

"I'm on nights," I explain, moving to sit up. I rub at my eyes and blink to wake myself further.

"Nights? Sorry, love. I thought you worked da—"

"I do." I yawn. "It's just for this week. I'm off from Friday to Monday."

"I called to say we'd love to have you for dinner. Would

Friday suit? I'm sure James can make some time too," my mother says hopefully. I haven't been home since I arrived in London. I do feel guilty about that, but so much has happened in these past few months. As much as I love having my own space and being my own person, I do miss my family.

I nearly decline, worried about what Henrik will do, but he can't stop me from visiting my parents, so I find myself agreeing. "What time?"

"Anything after noon. We'd love to spend some time with you."

"Great!" Leveraging myself up, I get out of bed and say goodbye to my mum. With an extra hour on my side, I spend a long time in the shower before I even contemplate getting dressed. I keep my hair down with the intention of pinning it up, then I tidy up my flat and leave for work.

I purposely arrive so I cross over with Amberley. Her face lights up when she sees me walking towards the staff canteen. "Urgh, day shift sucks without your pretty face!" She flings her arms around me.

"That bad, huh? Try wandering around this place at night." I laugh into her hair.

"I'd take that over Felicity any day," she grumbles.

"Time for a drink?" I push open the staff canteen, and she nods, following me. I fetch our drinks and find Amberley at a table. "I can't wait for Friday," I grumble, sitting down. I slide her drink across, and she grins at me.

"I don't envy you." She blows on her drink.

"Everything else been okay?"

"I guess—nothing to report, anyway." She nods over my shoulder, making me look around. "He's new. His name is Oliver."

Oliver is tall, blonde, and about our age. "Cute," she says, and he is, in that boy-next-door kind of way. He twists our way, and Amberley lifts her hand, calling him over. "He started yesterday. Seems nice enough." Oliver makes his way

over, and Amberley smiles up at him. "I see you're back. Glad
we didn't scare you off." She laughs.

"Nearly, but my girlfriend would flip if I left my job, and
that is scary." He grins, taking a seat. "I'm Oliver." He looks
at me.

"Lauren."

"So, you're her partner in crime?" He smirks at us both.

"The one and only." I laugh, cupping my chin and fluttering my lashes.

"Amberley said you're on nights this week?"

"Yeah, back on normal shifts next week."

"I'm with security," he tells me as I sip on my drink.

"Enjoying it?"

"Yeah, this hotel is far more upmarket than any other
place I've worked. I was hoping to meet the boss. Isn't he some
kind of super-rich hotel god?" Or a massive twat.

I sip my drink. "Has he not been in?"

"Nope," Amberley sighs. "He is mega-rich. I read somewhere he purchased holiday homes in Mexico and Aspen this
last month." Oliver whistles. "Yeah. Oh, to be rich," she
murmurs.

I check my watch and realise I'm due to start shortly. "I
better get sorted. Nice to meet you, Oliver."

"And you."

"I'm going to walk with Lauren. I'll see you tomorrow,
Ollie." Amberley gets up with me.

"That name is reserved for my future wife."

"Well, then, tell your girlfriend she has competition."
Amberley winks jokingly. Oliver shakes his head, and I let her
link arms with me. We're more than halfway across the
canteen when Cain walks in, eyes seeking me out.

"Lindel, a word." Since when does he use my surname?

"I'm due to start my shift. Is everything okay?" I smile,
despite Amberley frowning at our boss.

Cain scratches his jaw, and my eyes are drawn to the

shadow of hair there. "I'm aware. I suggest you hurry up and follow me, then." He turns on his heel and saunters off, a hand in his trouser pocket, looking mega-rich and like a multi-holiday-home owner. Posh wanker.

I eye my friend and pretend to adjust a tie I'm not even wearing. "Look at me. I'm a pompous twat," I whisper and Amberley giggles. I peck her cheek and jump when he snaps my name. Rolling my eyes, I turn and walk quickly to catch up with him. I follow him silently across the lobby and to the elevators at the far end. My boss stands with his back straight, legs firmly apart, as he waits for the lift to open. I manage to reach him in time and get in the lift before the doors close. There are two other people in the lift, both from cleaning, so we all stand in silence, too afraid to speak with Cain in attendance. They rush off on level three, and we carry on to the top floor, where he walks towards his office. No pleasantries—just pure, spine-tingling tension escorting us all the way. He holds the door for me, and I smile as I enter. Is this about Perry's? It must be.

"Have a seat." Cain closes the door, and I watch as he walks to his desk and takes a seat.

"Will I need one?" I ask, trying to gauge what is going on here.

"I hope not."

"Then I'd prefer to stand." It also allows me the distance the chair wouldn't. I cross farther into the room, closer to him, but a foot or two away from the back of the seat he offered me. Tilting his head, my boss pushes up from his chair, and I widen my eyes as he moves around the desk, circling me. I move with him so his desk is now behind me, and he is standing less than a metre away.

"What happened with you and DeLuca?" he demands.

My head snaps back. Is he serious? "I'm sorry. If this isn't work-related, then I really do need to get back downstairs." I try to side-step him, but Cain's foot lands in front of mine. His hand takes my elbow.

"Lauren, did you sleep with him?"

"That's none of your business, Cain!" I snap. He is towering over me, his face a mask of irritation. He grits his teeth loud enough that they grind. Jeez!

"Maybe not, but I want to know."

"Well, tough, you don't get to know." I take his hand and secure it so I can remove myself from his grip. "This whole thing," I motion between us, "is not doing anything for me. You really need to work on your bedside manner." I laugh scathingly. I bet his bedside manner is porn-worthy.

"My bedside manner is impeccable. You'd know that if you stopped arguing with me every time we fucking spoke."

"Oh, sure. Real impeccable," I scoff, walking away. "Cain, I really love working here, but honestly, I'm not sure I can work for you any longer."

"Good. Quit. Then I can finally act on my attraction." He walks to me with purpose and cups the back of my head. "Is this you finally voicing your resignation?" His nostrils flare, and his eyes light up with the kind of heat I've only ever wished to see burning back at me.

"Cain," I whisper, stunned by his direct approach.

"All I need to know is if you're resigning and if Matteo touched you?" His eyes drop to my mouth. I bite it, and he hums deeply. His thumb runs along, encouraging my teeth to let go of my lip. "Answer me." If I resign, I'm giving him more access to me. If he knows all Matteo and I did was share a drink, he will be relieved.

"I'm not resigning. What happened between Matteo and me will stay between us. I don't kiss and tell." I blink up at him, and his gaze narrows.

His laugh is short. "Funny, he said the same thing." His thumb is back, and I stare up at him. "I want you, Lauren. I've tried to keep things professional."

It's me who laughs now. "You've been a prick," I tell him.

"I don't think the good doctor did anything more than kiss you." He frowns, watching his thumb dancing over my mouth. "Tell me, did he kiss as good as you thought I would?" I gasp, and Cain smiles. "You walked out of Perry's because it was easier than letting DeLuca down with the truth. You want me." He adjusts his stance, bringing us into contact, and as his thighs line up with mine, I shiver. Double fuck!

"I don't," I lie. My chin lifts, and Cain narrows his eyes, trying to fathom if I'm telling the truth as my voice suggests, or lying through my deceitful little mouth. His gaze flicks up, and he smirks at me before pulling my lower lip down as he leans in. I stand, immobile, as he closes the distance.

"Aren't you going to stop me?" he muses softly, "or are you desperate to know what it will feel like, too?" His eyes glimmer with satisfaction, and when I don't make any move to stop him, he lowers his mouth to mine in a searing kiss. His tongue sweeps in, and I moan and kiss him back. I want this. I want him, and if I'm really being truthful with myself, I have wanted this man ever since he insulted me that first day. My face is crushed between big hands, and I grip his suit jacket as he plunders my mouth and my lies into submission. I couldn't refuse him if I tried. And no, Matteo wouldn't hold a light to Cain in the kissing department. For every ounce of pressure I apply into his kiss, I find Cain applying twice the dose back. "Are you ready to hand in your notice yet?" he purrs between a rough kiss. He holds me close, pressing every part of himself into me as though he can't quite get close enough—as though to adjust my position would be to refuse him something that is fundamental to his being. I shake my head.

"Liar. Don't ever tell me you don't want me as much as I want you." His thumb crushes my lips. "I wonder what you look like when you come apart." Gasping, I try to regain my composure, but he is dragging up my skirt and hauls me up his front. My legs instinctively go around his waist. "You've been causing me all kinds of trouble, pretty girl."

Shock spews from my lips in a throaty moan. Trouble. That's what I'm going to get into if this continues, but I can't pull myself away. Don't want to.

Large hands palm my ass, fingertips dig into the flesh as his mouth works passionately over mine, teasing, seductive, and laden with intent. If we don't stop now, we'll be naked and in violation of the fraternisation policy. Scrap that, we already are in violation. I lace my fingers deep into his hair and whimper. I want this more than I dare to admit.

"Cain." I pull away, sucking in a lungful of air. "I'm due to clock on."

"We're in a meeting. You're technically working." Bold blues meet mine, twinkly and hot.

"Not helping," I choke as his mouth finds my neck, and his teeth drag down the sensitive flesh.

"I can help you out of your clothes," he utters roughly.

A sudden knock at the door has us springing apart. I struggle back to my feet. "That should never have happened. I need to get downstairs." I press my lips to my fingers as Cain asks for a minute. I'm officially late for my shift. A shift I could very well lose. Cain steps forward, but I dodge his touch. "This was a mistake. I'm not resigning." My lip disappears behind my teeth, and his eyes squeeze into determined slits.

"You know, I could fire you for what just happened here," he speaks softly, teasing. It's not surprising that my boss likes to play dirty. If I've learnt anything about him in these past few weeks, it is that he is cutthroat. That knowledge doesn't stop me from feeling combustible around Cain, something I've never experienced with another man. The irrational, lust-infused side of me wants to quit on the spot, screw any responsibilities and give in to my base desire. The other part of me knows it will only end badly.

"You kissed me," I whisper, dismayed and annoyed that I can't tell if he is being serious or not.

"But you kissed me back." He shrugs, watching my expression. I gasp, shocked, and his face twists in regret. "Lauren, I would never fire you for something I did. I was...fuck, you get under my skin. It was a joke. I'm sorry."

"But you do want me to quit?" I croak. He wants me and the only way he can have me is if I quit. He grins apologetically and I narrow my gaze, too worked up to see the funny side of it. "If you're going to fire me, then do it," I spit. "But the second you do, don't ever expect to see me again." Cain removes his arm, allowing me room to move. "And for the record, I find DeLuca very attractive, and no, you don't kiss as good as I thought you would," I lie. Cain's face snaps into annoyance, and I bolt out of the office and past a prim-looking older woman as I rush down the hall to the elevator. My lips are abuzz with his touch. My heart is screaming a happy dance, even if my head is chaotic and unnerved. Cain Carson-Ivory is so much more than some mega hot-shot hotelier. He's dangerous and seductive.

⁓

I don't come into contact with Cain again, and by the time Friday comes around, I'm desperate to escape London and be home with my family, even if it means spending the day with my overbearing brother, not to mention putting us all at risk. If word gets back that I'm in town, Henrik will be angered, but he never verbalised I couldn't visit my parents. My drive is long and slow and allows me too much time to think about the past few weeks. I wonder what it would have been like if Cain had never taken over the hotel. What it would have been like if his assistant hadn't interrupted us.

I cruise down Main Street and find a space to park outside

Waitrose. It's a fairly warm day, so I've teamed a maxi dress with my pumps and pulled a knitted jumper over the top to finish the look off. Collecting my bag, I exit my car and make my way inside. Heads twist my way, but I affix a smile and give them the Carson-Ivory treatment. Some smile and greet me warmly, and others look at me with sympathetic eyes. It's like I never left.

I head for the drinks aisle and select a chilled bottle of wine just as Martin and Kristy turn the corner hand in hand.

So much for missing me. His eyes spring wide, and hers dart away. I only manage to roll mine as Martin unhooks himself and walks towards me, but my mind is back there— back in that room as I caught them betraying any word of love or support they had once professed to have for me. I can still remember asking them how long they had been lying and sneaking around behind my back. Martin had rushed to me then, as he is doing now. Only this time, Kristy grips his hand, and he stops. If I didn't know him so well, I'd almost believe he was regretful. Three months. It had destroyed me.

"Lauren. Hi." Martin sounds uncertain.

"Please stop messaging me," I say calmly. Kristy snaps to look at Martin, who is watching me with sad eyes.

"I just want you to know that I am sorry," he says as Kristy palms his upper arm. I don't pay her any attention.

"I'm not." I give them a genuine smile. "Take care." I stride off and find my smile stretching. It has absolutely everything to do with my gorgeous boss.

I feel lighter for coming face-to-face with them, liberated even. I smile as I pull into my parents' driveway. The two-storey family home sits nestled in a cul-de-sac, and the weeping willow with rope swing still guards the front lawn.

A small ding has me rummaging for my phone. I expect Martin or Kristy, but it's worse.

· · ·

I do hope you don't plan on staying long?

Just visiting. I will be gone before dark.

Make sure that you are.

My eyes water slightly as I read over the messages. They may be from an unknown number, but I know who is on the other end: Henrik. He and his family have run this town for a long time, ever since they developed the country club and moved into a gated house up on the hill—where the money lives and where he can be lord surveyor, watching over his town. He has gained complete rule. I was too young to watch it happen, and I knew no different or nothing of his callousness. In some ways, I'm glad I was able to escape the life I thought I would have had if I had married his son. I'd been ecstatic when I told Kristy of our engagement. Now, I know why she wasn't overly pleased for me.

Kristy can enjoy his wrath. He can't blackmail me forever.

Hearing my car, my mother comes to the front door and waves happily. She is a slight thing with a white pixie cut and big brown eyes. She wipes her hands on her apron as I get out of my car. "Hey, Mum."

"Oh, Lauren, love. Let me get a look at you. How's your head?"

"Mum, it's fine." I laugh. She meets me at the bottom of the path with a tea towel in hand and a bright smile on her face. I lift my fringe. "See." I show my very normal-looking forehead.

"We were worried about you, Lauren." Her concerned eyes search mine. She means my breakup too.

"No need. I'm fine." I lean back in my car and pick up my bag. "How's Dad?"

"He's inside." My mum leads the way. "Robert, Lauren's here!"

"James not here yet?" I check for his car in case I missed it.

"Running late."

Once inside, I find my dad with his glasses on, watching the football, a beer at the ready, and a discarded crossword to his left.

"Hey, Dad!" I smile, approaching him, and dropping a kiss on his cheek. "Who's winning?"

"Would you even know the teams if I told you?" He twists, looking at me over his glasses.

"Well... erm... no." I laugh.

My dad pushes himself up from the chair. "Let me get a look at you. Your mother said you had an accident?"

"I walked into an opening door. I was taken to hospital with a very minor concussion. I feel fine now," I rush to say when his eyes widen in worry.

"Lauren, why on earth wouldn't you call us?" My dad's angry tone shakes through the house. "And if not you, then your boss or a friend should have informed us."

"If it had been any worse, they would have, but honestly, it was fine."

My mum pops her head around the door. "Drink, Lauren?"

"Please, can I have some tea?"

"So, Dad. How's golfing going?" I change the subject, eager to move on from my bump.

"I don't like the instructor," he mutters.

"That's only because I'm better than you." My brother James saunters in, grinning at my dad. His eyes slide over me with little interest. He's always been that way. Out for number one. The golden child. I'm no threat to him, so he pays me no mind. Not to mention that he doesn't agree with my life choices, and refusing him the opportunity to boss me around in his company still pisses him off. *If only he knew the truth.*

"Wait until I invest in some good clubs and not those worn things you gave me," my dad relents, smiling fondly at my brother.

"How about a round tomorrow?" my brother asks, walking past me without so much as a hello. Turd. I watch him secretly, wondering what it is that he has done to enable someone like Henrik Johansson to blackmail me into silence. The more I observe his arrogance as he boasts to my father, a cocky smirk on his face, the less I want to be here.

"I'm going to go see if mum wants any help." I stand, leaving them to watch the game. I love my brother, but I can't say I like him much. Years of watching my parents fawning over him and being compared to him was enough of a reason to start out on my own. Add in Henrik, and it was a no-brainer.

CHAPTER 15

Lauren

"How's work?" Mum asks, elbow-deep in bubbles. My mind catapults back to Cain's office and how I was wrapped around him whilst he moaned into my mouth. My cheeks heat, but I clear my throat and dry the pots for her.

"Good." I smile. "Just tired from night shifts."

"You'll have to bring your friend next time."

"Amberley?"

"Yes, that's the one. Is she enjoying it, too?"

"Yes, it's a really lovely hotel."

"Maybe another time, your father and I can come and visit, and you can show us." I smile at her and pass her a tea towel to dry her hands on.

"Sure, let's arrange something." They would hate my flat —maybe I could take them to a nice restaurant. I frown into the sink, thinking of a suitable place when James comes into the kitchen. My mum pours my father a drink and takes it to him in the sitting room.

"You and dad playing golf, that's nice." I smile, not sure what else to say. We're not close enough for me to know what's going on in his life, or vice versa.

"Don't be like that. You chose to move away," he scorns, getting a drink and not even bothering to let me respond. I watch him walk out and grit my teeth. This is how it always is, jibe after jibe from James. He will charm my parents stupid and make me look like a pointless twit. I finish making my tea and join my family in the sitting room.

"I would have done that, Lauren." My mum tuts seeing me with a drink.

"It's okay. Dinner smells amazing!"

"It will be a change from takeaway, I'm sure," James mutters.

"Oh, Lauren. You don't eat that rubbish, do you?" My father frowns over his glasses.

"No. I cook most evenings unless I'm with friends."

"Beans on toast doesn't count," James interjects. Given he is six years older than me, he is a childish twat.

"Good job, that's not what I eat," I say as I lift my cup and take a sip, happily swallowing the insult working up my throat.

"So what do you eat, then?" James demands. My oblivious parents don't even bat an eyelid at his needling. They are just happy to have me home.

"Why?"

"Well, since you left, you've probably lost a stone," he delivers, and both my parents snap around to get a look at me. Great. Thanks, James!

"Oh, Robert, she has!"

"Do you need some money?" My father wants to know.

"No." I spend the rest of the afternoon fielding questions about my diet and day-to-day activities. By the time I leave, my parents have arranged to come and visit the following weekend, unhappy with my life. I feel exhausted and can't wait to crash when I get home.

Night shifts and a day with my family have left me feeling drained, not to mention the whole Cain situation. I left London to catch my step, and now I feel worse.

—

I arrive home to find Amberley slobbing out on my sofa. She's had a key a little while now but rarely uses it.

"Oh, thank god!" She jumps up. "Where the hell have you been? I've been trying to call you!"

"With my family." I check my phone as multiple messages and missed calls ping through. "No signal."

"You looked wiped."

"Feel it." I yawn.

"Oh." She pouts. "I was going to ask if you wanted to hit the town. I'm feeling the need to dance the week away."

"I don't know. I'm shattered." I flop down on the sofa, and she joins me, pulling me in for a hug.

"How about you grab a shower, and I make you a coffee, and if you still feel tired, we can slob out?" I'm pretty certain we will stay in. I nod and opt to stay put for a few minutes, too comfy to move.

"Parents okay?"

"Yeah. It's just James. He kept twisting things, and my parents got stressed. I don't know why he does it." I sigh. I've even confronted him before, and he laughed, telling me I had finally become the woman he expected, as I was concocting something up that wasn't even there. Since then, I've given up. I haven't the time for games, and I barely see him, so it's not much of a concern for me.

"Maybe he's unhappy, and seeing how free-spirited you are pisses him off." He is hiding something, that I know.

"I'm hardly a free spirit," I scoff. I've never confided in her about my ex or his father. I didn't want to see her pity. I was a victim to it back home. Here, I can be anyone but that person again.

"Freer than him. He has met every expectation your parents put on him, and you just walked away. I think he is jealous. My sister is the same. She is always trying to prove she is better than me." I never really thought of it that way.

"Sorry, I didn't know that." Amberley shrugs, and I pull her in for a hug before I head for a shower. "Make it a strong coffee!" I holler from the bathroom.

An hour later, we are sitting on stools at a cocktail bar. I'm glad I decided to come out, despite still feeling tired. My mood has lifted, and Amberley and I are three tequila shots down. We've laughed about work, shared stories, and she has just revealed a sexcapade incident that had us both nearly falling out of our seats.

"Blurgh, whose idea was shots?" She scrunches her face up, shuddering.

"Yours." I giggle, having a sterner stomach.

"Shots are the devil."

"I love tequila," I chirp.

"That's because you're weird. You probably like being flogged too, or some kinky shit like that," she casually says, and I burst out laughing.

"I've never been flogged in my life!" I splutter, my eyes tearing up as I titter in my seat.

"Bet you would though." She giggles, and I go red at the thought of giving in to Cain's request.

"Anyway, you can't talk. I can't believe you slept with your boyfriend's brother." I snort, still finding it funny.

"He was a twin. I didn't know!" she defends. "Anyway, Hugo should have fessed up instead of fucking me blind. I knew then it wasn't Darren—he never could make me come," she garbles, already laughing hysterically. I spill my drink as I laugh at the thought.

"What a way to find out!"

"Best way." She smirks. "Shall we move on? I'm ready to dance."

Much to my dismay, we arrive outside Perry's club, and Amberley coaxes me inside. "Honestly, I can't think of anything worse than clubbing where our boss frequents," I mutter in her ear. I don't confess that I'm scared he will be here or that I secretly want him to be.

"If he was anything but a hot, rich sex god, I'd agree." My eyes snap wide. Does she fancy Cain? "Why are you looking at me like that?"

"Do you have feelings for Cain?" I stutter.

"What? No." She laughs. "Sure, he's hot, but he's a bit too serious for me." She shakes her head, and I deflate in relief. "No!" she gasps. "You like him?"

I shake my head vigorously. "No... I... it seemed like you di—"

"Cut the bull, Lauren. Shit, you really like him. He's a bit of a dick to you, though," she contemplates, leading us inside. The music thumps, and I hook my arm through hers, searching frantically for the man in question.

"He's oddly decent one minute, then this moody twat the next." I sigh, shrugging, not wanting to admit I do, in fact, have very confusing feelings for our boss. I refuse to admit our kiss, too. Amberley will hyperventilate. How would she feel if she knew he'd eaten dinner at mine and that he'd confessed his intention to act on our attraction?

"If he does appear and starts giving you a hard time, we can leave, okay?"

I nod and join her at the bar, order our drinks and pay. "It's packed in here," I shout as a group of boisterous men stagger to the bar, chortling loudly.

"I know. Let's hit the dance floor." Amberley begins shimming her way to the floor, and I follow. Kendrick Lamar is pumping through the club, and people grind and sway to the base. I find my rhythm quickly and mouth the words to my friend as she sips her drink and rocks to the beat. I'm verging on drunk, and the music is riding on my good mood and filling me with confidence.

A guy comes up and shouts over the music. "I'm Eddy."

"Lauren, and this is my friend Amberley." Eddy smiles at Amberley and leans back in to talk to me. We noticed them as we headed to the bar not long ago.

"Do you want to join me and my mates? We're just over there?" He uses his bottle to point in the direction of a group of men. I flick a look at Amberley, and she gives a slight nod. She's out to get laid. I roll my lips, dispelling a smirk.

"Okay, sure." Amberley wiggles her brows, and I hook my arm with hers, following Eddy across the floor.

"This is Paul and Ian," he introduces us.

"Lauren." I smile.

"Amberley." My friend hops up onto a stool as Eddy pulls me one out.

I smile at him and step up as a pair of large hands clasp my hips roughly and pluck me off. I'm deposited firmly on the floor, a wall of heat enveloping my back as a hand slides around to splay on my lower stomach. "Lauren." Cain's tone is a warning. I blink at my friend in shock, wide-eyed, as Cain's breath skims my neck. "Join me in VIP." It's not a question. Amberley's face is a picture. She gawps at our boss.

"I'm good here, thank you," I squeak, stepping forward as butterflies erupt in my stomach, but his hold tightens, and I'm pulled flush to his front, my bottom landing just short of his groin. He grunts and grips the material at my navel.

"I disagree," he snaps.

"She said she's good here," Eddy scoffs.

"She's none of your business," Cain spits. Twisting me behind his frame, he slides his hands into his trousers, the picture of calm, despite his tone being knife-sharp. His casual indifference to the three men glaring at him makes me shiver. I peep at Amberley, and she is grinning like a maniac. She's soaking this up like an addict taking a hit on their latest fix. Even with his hands tucked away, clearly putting him at a disadvantage to these other men, I know Cain would flatten them without much effort.

"VIP sounds great," I cut in, trying to diffuse the situation. "Amberley?" I ask, checking she is okay with how this night is quickly unfolding. A small girlish part of me can't wait to rush up to VIP with him.

"Sure. Night, guys," she chirps, and Cain steps aside to let Amberley past. His hands remain briefly in his trousers, and he looks hot as sin in his open-neck shirt and jeans.

"Okay, so that was hot," Amberly whisper-shouts in my ear. "What haven't you been telling me?" she accuses, and I bite my lip, unsure what to say. It doesn't matter anyway, because Cain takes my hand and threads our fingers. I gape, shocked by his open display, and her eyes bug. "You better start spilling, Lindel!" she spits quietly.

My small hand flexes, a soft thumb runs back and forth along my pulse, and he presses on the spattering beat, absorbing it into his own hand. I suck in a shallow breath, flicking a look up at him. His lips tilt ever so slightly before he lowers to run his lips across the shell of my ear. "Nervous, pretty girl?"

My lips part, his thumb keeps on rolling across my wrist, and I manage a small swallow. What the hell is happening right now? Cain nods me on, and I turn slowly and blink up at Amberley, smirking at me from midway up the steps. Cain encourages me up, and once we are above the club, I chew the inside of my cheek to stop from squealing in giddy excitement. I twist into him with the intention of gaining clarification of what this means, but he leans down and renders me speechless, saying, "You look undeniably fuckable. I watched you dance."

"What?" I blurt. Did he actually just say that out loud?

"You mean pardon?" He raises his brow.

"Yes, pardon?" I splutter.

"I'm going to fuck you," he informs me with cool certainty.

"Yes," I agree. "Wait, no." I give my head a stern shake. "Okay, I did mean yes." I concede, blushing. "Are you drunk?" I garble nervously. I don't want to be a drunken mistake.

A mile-wide smile brightens his face. He steps in, crowding my space. His fingertips slide below the shoulder strap of my dress, but his eyes never leave mine, and I feel his heated promise right down to the delicate throb in my pussy. He twangs the material and drops his head to level his lips with my ear. "No, I'm not drunk. I've thought of nothing else since your accident. Thought of nothing but how you'll taste and smell. How you will sound when I sink myself into your cunt."

"Oh." Oh? Surely. I could have come up with something better than that, or at least some faintly sexual reply. What a lame twat. I blush, and Cain smirks.

"Any questions?" he wonders, bemused, tucking a large curl over my shoulder. I shake my head, completely enthralled by how good his mouth looks when he talks.

"What about your non-fraternisation policy?" I glance around, ensuring no one hears us.

"It's outside of working hours."

"I know but—"

"After hours, you're mine, Lauren. I think I've been more than patient."

I scoff loudly, and he has the decency to grin. He nods me towards Amberley, who is watching with fascination.

I rush over to her and squeak something unintelligible.

"Again, but in English." She laughs.

"I'm going to fuck our boss," I tell her, having a complete brain-to-mouth malfunction, my face flaming beetroot red.

"Lucky bitch. What the hell did he say?" she whispers quickly as he comes back over with Perry at his side.

"Alien!" Perry calls and scoops me up in a hug, walking us towards a booth.

I slide in beside my friend, but Cain moves in next to me and pulls me onto his lap. The distinct bulge in his jeans sears my arse. My thighs clench, and he grunts, shifting, but it only adds to the growing pleasure raining down heavily in my womb. A few moments later, a waiter approaches with a tray of drinks and some water. I thank him and pick up an icy cocktail. It's delicious.

"You look incredible, Lauren," Cain whispers into my ear, and I shudder. Perry is smirking as he watches us, and I give him the finger around my drink.

"Now, now. Play nice!" He chuckles.

Hands slip around my waist and splay over my thighs, and I lean forward to put my drink down, not at all confident I will be able to keep it in my hand if he keeps touching me. "We're having this one drink, then I'm taking you home with me." Fingers trace the seam of my dress, their languid strokes spiking my temperature and sending a wave of electricity straight to my core.

"What about Amberley?"

"Perry will make sure she gets home safely."

"I'm not sure your home is such a good idea." It feels too personal. He's my boss, after all. I shouldn't be doing this full stop, but I can't stop. Not now.

"With all due respect, your pull-out bed doesn't really bode well for what I have in mind."

"Which is?" I ask sheepishly.

"I want to do very bad things to you. Things an employer has no right doing to someone who works for him," he murmurs and runs his chin along my neck—the rough scrape of his bristles makes me shiver with anticipation.

"Oh." I squirm in his lap, and Cain grunts, holding me still.

"I have no issue with exhibitionism. However, if you do, I

suggest you sit still." I go ramrod. "Good girl." I peek at my friend, but she is tapping away on her phone, and Perry is slouched back, staring out over the sea of people gyrating below. I take my time finishing my drink, but as soon as the last drop slips down my throat, Cain stands, and I gasp. "We're going. Amberley, I would hope, given your job role, you can master the art of discretion." She blinks at our linked hands and nods. "Perry will see you home."

"No need. I've ordered an Uber."

I feel terrible. She asked me to come out, and I've ditched her to hook up with our boss. "Do you want me to come with you?" I ask, but Cain slips a hand around me, pulling me back to his front.

"No, don't be silly. I'll ring you tomorrow. Love you." She stands and pecks my cheek. I search her eyes, worried she's upset, but she winks, and I swallow the girlish grin rippling across my face.

Cain escorts me out of the club, using a side exit that opens up into an alleyway. There is no big queue or bouncers. My hand is tight in his grasp as he begins walking up the alley. "You do know that I wouldn't have let you go with her?" He smirks, lifting his brow at me. I've never seen him smile so much. Is it because he has finally got me where he wants?

"Is that so?"

His wide smirk is answer enough. "I'm parked just up here." The alleyway opens up into a private car park, and a set of lights flashes up ahead, and we move towards a black, shiny Maserati. I'm sure this is where I'm supposed to be filled with doubts and talk myself out of making a very bad decision, but Cain is the kind of bad that is so good it curls your toes. Like the gentleman I hope he is, he walks me to the passenger side, but it's for his benefit. He nudges me against the vehicle, knocking the wind out of me. "Just to iron out the finer details—this is a one-night thing. It has to be."

I honestly hadn't expected anything else. I'm not naïve

enough to think my boss has feelings for me. This is lust-fuelled. "I get to keep my job," I dictate. I'm not asking. If he doesn't agree, he doesn't get me.

"You keep your job," he confirms. Wide hands cup my face. "For the record, I don't plan on being gentle. I've wanted you for too long to go slowly." His thumb tilts my head so I'm meeting his gaze head-on. Was I expecting gentle? Nope. Never. Cain does not strike me as the kind of man who smothers with flowers and kisses. He's aloof and cold at times. A little high and mighty. He plays dirty, and I bet he fucks dirty, too. "Last chance to run for the hills." His voice drops to a rough caress, and I lick my lips for the kiss I know is coming. I give a simple shake of my head. When he closes the space, I tilt my head, my neck rolling back to cup the roof of the vehicle, his fingers thread with my own, and then he is lifting them and pressing them flat into the cold metal. He pushes his legs between mine and folds himself above me. Every inch of him is hard. From his wide chest emanating heat, heat that wraps me up and fights against the icy material at my back, to his thick cock pressing hard into the apex of my thighs, bruising and big.

"Cain—" I'm breathless. My heart is dancing an unknown beat, and when he grinds me into his car, I gasp, but the wind chases it away. Lowering his head, he bites my jawline hard, and I whimper. His tongue softens the blow. He teases the tip along my jaw and back down to nip at my mouth. I turn into his touch, and his lips crush mine in a low growl. His tongue sweeps into the depths of my mouth, and his hip grinds roughly. My moan is met by a harsh hiss of his own. He kisses me senseless. It's long and hard, and I'm panting by the time he lets us come up for air. His hands trace down my arms and lower still until they are running down my breasts and to the seam of my dress. His hooded eyes watch me with intense need. Fisting the material, he pulls it up over my hips, leaving it to bunch on my waist, and the cool air swirls like a thousand kisses, easing the heat pulsing between us. Panting, I watch in silent anticipation as he disappears before me and crouches down. His warm breath fans along my thigh, light kisses feather my skin, and he nips and sucks hard on my inner thigh. I buckle, and he plants a firm hand to my waist, keeping me upright. His nose dives into the soaked material between my legs, inhaling deeply, his fingertips bruising my flesh as he holds me still. A hand glides over my legs, and then he is sliding my sodden knickers aside.

"Is this for me, pretty girl?" A wide finger slides between my slippery folds, not deep enough to breach but enough to have me choking out a plea. My chest is flaying, and I whimper as he circles my slit in torturous strokes. He flips me suddenly, and I yelp and slap my palms flat to the roof, holding myself still. He cups me from behind. His hand dances back along my opening, causing my fingers to curl into fists, my ass arching to allow him better access. "So eager, so wet."

"I need more."

His finger drives deep inside, my walls gripping hard and holding him still. "Fuck, Lauren," Cain rasps. His finger works in and out—his teeth a rough bite on my neck. "I'm going to fuck you here if I keep touching you." He slips his finger free, and I whimper. He kisses my shoulder and covers me with my damp panties.

"Get in." He opens the door, and I slide in and blink up at him. Raising my hips, I tug at my dress. He grips my hand. "Tell me to be a gentleman and take you home!" He is panting roughly. His hand vibrating against my own.

My answer is to pull his hand between my legs and whimper when he massages my clit. "Don't you dare take me home." I writhe and clutch at his wrist as liquid heat pools in my pants—my skin feels alive. His palm flattens, and he ducks into the car and grips my cheeks fiercely, dragging my face to meet his. My head knocks back as waves of pleasure crash across my skin, the electric heat reacting to the dampness in my core. He keeps my eyes on his as I come against the heel of his hand—a sharp but sweet cry swirling between us.

"So many bad things, Lauren," he growls, slamming his mouth to mine.

CHAPTER 16

Lauren

Twenty minutes later, we are travelling in an elevator. Cain pinches my chin lightly. "I'm looking forward to getting you out of that dress," he remarks as the lift slows to a stop. "I can smell your pretty little pussy on my fingers."

After being subjected to his cold shoulder, I wasn't expecting this heat or how dirty his mouth is.

We step out, and I eye the corridor, feeling foolishly brazen with all the alcohol in my system. He leads the way, and I begin to unzip my dress as I follow him up the hall. I want to shock him. I want to be remembered after this night. Not just some woman he has added to his no doubt already over-flowing entourage. I want to be the woman that he thinks of as he walks these walls. Cain stops at the only door at the end of the hall, and as he does, I step out of my dress and hold it up so it hangs limply from my finger. The door clicks, and he turns to invite me in, but his eyes pop open. "Surprise." I smirk.

He snatches the dress and yanks me inside. "I wanted to do that."

"Oops." I roll my lips, trying not to giggle at how annoyed he looks. Annoyed and aroused. My response irks him further. Too entertained by his disapproval, I run my hands up his chest and purr, "I can slip it back on?" His fingers feather up my back.

"No need," he rumbles. "But you can take these and put them in the bowl in the kitchen." He holds out his keys for me to take. Confused, I lift my brow and allow him to drop them in my open palm. I spin on my heel and begin to strut down the hall, perplexed by his sudden change. "On your knees." His deep voice rolls out the order. I falter in my steps and look back with my mouth open. "Having second thoughts?" he says, shrugging out of his jacket, and I suck in a deep breath. We stare at one another for a moment, Cain adjusting his cufflinks and me gripping his keys hard enough to break skin. "I want you on your knees. You wanted me to see your body. Well, this is how I want to see it." And with that, his eyes drop to the floor. "Crawl." Heat blooms over my skin right from my toes up to my scalp. I should feel humiliated by his request. It's demeaning, but seeing the glitter in his stare, I find myself lowering until I'm on all fours.

His jaw clenches, and my sex reciprocates. "We've come full circle, pretty girl. This is how we first met," he murmurs, watching me closely. Realisation flashes, and I bite my lip. I was, in fact, on my knees when I met him. "Don't keep me waiting." He nods down the hall, and slowly, I begin my crawl. The silky, smooth floor glides beneath my knees, and I grip the keys tightly to stop them from scratching the surface. I want to look back, but there is no need. I can hear the tread of heavy footsteps behind me. My stomach clenches, and my heart does a weird stutter. "You're stunning, Lauren. You were then," he admits roughly. Ugh, God, stop talking. I'm hornier than I've ever been in my life. In fact, if I get any wetter, I'll be sliding over this damn floor. I reach the kitchen and look up for the bowl. Shoes step into my vision, and I crane my neck to find Cain bursting with satisfaction down at me. "Keys please?" He holds out his hand, and I raise mine to hand them over, but he takes my arm and hauls me to my feet. I gasp and grip hold of his shirt. His hand delves into my hair, tugging forcefully. "I could see your plump pussy between your gorgeous cheeks."

"Cain." I pant.

He takes his time, giving me a lengthy once-over. "I'm wondering which part of you I want to taste first." He reaches around to unclip my bra and slowly drags it down my arms, his eyes greedily taking in my pebble-dusted flesh and rosy nipples. He cups my breasts, his thumbs rolling over the sensitive beads. My head lolls back. "Any preference at all?" he muses and deposits me on the kitchen island. I arch away from the stinging cold burn and into him. "Perhaps you want me here?" His hand slides up my inner thigh until his thumb is running up my thong, over my clit.

"Oh." Yes, I want him there. Cain tugs me to the edge of the counter, and I squirm, knowing what is coming. Wide palms slide up my thighs and prise them apart. His cobalt blue eyes are darker than a stormy sea and just as turbulent when his gaze zeroes in on the damp patch. "Fuck, Lauren." His whisper-soft groan sends tiny sparks of heat to lick across my skin, and his fingers ignite them further when he presses them harshly into my skin.

"Perfect." He trails his gaze down my body and drops a finger on my collarbone. "Such delicate skin. I already know you blemish easily." His eyes flick to mine, gauging my response. I moan, and my head dips back as his fingers run down my chest and between my breasts. "I can smell how wet you are for me." I arch and moan. I want his mouth on me now.

"Cain, please." I try to move and capture his mouth. I need contact and the heady sensation that accompanies kissing this man. Every time I close the distance, he retracts, and as soon as I move away, he leans in, taunting me. Dammit! "Kiss me," I whine. I'm not above begging. I will beg this man until I'm crying.

His fingers keep moving their way down my body. He circles my navel, and as soon as his fingertip runs along the seam of my thong, I shiver. With a growl, Cain slams his mouth to mine and kisses me passionately. His hand dips below the surface, and my eyes snap open to find him watching me vividly. He's so close, but not quite there. I spread my legs, encouraging him. "Tut, tut." He hums and withdraws his hand.

"No!"

Cain spins me quickly, and I scream out, fearing I will fall, but he flattens me to the surface and lifts one leg as teeth sink into my thigh, and I buck, crying out. As soon as the sting is there, it's gone. His tongue makes a languid sweep, softening the bite, swallowing the throb of pain.

"I've been looking forward to fucking you. In fact, I have wanted nothing more than to fuck you since you walked into that damn door. On both knees, pretty girl." He massages my bottom and coaxes me onto my knees on top of the counter. Panting, I press my face into the cool island. My knickers snap, and cool air rolls over my heated skin as goosebumps tidal wave over my body. His groan is pure satisfaction. Thumbs sweep along my seam, parting my lips. "You're weeping." And then his mouth is there, and his tongue spears deeply.

"Oh god!" I sob when Cain presses his face forcefully between my legs. His tongue and teeth ravage me, licking and sucking until my limbs tremble, and I beg for more. A heavy arm splays over my lower back, tilting my arse into a higher position and opening me wider to the assault of his tongue.

"You're so swollen, so fucking wet."

"I'm going to come," I gasp, shaking as his tongue and

mouth slide all over my lips. "There. Oh god, there," I cry. I need more. "Cain!"

He stops, and I sob in despair. "I know," he coos as he runs a thumb along my sex and dips it inside, his fingers pressing against my clit. Desire blooms thick and fast, and I rock back against his hand. He presses his thumb inside, right down to the knuckle.

"Cain, please."

"You're not ready." His fingers apply pressure, my head lolls, and I writhe on the countertop, rocking as he pumps his thumb in and out. "Your pussy is milking my thumb. You're tight as fuck. There is no way you're ready to take my cock."

"I am. I will." I whimper.

His hand slips away, and a delicate kiss is placed on my throbbing sex. It's too delicate, too soft, not nearly enough to bring me to the edge and one kiss too many to torture me further.

"Come here." Cain's low voice sends a ripple over my skin. Twisting around, I scoot to the edge. "Kiss me." Two words have never had so much power over me. I close the distance in a heartbeat and latch my mouth to his. He wastes no time in securing handfuls of my ass and lifting me off the side.

I wrap myself around him and sigh when his lips find the small hollow of my neck. The pleasure starts with the sting of his bite and skitters down to spark a furious throb inside. Grinding into him, I beg for him to give me what I need. His grip is harsh, his face set in a determined frown as he uses his hold to leverage me up ever so slightly. The wide crown of his cock teases through his clothes. He works my hips in small movements, up and down the ridge of his shaft, as his mouth seeks out a nipple, and his teeth play havoc with the sensitive nub. I jerk, moaning, the pleasure swirling up from the depths, tethering to the ache in my breasts. I grind down, staring open-mouthed as Cain drags my nipple through his teeth.

Every molecule in me is vibrating out a chorus of gratitude as my orgasm rips through me, and I cry out his name, my throat raw with need. He allows my hips no rest, dragging them back and forth as my sex pulses—the pleasure ebbing between us. Cain watches, his forehead furrowed as I climax in his arms. "Better?"

I slam my mouth to his, biting and licking at his lips. We ascend, and I blink to find the kitchen disappearing as we head upstairs. Cain's long strides have us entering his bedroom.

He lowers me, our mouths still fused. "Knees, Lauren," he grunts, undoing his shirt and unbuckling his belt. I watch, transfixed. "Knees, now!" I sink down to the floor in time for Cain to fist his cock and hold it at lip level. His free hand teases the strands of my hair, then delves deeper and takes hold of the silky curls. "I expect tears and not a drop wasted." He pants, adjusting his stance and opening his mouth when my tongue dips out to wet my lips.

I moan as his musky scent hits my nose. The wide tip runs across my lips and a salty tang bursts over my tongue when I dip it out for more. Hissing, he jerks forward, fills my mouth full and begins fucking it slowly until he is swelling and groaning. "Damn, you're good at this." Hot cum spurts down my throat, and I swallow greedily. My jaw aches, and my teeth are sensitive. His guttural groan skates across my flesh and sets my soul alight. Desperate to hear him moan again, I dig my nails into his arse cheeks and pull him deep into my mouth, hollowing my cheeks and suckling greedily.

He pants, large hands smoothing my hair, and his thumbs rim under my eyes, chasing tears away. "Such." He thrusts. "A good." Thrust. "Girl," he chokes out as the last bit of cum dribbles down my chin. I grip his cock and suck harshly. "Fuck!" he barks and rips himself free before tilting my head and thrusting his softening cock back in. Cain holds himself still, his cock twitching in my mouth. "Dirty girl." He grins down at me. I smirk around his cock, my eyes stinging from the makeup now swimming in them. "Go, get on the bed." He slips free, and I crawl out from underneath him and scramble my way to the bed.

The sheets are cool and silky beneath my limbs and, sighing, I roll over the surface and twist to find Cain with his head bent against the wall—still. Is he having doubts?

The harsh sigh he expels tells me as much. "You're going to ask me to leave, aren't you?" I whisper. His already tense shoulders lift even farther, and I flinch.

Cain doesn't move. His head never lifts, but the way in which he says my name, full of regret, has me sliding off the bed and walking hastily down the hall to find my clothes. Unbelievable.

Gritting my teeth, I drag on my dress and shove my discarded knickers back up my legs. Sure, but soft footsteps sound behind me. "That one experience is enough for me to know I will need more than one night, Lauren. More isn't on offer."

I refuse to look at him—allow him to see the hurt he has caused. "From now on, stay the hell away from me." I leave, and he doesn't stop me. How he manages to run a multi-million-pound company when he can't even make his mind up astounds me. Surely, we can have sex and carry on as normal adults? I certainly can.

I stomp my way down the hall, shaking from head to toe, when Cain bypasses me in his boxers. "Leave me alone, Cain."

He flings me over his shoulder. "I think you're turning me into a fucking pussy," he scolds.

I wriggle and slap his arse. "Get off me!" I growl. "Put me down." Cain powers us back down the corridor and into his apartment.

"I had a small blip. Something I can only explain as being your fault," he mutters, ignoring my protests.

"My fault? I think you're suffering from PMS. I have a spare tampon if you need it."

"You'd think after choking on my dick, your jaw would be too sore to talk." His fingers massage my arse, and he groans happily at the handful.

"Even if it was, I would still talk back." He takes the stairs two at a time. The upside-down structure makes me feel sick.

"And that's precisely why we are in this predicament." He lifts my dress so that his hand can make contact with my bare skin. I jolt in his grasp.

I jab my elbow into his back, enjoying the sound of him groaning in discomfort. I like it so much that I do it again.

"Pack it in!" he snaps and flings me onto the bed. His face is a mix of confusion and lust. "I need more than tonight. Give me a weekend?" he asks, reaching to hook my knickers around his fingers and sliding them down my thighs.

"No." I kick his arm away. "I'm not a toy, Cain. Either we agree to a night, or I leave." He glowers. I growl. With a defeated groan, he drops his face between my thighs and drives his tongue deep inside. Oh, dear god!

He moans, lapping at my folds and suckling my flesh into his mouth. Shivering, I grip onto his wide shoulders and cry out when he unexpectedly drives more than two fingers inside me. "Lauren, my hand is drenched."

"More, please. I need more." With a few precise pumps and a flick of his wrist, I suck in a breath as my orgasm washes over me with a sweet roll of ecstasy. Cain pumps his hand as wave after wave crashes over me. I'm delirious, lost in a sea of sensations. He flips me and pulls my cheeks wide, groaning about how pretty I am. I squirm, but then the blunt tip of his cock is there. I whimper, my legs shaking like a leaf caught in the wind. He slams deeply on a rough bark, filling me in one deep thrust. I squeal as the pressure of his cock torments, the sting still throbbing between my legs. "Too much," I gasp, overcome by emotion. He pumps out, then stretches me.

"Give me more time." He starts slamming away behind me. "Let me show you how much you can take, pretty girl." Cain adjusts his body, applying enough pressure to manipulate my body to whichever position he pleases. "Your cunt is so fucking tight," he chokes out, grinding deeply.

I groan and push back, becoming accustomed to the pressure in my womb and the width of him. My fists grip the quilt as his thighs slap against my arse over and over. His thumbs run between my cheeks, and I yelp, pulling away, but he grabs me hard, holding me still. "Oh, Lauren, if your pussy is as tight as this." He swivels his hips, and I whimper, pressing back to welcome the onset of another orgasm. "Then I know," —his thumb presses into the tight bud—"here will be like a vice. I'm having you. All of you."

"Cain," I murmur uncertainly. I can't, not tonight. I shake my head and wheeze when he pulls out to the tip and slides back in on a short, sharp bark, making me cry out in pleasure. I'm so close, and he knows it because each time my orgasm unfurls, he pulls away, allowing it to disappear back into some dark recess of me. "I need it." Each rough thrust jolts through me. The impact at the base of my spine, and the hard slap as his hips pound into my pussy, has my body shuddering. He slides in with ease, my arousal soaking our connected flesh.

"If you could see what I see." His palm connects with my arse cheek. Smack!

I garble a response.

"You're stretched to the max, pretty girl."

"Cain, I'm close. You feel so good. So deep," I cry.

I'm scooped up, and my back sticks to his sweaty chest as he rests us on his knees. "Watch," he growls in my ear. My eyes dance open. London is spread out like a blanket of lights, and amidst the sky, there we are in the reflection, fucking in the stars. I begin to move, but it's not enough to appease him. His hand slaps messily between my thighs, and I arch in his hold, my eyes splintering into a myriad of colours as the pain mixes with my pleasure.

I shock myself when I say, "Again." A loud smack vibrates through the room, and my body slips into a place of calm. My mind shuts off, my body slips away, and I'm blanketed by the most serene sense of powerless pleasure. "My thighs are fucking soaked."

I choke out a deprived cry and swing my arms back to hook behind his neck as I ride him with vigour. I should probably thank my parents for putting me through gymnastic school because I doubt I could bend like this if they hadn't.

"Cain, now, now," I cry, feeling the deep twist of pleasure curling in my womb. Attuned to my needs, he grants me my wish. Smack! I sob and shake as an orgasm bigger than even myself ricochets through me. I slip into a blank void. The stars kiss my skin, and his touch sends me there.

"That's it, take it. Your eyes are so fucking dilated. Do you love taking my cock?"

Choking out a sweet cry, I nod. Cain grunts, pulling my hips down in three sharp pounds and calls out in pleasure behind me. His cock swells and jerks as he fills me full of cum. His hands roam over my body, one kneading my achy breast and the other slipping all over my swollen folds. "I need a weekend, Lauren," he finally gasps.

I shake my head, disturbed by how much I want to agree. That wasn't just regular hook-up sex. Cain and I have serious chemistry.

"Stay the rest of the weekend with me, pretty girl."

CHAPTER 17

Cain

A small palm is spread across my chest, and light, painted fingertips crown delicate fingers that not mere hours ago were cuffed around a part of me that is still aching for more attention.

She agreed to the weekend, and I relax into the mattress, knowing that I can enjoy the next two days with her behind the safety of these four walls. She snores lightly—a gentle huff expelled from her bruised lips. Asking for the weekend is dangerous, but not having her for longer was out of the question. I've never wanted a woman with this ferocity. Never craved to be inside a woman as much as I do her. I want her body as much as I require my next breath, but given the choice of the two, I'd fucking pick her and die a happy man. Shaking my head, I peer down at her, slumbering peacefully. She's a distraction—one that has cost me too many hours of contemplation. I have no doubt that this is pure, basic, and unfiltered lust. It's addictive and mocks any previous encounters. I've wanted women in the past, and then there is Lauren. I'll give myself the weekend—sate this aching pull she has on me before I give my attention back to what really needs it. Royce. Carefully, I move her arm and pull the quilt over her bare shoulder, and leaving the bed, I move into the en-suite and flick the shower on. I expect some kind of movement by the time I'm showered and wrapping a towel around myself, but she is still sound asleep when I walk back into the bedroom.

It's still early, so I let her sleep and make myself some coffee. Danvers, my lawyer, has left me a voicemail, so I hit play and smirk as he advises me that Royce Ivory, my spineless stepfather, is making demands through his lawyer. The only thing he will get to keep is my mother. The rest is mine. Carson Court is my father's home, my true fucking birthright. I have this unethical desire to burn the place to the fucking ground, lay coal along the halls, and burn every memory embedded into the walls to ashes. I crave to demolish it and build new foundations, but then it would no longer be the home of a boy who loved to skid along the marble floors or hide in the empty rooms. It would no longer be the home of a boy who lost his father and grew into a man feverish with revenge. I could bury Royce ten times over now and plaster his fucking soul to the gates just so I could drive through him and be smug in the fact that he, too, would have to watch from the iron bars as someone else lived the life he loved.

I thought this news would bring me satisfaction. Almost cleansing, but if anything, my anger spikes, screaming its way through my mind and reaching out to tell the one person it can't—my father. Dropping my head, my chin flush to my chest, I blow out a long stream of air. The anger doesn't dissipate but clings to me as tightly as I did my bleeding father's hand. Striding across the room, I aim for the gym to work my mood away. I should be celebrating, could be, but Lauren doesn't deserve my raging emotions.

It's an hour or two when I hear the low moan of someone stretching from upstairs. By the time I make it to the top of the stairs, Lauren is sitting up with the quilt bunched around her, her hair a tumbling mess, and her face hidden as she rubs at her eyes. "Tired?" I rest my hip against the frame, my muscles burning from my rigorous workout.

"I'm broken," she grumbles. "I think you went to war with my limbs because I ache all over." She flops back and huffs dramatically. Her response is so unexpected that my eyes widen, and a bark of laughter shakes through my chest. Her lips kick up, but her eyes are still puffy.

"Ready for round two?" I muse from the doorway.

"No, I call a ceasefire. I need a spa day and therapy."

My laugh is loud and short. Fucking comedian. My feet dig into the floor. I could easily clear the room and pounce on her to fuck the last of my anger out, but her sleep-stained eyes and croaky voice keep me at a reasonable distance. The light and feminine fragrance in the room softens the scent of sex. There is not an inch of her body that I did not have my hands or tongue on last night. "I'll make some coffee. Go and grab a shower, then come find me for some therapy," I suggest.

"Are you not going to join me?" Her face appears from beneath the covers.

"No."

"But you're all sweaty. Have you been working out?" She sits up, the quilt tucked neatly under her armpits, her breasts squashed high so the soft curve is plumb against my bedding. Taunting me, teasing.

"I have."

"So, come and shower with me." She flicks the cover off and stands, walking towards me. My eyes zero in on the sway of her bare hips and the nicely trimmed hair I had my tongue tangled in last night. "Cain." She smiles, tucking her finger down the front of my shorts. "There's a lot of intention in those eyes and minimal action." Another fingertip glazes over my damp pecs, her nails gently curling.

"I thought you wanted a ceasefire?" My brow challenges her as she smirks and shrugs a shoulder. My restraint is commendable. However, I can't help wanting to touch her, so I cup her hip and let my fingers run up and down the slope of her arse. My fingers dance over the slightly raised line of welts. Hissing, she pouts her lips and smirks at me. I had sunk my teeth into the creamy flesh and licked the bright red mark before sinking into her warm cunt and losing myself in her tight pussy for hours. We had fucked, napped, fucked some more and when she had begged me to stop, cried out for me to let her rest, I'd spread her slippery thighs and feasted on her swollen slit.

"Are you really going to let me try to seduce you, then just leave me hanging?" She blinks innocently up at me. I slowly straighten from where I'm leaning.

"I have all day to fuck you, and I want you to trust me," I say as those same delicate fingers palm my growing cock. My stomach tenses. "Bu—"

"So fuck me. That's what this weekend is about, right?" Her small fist pumps me slowly. "I don't plan to waste valuable time with small talk." She tells me just so. Fuck, could she be any more perfect right now?

I grab just below her arse cheeks and hoist her up. "You're not sore?" I ask, walking us towards my en-suite.

"I could ask you the same thing?" She quips her brow.

"I'm trying to be a gentleman here," I drawl.

"Don't bother." Her laugh is dirty, her head thrown back in a way that exposes her throat, her skin grows taut, and her eyes glitter with humour when she looks back at me. I watch her through hooded eyes, and her smile is slow, flirtatious. Her arms twine behind my neck, and her fingers sink into my hair.

"I told you my bedside manner was impeccable," I murmur as she drops forward and sucks my lower lip into her mouth, big eyes watching me coyly. I turn the shower on and walk us straight under the spray. Her hair moulds into a silky curtain against her skin. She flashes a cute smile at me, and it's at this moment that I remind myself why I wanted more than one night with her. She is inexcusably pretty. Delicate and dirty. She may dress demurely, but she fucks me like she hates the thought of only having a weekend. Like she is determined to walk away with my fingerprints inked into her skin and the sounds of her name leaving my lips as it plays on repeat in her ear.

"What about your shorts?" Her voice distorts when she tilts her head back against the water funnelling around us. I ignore her question and latch my mouth around her nipple and draw it into my mouth with a deep pull, my tongue massaging as my cheeks hollow. "Shorts, what shorts?" she moans, gripping my hair roughly.

"Lauren, stop talking." I laugh, stepping to press her into the wall and undress. My shorts slide down easier than I expect. Her fingers delve into my hair, tilting my head away from her breast. "Yes?" I grin.

"Will it be weird if Perry and I stay friends after this weekend?" she asks, genuinely concerned for their friendship.

For fuck's sake.

"I do not want to discuss that clown when I'm seconds from having sex with you."

Her small nose wrinkles. "What, no foreplay?"

I capture her mouth quickly. Her gasp swells around my tongue, and I swallow it down. Her lips are soft, bruised, and when her tongue laces with my own, I grind my cock into the apex of her thighs. Her pussy parts, her wetness coating my flesh, and she whimpers, her eyes flickering against the spray, as I watch her gaze evaporate into a slumberous blur. "Your eyes are so fucking glazed."

"Touch me." Her voice is liquid, and her breasts brush against my chest. I keep my cock flush with her clit and grind my hips, teasing my cock. She'd sucked on the tip for an age last night, bringing me close to climax, and I'd held back, watching her tongue lap at her creamy cum coating me. I wanted to thrust to the back of her throat and claim it as my own, but there is something to be said for delayed gratification because watching my painfully hard cock sliding slowly in and out of her mouth had been biblical. Licking her parted mouth, I reach around and run my finger over her slick entrance. "Ah, Cain. I need to feel you inside."

"You're swollen," I groan, brushing my finger back and forth across her entrance. I dip my finger in, and she hisses, sobbing softly at the intrusion. "Lauren, you're still sensitive."

"I know," she whimpers, flexing her thighs to open herself wide for me, and my finger slides deep. Her mouth drops open, her head lolling back. I coax my finger in and out, and when I press in for a third time, I add another finger, curling to massage her g-spot. She cries out, her voice splintering around the shower. Her narrow hips gyrate, and her fingers bite into my scalp,

"I want your cock, " she begs, fucking my hand.

"Fuck." Slipping free, I gather her arse cheeks and spread her as her hand grips my cock and positions me at her entrance.

"Cain?" The sound of my name spoken from another pair of feminine lips has Lauren going stiff in my arms.

"Fuck."

"CAIN!"

Lauren struggles out of my hold and races to grab a towel. "What the hell?"

I move to reassure her, but she flinches away. "It's my sister!" I hold my hands up as she attempts to cover herself, moving away from the doorway. "Lauren, I'm not the type of man to fuck around with multiple women." She stares at me, worrying her lip beneath her teeth. "Just a sec!" I call, knowing Kat will have no qualms coming up here.

Lauren dabs her face. She looks ashen, and I realise there is more to this. I know all about her scumbag ex. I may only have basic intentions with this woman, but I'd never disrespect her like that.

"No, not just a sec!" Kat snaps, walking into my room. I yank Lauren's towel and wrap it around myself, leaving her exposed, but out of view. She squeaks and scrambles to grab another, shooting an angry look my way.

My sister screeches with embarrassment. "Kat, fuck off. I'm not alone," I snap. Her face flames bright red, and she quickly U-turns and rushes back through my apartment. "Make some coffee!" I shout.

"I'll wait for her to leave," Lauren murmurs, embarrassed.

"I'd rather you didn't. She'll be nicer to me if she meets you," I say honestly and tug her to my chest. "Finish showering and come to join us." I dip and press a kiss to her mouth. Her lips are flat against mine. Gripping her jaw, I lift her face to mine. "Don't," I warn, "don't give power to those kinds of thoughts. You're here because I want you here. I asked you to stay because what I'm feeling doesn't just go away in one night. Nor will it disappear after a weekend."

Her mouth opens, but I drop a kiss to her lips, silencing her. Our eyes speared together. "I'm a one-woman kind of man. So, for the short amount of time you've extended to me, I'm yours, and you're mine."

She searches my eyes, her chest rising in quick sharp bursts.

"Okay?" I say softly.

"Okay."

I pull her towel away and slap her ass. "Don't be too long,"

"She seemed upset," Lauren ventures, stepping back under the spray.

"She'll be sweet as pie when you appear," I mutter, drying off and pulling on some fresh shorts and a plain tee before heading down to the kitchen, where Kat has the decency to look regretful. "I get you're angry," I bite, glaring at her. "But don't *ever* let yourself in here again unless it's an emergency," I tell her as I take a seat at the island.

"I didn't think you'd have company." She presses her lips together, trying not to laugh.

"Even if I didn't, you have no right to storm in here. You came into my room, Kat. What the fuck! Do you have no respect?" I demand quietly.

"You can hardly talk. You're taking everything from us."

"I'm taking what was always mine. I already told you that you can stay at the house."

"I asked them about your dad." Her lips downturn.

"Let me guess—I'm a liar." With no sign of coffee, I leave my seat and make some, knowing Lauren will more than likely want a cup, too.

"They said you're trying to turn me against them." She looks up from where she is pulling some tissue apart. Her eyes are red-rimmed, and her face drawn.

"I can show you the death certificate, the bank transfers, the messages, and anything else you need to understand the depth of what your father is capable of."

"If I believe you, then it was all a lie, you know," she whispers painfully.

I circle the island and pull her into a hug. "It's easier to be angry at me than to accept the truth about him."

She nods and sniffles. "If he knew I was here—if either of them did—" her voice catches, and I grit my teeth.

"Have they threatened you?" I ask. It's one thing that has bothered me—what will they do to her when they find out she has a mind of her own? She gives a small shake of her head, but I know what she is thinking: if her father is capable of the things I have told her, what else is he capable of doing?

"Hello?" Lauren appears. She tucks her hair behind her ear and cups her waist, looking as young and vulnerable as Kat. She's got one of my tees on and her feet are as bare as her face. Kat wipes her face and beams past me.

"Hi, I'm Kat."

"Lauren. I can give you a few more minutes?" she says, seeing how emotional my sister is.

"No, it's okay." I walk over and join her, and she pulls an uncertain face. "It's fine," I whisper, leaning to kiss her. She's tucked my tee into the back of a pair of my shorts.

"I have no clothes with me," she admits.

"I know." I grin, "Coffee?"

"Please." With a bright smile, she moves past me and tentatively takes the seat next to the one I was occupying. I wait for her to flick those pretty eyes my way, and when she does, I smirk, knowing I'm the cause of discomfort from her waist down. She gives my sister a sympathetic smile and rests her elbows on the granite surface.

"Milk, one sugar," she tells me.

"So, how do you know each other?" my sister asks. Lauren looks at me, and I lean against the counter as the machine whirs and grinds the beans.

"We met through work."

"Oh, the employee." Kat grins and twists to Lauren. "My lips are sealed." She motions across her mouth.

"Erm, thanks," Lauren garbles.

"So, what are your plans for the rest of the day?" I ask her as the main door clunks shut.

"Lovers, get dressed!" Perry calls, and I groan as Lauren looks at me helplessly.

"Kat, you're on coffee duty," I state, walking to block Lauren into the island. "I'd like to say it's not always like this, but it is," I admit, grinning.

"It's nice,"—her fingers play with the seam on my tee—

"but I'm going to order an Uber and get out of your way." Her neck is craned to accommodate me crowding her.

"No," I say simply. I lean over and press a kiss to her mouth as my friend strolls in with several paper bags. "Anyway, he has breakfast," I murmur against her mouth.

"I feel a little awkward," she whispers. I grip the back of her neck and press a deep and suggestive kiss to her mouth. Her hands tangle with my top as effortlessly as my tongue attacks her mouth.

"And now?" I hum.

"Worse." She chokes, pressing her face into my neck. "This was supposed to be a naughty little weekend heist," she whispers, flustered.

"It is. They won't say anything, and no, it won't be weird if you and Perry remain friends," I tell her as her eyes dance about the kitchen nervously.

"And us—this feels weird." Unease holds her face in a strained smile.

"We can talk about that later. Just relax." I peck her lips and step away as Perry starts getting things out.

"Hey, Kat. Looking tear-stained as ever, what gives?"

"Hey, Perry. Less of a dick today? No, oh, what a surprise," Kat spits back and stirs the coffee loudly to drown out Perry when he blows a stream of kisses down her ear.

"They always like that?" Lauren laughs.

"Always." I sigh.

"You are, without a doubt, the most irritating man," Kat fumes.

"I think Lauren would disagree with you there. She can barely tolerate your brother," Perry quips and winks at Lauren.

"Well." She laughs, pulling her top over her bare thighs. "Office Cain is definitely more irritating than penthouse Cain." Her cheeks warm, but I move to put my lips against her ear.

"I was only irritated because it's painful having to look at something you can't have."

"Couldn't," she muses lightly as Kat places our coffees down.

"So, what's on the agenda?" Perry joins us at the island with two plates of pastries in his hands. "The cinnamon swirl thing is mine."

"Meaning?" I query, ignoring my friend. Is she suggesting she wants more than the weekend? I can't allow myself the luxury of getting involved with her or anyone else.

"Nothing. You said can't, but you have, so—" She blushes, her voice filtering off into a barely there whisper. I spoke the truth when I said the weekend wouldn't be enough for me. Seeing her around work will only torment me further, and I loosely debate what it could be like if I did allow this to blur the lines. If, for a short amount of time, we did let this progress into something more casual. The thought of fucking her over my desk sends me dizzy with tangible excitement.

"For a moment, I thought you were offering to be more accessible to me at work," I speak quietly, low enough for only her to hear, testing the waters.

She licks her lips, and I know, like me, she wants more than a weekend. Her eyes slip to see if we are being listened to. "Cain," she murmurs, unconvinced.

I lean right in, and my hand slides up her legs and under the seam of the shorts, where I find her pussy bare and wet. "You could use your lunch break to venture up to my suite. I would be more"—I slide my fingers along her lips, and she grabs her coffee, quickly taking a small sip, her breathing uneven and laboured—"than happy to find you there." I peel my hand away and lift my own mug with my clean hand, and the other one picks up a pastry. She watches me wide-eyed as I take and bite, then lick my fingers clean. Winking, I push the plate to her.

"You okay?" Kat asks Lauren.

Clearing her throat, she smiles brightly. "I'm fine. I was just saying that I need to get dressed."

"Amberley is on her way with some clothes," Perry announces. I drop my cup on the side with a crash. "What?" Perry says, smirk in place.

"I had no intention of having more than one guest this weekend," I deadpan him.

"Tough shit, you're getting four," he retorts, then smiles at the girls when they laugh. "We can grab lunch," he suggests.

"I'm not sure that's appropriate," Lauren manages to say before I do.

"If anyone asks, you're Kat's friend, and we happened to end up in the same spot. Seriously, it's not a big deal." Perry's flippant attitude pisses me off, and when Amberley arrives a few minutes later, I almost lose my cool because she gawps at my home like she just found the recipe for immortality.

I eye Perry, and he looks a bit sheepish for having invited her round.

"Here, I packed some makeup too." The bag is placed on the side, and Lauren grabs it and jumps down from the chair, leaving space for her friend to take a seat.

"Excuse me." Lauren walks away quickly and takes the stairs.

I watch her legs disappear before I turn to look at all three sets of eyes, smiling awkwardly. "I don't like any of you." I knock back the remainder of my coffee as Perry smirks knowingly at me.

"Oh, come on, Cain. It's fun. I've not spent time with you in ages, and lunch sounds good," Kat chimes. It's certainly nice to have Kat eager to spend time with me and not want to poke my eyes out.

"Excuse me," I mutter and stalk away. I take the stairs two at a time and find Lauren sifting through the bag—her belongings splayed out on my bed.

"It's weird. Work is going to be weird," she blurts. I cross the room and yank her to me, smashing my lips to hers. "Cain," she pants.

"I'm so fucking hard for you." Walking her back, I bump into the drawers and pull her shorts down, my mouth frantic on hers.

"What if someone comes up?" she whimpers, pulling at my clothes.

"They won't. Trust me." With our lower-body clothing items gone, I tug her to the edge of the unit and line myself up.

"What if—"

I sink deeply, her pussy quilting my cock and hugging me tightly. Our jaws go lax, our eyes glittering with pent-up arousal. "Lean back." I groan and watch as she leans to accommodate my request, her small hands gripping either side of the wooden furniture.

"Oh god," she whispers. My gaze drops to her pussy, spread wide, her flesh plump around the thick edges of my cock.

"Lauren, if you could see—you take my cock so fucking good." Her eyes watch me with quiet excitement. I flash her a dirty grin and push her legs to hook around my waist.

"Try to be quiet." I grunt, pressing my mouth to hers as I grind into her pussy.

She garbles, gasping and moaning sweetly, but I eat up her sounds as her cunt eats up my cock. She's tight and swollen, and I can't get enough of her. I drive my hips forward, my erection sinking into her creamy warmth. Choking out an expletive, I grab at her jaw lightly and devour her mouth.

"Fast and hard." She pants against my lips. I slam upwards, and the drawers groan in protest. "Shush!" she giggles.

I rut into her, and the drawers creak again. Fuck.

"Hands on the wall," I hiss, slipping out and pulling her down. I turn her and tilt her ass.

"Cain, quick." She bends, and I sink back in and grip her hips. "Oh god, oh god." I pound deeply and groan at how easily she lets me fuck into her. How she is pushing back to take the brute force.

"Are you going to come for me, pretty girl?"

"I've been on the edge of an orgasm all morning," she mutters dryly.

Laughing, I grip her hip in one hand and her shoulder in another and fuck her roughly. Her moans are low. Our flesh slaps, and she whimpers plea after plea for me to make her come. Her thighs tighten. Her hand flays to grip me close, and then her pussy is suckling my cock as her legs give way and a long, sweet cry escapes her parched lips.

"Fuck, Lauren." My balls draw up, and the base of my spine tingles as I slam into her twice and grunt through my own release. She's fucking perfect.

Too perfect.

CHAPTER 18

Lauren

Lunch is a swanky affair in a restaurant neither Amberley nor I can afford. I purposely sit away from Cain, placing myself between his sister and my co-worker, taking some level of comfort in knowing Amberley is with me. She is chatting animatedly to Perry, and Kat is sitting sullenly beside me. I flick a look between her and Perry and see her mouth turned down as she quietly observes the interaction happening opposite her. It's clear as day that she has feelings for Perry. My eyes slip to Cain, who, in turn, is watching me closely. I give him a small smile, but truthfully, I didn't want to come out for lunch. Amberley is in her element. She's dining with Cain Carson-Ivory, and if the short journey here in her car has taught me anything, it is that the man I have been doing inexcusable things with is much more than a hotel god and a soul-tingling lay.

He really is one of the richest people to grace our planet, according to Forbes. Amberley thrust the article under my nose as we cruised along after Perry. My fingers had trembled as I read the entire two-page spread with sick swirling in my stomach. Fame and wealth had never troubled me—until now. My breath stutters out as I recall the staggering figures on the glossy pages, the never-ending string of hotels, complexes and resorts he has to his name, and the properties he is estimated to own, commercial and domestic. He is reputed internationally, a formidable businessman, and an untouchable adversary. I have touched him, and if he is half as assertive in the boardroom as he is in the bedroom, I feel nothing but sympathy for his competition.

I feel the colour leech out of me, my skin puckering into tiny blisters as a cold sweat sweeps my frame. We've been seated out of the main view, discreetly tucked away, whilst several waiters attend to our one table. I've barely touched my drink. I couldn't swallow a drop. I already feel like I'm drowning.

"Excuse me, where are the bathrooms?" I manage to ask a waiter. I stand and am ushered through the restaurant towards a set of doors. I walk quickly to the ladies and slam my way through the entrance. Gasping for air, I clutch at my stomach, my eyes swimming with embarrassment. The penny has finally dropped, and I'm the rusty conclusion. The truth of my stupidity slaps me as hard in the face as the door Perry had swung into it. What the hell am I doing? Glancing around, I check I'm alone and move to the washbasins, running the tap until it's icy cold, and I hold my hand under the stream before pressing it to my neck.

"What happened between my place and here?" Cain's deep voice catches me by surprise.

I jump, not expecting anyone to enter, least of all him.

"Jesus," I choke, yanking the handle for the water and turning it off. "You can't be in here." I take in his tall frame and neatly pressed shirt in the decorative mirror, then the clean and harsh cut of his jaw. His shoulders are wide enough to cause discomfort, and my thighs are a testament to that. My body is victim to the only kind of assault I would ever welcome. I stare back at my beautiful boss with his discerning gaze and wickedly handsome smile. I never stood a chance. Martin and I never had this kind of chemistry. I don't trouble myself worrying that Cain may have shared a similar buzz with women before me. What we shared last night, unexpected or not, has crashed into my skin like a cresting wave. The essence of his devotion to my body has seeped into my pores and made its way into my veins. It's still pumping through me, heavy, greedy, and in search of its owner. And now he is here, I feel it reach out like an invisible arm to take hold of him. Poseidon himself couldn't wash away this feeling.

"What happened?" His demand is softened by the concern veiled beneath heavily lashed eyes—eyes that have watched me, *seen me*. I'd come undone for this man. Unzipped my skin and let him into me. I hid nothing and gave him everything.

"Nothing," I croak, dropping my gaze and wishing I could be sucked down the plughole with the last little trickle of water as it washes away. The gold, polished taps gleam under the crystal chandeliers brandishing my shame in a healthy glow, and my shoes have sunken into the plush carpet that I want to disappear into.

"Bullshit. Half an hour ago, you were crying my name, and now you look like you're about to be sick." *Again.* He need not utter those words, but they hang off his tone.

"Cain, please." I offer a wobbly smile. "I'm just tired and hungry." My response has little effect. In fact, it only seems to anger him. I turn and face him as I dry my hands. Confusion pulls at his forehead, engraving fine creases across his face, but his mouth is drawn into a harsh, flat line. Shaking his head, he sighs softly as he allows a beat to pass between us, an opportunity for me to voice my plight.

"Don't insult me. You're a lousy liar." He walks to me and

brackets me into the countertop. Legs braced either side of mine. Hands planted to keep me caged in. "Talk to me." His hand comes up to cup my jaw. His fingers heat the ice away and remind me that he held my face similarly in the early hours of this morning as he had ploughed himself into me, pushing, pressing to gain depth, his jaw lax and full of praise as he held me fast and watched me come apart beneath him.

I shake my head, flustered.

"Lauren." It's a warning, white-hot and unavoidable.

I lick my lips, bringing my eyes up to meet him from where they were lost in the smattering of hair at the base of his throat. "Amberley showed me this article about you." I swallow sickly. "You're stinking rich. This place—I can't eat in a place like this." I cup my throat, distressed. "I can barely afford my bloody rent." I laugh humourlessly. Cain holds my face. His gaze darkening to the shade of the bowels of the ocean.

"I thought we were going to talk about us later?" He steps in, flattening his thighs to mine.

"There is no us. This was a mista—"

"Don't," he warns icily.

I suck in a short breath. "Let's get back to the table," I suggest. Lifting my chin, I hope to break the contact, but he doesn't budge. The heat radiating off him sweeps across my pebbled skin.

"We can leave if you'd like?" I shake my head. I don't want to cause a scene or make this any more uncomfortable than it already is. Money has never been a grudge I bear. I never found myself overly impressed by it or intimidated until working at the Carson-Ivory, and even then, I was able to detach myself, unaffected by the glamour and status I was faced with. But those faces never crossed my threshold, didn't step into my life, and they certainly never shared a meal or stared in rapture as I was devoured from the inside out and cried shamelessly for more, for more pain, more pleasure.

Somehow, along the way, I had forgotten who he was and how we were connected. Somewhere between hitting my head and waking in his bed, my sensibility had evaporated. The depth of my choices and the width in which their consequences could spread have brought me to a grounding resolve. I need to walk away from this man.

"I'm going to go home with Amberley after lunch," I say to him. "This was a mistake."

"So, because I have money, it was a mistake?" he scoffs incredulously.

"No," I whisper, my face burning. "I think what you've accomplished is incredible. You're obviously very intelligent, successful." My throat aches uncomfortably. Cain's gaze is relentless, forceful in his challenge to push the truth out of me. "I… I'm not like you. You're my boss, Cain. That's why this was a mistake."

"Let me tel—"

Amberley swans in, and her mouth forms an 'O' as she sees I'm not alone. "Sorry," she winces, "do you want me to step into the hall?" She points over her shoulder, and I take the coward's way out, ducking under Cain's arm and sprinting for the door. I side-eye my friend, silently begging her to follow me.

"And the purpose of you showing her the article was? You made her feel like shit, Amberley." I hear Cain scathe as I put space between us. My head bowed low. Perry and Kat are in a heated conversation when I return. I'm glad I'm not the only one in a mood. Both Cain and Amberley return shortly after, and her fingers slip into mine beneath the thick white cloth— her hold fierce, protective. I twist enough to share a smile with her. She mouths a sorry, and I shrug, feeling utterly exposed. A waiter comes to take our order. Distracted, I lift the menu, and my eyes almost cannonball out of their sockets. I scan for the lowest price and order a plain burger when I see the salads are no less expensive. Tension pulses from our table, and I can sense even the servers are feeling the pinch of it. I try to be upbeat and chatty, but when I catch sight of Cain glowering at my friend and then staring annoyed at me, I sink a little in my chair.

"So, why the fuck is everyone in a mood?" Perry pipes up, lifting his drink and taking a sip. We all sit in awkward silence. "Yeah, don't all try to talk over me at once," he scoffs, laughing as we each look for something to say.

"How's BANK?" I ask him.

"Still standing." His reply is quick and to the point. "What the fuck is going on?" he demands.

"Lauren and I are leaving. Can I take your car?" Cain stands and stares down at Perry.

"Sure." His friend shrugs.

"No, we're not," I say loud enough for only our table to hear. "Sit down."

"Lauren, we're leaving. I'm not above making a scene, so unless you're up for a challenge, don't fucking try me."

"Cain," I plead.

"Now," he demands. I flick a cautious glance around the table. Perry is grinning like a fucking hyena on the other side of the table. Kat is pressing her lips together to stop from laughing, and for once, Amberley looks gobsmacked, if not a little guilty.

I collect my bag and stand slowly. "Excuse me," I whisper haughtily, hooking the strap of my bag over my shoulder and walking away at a speed I feel is neither too slow nor fast. As I breach the door, Cain cups my elbow and steers me towards the valet, who pulls up with Perry's car. "That was embarrassing and completely unnecessary," I grate.

"Yes, it was. Imagine being told you're too rich to fuck," he drawls as the doors open, and I stare, open-mouthed, as Cain loops around the bonnet and stands watching me from the other side. The valet slips from the vehicle. "Allow the nice man to escort you to your seat," he mutters, and I jump into action, smiling at the valet who waits for me to secure my belt before he closes the door and Cain peels out of the circular drive.

We don't talk on the journey. The radio is untouched, and although there is a world of noise happening outside, the car is a catacomb of silence. By the time we pull into the underground parking, I'm feeling even more foolish and awkward. Before I have a chance to open it myself, Cain walks to swing open my door.

"You're angry with me?"

"I'm not angry with you. I'm angry with your friend, and I'm disappointed that after we spent a night together, you would use money as a reason to cover for your insecurities."

"I'm not!" I snap, indignation hot in my voice.

"No?" He dips his head so we are face-to-face, inches apart, breath tangling together. I square my chin, but his eyes take the action in with a dazzle of amusement. "You admitted Amberley had shown you the article—you said I was stinking rich. I am." He growls lightly. "I could secure a jet in less than a minute, be on it in twenty, and be balls fucking deep in the most expensive pussy the world could buy, and yet, I wanted to fucking spend the weekend with you," he points out.

"I hardly need to hear about your weekend escapades," I spit, my face aflame in light of his directness.

"I don't have escapades, Lauren. I was spinning a fucking line. That's what you read, right? That I could jet to Dubai and buy whatever I wanted ten times over? Or that lunch in a restaurant that you can't afford is pocket change to me?"

"What is your point?"

"My point is, yes, I do have money." His gaze burns like hot, glowing pokers. "But the only thing I wanted this weekend isn't for sale. She doesn't want to buy me either, and for once, just fucking once, I was glad to be able to enjoy a woman's company for the simple fact that we share something that is priceless," he hisses in my face. His eyes are an even deeper shade of blue as anger swirls, whipping up a storm, and my mouth turns down, feeling shameful and small. He's talking about our chemistry, the tangible rush crackling and buzzing between us, the desperate need we feel to devour one another in those intimate moments when not a soul but us is watching, and we can see nothing but each other. It's an addictive feeling. A dangerous drug nature created, and indulging does not cure it, and distance would not dismiss it either. It's without visibility and louder than any explosion.

"I'm sorry," I whisper.

"Do you think if I cared about our differences, I would be entertaining this attraction?"

"I said I was sorry. Amberley wouldn't shut up about you on the way over, and it freaked me out," I admit, swallowing thickly. "I was reading the article, and she was going on about all this stuff she had read online"—his face shutters, and I grip his arm—"and I know, I know not everything the media shares is true, and that this is a…a..it's a—"

"Weekend heist." His lips finally develop their usual curve as he smiles softly and intimately.

"Yes, but you are painfully rich, and for a short time, I forgot all that…forgot you are my boss. Seeing the article. Hearing her. I panicked. What if someone finds out? I could lose my job. I'm doing okay for myself. I like London. I don't want to jeopardise the small life I'm creating for myself."

Cain drops to his hunches, unclips my belt, twists me in my seat, and cups my bottom. "I wouldn't let that happen, Lauren. I may not know you all that well, but I do respect you enough to ensure nothing like that would happen. Next time, before you read anything, ask me."

Nodding, I roll my teeth along my lower lip. "Please don't be mad at Amberley."

"She's lucky she still has her job," he rattles before helping me to stand and threading our fingers. I drop to stare at our linked hands as he locks the car and begins walking us to the elevator. His fingers are long enough that they envelop mine and hold my hand in a soft shackle. His thumb is lazily rolling across my skin, dancing on my pulses and tickling my palm. When we step inside, he pulls me to his chest and drops to kiss my mouth softly. "Us," he begins quietly as we ascend, "has been a welcome surprise and one I shouldn't act on. I'm violating more than one policy and setting a really awful example by indulging in you."

I let him press a short but sweet kiss on my mouth. "I'm not expecting more from you. I knew what this was…is," I correct. "I'm not in the market for a relationship, and I hope, come Monday, we can remain professional. I really do love working at the hotel, Cain." I hold his gaze, hold it long enough to fight the haze of desire and ensure he hears me and believes the truth in my words.

"Out of all of my employees, my assistant included, your job is the only one I have a vested interest in. You're putting yourself at risk, but your job is safe, Lauren."

"Okay," I whisper.

The lift comes to a stop, and we exit, our hands knotted together in some unspoken bond. We know what we are doing is wrong. Know that the rules he enforces and the documents of agreement I signed have been excused under the rush of lust. When he reaches the door and keys us in, my hand flexes softly in his.

I don't know what I expect when we enter, maybe for him to suggest arranging some sort of lunch, so when he backs me slowly into the door and slants his mouth over mine in a bruising, slow kiss, I gasp, surprised. He holds my face, his thumbs dancing the column of my throat as he silences any fear, any awkwardness with a searing kiss that blooms from my mouth and roots in my toes. My hands slide around his waist and tuck under his shirt, and I run my nails over his skin, my body mellowing as my limbs soften and I melt against him. My nails claw and dig deeply as his tongue takes a lazy and heated run of my mouth, and when my eyes flutter open, he is dining out on my response. "See, priceless."

"Tomorrow, we're not leaving this apartment," I hum as his teeth nibble along my lower lip.

"Not even the pope himself could pull me from between your thighs,"

"He might want to watch." My voice catches. His eyes are glinting with humour.

"I wouldn't allow it." His mouth lowers, and his tongue careens down my neck. "If I had more to give. If there wasn't the weight of the world bearing down on my shoulders, I'd never allow another man the luxury of you."

I slam my eyes shut, trying to forget his words.

"Have you ever wanted something you know you can't have? Needed to own something you know isn't yours to take."

Yes, I do now.

His words could crush hearts worldwide, and the damn devil is speaking them to me, luring my sensibility to sleep and waking up something far more basic, far less attainable. His eyes are molten. I find myself answering when I know I shouldn't speak as freely as him, know I should guard myself because this man has the power to walk away unscathed from this. He can say whatever he likes to whomever and be damned about the consequences. I'd be no match as an adversary.

"I'm already regretting this, and for all the wrong reasons." *How am I supposed to pretend this weekend never happened?*

"It seemed like a good idea, didn't it?" he rasps.

I give a light but agreeable nod.

CHAPTER 19

Lauren

The dip of the bed and the weight of Cain's arm rouse me from my deep sleep. His fingers stretch wide, reaching to cover as much skin as possible and ground me to the mattress. I twist my neck to find him lost to the sleep that so easily claimed me. His hair is shaped by my desperate fingers. I told myself I wouldn't allow my thoughts to plague me until I was in the safety of my own home. Only then, behind those four walls, would I let the memories of this weekend tear into me. But behind the cloak of darkness, I find them begin to nip, cutting past the thin barrier and eating into me. My breath stutters out, and my tongue darts to dampen my drying mouth. I'm a practical woman, sensible and loyal to a fault, so it irks me that I have given into something I have dismissed so easily in others. I greedily absorb his features, the smooth bow of his forehead, the harsh but flattering slant of his cheekbones, his wide fanned eyelashes and straight nose, all leading down to a full and sinful mouth. His jaw teases the idea of stubble, its shadow lurking below his skin. Pulling my lower lip into my mouth, I contemplate just how irresponsible I've been—how selfishly stupid I am. We've come a long way from snapping insults at one another. We'll go full circle again. Cain will not hold me in special regard. If anything, he will ensure the only person who speaks my name with any detestation will be him and him alone—only I now know those words to be a lie. For every insult, below the surface, has been a compliment he could never utter, a desire he dared not voice. A chasm of truth we know should have stayed as false as our invalid dislike.

It really did seem like a good idea. Until it wasn't.

The *wasn't* is a truth I choose to stay in denial from.

It's a realisation that neither of us can afford.

Because this became something more than we expected.

Cobalt eyes break my train of thought, their deep shine a glimmer against the minimal light glowing from the hallway. My lip pops free, and Cain smirks, one side lifting in a boyish smile. It's a far cry from the kind of smile that smugly pulled his face into anguished pleasure as he watched me scream for him. "Give me your thoughts," he demands gruffly. Sleep is a heavy glaze in his eyes, a warm bruise in his throat. His hand squeezes my side, and his heavy leg pulls me closer, the rough hair a pleasant change from the silk sheets wrapping around the rest of me. "I want inside that pretty head."

I shake my head softly, declining him. If I'm to leave this apartment with some sense of pride, it will be with the knowledge that I kept my heart and head intact. "My body you can have. It's yours for the weekend. But the rest is mine."

He moves fast to part us, and he pins me to the mattress, drawing a shocked gasp. He braces above me, my wrists locked and loaded above my head, as his knee knocks my legs apart. "I've seen enough truths in your eyes to answer my own questions." His cocky smirk is long gone, and he stares at me with an openness I have yet to share with another person.

There is no gratification in his tone. Arrogance has no place, so he keeps it at bay as his gaze dances between my eyes, waiting, watching for my response. His eyes fasten to mine with intent, eager for my reply, greedy for my thoughts.

"Don't complicate this, Cain," I whisper, my voice trembling as his hips dip back and forth, his erection gliding through my wetness.

"You complicated it." He sinks inside, driving to the hilt on a practised thrust. His jaw goes lax as mine widens to give birth to a lengthy moan. "The second you pointed your finger in my face." Hands cuff my wrists in a tight grip, and hips peel away, drawing his long cock out of my pussy, the thick tip still snug until he plunges back in, stretching me wide. "Lauren," he grits throatily.

"Again." I jolt forward, wanting his mouth, but he dances away, locking his arms and dipping his chin to watch as he rocks out all the way before sinking back inside with a low grunt.

"Fuck, you want to know what I think is in your head?" His thrusts are long and slow, his groin knocking against mine in a fluid roll. His eyes pierce mine, glittering, testing, challenging, and he rolls his hips, his shoulders bunching and knotting as muscles tense, ready for impact. I whimper, eager and hesitant for the amount of pleasure coming my way. "I think, *Lauren*—" He makes sure to hit as deeply as he can go. Pressing his body flush to mine. I arch, opening myself up for another slide and thrust, and he pins my hips to the bed as he rocks in, chasing the wind clean out of me. His vivid eyes are lit up like a blue flame, burning, flickering with too many truths of his own.

Shaking my head, I refuse to give him what he wants.

"I think you thought you could walk away from this." Sweat beads below his hairline. My fingers are greedy for the silky strands and flex in his hold. He withdraws, and I bow off the bed, my hips following his path, desperate to hold the connection. He jackknifes back in, and my eyes open wide, my mouth gaping. He dives forward, sweeping his tongue in and savouring my cry for more. He eats my words, licks them up and swallows them whole, his hips pistoning in and out. The steady slap of flesh and the shared gasps are chased away by his deep moans and my higher mewls echoing through my head. His lips are on my mouth and neck, sucking, nipping and whispering filthy words. "I think," he pants thickly, "you thought wrong." He rams to the hilt, snapping the last of my resolve. It glitters and bursts through me, pulling all the pleasure to the apex of my thighs and bursting apart.

I call out, my voice raw, pleading.

"Pretty girl, you're so tight. Fuck." He thrusts inside, several deep, harsh pounds until he is going stiff above me. His head drops, and his eyes are sparking like my own. "I was wrong," he chokes. "Lauren, I can't get enough of you."

His cock twitches, and I mewl, pressing against the restraints he holds me in. I capture his mouth, moaning greedily. "Let me touch you," I manage to gasp between his deep kisses. Kisses that blaze through my soul and snare my heart into a vice. His grip loosens, and I slide my palms up his back and drive them where I need them, my grip on his hair holding his mouth to mine. I press into him—my eyelids held fast to hide the emotions clouding my vision. He gently rocks in and out, our creased foreheads sticking together. The friction draws the last swell of my orgasm to wash through me.

"I love how you milk my cock—so fucking greedy." His mouth demands a deep kiss, and his hands mimic my own, gliding along my spine and weaving into my damp locks. He nudges himself deeply, holding himself to the hilt and shaking his head in awe. "I want more weekend hook-ups," he confesses into my hair.

My heart gallops and bangs unsteadily against my breastbone. However, Cain relaxes, and my body accepts the extra weight, purring at the heady sensation it evokes.

He's granted me an opening. One I have mentally fought against, refused to allow my mind to dream up. It morphs into something more than an idea, and it becomes a living, breathing organism that pulses between us. I want for only a moment to hold it and believe I'm not alone in this, not conjuring up some misplaced belief that we actually share something deeper. I hold it and bite my lip. I want to fall into this void with him. "Me too," my light whisper hangs suspended in the air, our dilemma as physically unavoidable as we were. I see it now, the tangible thread bouncing between us. We pant quietly, fingers gliding across sweat-coated skin.

Cain lifts his head and cups my jaw. I want so badly to look away, to keep my thoughts as my own. I want more of this man. I want him to be more than my boss. I want more weekends wrapped around him in his big bed, silk sheets soothing my skin. I want him to look at me like he is now without the fear of being caught. Sucking in a deep breath, I swallow against his hold and shake my head in self-incrimination. I should know better than to get tangled up with my boss, but my head and heart have no place when my body is betraying every part of me.

"I never wanted to fire someone so fucking much in all my life," he blurts roughly.

And that's the problem. If we want more, I have to give up my career.

My laugh is accompanied by a shaky smile. "I love my job," I remind him, entwining my fingers into his wet hair.

"I know, pretty girl," He drops, pecking my mouth softly. "I still want to fire your sexy ass." He smirks against my mouth. When he rolls, I snake around him and let him flip us until I'm straddling his hips. I stare at him, a little smile stretching my mouth up at one side as he hooks his hands beneath his head and lazily rakes his eyes down my naked body.

"I have to admit, I wanted this to be bad so I could make my excuses and leave."

"Jokes on you." He chuckles. "There's little you could say at this point to make me believe otherwise." His leg lifts, and he gently knees my backside, jolting me forwards so he can capture my mouth.

"So what does one do in a place like this when you're not fucking?" I muse, leaning back to rest my hands on his thighs.

Laughter rips from his mouth. His head doubled back, exposing the thick column of his prickly throat. "Work," he drawls.

"No, seriously." I grin. "What do you do?"

"I work."

Wrinkling my nose, I hold his gaze, assessing how much truth his reply carries. For a man with exceptional wealth, I was expecting something a little more glamorous. The truth is sad, but money doesn't sleep, and Cain wouldn't be where he is today if he didn't exploit every waking hour to grow his business. "No hobbies?" I pry.

Something dark and painful flickers across his gaze, and he shifts and runs his hands up my thighs. "I like going to the gym." His rough voice snakes into my gut. He doesn't want to touch on anything personal.

Biting my lip, I thread my fingers with his own. "I would have thought a man like you would have a gym here?"

"I do."

"And how does Perry feel about that?"

"I believe he threatened to never talk to me again."

"He's full of shit." I laugh.

"You're fucking beautiful." His compliment is so unexpected that I drop forwards and hide my face. "You don't agree?" He nuzzles my neck and uses his weight and our hands to flip us so his body crushes into mine, hard, smooth and heavy. "Tell me who made you believe otherwise. I want to wring the little fucker's neck." He bites into my shoulder and moans happily. Laughing, I wait with a grin in place for him to sit up and look at me.

"No little fuckers," I breathe. Martin doesn't count. I left all that behind me. Him and his bastard of a father.

"No?"

I shake my head. Outside of the bedroom, our lives are ours alone. I have no intention of sharing my life with him. Just like him, I am keeping my cards close to his chest. I've been burnt hard enough before. I'll play his game and keep my poker face in place. It's what will make this easier in the end.

My stomach rumbles and Cain's brow raises humorously. "Let me get you something to eat."

"The service is kind of shabby," I proclaim, and he scoops me up, chuckling.

—

Cain took himself off to his office a little over an hour ago, and I can hear the deep hum of his voice as he speaks with his lawyer. One call and his playful and passionate demeanour had evaporated. A cloak of agitation had washed over him, and when his shoulders had risen, I'd wrapped my arms around his neck and told him to go and deal with whatever was bothering him.

"It can wait."

"Can you?" My laughter was met by a pointed stare. "Go. I will watch something on that obscenely large TV."

"I'll be an hour, tops."

When he doesn't appear, I decide to open the envelope Amberley had thrown in the bottom of the bag she had arrived with earlier this morning. Dropping down in the chair, I tear the heavy paper and peer inside. A stack of paper and something shiny glints back at me. Turning it upside down, I let the contents slide out, and a small key drops out onto my knees. Frowning, I hold it up, expecting an explanation alone from the small object, but it's a bog-standard key. Leafing through the papers, I begin to read, but the words, although manageable, aren't sinking in, not fully.

"What's that?" Cain's deep voice pulls my head up from where I gape in shock.

"If I'm reading it correctly, a new apartment. The building I live in is undergoing repairs," I explain, scanning the last few sentences. "My flat has damp, and whilst the work is carried out, I'm being moved up a few floors." I pass the paperwork to him as though it's the most natural thing to do. He, a man with a cash revenue big enough to sink my apartment block into the ground. Our worlds may have collided briefly, but he takes it, humouring me.

He picks me up and lowers into the chair with me in his lap. "Good." He begins reading the document as I chew at the skin on my lip.

"I can't see anything about the cost—it's larger than my current flat." I worry, flicking through the pages at the corner as he absorbs the first page.

"You're to be out by Wednesday," he states.

"They've hardly given me much notice," I point to a contradictory sentence in the document. "What does that mean?" I huff, irritated by the circling instructions. Each means something else, and neither one makes much sense.

"That it's a permanent move, and your lease has been extended. Basically, it's a rolling contract—no inflation. You'll be paying what you do now," he summarises.

"But it's much bigger."

"And you were overpaying for the shi—"

"Don't finish that sentence," I snap out quickly. He was going to say shithole. I love my little apartment. Sure, the building is a dive, and the area a little sketchy, but I made it my own.

"You were being overcharged, trust me," he drawls. And I do. He owns multiple properties. His entire career is based around real estate.

"London's not cheap," I defend.

"But some people are, and whoever owns that building was fleecing you."

I suck in a short breath and shift, crossing my legs and flicking through to something else I read. "So I can move in today?"

"Sure can. You've got to be out of your apartment by Wednesday," he confirms.

"But I don't have enough furniture," I blurt.

Cain laughs. "Take the week off, move in and buy what you need." His flippant response has me going rigid in his lap.

"I can't do that. I just returned after having time off." I tug the papers out of his hands.

Cain hauls me back into his chest. "Lauren, you're entitled to a holiday. Take it off and get settled in."

I shake my head and relax into his hold, reading the contents of the document. "How long will the renovation take?" I say out loud. Cain is more likely to be in the know than me.

"All depends on the funds."

I riffle through the document and find nothing to enlighten me further. There are no pictures of the flat, just a basic description noting the room sizes and amenities.

"Did you want to go and see it?"

CHAPTER 20

Cain

It's late as we pull up, and my car thrums to a stop, the engine purring quietly. Lauren spent the entire journey trying to find ample excuses as to why she couldn't move, and the rustle of the papers had been our only music. "I didn't even know we were expecting restorations to happen—no one has complained." Her breathy voice floats around the car. She's anxious, and it's not an emotion I like to see in her.

"Someone must have." I take the paper away and watch as she palms the key in her clammy hands.

Someone like me.

Visiting her apartment once was enough to take Perry's comment into my hands and mould her life into something I could feel comfortable walking away from. Perry has embraced Lauren fully into his life—it may have stemmed from guilt, but they have developed a friendship that I know will be difficult for me to stomach when our time is up. She won't leave the hotel, and she'd never forgive me for firing her.

It's a catch twenty-two of my own fucking doing. The only one reaping the benefits is my friend. He gets to keep her. I swallow thickly and stare out of the window, my hands tightening on the wheel.

Sensing my irritation, Lauren's hand runs down my thigh, and there isn't a part of my body that doesn't feel it, welcome it, or thank her for the contact. In a perfect world, she wouldn't work for me. I wouldn't be seeking revenge on a man who ruined my father—seeking out retaliation and anticipating the demise of another with sick, dark satisfaction. I'm not an overly nice man or a whole one. Royce will come back screaming like a banshee. His ego allows for nothing less. I don't want that for her. I rest back in my seat, our eyes reflecting in the dark windscreen, and I give her a lazy smile.

"I know it's not the kind of place you'd live in, but it's not as bad as you think." Pink-tinted cheeks glow under the streetlamp. There is a loud smash in the distance, followed by an agonised scream as someone shouts. Rolling my neck, I pin her to the seat with my unamused eyes. "Probably a cat."

She shrugs nervously, eyes searching the streets for a feral animal wreaking havoc.

A hooded figure runs past, another one shortly after, as a series of shouts erupts. "Big fucking cat," I drawl. Fury licks its way through my stomach. I want to say much worse. I should have moved her somewhere new altogether—put her in a place on my side of the city. Somewhere safe, proper. I had considered it, but then she would have caught on to my deceit and refused. This way, I can keep an eye on her from afar.

"Honestly, it's not bad. Besides, Big Deeks looks out for everyone," she says simply.

I whirl on her in the car like a tornado. "And who the fuck is Big Deeks?" I condemn Justine to hell. There was nothing in the report about some alley crusader keeping watch on the tenants.

Lauren twists, frowning through the window, then points

in the direction of her building as a huge figure ambles across the lawn in the distance. "He lives in the apartment below me —or did. He's a big softie, really." Her smile is soft, trusting.

I hum—big fucking Deeks. I want to meet this fella.

We step out of the car, and I escort Lauren towards the building. A group of teens loiter by the entrance, and as we approach the main doors, the figure steps out from under the tree line. He's huge and bald.

"Hey girl, you good?" His wide smile reveals pearly teeth, and a gap appears where a cigarette now sits.

"Hey, Deeks. Yeah, I'm good. Thanks for the casserole." She beams.

He fucking cooks for her? Blind, contagious fury ripples through my chest. My shoulders stiffen, and I glare at the man. The piece of shit has the audacity to grin at me.

"It's all good."

"I'll drop the dish back soon,"

"Who's your friend?" Deeks asks, watching me with revulsion. He's pegged me as a corporate kiss-ass, but I'm just as much a thug as this fool.

"A friend," I retort, threading my fingers with Lauren's, but she pulls her hand free, and the colossal man chuckles, sucking on his fag.

"You sure about that?"

"Stop being a big oaf," Lauren chides as she strides to the huge fella and pecks his cheek, whispering something in his ear. His eyes widen, clean and as blue as my own. He nods, and Lauren steps back. I want to know what she said, but swallow the question down. It doesn't stop it from buzzing around my head like a swarm of bees. It's obvious she is comfortable around this guy, as he is her, and I don't like it. I square my shoulders and bracket Lauren, a wall of security thrumming with anger behind her.

"Did you get a letter about the restorations, too?" she asks, changing the subject. I place a hand on her hip, ignoring how she stiffens under my touch and flick a warning look at the teenagers staring at us.

"Yeah, the building has been taken over by some big shot." Knowing, clever eyes slip to mine briefly. "It's part of a government-funded programme."

"I'm moving apartments," she confides. "I have mould."

"Is that so?" Deeks eyes me with intent. He knows it's me. He pulls on his cigarette and blows smoke into the air. "As long as you're being looked after, girl." I tilt my head, silently confirming his suspicion and his own dips, sharing my small nod. For all he knows, I could be fucking him over and the rest of his fan club. I'm not, but I kicked someone out of the flat I intend to put Lauren in.

"Let's go and check out your apartment." I squeeze her hip, and she smiles at Deeks and his youth club entourage. The man has got to be in his late thirties, but the hollow lines and constantly furrowed brow suggest he is wise beyond his years. He's lived a life of pain, and I may be the one wearing a thousand-pound coat, but we have that in common, at least. That and Lauren.

I follow her up the steps and hold open the door for her. My eyes want to slip back to where holes are being drilled into my back, but I keep my focus forward. Lauren is running her fingers through the long ponytail sitting high on her head, and I want to reach out and tug her back, whispering my grievance with that particular action. Before I can act on my impulse, she drops her hair and twists, looking back at me with a guarded look in her eye. Silently warning me to keep my hands to myself.

Signs are already in place detailing the work to start in the next week. One of the elevators is taped off, and a few residents are reading a notice farther down the hall. "And how much is this going to cost us?" one man says. Lauren worries her lip, and we take the only available lift. It was the first thing I demanded to be fixed. She crosses her arms when I step in beside her. "You shouldn't have held my hand," she whispers.

"I shouldn't be fucking you, full stop," I drawl, smirking when she wrinkles her nose. She'd prefer I not be so crass, but I'm only speaking a truth we are both guilty of.

"This was silly to come here. You should have dropped me off," she mutters.

"If you wanted that, you wouldn't have accepted my lift. I'm here because you trust my opinion," I enlighten her, and she leans a shoulder against the metal enclosure. "Although, I have to say, you have questionable taste when it comes to your friendships."

She straightens so her back is flush to the wall, giving her a direct firing line to pin me with her big eyes. She rolls them, and I choke back a laugh. "I'm not stupid. I know he isn't the most savoury of characters. I think he's in a gang," her voice quietens, "but he helped me move in, carried my stuff up three flights of stairs, and never once crossed my threshold." Lifting to twiddle her ponytail through her fingers, she shrugs. "Something about that made me trust him. He has no need to watch out for me, yet he does."

Probably because he is suffering the same fucking ailment Matteo and I suffer from. He wants her.

She's mine. I've had her, owned her, branded her skin, and licked her tears away as she crumbled beneath me. She'll always be mine. She's in my employ, and I own her building. If she so much as catches a cold, I'll know about it. I've always been a possessive man, namely towards the things that I know are my birthright, things that would have been handed down or worked on together with my father: his business empire, my inheritance.

I don't like to share.

I would rather dismantle a company than allow it to be in the hands of a scumbag like Royce.

However, women have never captured my attention in a

way that my revenge has. I did not wish to possess or lay claim to them. Until now.

Swallowing thickly, I observe Lauren from beneath my lashes as she watches the light on the elevator buttons ping-pong across the panel as we get higher. She's naturally beautiful, delicate, and pure. There is something fiercely erotic about her—in the tilt of her chin, the innocently playful glint in her eyes, and the almost angelic way she moves.

I was loath to admit it when we first met, but she is the first woman to sucker-punch me on sight by just being unapologetically her.

I'll let her go because I know if I take from her, she will never forgive me, and it would thrum between us like toxic waste. If I allow it to be her decision, she'll come back. I respect her loyalty to the hotel and admire her work ethic, but she will soon realise those things mean little to her if she wants to keep me.

I endeavour to spend the rest of the weekend showing her, in every which way, why she should leave my employment.

I'm not a man that has thought of the future with anything but revenge in mind. I do not know what that future holds for Lauren and me, but for the first fucking time in my life, I want to find out. Once the threat of Royce is dealt with, I can finally give in to my other passion.

Her.

"He causes you any trouble, and I want to know." He won't because Deeks and I are going to have a little heart-to-heart. If I have to ram his casserole dish down his throat to make my point, then I will gladly cook a fresh meal to do so.

"Okay," she whispers, but her eyes pull together. She doesn't understand why I would care or ask. In twenty-four hours, I will be her boss again, nothing more, nothing less, just a memory she will touch herself to. It has to be this way. She can't think I can offer more, because she is a weakness my step-father will use against me without hesitation.

"You'll call me," I reiterate as the elevator jolts to a stop and the doors creak open. The hallway opens up, dark and smelling of damp. It's like something out of a bad horror movie. "This looks inviting," I drawl, and she snorts dryly.

Stepping out, the lights flicker on and Lauren stalls, looking down the entire length. "Are you sure this is the right floor? I don't think anyone lives up here?"

"You do." I shrug. But the answer to her question steps out a door farther down the hall, where an older lady shuffles towards us.

"Excuse me. I'm looking for 43B?" Lauren smiles. The lady ignores us and grumbles as she scuttles past. I drop an amused glance down at Lauren, who is biting her lip.

"She seems nice." I laugh, hooking my hand with hers and gripping it when she tries to pull away.

"Cain."

"No one is here. No one cares." I nod towards a door a few feet away. "Odd numbers are this way." I already know where the flat is. I've even been inside. I keep her hand in mine and take us down the hall and to the door at the far end. Lauren presses the key in the lock, and something close to elation warms my chest as she pushes her way in and makes a little sound of glee. "Still want to keep your little place?" I muse.

Her head shakes, her ponytail swinging happily. I reach out and grip it, pulling her back. She hits my chest with a muted grunt and blinks back at me over her shoulder.

"This has been driving me insane." I twine the silky locks around my arm and dip to press a kiss on her mouth. She opens up, letting me dip my tongue in. Her hair in one grasp, throat in another, I devour her until she is glassy-eyed and panting for more. "Do you like your new place?"

She frowns, and I berate myself for sounding too prideful.

"You're right. It's much bigger," I add, covering my tracks, pushing us inside and letting the door swing shut. Her head is swaying around to take it all in. Although the place is not fully furnished, I did have some pieces delivered and installed when the contract was completed. It's open-plan like her last place, but a dining table separates a large L-shaped sofa from the kitchen, and new appliances gleam under the modern light fittings. There is a narrow hall heading away from the main living room, and Lauren wanders down, peering into a newly tiled wet room and, farther on, a large double bedroom with a fucking proper bed in it.

"Did the paperwork say when this was being removed? God, my little sofa bed is going to look so silly in here," she laughs, walking to the window and peering out. My throat closes up when I realise she thinks all this stuff belongs to the original tenant. I had no qualms about removing him. The man was incapable of paying rent and was using his status as the owner's nephew to exploit other residents. "It's definitely a better view. No more staring at a grey stone wall." Her soft voice pulls my eyes back into focus, and twisting to face me, she leans her hands on the windowsill and smiles at me. "So, what's your verdict?" She beams.

"The apartment comes partially furnished, it said in the paperwork." I take great pleasure in enlightening her.

She pulls back, her brows furrowed. "It does?" Her lip disappears behind her teeth, where she holds it fast, her eyes dazzling with excitement.

"So, your sofa bed can stay downstairs." I'm going to burn the damn thing.

She walks over to the bed, the mattress still wrapped in a protective film, and sits down, making the plastic sheet rustle. Her palm runs over the mattress. "I don't have big enough bedding." She bursts out laughing and drops back, staring at the ceiling.

I stalk towards her, pressing my knee between her thighs and collecting up her hands to press them above her head.

"The apartment has my blessing," I state, dropping to kiss her as a wide smile breaks out, lighting up her face.

—

"If a bottle of your shower wash goes missing, I will claim insanity," Lauren hums, trailing her fingers along my arm from where it is resting on the side of the bathtub. The bubbles cloak my skin, silky and gentle, as she draws a smiley face and drops her head back into my shoulder, her wet hair trailing over my pecs and floating in the water.

"Claim it all you want. I know where you work and live. I'm certain I could retrieve it with ease."

"Maybe I want to take something with me to remember this weekend." Her softly spoken words are laced with vulnerability.

"So tell me something about you that no one else knows, and I'll give you a part of me in return." The water laps around her navel, her breasts kissing the cooler air. I trail my fingers up and down her stomach. "Tell me something intimate," I rasp. My finger rings her belly button, and her foot rubs the length of my shin as she shifts to encourage my hand lower. Her breast grazes my arm and her breath hitches. I keep circling her stomach, trailing my hand down to her pussy and pulling away just as her hips tilt for more. "Tell me," I let my hand explore, "a secret, Lauren." Her head lolls back, her breasts arching high. Her slit is swollen and slick with pleasure. Dragging my finger along her lips, I nip at her neck. "If you want my fingers to fuck your tight little pussy, I want your words." Back and forth, my fingers roll, spreading her wide and teasing her entrance.

Indecision splinters across her gaze. She swallows, and I want to cup her throat and stop whatever was being washed away and demand she confesses her fucking sins to me.

"Matteo doesn't kiss as well as I thought you would," she blurts, her cheeks burning red.

I growl at the sound of my friend's name on her plump lips. I advance on her, biting her lip between my teeth and rolling it, the bite of pain a warning. "I said tell me something no one else knows." My tongue sweeps in possessively. "I already know this." My eyes spark smugly.

"Matteo and I never even kissed. I wouldn't have gone through with it. I wanted you to drive me home." Her breathy confession has heat tingling at the base of my spine and my cock stiffening painfully hard. I give her no warning and drive two fingers deep inside, curling them as I pull away and fuck them back in. "Yes." Her choked plea clings to the ceiling.

I drag her mouth to mine and claim her lips as my own. Spearing my tongue deeply as I plunge my fingers in and out, her warmth clinging to my hand. I cup her breast, massaging the pale flesh and rolling her nipple between my fingers. Her hips fly upwards. Her moan cemented to my lips. "I own all your whispers, all your tears—every little gasp has my name on it." I thumb her clit as I work my fingers in and out, adding pressure as I roll my fingers deep. "I own this body—every orgasm is mine and mine alone." My fingers are slick with her wetness. I slide them along her clit, lifting her hips out of the water so she can watch me work her pussy. She chokes out a sweet moan. "Every time you break apart, it's my face you will see."

"Yes." She nods, a low sob expelled from her throat.

"Whose pussy is this?" I spread her lips wide and groan. Dipping my finger in, I lift it to my mouth and suck deeply, her head twisting to watch, her eyes wide with need.

"Oh god, yours... it's yours, Cain."

Slipping my hands under her thighs, I lift her up and backwards, and my erection throbs as she takes it in her grasp, lining me up before I let her sink down. I snap my hips upward, surging deeply. Her gasp of pleasure rivals my bark. "You're damn right it's mine."

She pleads for more, twisting to find my mouth. I want to give in to her, but the idea of bringing her to climax slowly, delaying our release, bringing us to the edge over and over, only to hold it out of reach, is far more tempting.

I fuck her until her skin is wrinkled and her legs are boneless. I fuck her until the bath groans in protest, and our cries of desperation could crack the tiles. When my release finally comes, it chases hers, catching it and locking us together. The water has long since gone cold. The majority sloshed over the sides and sinking down the drain. Lauren's pants are short and soft, yet my own are being sucked down in pained lungfuls. Her legs are hooked over the edges, her head hanging over the side as I rut into her, never getting deep enough. Her chin is cupped in my hand as I kiss her through the madness. Lashes flutter, and big eyes blink shyly at me. Smirking, I slip out of her, pecking her reddened lips when she hisses in protest.

"I watched my father kill himself." My chest heaves as I grapple for air, my body slick with sweat. My damp forehead rolls over hers, avoiding the astonishing pain I've shocked her with. "I think he would hate the man I've become," I confess woodenly. My voice is devoid of emotion. I sink against her body, her creamy skin supple and comforting, her limbs wrapped around me, holding me tightly as we breathe harshly.

She pulls in a small breath, daring to respond.

"Don't say anything." The finality in my words has her chest deflating. "Now I know who owns all your pleasure, and you know who owns my pain."

We don't speak. We hardly breathe. Lauren holds me as we lay uncomfortably in the large tub. I think I nod off at one point, and when I finally lift my head to look at her, she is already asleep. Carefully, I ease her out of the bath and carry her to my bedroom.

CHAPTER 21

Lauren

When I wake, the moon is still riding high, clouds thick and fluffy, spread across the sky. Cain's light snoring breaches my ear, and I lay still for a moment, taking stock of my body, unsure why I'm awake when my limbs are achy and tired. My stomach protests, grumbling heavily. Turning my head, I blink as my gaze adjusts, allowing me to focus on the man sprawled next to me. His arm is thrown over his head, his chest wide and inviting as he sleeps with his other hand resting on my hip. He looks calm, nothing like the man who bared his deepest secret to me with sweat drenching his hair and the scent of sex floating around us.

"Now I know who owns all your pleasure, and you know who owns my pain."

Something heavy and painful sits low in my stomach. I can't imagine the grief of losing a parent, let alone bearing witness to one who took their own life. My heart aches for Cain. I wanted to say so much to him, but nothing I could say would repair the pain—no words would salve the wound he was walking around with.

Easing out of his hold, I shuffle along the top of the mattress and sit up, holding my breath. Cain doesn't move, but I twist to ensure I haven't woken him. Tiptoeing across to the chair, I quietly pick up his shirt and slip it on, buttoning it up as I make my way downstairs to the kitchen.

The penthouse is still. The bank of windows stretches to the furthest side of the room, but no sound is permitted past the thick glass. Moonlight streamlines inside, sending a healthy glow into the main living area, and my eyes adjust further to the darkened space. There is no creak as I descend the stairs, just the soft pad of my bare feet. I find the switch for the under-cabinet lighting and move around the kitchen, preparing everything I need to make a milky drink. Then it's just me and the moon as the city sleeps below.

I find a spot on the sofa and curl my feet under me, sipping my drink and only then do I let the shock from last night burn through me. My heart breaks for the man who looked as broken as he did handsome. He doesn't want my pity or to see his pain reflected back in my own gaze. I don't know why he confessed those things to me. I could blame it on lust, although Cain doesn't strike me as the kind of man who falls victim to something so basic. Whatever his reasons were, it was shared in confidence. It's another thing I will take with me. Something to never be shared—only to be wrapped up in layers of trust and buried in the bowel of my heart. Placing my empty cup down on the coffee table, I lean into the cushions and sigh. I could wake him, but I won't. I need a moment, just some time to process. Pulling a throw over me, I close my eyes and pretend the weekend is only just beginning again.

It seemed like a good idea until it wasn't.

Until I gave him my pleasure, and he bore his pain.

It was a lust labelled as hate.

A moment we allowed to get away from us.

It was my best mistake.

⁓

I wake as the surface below me dips, my eyes fluttering to find Cain knelt above me. The shirt I'm wearing is being pulled at, growing taut against my ribs as he begins to unbutton the top few buttons. "You couldn't sleep?" His voice is rough.

I shake my head as he works the last few buttons, parting the shirt, and my stomach hollows as he drags his hungry eyes down my body. "I was thirsty."

"You should have woken me," he berates, leaning to press a soft kiss just below my navel. His stubble scrapes across my skin, his tongue dips out, his lips kissing the wet path away. He rests his chin on my pelvis and stares up at me. "Let me fire you."

My fingers spear his hair and curl loosely, gripping the strands, laughing as I shake my head. "Again?" I lift my brow, lips twisting up at the sides.

"Don't remind me." He rolls his prickly chin across my skin, his hands spread around my thighs, lifting them to drape over his shoulders. Turning his head, he presses a wet kiss to the sensitive skin. His fingers glide over my skin, a soft contradiction to the rough scrape his beard is marking me with. His teeth sink into my inner thigh, and I jack-knife off the sofa, gasping in pain. My fingers tighten, pulling hard at his hair, but he sucks the clump of flesh into his mouth, soothing the pinch.

Hissing, I writhe and moan as his fingers dig into my skin, holding me in place, and when he pulls away, the angry red welt burns. Groaning, Cain flattens his tongue and licks it until it no longer hurts, but everything else throbs. It's not the first mark he has left on my skin. My hips are covered in faint bruises from where he has pinned me to his lap—my breasts littered with tiny love bites. His tongue rolls up my thigh, his nose burrows deep, and he inhales.

Cain's mouth drags along my pussy, his tongue dipping out to kiss me just as passionately as if he were focusing on my face. Sweet trickles of pleasure purr across my skin, and my hands fasten in his hair as he devours me, licking, sucking, and fucking me slowly with his tongue. It's almost too much, too prolonged. There isn't enough pressure or pain, I realise. Everything about his attention is slow and steady, attentive and teasing. He spears his tongue deeply, groaning, the vibration rumbling through me. "I need more." I breathe shallowly.

His lips pull wide, and he shakes his head, beginning his assault all over again, slow and brutal. Pushing me to the edge and altering his attention so my orgasm drops away. Grabbing handfuls of my ass, he moans into my pussy, sucking on my lips and flicking languid licks to my clit.

"Please, I'm so close." I grind into his face, sobbing, when he shakes his head again. There is no sense of urgency. No desire to chase the same high we have been addicted to all weekend. Cain maps out every millimetre of my pussy with his mouth and tongue. When his fingers trace a line down the centre of my ass, I stiffen and peek down at him. His grin is devilish, and I simply shake my head. His lips pout as he fights a dirty, knowing grin and continues to fuck his tongue in and out. My wetness glistens on his lips and drenches my thighs. His finger massages my back hole, never dipping inside, but the added sensation has my back arching and my legs quivering. His mouth moves to my clit, and he sucks me deeply, suckling until my orgasm is rushing upwards. I choke out a sob, terrified he is going to deny me of this one too. I stare at him, pleading, and he sucks hard, giving me what I need. Pleasure, sweet and long, washes over me in waves, bursting apart from my thighs and drenching me in ecstasy.

"Good morning," he rasps, mouth trailing up my trembling stomach and latching onto my breast.

"The best morning," I pant.

"Even though I'm a prick," he jokes.

Laughter bubbles in my gut. "The biggest. A massive cacti." I grin.

His smile is slow, his chuckle low, and he begins his assault all over again, moving between my breasts, licking, biting, and nibbling my nipples. His hand caresses my leg and slips between us, two fingers spread my lips, and he flicks a heated gaze up at me. "You're throbbing." He swallows thickly. "I can feel you pulsing against my hand."

I half moan, half sob as his intense gaze rakes over my face, watching as his fingers plunge inside, slowly stretching me. "Cain." I wheeze.

"Yes, Lauren?" His hand works me, just as his mouth did, long fingers slowly fuck into me, his palm pressing to my clit and teasing to the possibility of an orgasm, only to watch it fall away when he stops, grinning as I pant and choke out my frustration. His fingers gather up my slick pleasure and slather it across my chest. The musty scent pours into my nose, and Cain swears, shifting on the sofa, and I get the first look at how aroused he is. His cock is thick and long in his boxers, the head wide and angry as it pushes free of the waistband.

"Fuck," I whine.

With my chest glistening like his mouth, he drops his face to my breasts and begins kissing and sucking. His fingers find a place between my legs, and he fucks me slowly and deeply, curling his fingers against my inner walls and pressing his palm to my clit. Shivers of slick heat douse my body and slide across my stomach, hanging heavy and low as another orgasm begins to build. His free hand holds onto my breast, and, pushing a nipple into his mouth, he drags it between his teeth as I teeter on the edge, moaning over and over as my orgasm balances on the pinnacle but doesn't slip over.

"Please!" I cry. My nails are sinking into his scalp.

He sucks hard, and I fly over the edge, screaming his name. "Lauren, you're so fucking sexy." His mouth slams against mine, devouring me. "Such a good girl."

"Oh god," I writhe and whimper as my body shudders.

"I love watching you come. Love hearing my name on these lips." He licks and kisses, grinding into me.

He drives his tongue inside, and I tangle mine with the hot curl of his. He shifts, ripping his boxers down and then the wide crown of his cock is there, slipping between my pussy, and sliding up and down my slick entrance. He grips under my jaw, the other hand fisting my hair, and then he sinks deeply, rearing back to watch my face convulse in bliss. The long, slow thrust is dedicated to making me feel every inch. I gasp into his mouth, my eyes wide as he stares back in awe. I slam my eyes shut, scared to see those feelings burning back at me.

"I know. I fucking know." He chokes, lifting his hips to drag his cock out to the tip, and the pressure at my entrance throbs before he plunges back in, shaking my face to get me to open my eyes. "Look at me."

I refuse, my head barely moving in his grip as he holds me tightly. He plunges back in harder, hitting deeply, and my eyes snap wide, a low cry slipping free. "Cain, I can't," my whisper breaks through the crack in my lips.

His eyes glint and burn as he watches me, his brow furrowed, his mouth lax as he pants roughly through each deep, slow thrust. His hips roll into mine. His thick thighs owning me with a gentle confidence that I didn't know he possessed. He's spent the weekend fucking me with little to no shame, pushing me to my limits, marking where he sees fit, and revelling in the loss of control we both share.

But this is different.

Something palpable exists in the air and clings to the tense brush of his shoulders.

It guts me whole and exudes from him in heavy, unapologetic waves.

He's going to ruin any sliver of dignity I have left.

Mould it in his bare hands and send me back home a different woman.

"This is only the first of my goodbyes today," he says softly.

I suck in a pained breath. His fingers tighten around my cheeks, and he kisses me hard. He pumps his hips in at a different angle, and the slight change pulls out a sharp cry of pleasure, and he shakes his head.

"I don't want to have to say goodbye to this pussy." His smile is soft and sad, and I bite my lip. "You feel so good. Can you feel how you hug my cock?" He kisses me roughly and thrusts in twice, the pace no different but harder, forcing me to feel him everywhere. My insides cling to him, and a rumble of pleasure rattles around his chest.

"Yes," I huff through gritted teeth.

I don't want to have to say goodbye to this pussy.

Not me, my pussy. It's the brutal truth I need to hear.

"You've made a mess on my sofa," he admonishes, biting my lip, and swivelling his hips.

I sob, and he pumps in and out quickly. I hook my legs around his back and beg him to give me what I need. Sweat is settling into his scalp, making it hard for me to stay hooked to his strands. I rock my hips into his. Slamming my smaller body into him, trying to build friction. Cain tuts and kneels up, leaving my mouth bereft. The angle has me hissing, and he opens his mouth, groaning in pleasure as his eyes glitter down at where he is stretching me widely. "You're so fucking swollen," he tells me, shifting to pull my hips into his. His muscles ripple and tense as he runs his hands up my thighs and spreads them wide so he can fuck into me with slow, deep pounds. My tits bounce, and his neck lolls back. "Pretty girl," he warns. "You feel too damn good."

"Say goodbye!" I cry as he pumps deeply. Bright blue eyes snap to mine, and I hold my hand to my mouth as pleasure ripples everywhere. "Please, say goodbye." I stifle a sob, over-whelmed with emotion, attacked with sensation. I shake my head as tears prick my eyes, and I beg him for an orgasm that I know will wreck me.

His hips rock like a swaying boat, surging into my pussy. Each velvet thrust has my eyes rolling to the back of my head, my hands grappling to touch him, but he denies me that too, and gathers them up, pounding deeply. The wet slap of our bodies connects in a sweaty frenzy echoing around the elevated room. Cain growls as the noises quicken, my thighs tighten, and my cry is agonised, sweet, and loud for all to hear. He erupts into expletives, fucking me hard and fast, and his mouth is suddenly on mine, his tongue stabbing inside, sweeping up the tail end of a sob, as his cock lengthens and hot streams of his cum fill me up.

I hate this.

I don't want to say goodbye.

I don't want to fall victim to lust, either.

I know I can't let myself be dazzled by his words. The low hot confessions he has made over the course of my stay, the softly spoken promises, the devious pleas, the dirty praise, and hooded eyes following me wherever I go will remain in these four walls, burnt into the plaster and hidden in the cavities for none to see.

I don't want to have to say goodbye to this pussy.

It's just sex. Nothing more. Nothing less. There is no emotion here, only the intoxicating heat of lust boggling our minds.

I twist my head away, blinking furiously as he pants into my neck, his chest heaving with exertion. My hands splay in his hair, my body shuddering as my orgasm ebbs between us. Cain's thighs tense, drawing out the pleasure before he relaxes into my body and plants a soft, wet kiss in the crook of my neck.

"That was still good morning." His deep voice is charred by desire. Big hands circle my back so his arms are wrapped around me tightly.

CHAPTER 22

Lauren

It's late at night when Cain parks his car outside my block of flats. The journey has been quiet, the tension thick enough to taste. The engine stills, and I smile, twisting to face him, "Thank—"

"I'm walking you up," he interrupts, jaw locked, eyes hard. His hands are as stiff as granite on his steering wheel.

"Oh, okay." Elation erupts in my breastbone, fluttering wildly.

Cain walks me to my apartment and waits patiently whilst I key us in. This little space used to bring me such comfort, but I feel a great sense of loss as I cross the threshold. I find a place for my bag and hang my keys up, turning to find him clicking the door shut and looking at me with a closed expression on his handsome face.

"Thanks for the lift home," I say breezily.

"Come here," he rumbles. He meets me halfway, and his hands hook above my arse, knotting us together. I let the heat of his touch immerse into my skin like a lotion, never wanting to forget the sensation. My own find a place around his neck, but it feels too personal, so I slide them to his chest. Smirking, he nudges his chin. "Don't get shy with me now." His laugh is low and sexy, and it has the corners of my lips pulling upwards. I return my hands to his neck and blink up at him, waiting. "Are you ready for goodbye?" he hums.

I nod, but what I really want to do is shake my head vigorously.

"Liar."

"Cain," I sigh.

"I know." His tone matches mine, twisted with longing and regret; he drops his lips to mine, and his hands move to cup my face. It's not a hard kiss, but it's passionate, nonetheless. Packed with slow heat and everything we never said. I hold on and fight the surge of emotion racing up my chest. When I suck in a pained breath, he pulls away and drops his forehead to mine. "You'll ring me if you have any problems."

I hum a yes, untrusting of my own voice. I can't bring myself to meet his eyes, and he doesn't force me to either. I have no intention of ever calling him. It's a cut that needs to be severe, final.

"Goodbye, pretty girl."

"Goodbye, Cain." My voice cracks, and I swallow the remnants of vulnerability away before I say something stupid like, stay.

With a quick peck to my lips, he gives me a little wink and walks out of the door. It clicks shut, and I sit down on the sofa, perplexed. Sadness washes over me, along with a flicker of misplaced hope. I bat all those emotions away and cling to the happiness I felt only a few short hours ago. I want to hold on to those feelings a little longer before I'm sucker-punched by the ache of loss. This weekend was the best but worst thing to happen to me.

I never wanted to regret saying no to the man, but living

with the knowledge of what yes allowed me to experience will forever haunt me.

It's a little while before I find the energy to move. I've let my emotions get away from me and held onto the small bubble of hope floating around in the back of my mind, hoping that Cain would decide to act on wanting more than a weekend. I laugh humourlessly—my apartment could fit into his en suite. I'm most definitely not the kind of woman he would settle down with.

I'm the weekend heist kind.

The kind of woman he can pretend to want just to see how the shoe fits. But women like me know the shoe never fits. Besides, most of his shoes look handmade.

I could spend the rest of the evening moping around. It's all I really want to do, but it would do me no good, and Cain is probably going to fumigate his penthouse to remove any memory of me so he can carry on with his life. I tell myself all the things I think I need to hear to wrestle with the reality of not having him in my life.

I need to pack. Heading to the kitchen, I dig out some bin liners and the flat-pack boxes wedged under the sofa and begin putting my little life into them. Filling a small holdall with necessities that I will need over the next few days, I put it aside with my work uniform and some loungewear, then I begin heaving boxes to the door and prop it open so I can start to cart them up in the elevator. I'm sweating and out of breath, but mostly, I'm doing everything I can to keep my mind from slipping into a miserable void.

Heavy, slow footsteps bring my head up as I grunt and pant, pushing one of the heavier boxes out into the hall. Deeks' face appears at the top of the stairwell. "Where's the elephant?" he remarks, amused.

"I could ask you the same thing." I heave another box out. His laugh echoes through the empty stairwell.

"Need a hand, girl?" He ambles towards me, and I nod,

wiping the sweat from my brow. His eyes zero in on the smattering of bruises on my upper arms where my t-shirt has become stuck to my skin.

I tug the sleeve hem. "I'm fine, it's—"

"Complicated, right?" That's what I had said last night to him when he was poking at Cain, trying to rile him. That he was my boss, but it was complicated.

"Right." I slap a bright smile on my face, throwing him off guard. I appreciate his offer of help, but I don't want to accept it. Cain was adamant I call him where Deeks is concerned, and I don't want to have a reason to call Cain. "I'm good, but thanks." I shove at a box, and it topples.

Deeks makes his way to me and sets it the right way up. "No can do. Mr Complicated asked that I keep an eye on you."

"Well, he asked that I call him if you cause me any trouble," I retort flippantly, "wait, what?" I splutter when his words suddenly register. "Why did he ask you to keep an eye on me?" I'm dumbfounded.

"I'm guessing it's complicated." Big Deeks drawls, and I huff, confused. "So, where are these boxes going?"

"To 43B." I sound petulant.

An ear-splitting whistle rings through the corridor, and the thunder of shoes makes its way up to us. "You heard her, 43B." Deeks winks. It catapults me back to Cain, winking goodbye, and I drop my head, but not before I see a handful of lads around my age, if not younger, lifting my boxes with ease and disappearing up the stairs and in the elevator.

"Oh, wait. I need the key." Jumping up, I find the new key, and Deeks helps me carry some clothes on hangers up the stairs.

What I expected to take me all evening is compressed into two short hours. My new apartment is full of boxes. The only thing left downstairs is my sofa bed. The guys managed to heave my fridge up a few levels, and all I need now is new bedding. "That's it, Deeks." I lift onto my toes and peck his cheek.

"Don't forget where I am if you need me."

"I won't." He steps out into the corridor, closing me in with a slight click of the door.

The silence is unexpectedly deafening, so much so that I smack my lips together and swing my arms, unsure what to do with myself now I'm in my new place. I ate with Cain, so I'm not hungry. Instead, I prepare my uniform, grab a shower in the wet room and crawl into bed, folding my quilt over me so I'm not lying directly on the mattress.

I don't know whether it's the new surroundings or the fact that I have spent over forty-eight hours wrapped around that man, but I am shocked by how utterly alone I suddenly feel. The unwelcome feeling stays with me until my eyes become droopy in the early hours.

———

Amberley is waiting eagerly for me as I arrive at the hotel. Her eyes are wide with apparent excitement. "Is that a limp I detect?" She laughs, dancing over to me and slinging an arm around my neck. "I'm sorry about the article. It was stupid."

"It's okay." I shrug it off, embarrassed by how insecure it made me.

"Spill!" she pleads.

"I have so much to tell you." I press my lips together to contain my excitement. I have so much news—from Cain to the apartment.

"Priorities first." Her hands swing away, and she walks backwards, wiggling her brows. "Is he big?"

"Amberley!" I chide.

"Oh, come on. He is, isn't he?" I shake my head, and she links arms with me. "His penthouse is gorgeous."

"I know. I also have a new apartment." I'm quick to change the subject because I am trying to keep the sadness away. It's been constant since he winked and walked away.

"He didn't! Holy shit!" she exclaims as we enter through the back. She thinks Cain brought me an apartment.

"What? No," I laugh. "I have mould. Well, not me, the flat," I laugh. "I've been set up in a new apartment. It's bigger and newly decorated."

"Seriously?" She grins. "Can't wait to see it."

Unlocking my phone, I hand it over, and she begins thumbing through the pictures of my new place. She gives an appreciative whistle that has me leaning to see the photo, but I choke out an apology when I find it's Cain in his workout shorts. I captured it in a moment of weakness when he wasn't looking.

"Don't apologise." She hums. "I can't believe you're fucking that. Lucky bitch." She grins. I pull it away, hiding my screen as a few colleagues walk by. The staff room is quiet, with only one other person putting their bag away, a lady from housekeeping. She smiles as she leaves, and Amberley leans against the lockers. "So, when are you seeing him again?"

"I'm not," I say quietly. I put my bag in my locker, and Amberley stares at me as if I have two heads and more eyes than a spider.

"Lauren, why the hell not?"

I shrug. "It's what we agreed. One weekend. No-strings fun." I don't look her in the eye because I know my true feelings will show.

"You or him? He couldn't keep his eyes off you."

"It is what it is. I knew what I was getting into." I smile softly. "He's my boss," I whisper.

"Are you okay?" Her voice lowers, and her hand rubs along my spine.

Nodding, I beam at her. "Of course. Honestly, I think you're more upset than I am." I laugh, feigning indifference. I check my watch and lock my locker. "Come on. We're due to start." Amberley doesn't say anything, and we walk in silence down the corridor to the foyer.

I was excited when I woke up this morning, keen to see Cain. I know we called it quits, but there is a small part of me that hopes when he sees me, he'll think better of his decision to leave. I've never experienced this deep ache, even with Martin.

My past relationship felt more like an intimate friendship, and now I think of it, it only hurt because I couldn't believe Kristy would do something like that. She never reached out after I left Martin—if anything, she secured herself to him more.

The deep rumble of Cain's voice has my steps slowing. I look at my friend nervously, and she nods at me reassuringly. He's standing, talking to Felicity at the main desk, and greets Amberley as she rounds the desk. He says a few words to them, and just as our eyes are about to meet, he looks away and begins tapping on his phone as he walks. Pain stabs at my chest. Embarrassment ripples across my face, and I stare at the ground as hot tears prick at my eyes.

He fucking blanked me.

Amberley rushes over. "Breathe," she utters softly.

I quickly replay it in my head, trying to rationalise his behaviour. "He blanked me," I whisper, my throat closing around the words.

"He's a prick. Shit, I'm so sorry, Lauren." My shoulders droop in defeat. He seriously just blanked me.

"What's going on?" Felicity mutters impatiently.

"Lauren has a headache," Amberley's lie is swift. "She's just going to grab some pain meds. She needs to be careful after her concussion."

"Concussion?" Felicity frowns.

"Yes, the other week when I left, I was concussed," I remind her.

"Oh, right, yes, hurry back." With that, she twists and returns to her duties.

Amberley pushes me back to the staff room and whirls on me as soon as the door closes. "I'm shoving laxatives in his fucking drink!"

"No, don't." My laugh is strained. "I'm just in shock. He went from disliking me——"

"He never disliked you," my friend interrupts.

Ignoring her, I carry on, "——to completely doting on me. Honestly, Amberley, he treated me like a princess. Our chemistry was off the charts. We couldn't keep our hands off each other," I admit, sniffling. She hands me a tissue, and I wipe my eyes and nose. "What the hell was that?" My hand wafts towards the door. "I expected him to be standoffish. Polite, but not that. Never that."

"He's a prick," she rationalises.

"A massive cacti," I whisper.

"What?"

"Nothing." I shrug, looking at her with a watery smile. "I'm an idiot."

"No," she says passionately. "He is a 'see you next Tuesday,' the biggest one ever."

"God, I feel so used," I choke, my neck heating as I remember how easily he dismissed me out there.

"Take a few minutes and come and meet me out front. If you don't want to stay, I'll tell Felicity you went home."

"I won't give him the satisfaction," I say abruptly. "I just need a few."

She pecks my cheek and hands me another tissue before leaving me with my thoughts in the staff room.

I'm only alone for a few tense minutes before she barrels back in. "He's leaving," she tells me.

"Oh, okay, good." I sigh with relief.

"No *leaving*. He is flying out tomorrow. He's leaving and returning to his New York office now that the CI has been set up. I fucking hate him. I hope a nest of ants takes up residence in his fucking penthouse," she seethes.

No wonder he wanted a weekend with me—he didn't plan on seeing me again.

Shaking my head, I slump down on one of the chairs.

It shouldn't hurt, but it does.

I keep trying to remind myself that we agreed to a weekend. That's all that it was, but my heart objects, and I bite my lip.

"Shit, are you falling for him?" Amberley whispers, walking hurriedly to me. I shake my head, but a small part of me, deep inside, laughs darkly.

"It was just sex," I croak.

"Lauren, you and I both know there was more to it than that. He let you sleep in his room here. It's no surprise your feelings are all in a jumble."

"I need to clock on."

"Go home. I can cover for you."

"No way." I stand, and with it, my anger wakes up, a hard wall looming over me. "I'd say screw him, but I already did that."

Amberley's eyes snap wide, and then she laughs loudly. I smile, and she hugs me tightly. "Let's pray he gets diarrhoea during his flight."

"Okay." I smile. "The worst bout of diarrhoea ever," I affirm.

"Explosive." She giggles. "Come on."

CHAPTER 23

Cain

I watch the camera playback. Each time Lauren's face crumples, I rewind and hit play. Some would accuse me of being a masochist, but every time I witness the hurt fall across her face, I remind myself why I walked away. I wanted to forget her, but I forgot myself in the process. She offered everything and took nothing, but she owns me. There is a quiet resilience about Lauren that I want to devour. I lost a huge part of me when my father killed himself, but I found a small part of it when I was with Lauren. She deserved more than my dismissal just now. Leaving her last night has weighed heavily on my mind, and returning to New York will give me the distance I need to focus on Royce.

Danvers already emailed this morning to confirm the will we suspected was fake has been sent for testing. There is no way I will be able to search Carson Court, but I know Perry has been back over the weekend to try and secure the original. I'm just hoping Royce's password choice has been as predictable as his business strategy. If my father's safe is still situated in the study, it's likely it is locked in there.

On the screen, Amberley rushes to Lauren, and I see her comfort her friend and throw daggers at me over her shoulder. I felt them, sharp slices to my spine as I walked away. I fucking deserve them. I want Lauren, but I don't want her anywhere near Royce.

Amberley escorts her back to the staffroom. Slamming my laptop shut, I pack up my things and meet Justine in the corridor. She's travelling with me and is pulling a small case along beside her. Her hair is pulled into a severe bun, and her skirt suit is a navy ensemble. She's serious and efficient. I have no idea how she puts up with me, but I couldn't function without her. "The car is ready, and the jet is fuelled."

"Thank you, Justine."

My assistant double-takes. "Are you okay?"

"Because I said thank you?" I muse.

"No, because New York is suddenly the place to be?"

"I have work to attend to."

Her lips purse, but I don't elaborate. I texted Matt and Perry this morning, updating them about my plans to head to New York. I need to get my head in gear before Royce and my mother return from St. Lucia. I need the distance. No distractions. No pretty brunettes messing with my head.

One weekend with Lauren, and I don't even recognise myself anymore. We take the elevator down, and as soon as the doors open, I feel her eyes on me and the accusation she's regarding me with. I keep my head down, pulling my phone out to tap an imaginary message.

My father would be ashamed of me. I'm ashamed of my behaviour.

Perry is cursing me to hell and back. I informed him I put an end to things last night, and he has sent me one-word insults all morning.

Lauren and I exchanged numbers, or at least she let me

put my number in her phone before the weekend was up, and I made a note of hers. She hasn't called, but I know she is settled in her new apartment, courtesy of Kelvin Deeks. That bulldozer has been surprisingly useful.

Ignoring the latest insult from my friend, I scroll through my contacts, my thumb hovering over her number. I want to explain, but instead, I lock it and drop it in my suit pocket, exiting out onto the street, regret curdling in my stomach.

Our ride idles just outside, and Justine and I load the boot up before slipping inside to head straight for the airport.

~

"Anything to report?" I lounge back in my chair, my feet kicked up on the desk. It's been two weeks, and I've asked the same question each time I've spoken to Perry. What I really mean is anything to report on Lauren.

"London isn't missing you," he retorts.

My lip curls, and I fight the compulsion to ask him exactly what that means, but he beats me to it. My phone pings with an attachment. Opening it, I come face to face with Lauren's beautiful smile. She is dressed to impress and has loose curls weighing her hair down. Perry, Amberley, Kat, and Matt smile back at me from the image.

"When was this?"

"Last night, we arranged to meet at BANK." I nod but say nothing, absorbing the information like a hammer to the chest. Perry must sense my unease because he adds, "They cleared the air with one another, but that was it." *They*, meaning Lauren and Matteo.

Clearing my throat, I slide my feet back to the floor and adjust my tie. "Any news on the will?" He needs to find it.

"No, look, Kat is getting suspicious. I'm running out of excuses to go to the house."

"Perry, my sister is enamoured with you. She won't care," I remind him. I rub my eyes in irritation that Lauren and Matt went for a drink last night.

"Your shitty excuse for a mother returns this weekend. All hell is going to break loose. You need to get back here."

"I know." I sigh heavily.

"Just ask me," Perry mutters, annoyed. I've avoided any conversation surrounding Lauren.

"She seems fine." I sound petulant, and the smug prick laughs at me.

"You left your balls here. I think Lauren was wearing them as earrings last night."

"Eat shit." I grin.

"You both have more in common than you realise. She doesn't want to talk about you either. However, she did let slip after one too many that she had respected you for the wrong reasons, and she was more annoyed at herself for being such a poor judge of character." He sniggers.

Ouch. My girl is hurting.

"I thought I was doing the right thing."

"I get it. Things could get nasty with Royce."

"They will."

"She can handle it. Look how she dealt with her ex. She hasn't uttered a word about his poor choices, and she walked away gracefully. Cain, I knocked her out, and she had secured interviews like she was shopping for milk. She can handle it," he reiterates. "It's you that's having a hard time."

"I hope you're not expecting me to cough up a fee for your worldly advice."

"She's good for you. That's all I'm saying."

I snort and stand up, walking to look out across the skyline. New York spreads out far and wide. The dense concrete landscape is as endless as the sea I flew across to get here. I suddenly hate the distance, each building an obstacle, the sea a vast blue wasteland in my way. Panic grips at my chest, and I shake my head, refusing to give it any leeway in my mind.

I know this feeling, and I hate it. The power it holds over my emotions and the lack of control are debilitating. I clutch at Perry's words, gripping them like a life raft, keeping my mind grounded.

"You established that from us spending one weekend together?" I yank at my tie, sweat beading my brow.

"So spend more time with her," he drawls. "She's seeing her family this weekend. Amberley mentioned her not looking forward to it. Apparently, her brother is a dick to her."

This is unwelcome news, and my anxiety exacerbates. Amberley's insight gives me something to focus on. I might have to investigate James Lindel further. "I'll let you know when I land," I reply, avoiding the topic of Lauren, because I know I seriously fucked up.

I fucked up royally. I want Lauren, and that terrifies me.

"*You* eat shit," he states bluntly, before putting the phone down on me.

I spend the rest of the day hauled up in my office working. I'm emailing Justine about securing a flight home when David, an assistant, knocks and walks in. "Sir, I think I'm on to something. He's definitely having you tailed." He walks forward, handing me some papers. "He's using the company Saples & Co, and the will was drawn up by Harold Morris. I've emailed a copy to your lawyer. He's retired now, but around the time of your father's death, he received a hefty payout. It's got to be a fake." There is an element of excitement in his tone, but his eyes are as cold and hard as mine. There's a reason I hired David, and it wasn't just down to his work ethic. Royce has burned his family too.

Ivory is a poisonous snake. I wonder if Kelvin Deeks' talents extend to bodily harm because I want more than to financially ruin Royce—I'm out for blood.

"Thank you, David. I'll be returning to London in a day

or two, but keep me informed." He leaves me alone, and I read through the information, taking stock of the older man with snowy hair that my stepfather has paid to follow me. When I return to my desk, Justine has updated my diary, and I pack up my belongings to return home tomorrow morning.

I'm close to leaving the office when I dial Lauren's number, unable to let another day pass between us. I wait as it rings. She doesn't answer, so I find a seat on one of the sofas and connect the call again. She'll know it's me. I purposely put my number under No.1 Prick with a cactus emoji. I'm sure she believes I've lived up to that name more than once. I may as well embrace it.

"Hello?" she answers curtly.

"It's Cain."

"I know. I'm just not sure why you're calling me." She's not fishing for reassurance. Her clipped tone cuts like a blunt knife.

"To apologise." I plan on apologising properly when I see her. I'm going to apologise to her all night long.

"Why? We agreed to a weekend." That was my first mistake.

"We didn't agree to me being an asshole."

"Given the nature of our relationship, our professional one," she is quick to make that point, "it's best you don't call me again. And stop having Deeks check up on me!" She cuts the call, and I grin at the impatient sigh I caught at the end. Surely she doesn't think she can meet up with my friends and sever all ties with me?

I ring again, and she answers almost instantly but doesn't speak. "Can we meet for dinner? I want to apologise." I rest back in the seat and pull the phone away from my ear, checking we are still connected when she doesn't respond after a few tense seconds.

"You already apologised."

"In person. I want to apologise in person." The silence

lingers, and I run a hand through my hair. "I fucked up. I hated leaving your apartment."

"No," she spits softly, "you don't get to do this. I can't afford to get involved with you aft—" She sucks in a breath. After Martin. She doesn't say it, but I already know. Once bitten, twice shy. I happen to like the shy parts and all the fiery bits in between.

"And I can't afford to let you say no." My smile is apologetic, even if she can't see me. "I want to see where this goes, Lauren." I curse under my breath as she stays quiet on the other end—again. "I hate that I'm not there."

"It won't work. I signed your policies—a contract. I love my job. I won't risk my job because you decided you miss me *today*." I know the hurt she is projecting has as much to do with me as it does with her ex-boyfriend and shitty friend.

"Have dinner with me. I'm flying home tomorrow."

"Cain," she utters in a cautionary tone.

"Just dinner. Please?" I ask again, knowing if she doesn't agree, I won't give her the option to say no. I could quite easily turn up at her apartment. I own it, after all.

"Will you go away if I do?"

My grin is instant—she doesn't mean that. "I can't make any promises, but if that's what you want, I'll respect it."

She waits a beat before she responds, and my fucking chest hollows when she does. "Okay."

"I'll pick you up at eight?"

"Won't you be jet lagged?"

"I need to see you."

"I'll see you at eight, then." She doesn't hesitate in disconnecting the call, eager to put the distance back between us, but I feel the tension in my neck and shoulders ease at her agreement to meet.

Perry's words are sobering, if a little unwelcome.

She *is* good for me.

I just know I'm no good for her.

CHAPTER 24

Lauren

"This is a mistake." I groan, plopping down on my bed as Amberley hands me a pale cream shirt and holds it against me, confident with her choice.

"Just see what he has to say. It's dinner. Lauren, most girls would be bowled over by someone like Cain missing them from hundreds of miles away."

"He is asking for us to date in secret—that doesn't make me feel good," I admit, faffing with my hair.

"He can't fire you, and you won't quit. Give the guy a break." Her eyes roll into the back of her head, and I laugh. She leans in to give me a hug. "Look, I'm living my girlish fantasies out through you, so just date him for my sake, please?"

"Of course. What are friends for?"

"Fucking bosses in secret and getting us free club entry," Amberley quips, dryly pecking my cheek when I choke out a laugh.

I finish getting ready, and she passes me some perfume. "You'll be here when I get back?"

"Nope." She laughs. "You won't be coming back." Her hands find my shoulders, and she angles me towards the door. I give my reflection a quick once over and pull at the shirt tucked into my jeans. "He's here," she announces, with her face pressed against the window.

Butterflies erupt in my stomach. I give her a quick hug before I leave her, peering down at the car park below. My legs feel wooden as I leave my apartment and take the lift down. Cain is already inside the building, and his eyes do a quick sweep of my outfit. He looks good, tired, but really good in his tailored suit and sporting a little stubble.

"You look nice." His jaw convulses, and his eyes lift to mine, regret burning hotly.

"Thanks. Shall we go?"

"Sure." I expect him to hold the door, but when he takes my hand, I tense. "How's work been?" He keeps his tone light and relaxed, and it eases my nerves. Cain keeps our fingers entwined as we leave the building and walk to his car.

"Fine, busy." There is an awkwardness between us that was never there before. It's more than likely down to me still feeling snubbed.

As soon as we are in the car, Cain turns to me and leans to cup the back of my neck, his other arm resting on the steering wheel. My spine lengthens, and I grit my jaw, not wanting to give in so easily to him. "There's a lot I need to tell you, explain. I don't want you going into this blindly." His gaze drops to my lips, but I make a point of turning my head away and clipping my seatbelt in, my gut aching when I hear him cough softly at my dismissal. I don't want to come off as bratty, but I have so much to lose. "Did you do much today?"

"I met my family for lunch."

Cain sits back, and our eyes briefly meet. "Did you have a nice time?"

"It was okay. I don't really see eye to eye with my brother, so it was a little awkward." I pull at my ponytail and stare out of the window. Deeks is just getting out of his car, and he lifts his hand in a wave. I smile but duck my head. I'm not sure he approves of Cain, even if he did agree to keep an eye on me.

During the drive, Cain chats to me about New York, and we fall into an easy conversation about how much we have travelled, or in my case, haven't. "It's a great city," he remarks as we pull into the underground garage.

"I bet. Do you have offices elsewhere?" It feels peculiar to be talking about work like this. We made a point not to when we spent the weekend together.

"A few. Italy, Paris."

"How do you manage it all?" I laugh, following him to the bank of elevators.

"I don't. I manage people." The doors close us in, and he takes my hand and pulls me forward as I bump gently into his chest.

"Cain."

"I needed New York to think, not because I was unsure about you. I wasn't sure if you could handle being with me. I told you about my father." His mouth flattens as pain flits across his face.

"We don't need to do this now," I murmur.

"I really want to kiss you." He smiles and cups my face. "I'm a prick. I act before I think. I'm quick-tempered because I'm used to getting my own way, but it's more than that. I'm... there are things going on tha—" The doors whoosh open, and it catches me off guard, distracting me. Cain walks me backwards and slants his mouth over mine, groaning appreciatively. He doesn't demand I kiss him back, and his lips sit firmly over mine, but I don't pull away, nor do I reciprocate. I'm not punishing him. I'm just trying to be reasonable about this—level-headed. Slowly, he steps back and smiles hopefully at me. "I know I'm asking for a lot."

"You've not asked me anything," I point out, and for once, he looks perplexed. His head shakes slightly, and his lips quip into a smirk.

"Let's go and eat." He makes a play for my hand, and I let him, enjoying the feel of how his larger one envelops my own. My skin absorbs its heat—this one touch and his kiss back in the elevator have me feeling weak already. His penthouse is quiet, and the faint scent of garlic lingers. "My housekeeper has just left," he says when I peer into the kitchen as we head down the wide hall leading into the sitting area.

"I didn't know you had a housekeeper." I never met anyone the weekend I stayed.

"Carly works Monday to Friday, but she stayed late to assist with dinner." He unhooks my bag and pulls out a bar stool for me, then leaves me to pour us both a drink.

I decide, rather than waiting for him to address the situation, I'm going to ask the questions I want answers to. "Cain, why did you ignore me?" There's no malice in my voice, only genuine confusion. If he had gone back to being short-handed and rude, I'd have found it easier. I expected nothing less. It was how he always was with me.

My drink is placed down in front of me. He removes his suit jacket, draping it over the back of the seat, and he rolls his shirtsleeve up, revealing a toned arm smattered in hair. "I'm an idiot," he admits, moving to lift the other sleeve. Only then does he lift his head to look at me. "I knew looking at you would only make me regret leaving. Plus, I would have kissed you." His smirk is slight.

"I don't thi—"

"I would have kissed you," he declares boldly.

I swallow and turn away, lifting my glass and taking a small sip.

His hand reaches up to part the collar of my shirt, where a small blemish sits proudly on my collarbone. "Because I knew I'd see evidence of me on you, and it drives me insane."

I keep the glass between us as a barrier.

"Because you're the only woman to give herself to me like you did, and I can't walk away from what you have to offer."

"And what am I offering?" My head tilts, and his eyes twinkle sexily.

"Just you." He gives me an ironic laugh, as though something has just occurred to him. "And that's the biggest compliment I could receive. You give everything, and you expect nothing but this." He tugs me towards the edge of the seat and rubs my knee softly. "This is all I need. You and the peace you bring with that gorgeous smile. "

My lips tempt to quirk, but I hold it back. "So what does that mean for me? I still work for you, Cain?"

"I know. We just need to be careful and see where this leads." It's early days. I'm not expecting a declaration of love, but I do deserve respect and the security of knowing my life won't alter because his feelings do.

"And if it doesn't lead anywhere?" I scoff. "Will you ignore me again or push me to resign?"

Cain holds my gaze, and the firm set of his brows and the shine of sincerity in his eyes keep me hooked. "No, Lauren. If you want to get a contract drawn up, I will, but I'd like to think we are mature enough to deal with this our own way."

My eyebrow lifts in the air. He was anything but mature the other day.

"I think we've already agreed I was a prick," he huffs playfully.

"A massive cacti," I whisper, trying to avoid his eyes.

He leans in, infiltrating my space, forcing me to acknowledge him. "The biggest." His fingers pinch my chin, and he brushes his lips over mine. Soft, gentle, and everything I need him to be to make me relent and give in. "Are you ready for dinner?"

Nodding, I slip down, help him prepare the rest of the meal, and set some places at the bar when we decide to eat there. Cain serves garlic butter chicken and pours us another drink as I slide the vegetables towards him to plate up. I'm still hesitant, but Amberley was right when she said I wouldn't be going home. Now I'm here, with him, I don't want to leave. "You said some things are going on?" I cut into the food, and he nods.

"It's a shit show. It's going to get ugly, and I didn't want to pull you into my life when I'm expecting it to get nasty."

"Does it have something to do with how upset Kat was? I heard her mention something to Perry the other night." I don't like to pry, but with Henrik already controlling one part of my life, I don't want to set myself up for failure in another. I need to know what I'm about to walk into.

"Yes, her father was a business partner with mine. The business was already established when Royce came on board. Over several years, he syphoned hundreds of thousands of pounds from my father." His cutlery sits untouched on either side of his plate. "He lied, cheated, and pulled the company from under my father's nose, leaving him broke, and then he moved in on my mother."

"Was he prosecuted?" I gape, seeing how utterly enraged he is by this.

"No." Cain huffs out a disgusted laugh. "He moved into my family home, took over my father's life as though it had always been that way, and my father took his life. I was a teenager."

I sit back, completely appalled and heartbroken for this man. This certainly wasn't in the article Amberley showed me. This is so unexpected compared to the explanation I had assumed he would spout to win me back over. "I'm so sorry."

"I've spent years gathering information, educating myself, and doing everything to work against him and take it all back." Hard eyes move back to mine. "I plan to ruin him, Lauren. I won't stop until he is as penniless as my father was. I can't stop." I swallow at the vehemence in his tone. I desperately search Cain's eyes for something more than the burn of hatred for his stepfather. I was too trusting with Martin's family. Cain is on another level. Allowing this man access to my life and agreeing to a relationship is one of the most terrifying things I've done. Henrik is still a threat to my family. Cain is a threat to my heart. "This is the side of me I expect you not to like. It's the only side I know," he confesses bleakly. This is the side he said his father would hate.

"It's not," I say quietly. I know it's not. I need to believe that for my own sanity. The Cain I've come to know is as brutally passionate as he is proudly ruthless. Those are two things I can't afford to take on, but I can't bring myself to say no to him.

"Apparently, I have another side," he muses, turning to me. "A side I have reserved for one other person." He winks, and a slow blush creeps up my neck and helps my heart pump faster.

Self-preservation has me changing the subject. "Are you close to getting it all back?"

"The closest I've ever been. The reason I'm telling you this is because I trust you. At least I hope I can?" He levels me with a heavy stare. "Lauren, I want you in my corner."

It's a tense few seconds where I mentally roll off every reason why I should cut and run, and only one reason has me wanting to say yes.

It's staring at me with bright blue eyes.

"You can trust me," I pledge.

"It will get ugly. If you're with me, I need to know you can deal wit—"

"Cain, you can trust me," I affirm.

"I told myself to cut ties with you until this is all over." He prods some chicken and chews it thoughtfully. "I'm all about the weekend heists."

"I'm assuming you're telling me this because you truly

want this to go somewhere and not because we have some serious chemistry," I say, blunt but soft.

"I want this to go somewhere, Lauren," he confirms.

I close the space and press my mouth to his. I cut off the fear, the anxiety of being caught, and the uncertainty that being with him brings. Him trusting me with this information alone is hugely flattering. A bond passed between us during the weekend we spent together—it was unspoken and too precious to ignore. Thick arms wind around my back, lifting me to straddle his legs. His rich, woody aftershave snakes around us, and I breathe it in.

This isn't a mistake.

Whatever this is, it's real. It's delicate, but it's real.

"Royce is a complication I don't want for you," Cain rasps woodenly. His lips rub along my hair. "I need you to expect the worst. He's predictable, but I'm pushing him into a corner, and he will get nasty. I don't want him making a beeline for you." Cain tilts his head and pecks my mouth. My mind is catapulted to another man who made a beeline for me. Henrik. I have no doubts that Martin is aware of his father's blackmail. The fact that Cain is concerned about the outcome and not assisting in it has the knot of unease in my stomach unravelling. I almost blurt out the truth behind my move to London, but I swallow the words back down, hiding the truth because that's my fight to win. Although, withholding leaves a bitter taste in my mouth. Cain is laying his cards on the table, and I have mine neatly tucked away. Now wrapped in a bow of guilt.

"We just need to be careful," I remind him and myself. If our involvement gets out, not only will it jeopardise my job, but it is a complication I know Cain can't afford to deal with right now.

"Am I forgiven for my prickish ways?" he hums between kisses.

"I will deny all knowledge of what I am about to say, but,"

—he grins against my mouth—"I somewhat like your prickish ways."

"I fucking knew it," he declares proudly. "Every prick needs a prick tamer." His eyes glitter, and I bite my lip.

"They do. Although I refuse to work a probationary period," I stipulate my terms.

"Agreed. Anything else?"

"Staff meetings are to be conducted in the buff." I peek up at him.

His smile is almost jumping off his face. "Naturally." He nips at my jawline and groans deeply when I wriggle to get closer. "Daily reports are of the oral variety," he counteracts.

"Seems fair." I dip my head, giving him full access to my neck.

"And I want that ass." Large hands grip my bottom and squeeze.

I squeak with uncertainty.

"I'm having it," he confirms, sucking my bottom lip into his mouth. So much for trying to set boundaries and play it safe. Amberley knew I would give in. I should be ashamed, but I feel compelled to be around Cain. He is far nicer than the reports and articles detail him to be.

The man I have here is one I get to myself.

His fingers give another determined squeeze of my bum. "Negotiations can start tomorrow."

I pout.

"I'm a ruthless prick—business with me could get physical," he warns playfully.

"I don't doubt it." I run my fingers into his hair. "Take me to bed."

"Do I need taming?" Full lips quirk up at one side. I can't help it as I lean in and kiss him, moaning happily.

"You wish." I hum against his mouth. "You look knackered. You need sleep."

"Shower with me first?"

CHAPTER 25

Cain

D anvers is detailing each offence and how we can build a case against Royce. We have a meeting first thing Monday at Ivory Corp, and as soon as we hand the evidence over to the police, Royce is going to be wishing he never left St. Lucia. He was safer there. I know he returned home yesterday, and that he had an emergency meeting with his own lawyer.

His life is unravelling, and my poor mother has no new ship to jump to. The only person she can turn to is me, and I have purposely chosen to ignore each call or message she has sent me in the last few hours.

"Perry did well to get the original. Royce is finished. Cain, I did want to note that it's likely that your mother is aware of the forgery, and if not, I believe he will throw her under the bus to save his own neck."

"I suspected as much, too. She's been trying to reach me all morning."

"Guilty conscience, perhaps?"

"Not my problem." Danvers doesn't react to my blatant dismissal. Olivia stopped being my mother a long time ago.

"I'll see you Monday. Enjoy your weekend, Cain."

Dropping my head into my hands, I sigh heavily. Ruining Royce seemed much more fun when Lauren wasn't on the scene. Each time I picture bringing him to his knees, he has my girl in his grubby hands. Fear claws at my throat. If he so much as looks in her direction, I will implode.

"Everything okay?" Her soft voice pulls my head up. She's wearing one of my t-shirts, and the sight alone has my stomach twisted in knots. I need to contact Kelvin Deeks. I need Lauren safe and protected.

I lean back and smile confidently at her. "Sure is. Come here." I beckon her with my finger, and she pads to me quietly, her fingers tugging at the hem. "Sleep well?" I know she did. We both fell into bed, and she dozed off into a deep sleep, her arm slung over my stomach.

"Your bed is coma-worthy." Her smile is sleepy. She kicks her leg over mine and lowers to straddle me. Her weight sinks through the tension and chases it away. "Morning," she hums, taking in my features.

"Hey, pretty girl."

"What's on the agenda for today?" Those eyes fall to mine, and I suck in a low breath. I'm falling hard and fast for this woman.

"Whatever you want. I've invited the gang round for dinner later." Perry was adamant that he see Lauren. I figured it was best to remove any awkwardness and extend the invite to Matteo too. I know that Lauren will want Amberley here, and Kat has yet to respond, but with everything happening, I doubt she will leave her parents for the night.

"A night in with the lads! Is this a baptism by fire type of thing?" She chews her lip, a cheeky sparkle in her eyes.

"Oh, absolutely, although if it helps, Amberley is coming."

That gets her attention, and her face lights up. "Thank you." Her cheek dimples. "Kat?"

"Hopefully."

Her hands slip to hook behind my head. "She's struggling with all this."

Nodding, I stand, lifting her with me. "I'm wrecking everything she thought she knew. Her life was a perfect little bubble, and I stabbed a big fat pin in it."

"There you go, swinging that big prick around again," Lauren chides, and I laugh deeply.

"It's a danger." I widen my eyes playfully.

Her fingers trace the stitching on my top as she flicks her fringe aside and surprises me by saying, "What can I do to help? With Kat, I mean?"

"Just be you. She likes you, and she doesn't have many friends. Olivia treats her like an accessory."

"Who's Olivia?"

"Our mother." Her lips twist sympathetically. I don't want her pity. Carefully, I secure her face in my hands and lean in to kiss her softly. "Fancy a swim—we can go down to the indoor pool?"

"I'm not sure the residents of this nice building will appreciate seeing me in the buff. I didn't bring any swimwear. I don't even have fresh clothes," she imparts.

"I can have something sent up, bikini or swimsuit?"

"Just like that?"

I grin, but it slowly slips away when I see her resistance, so I kiss her again. "I want to go swimming with you."

Her mouth parts, the words lost on her, but her eyes say it all. This is new territory for her, and my life is one giant glitter ball. Once you get on, it's hard to get off. She's terrified to step on.

"Lauren—" my prompt pulls her big eyes back to me.

"Swimsuit," she utters shyly. I help her to her feet and

walk us through to the kitchen. "I put the coffee on. Hope you don't mind." Her voice is nervous—her gaze fleeting.

"I want you to feel at home here." I want to feel at home with her here. For all my intentions to keep her safe and away from me, now that I've given in to the possibility of us exploring this more permanently, I can't envision it any other way. I want her. Not just here, but also at Carson Court. If it was any other woman, I would be second-guessing my feelings and rejecting them, but she has a serene quality about her that my chaotic life has been missing. My family home will over-whelm her, so I don't mention it.

Taking back ownership of Carson Court finally seems possible, and stepping inside the other week only cemented my need to secure it for myself. Royce never changed a thing—he really did try to mould himself as the new Nicholas Carson. He was a piss-poor substitute.

Lauren makes our coffee, and I lay out a tray with pastries and some fruit. "What if someone recognises you?"

"We can use the pool on the roof if you'd prefer—swimwear optional." I grin.

"It's freezing!"

Laughing, I take a seat, and she takes the one beside me, sliding a cup in my direction. "It's not that cold."

"Maybe not for you." She shudders, and a thought occurs to me. I have access to plenty of pools. They don't have to be here in London.

"Let's skip swimming. I'll hit the gym, and we can slob out before everyone gets here later." I break a croissant and pop some in my mouth. "I've got some emails I need to attend to, but I'm all yours after that, okay?"

I've been in contact with Matteo since our bust-up over Lauren, but this is the first time we will all be together. He arrives with Perry and Amberley in tow, and any awkwardness I expect is shot to pieces when Lauren gives Perry and him a hug before linking arms with Amberley and walking off.

"You look like you're about to go to war," Matt muses, walking to clap me on the back. "I'm already regretting making a move because her friend is refusing to even look my way," he grumbles, and I chuckle, watching the girls disappear. I hadn't pegged the leggy blonde as his type, but his despondent frown is fixed down the hall on her.

"That's karma for touching what was mine." I smirk, leaving him behind as I search out Lauren. She is perched on one of the stools, pouring out a glass of wine. I stand behind her, and Perry passes me a drink. "Anyone heard from Kat?"

Muted headshakes stare back at me, but Amberley surprises me by saying, "I think she is trying to slip away." She pulls her phone out, and I frown down at the screen. Amberley types out a quick response.

We're all here. Can't wait to catch up :) x

"Thanks," I reply gruffly, sipping my drink. Lauren squeezes my hand, and we move to the dining table. I barely use the thing—any time the guys are round, it's either reheated meals from Carly or takeout. I helped Lauren prep all afternoon, and she has even set out some appetisers.

"You owe me forty quid." Perry holds out his hand to Matt.

"Are we not having takeaway?" Matt looks at the decorated table as my girl chuckles. "We always have takeout." He throws me a reproachful look.

I hold my hands up. "Hey, I was down for takeaway. Blame the boss—she was having none of it."

They exchange money, and Lauren plucks it out of my friend's hand. "You hardly won fairly. I told you I was cooking." Her pointed look at Perry has his ears turning red.

"You damn cheat!" Matt laughs, taking the notes from Lauren, who's holding them out to him. Amberley takes a seat next to Perry, and we all find our places, music softly playing in the background. It doesn't pass me by that this will be the only sense of normality I will experience with this woman, not only because of Royce but because she is too dedicated to her role at the hotel, and it inflates my desire to whisk her away to somewhere outside of London. Hooking my hand over the back of her chair, I lean in and nip her ear. "Thank you for doing this."

Her lips find mine and brush my mouth in a quick kiss. "It's nice. It feels good, all of us being here. I hope Kat manages to get away."

It's times like now, when I feel happy, that the pain rushes to the surface—my father will never get to enjoy this with me: meet my friends, Lauren, or witness my success. My mouth turns down, and I run my thumb over my lip, disabled by an acute sense of sadness. Perry frowns at me, and I shake my head, grateful Lauren is busy chatting to her friend and oblivious.

My unease extends to Kat, too. I'm battling with the guilt of putting her through this pain. I know I can't stop it— ruining Royce has become an addiction. I don't wish to lose her. Choosing me over her parents isn't an easy task.

An hour passes, and I'm about to ask Amberley if she has heard from Kat when the main door clicks and my gut swims with hope. My sister appears, and I stand, walking quickly to her. Small arms wrap around my waist, and I hold her to my chest, kissing her temple. "I'm glad you came."

"It's never going to be the same, is it?" Pain laces her tone, her voice a broken rasp. The worst of it is yet to come. Her father will go to prison, her mother will become the wife of a criminal, and Kat will feel as alone as I did all those years ago. She needs to know I'm here for her. That I'm not the bad guy in all this. Losing to a man like Royce has always unsettled me, but watching my sister become like them terrifies me.

"No, but I couldn't let him get away with it, Kat." My voice is thick with emotion, and her arms tighten.

"I know. It hurts, but I get it, Cain. I'm sorry for everything he has done. He's losing his mind with rage."

"He's got away with it for too long. I'm sorry you're hurting. I don't want this to ruin our relationship. It will be tough, but I'm here."

Her stiff nod relaxes the tension in my shoulders. I dry her tears away and offer her an apologetic smile. "We haven't started yet."

"I'm in dire need of wine." Her croaky voice wavers when more tears swell in her eyes, but she blinks them away.

"Luckily for you, Amberley is here," I muse, hooking my arm around her neck and walking us back to the group sitting around the table. Amberley is already on her fourth glass and talking animatedly. My sister finds a place next to Perry, who pulls Kat into a tight hug, and she grumbles that he smells like garlic. We laugh, and the sad tension she brought with her disperses.

Amberley offers to help Lauren serve, and I refresh the glasses. "Are you on call?" I ask Matteo when I notice he isn't drinking much.

"No, but I'm driving, anyway." He cradles his glass and leans back to watch the girls chuntering away in the kitchen.

"How are your parents?" I ask. I know he is due to travel to visit them soon.

"Insufferable." He smirks. He'd do anything to lessen their involvement. I, on the other hand, would give anything to have my father back.

"It will be good to see them. It's been years since you returned home."

"It won't be an enjoyable visit. They'll have women lined up out the door and will be trying to pull me back into the fold."

"Take a woman with you." I nod towards Amberley, and he frowns.

"I think the attraction is one-sided," he muses, watching as Amberley sings into a serving spoon and flicks sauce on her cheek. A slow smile tugs at his mouth, and then he is frowning again and rotating to face the table.

I lift a napkin and throw it at him. "Don't cry, mate. She'll come around." I snigger.

Glaring at me, he stands and folds the napkin. "Shut up, Cain."

I laugh deeply, and Kat twists to see what has humoured me, but Matt is already skulking off. "You love-sick fool!" I call after him, bending the napkin into a heart to mock him further.

"What's that all about?" My sister smirks, pushing up to see what I'm doing.

"Can't say. It's bro code."

"What about sister code?"

"That's different, and you know it is." I give her a doting wink and head into the kitchen to bring the plates through.

"Where's Matteo?" Lauren frowns when she returns to find his chair empty.

"Probably giving himself a pep talk in the bathroom." I snort evasively.

Matt stalks back in and levels me with a hard stare when he cops a look at my handy work with the napkin. "You're a prick, Carson."

My eyes slant to my girl, and she bites her lip as she lowers into her chair. I grip her chin, tilting her face to mine. "A massive cacti," I affirm throatily. "This looks amazing." There is an ease around the group, a quick and playful banter between us. Conversation flows, and Lauren is laughing by my side. It feels good. Matteo grins at something Amberley says, and then she is up out of her chair, demonstrating something to the group. We've barely tucked into the homemade paella when, as I ask Perry to pass the wine, there is a knock at the door. Frowning, I stand and check my intercom is working because Walter didn't announce a guest. "Back in a sec." I scroll my phone, but no announcement is listed. Perplexed, I pull the door open and scowl as Olivia, my mother, storms in, her heavy perfume stagnant and too sweet. Years of memories bombard me, and I blink furiously as the rage burns through my skull.

"Where is she?" My mother's narrow face is set in a tight pinch. Her blonde hair is secured in a severe knot, and the designer dress she has on is a crisp white. To many, she is the picture of innocence, the grieving widow who fell in love with her dead husband's business partner. But there is nothing pure about this woman.

I cut her up, refusing her further entry. "You don't get to walk in here. You don't get to just show up." I bare my teeth, too angry to control my dislike. "There is no one here who has any interest in talking to you, Olivia."

She sniffs haughtily. "Does referring to me by name somehow make this easier for you, Cain? I'm your mother!"

"You're anything but," I growl as Kat and Perry appear.

"Katherine, get your belongings. We're leaving," she snaps, vehemently pinning Kat to the floor with her signature scowl, reserved for those she is severely disappointed in, the kind of look that makes you squirm with anxiety. It works. My sister looks like she just swallowed an insect.

"Kat, stay." I keep my tone low and reassuring, but my eyes are stabbing straight through my mother. "You know I will look after you."

"Like you do me?" Olivia harps, dragging her eyes down

me in disdain. "Katherine, we're leaving now. Don't you dare turn your back on your father." I cough out a sardonic laugh. She was happy enough to leave me high and dry.

"I... I." Kat searches all our faces, indecisive about what her next move should be. Slowly, she edges forward to comfort Olivia. "Mother, please, this is all happening too fast," she whispers, visibly shaken. Her pained expression pales further when our mother gasps dramatically, bypasses me, and slaps Kat hard. The yelp that ricochets between us sets my blood boiling.

"GET OUT!" I roar, pushing a hand to halt my mother from causing any more damage. Perry holds my sister as she sobs uncontrollably, his face pulled into an angry scowl.

"Katherine, I didn't... I'm sorry." Olivia trembles, trying to reach for her daughter.

"That's assault," I lean down to hiss in her face, pointing out the camera angled down the hall. "Unprovoked. You fucking disgust me. What dad ever saw in you is beyond me. I won't let you hurt her like you did m—" I swallow the rancid confession. "—Him," I finish, refusing to give her an insight into my mind. Her eyes gleam, as hateful and as cold as mine. When they move to Kat, they soften with regret, and the truth I never wanted to admit stares back at me. My mother never once looked at me like that. She adores Kat, but I look too much like my dad. I'm too bull-headed—too much of a reminder and living proof of her mistakes.

"Kat, come on," I hear my girl's soft voice, the sweet encouragement to help my sister, even though she is putting herself in harm's way. I keep my eyes firmly on Olivia's. The slightest interaction between Lauren and me will be fed back to Royce.

Amberley appears and hooks an arm around my sister's back, ushering her away as Perry storms to the door and pulls it wide. "GET OUT!" he booms. I've never seen him so worked up. When she doesn't move but stares after her daughter, he powers toward her and takes hold of her elbow. "You just lost her. You don't deserve them—you never fucking did." The moment her heels cross the threshold, he slams the door in her face and stands, shaken, his shoulders heaving with unbridled fury.

I'm in shock, unable to move. I've not come face to face with my mother for over two years, and seeing her has provoked something deep inside, twisting up old feelings and causing my hatred to gurgle like boiling lava. Soft hands slide around my stomach, and my abs flex involuntarily as the distinct weight of Lauren's body presses into my back. I'm glad she isn't facing me because I can't look at her right now. "Kat needs you, Cain," she speaks softly. I thread my fingers with hers as my friend turns with bewilderment plastered over his face.

"We need that footage," he says, rushing past me, pulling his phone from his back pocket, no doubt calling down to Walter to have the footage sent up.

"I want to know who let her up," I snap. Whoever it was, was about to lose their job.

"Do you need a minute?" Lauren murmurs.

"No," I grip her hand and turn to walk us back to the others. Matt is already icing Kat's face, and when I walk to her, she sniffles and begins to cry loudly. I take over, holding the cold compress and tucking her into my side. "You did nothing wrong."

"She's never hit me before." She shudders, and I hug her tight and refrain from telling her that I wasn't surprised, not after having been on the tail end of my mother's palm.

"It's the only damn time it will happen."

CHAPTER 26

Lauren

I lie in bed with the balcony door partially open. I don't want to be alone with my thoughts, so the flutter of the curtains and low groan of traffic below helps focus my mind. Cain said he needed to blow off some steam, so I left him in the gym and had a shower after Kat excused herself to one of his spare rooms and the others left. He's barely met my eye, and I know it's because he is hurting. I'm hurting for him and for Kat. Things may be strained with my brother, James, but the love I have from my parents is unconditional, supportive, and nothing as destitute as what Cain has experienced. Witnessing this first-hand has only cemented my feelings for this man. He's viewed as a successful entrepreneur with the Midas touch. Handsome and respected. Tonight I got to witness just what pushed this man to be who he is—why he is so ruthless and aloof.

Rain begins to patter against the windows. Twisting, I

stare outside, lulled by the rush of water falling from the sky, and fall asleep.

Hands bigger than my own graze my skin and run up my stomach, and a soft kiss lands on my shoulder. "Cain?"

"Shush, go back to sleep." Tension pours from his body. His muscles are tight, and his voice is strained.

Gripping his hand, I pull it to my mouth, kissing the soft skin on his palm. The moonlight filters inside, and I see how raw his knuckles are. I kiss it again, and his lips find my shoulder for a second time. He shifts, and I feel the hard ridge of his arousal pressing hotly against my thighs. "Cain." I sigh, pressing back. His damp hair sticks to my skin when he rolls his forehead over my back.

"She's a real gem, huh?" He means his mother. He shifts behind me and hauls me against his chest even tighter.

"Kiss me," I whisper, arching into his palm as it drifts to my breast. "Just be with me, here, now." I offer him the only thing he doesn't have. Unconditional love.

"I fucking hate her," he admits thickly.

"It's okay." I twist, but he holds me still, his hand running to trace my throat. He tilts my head and leans to capture my mouth in a bruising kiss. I sense the pain behind it, the anger and injustice, as he sweeps his tongue inside and holds me so tightly that I might crack. So tightly that no one can take me away. I cup his jaw and give myself to him. Twisting in his arms, I hold my mouth just out of reach. "Cain, don't ever let this end," I plead, hooking my leg over his as he lines up. I take him all the way, and he fills me, stretching me wide with a deep ache. His mouth slams to mine as he grips my arse, grinding himself into me. We move slowly, kissing and licking. His fingers drag down my back, marking and possessive, and I shudder as my orgasm swirls and blooms, pulsing between us. "Cain, I…" I swallow my words. My almost confession is a raw burn on the tip of my tongue. His eyes hold mine, ripped of emotion. Vulnerable and wide. Does he know? Can he feel it too? I say it without speaking, but in the way that I take him inside and the slow but heavy kisses. My lip bows with emotions, and he grips my jaw.

"I don't want it to end either." They are not the words I so desperately want to hear, but they are close, so close that I can feel them curling into my heart. I splinter, my legs spasming and my body pulsing. Cain grunts my name, his cock flexing and swelling as he comes. Slumberous eyes lift to mine, and his mouth chases upwards to claim my own. I sag into him, and he flops back, holding me tight to his chest.

I'm in love with this man. I love his passion and beauty. I love seeing the cracks in his hard exterior and how he has let me slip between them, honouring me with the softer energy he keeps for his loved ones.

I protest when he lifts me to pull out, his tired chuckle making me smile. I grin into his neck and kiss and nip at his jawline. Cain rolls, tucking me into his chest. It expands in a big contented sigh, and I pull his arm, holding it to my chest. "Sleep, pretty girl."

I swallow any uncertainty, hoping that this is growing into something much more than the little secret we promised to keep after hours.

Something knocks me awake. The covers rip from below me, forcing my eyes wide as the low and unmistakable moan of pain permits the air. I sit up rapidly, demanding my eyes focus to see through the sheet of darkness around me. Another moan. I turn towards Cain, groaning in his sleep. Gently, I reach out, finding that he is drenched in sweat. *"Don't!"* his plea is cocooned in so much desperation, such anguish, that I know it's not my touch he is begging to end. I cup my mouth when he jerks in sleep, chokes out a gargled pain, and then snaps upright, gasping for air.

"Cain?"

"*No.*" He heaves breathlessly.

"It's Lauren. You were hav——"

"Fuck." He drags his hand down his face and sucks in lungfuls of air. Sadly, I watch as he grapples with his mind. I'm no therapist, but I can only assume seeing his mother has pulled some nasty memories to the surface. He turns into me, pushing me into the mattress and angling his mouth over mine in a hot and aggressive kiss. He doesn't want to talk—he doesn't need to relive it another time. He wants to forget, and I let him. I coax his sweat-slick body between my legs, and he curses with relief as he replaces those memories with a new one.

———

I'm cleaning the dining room when Kat appears the following morning. Her cheek is still smarting, but I don't let her see how much her mother's actions have perturbed me. "Hey, do you want a coffee? I'm nearly done."

"I can do it." She wrings her hands, seemingly embarrassed.

"Okay, give me a sec, and I'll join you."

"You don't need to do that, you know. Cain will moan that you're cleaning up." Her eyes widen at the mess.

"He'd better thank me," I scoff, carrying the last of the plates through to the kitchen to load the dishwasher. "Anyway, I made the mess." I smile. The aftermath of Cain's nightmare is still hanging heavily around my heart, and I have a new sense of protectiveness for him. He's been fighting his battles for as long as I've been breathing, but I want to be the one he seeks solace in—with his words and body.

"Sorry we ruined your dinner," Kat's voice tapers off, and she stares down into her empty cup.

"There's nothing to be sorry about. I know yesterday was

a bad day, but let's do something nice today." I keep my tone light and click the machine on. "I mean, if you want to?"

"I don't know. I'm still processing," she murmurs, the coffee machine drowning her out.

I round the counter and push my cup towards her. "When I say nice, I mean copious amounts of ice cream, trash TV, and cheap wine." She smiles, but it slips at the mention of wine. "Or really good wine. I'm not too picky," I confess.

I manage to pull a small laugh out of her. "Okay." She flicks a sad look my way. "Thanks, Lauren."

I give her a quick squeeze and leave my cup with her as I find some things for breakfast. Hardly anyone ate last night because the meal had gone cold by the time we returned to the table. "Does Cain like pancakes?" I wonder aloud, pulling some things out of the fridge. "I feel cheeky rummaging through his fridge." I blush, putting it all on the side.

"I'm sure he does. He won't mind. It's you." She shrugs as though that fact should be obvious.

"I don't want it to seem like I'm taking over—things are still very new." I shouldn't be talking about this with her, mainly because she isn't in a good place, and she has far more serious things to concern herself with than my new relationship.

"Cain doesn't date, and not because he is a commitment-phobe. He loves hard, without reserve, and he will pour everything he has into you. He gives his all and then some. He's just so used to having it all taken from him." Her voice catches, but she stumbles on. "I'm learning that now—things about him I didn't understand now make sense. Did you see how my mother looked at him?" She shakes her head, clearly distraught. "But you, you're different. Sure, he's had a few flings, but my brother doesn't make decisions lightly, and if I know him as well as I think I do, you are the best thing to happen to him. I like seeing him happy." Kat breathes out a ragged breath. After a few moments, she holds out my cup, and I take it wordlessly, my lips rolling together as I try not to blurt my feelings to her.

"He was worried you wouldn't come. He was so relieved to see you," I offer back, trading secrets about him. "He's scared of losing you, Kat."

"He won't."

"I know. I wish my brother and I had your relationship. James and I can barely be in the same room." I roll my eyes and follow her to the sofa. "You think Perry is a pain in the ass? Well, James is the steroid version, but meaner," I scoff, and Kat's face slides into a frown, her fingers rubbing over her lips. "It's nice to see the love you share. I wish I had that." After Olivia ripped through the penthouse, I strongly contemplated coming clean about Henrik. I wanted to divulge it all to Cain last night, but things are moving in the right direction, and I don't want to back peddle and get stuck in the past. My life is here, in London. Henrik isn't a threat to me. Not now that I have started over. He can't hurt me or my family.

He has no reason to.

"Talk of the devil." Kat kicks up her chin, and I roll my neck as Cain walks down the stairs in his swim shorts.

"Morning." He winks, heading straight for me, gripping my face from behind, and planting a rough kiss on my mouth. It's as though he has expelled the nightmare from his mind— that and his mother's appearance. He scuffs his sister's hair. "I'm going for a swim, coming?" He looks at us both expectantly. Kat's nose scrunches up, and I shake my head aggressively. His eyes are pulled to the ingredients on the side. "Are we having pancakes?" I search his eyes for any sign of tension, but he is back to being closed off.

"Maybe."

"Maybe is good." He leaves us both, and I watch him until he disappears and exits through the side door. An icy chill sweeps inside, and Kat and I protest. I'm glad his mood has improved since last night—seeing his mother really ate away at him.

"You're in love with my brother." I jerk to look at Kat, watching me intently. The corner of her lips quirk up in a slight, knowing smile. I flounder, my mouth working wordlessly. She giggles, and I groan and throw a pillow at her. "My lips are sealed." She mimics locking a key at the edge of her mouth.

I want to dismiss her claim, but instead, I get up with the excuse of needing more coffee and head to the kitchen, her soft laughter chasing me away. I busy myself by making pancakes and pouring several glasses of fresh orange when Cain appears, dripping with water. Ducking my head, I keep my focus on chopping strawberries and bananas. "Tonight, we'll get takeaway," he promises.

"Okay." I hadn't said as much, but I planned on going home later. I need to do some washing and clean my flat.

Kat joins me, and we start piling up our plates and begin eating without him. He returns moments later, joggers on and a towel slung around his shoulders. His hair is saturated, and he smells of chlorine. "I need to catch up on some work bits. Will you both be good until I'm done?" He stacks his own plate high and stabs a strawberry from my plate, stuffing it in his mouth and smirking widely.

"We're going to hang out," Kat announces, and swirls her pancake in syrup. I've already cleaned my plate and am finishing my coffee. I know they didn't get a chance to talk much last night without everyone else present, so I make my excuses and give them the time they need.

"I'm going to get a shower, if that's okay?"

"You don't need to ask." Cain frowns at me, and after I put my plate in the dishwasher, I leave them alone, but I can feel his eyes glued to my back.

Amberley brought some clean clothes for me yesterday, so

I lay them out and then step into the en suite and get in the shower.

Yesterday was unpleasant, with too many emotions to sift through. I meant what I said to Kat. Seeing her and Cain's relationship gives me a small notion of hope for James and me.

"Lauren?" I turn under the spray to find Cain walking towards me. "You okay?"

My smile is wide and intimate. "Yes, I just wanted to give you some time with Kat." I brush my hair out of my face and tilt my head under the stream of water, watching him. His eyes grow heavy and trail down my torso.

"I've got all day to talk to Kat. I want to talk to you." Gratitude simmers in his deep blue gaze, and my heart curls with happiness.

"Those eyes don't look like you have talking on your mind," I drawl. "And neither does that." I point at his tented swim shorts.

"I don't have to *speak* to tell you the things you need to hear."

CHAPTER 27

Cain

I enter Ivory Corp with Danvers and Justine at eight sharp. The open high foyer and deep rich wood are an upgrade from when my father owned this building, but I can still see signs of Carson Limited, and it makes my chest swell with pride. My father built this company, fostered it from the ground up, and Royce would never be in the position he is now if it hadn't been for Nicholas Carson. He was a rising star in the investment world, and he had a sixth sense for the big game, but it failed him with Royce. Now I was here to take it back. We even dropped by the police station with stacks of evidence to make a lawsuit against Mr Ivory. After today, his name will be dirt, his reputation and credibility a forgotten entity, and then there will be just me. The only man with the name Ivory that holds any merit.

I eat up the marble floor with the confidence of the owner —the place is as good as mine—and I have complete faith and assurance that Ivory Corp will return to its rightful owner. I acknowledge the receptionist with a polite nod as I continue on my way to the elevators. Danvers presses the button, and we rise to the top floor. I know that Royce called an emergency board meeting. Unbeknownst to him, he is missing one member.

"The first thing I'm going to do when the company is back in your name is watch the security footage of you walking in and him being escorted out." My lips twitch at Justine's excitement.

"If the police act swiftly, we may be lucky enough to see him escorted out in the only way he deserves," Danvers pipes up. I'm paralysed by adrenaline. Every thought I've had up until this point is spinning like a tornado through my mind, ripping up all wounds and breaking down others. I don't trust myself to speak, not until I see him.

When the elevator doors open, Austin Keeland is waiting nervously. He's my inside man and has been feeding me what little information he can. "Lead the way," Danvers says to the other man when he clocks my grim smile.

I've anticipated this moment for years. Lay awake through my teens, concocting all kinds of retribution against my stepfather, and it's all come down to this one moment. Tucking my hand in one pocket, I stride past the glass meeting room as several faces snap up in disbelief and some with fear. Royce double-takes and stands slowly, placing his hands on the long smooth wood. He's aged considerably, and I like to think I'm a contributing factor. "Don't stand on my account," I drawl as I enter and take the seat at the head of the table directly opposite him. His jaw grits, and I swallow a smug smile.

"What the fuck do you think you're doing here?"

Danvers and Justine fold into their seats beside me. "I'm a board member, kindly appointed by your dear associates here." My eyes cast around the table of executives who I have been schmoozing for months. The many that have recognised when a ship is sinking and know to join ranks elsewhere. My loyalty to them is limited, but they need not know that yet. "Also, a majority stockholder. I earned this seat. *Legally.*" I dip my chin and glare at him. "So, Royce. How have you been?"

"This is some kind of sick joke, right?" he fumes, lifting his phone and demanding security come to remove me.

"A sick joke would be a man syphoning hundreds of thousands of pounds from his business partner, bedding his wife, and forging his will to accumulate his assets." Leaning forward, I cup my hands on the table and lift the corner of my mouth in a sinister smile. "The punchline would be me spending years compiling evidence and taking it all fucking back." Royce's face washes of any colour, and several of his employees snap to glare at him. Did he really think I was only coming for the house in St. Lucia? It had been Danvers' idea to target the property abroad whilst they were away.

"Is this true?" the woman nearest to him snaps.

Austin plugs in my USB and hands me the remote as I thumb through a small margin of the evidence. "My god," a thin-faced man close to him breathes, standing in horror. "You've ruined us all."

"This is all a misunderstanding," Royce splutters as page after page swipes by before him. "He's making it up."

A video of an old man confessing to forging the will pops up, and Royce tries to run for the door. I want to lunge at him and smash his face into the glass, but several officers appear and halt him.

"I may have tipped off an old buddy." Danvers smirks and swivels to watch as the police move in on my stepfather.

"Royce Ivory, you are arrested on suspicion of identity theft, money laundering, and fraud."

I stand, buttoning my jacket as my stepfather is carted away, shouting for someone to call his lawyer. Elation erupts in my chest, but I squash it. The fight is not over yet. I will win at the drop of a hat. Danvers is the best at what he does, and I've played a legitimate game. I have everything to gain and nothing to lose, but I intend on dragging him through the courts until he is left with only the clothes on his back.

Turning, I hold out my hand, indicating for those who are now standing to sit before I address the room. "Shall we?"

—

It's been four days since news of Royce's arrest broke. Four days of paparazzi stationed outside the hotel and my penthouse. One thing I did not anticipate was the lack of opportunity to see my girl. Never did I think I would resort to facetiming a woman just to see her, but I have called Lauren up each night. I'm whipped, and oddly, I like it. Last night only formed another roadblock, with it being The Luxury Hotel Awards. Lauren had already sent a message saying goodnight by the time I had returned home, so I'm even more perturbed that I haven't spoken to her.

The constant pressure to build a case, to manipulate the field, and to find an angle to bring everything my father built to fruition has come to a cease-fire. And with no Lauren, I'm at a loss for what to do with myself. She never mentioned my nightmare and never once viewed me with pity. The nightmares are back, tormenting my mind and infecting what small amount of quiet I could find in my sleep.

Olivia refused a therapist when I started to wake, screaming. She didn't want anyone to know the truth that lay behind the doors of Carson Court. To the outside, our life was as elegant and perfect as the gates that kept our family mansion secure from the public. As soon as I was old enough to seek support myself, I found therapy in the only thing I knew could help me: revenge. It irks me that I'm close to my goal, and my mind is reverting to old ways.

When I arrived at the hotel this morning, Lauren wasn't at the front desk, but I know she is working today. I scan the cameras and frown, unsure where she is. Picking up my phone, I tap out a message.

Morning, pretty girl x

It takes a further few minutes to locate her. She is down at the health and wellbeing centre, assisting the staff with something on the computer. As soon as she can excuse herself, she steps away and looks at her phone.

How was the awards show? Win anything? x

I lean back and kick my feet up, typing as I watch her huddled against the wall, smiling down at her phone.

It was the same as always. Tiring. Two awards.

Her eyes do a quick sweep of the corridor. Then she is typing furiously, her mouth curved up in a knowing smile.

Want to know a secret?

For the most part, I don't like secrets, but I like the smile on her face, so I send a question mark, grinning like a fool too.

I'm not wearing any panties.

. . .

I swing up out of my chair and glare at the screen. I've not been inside her for days. I don't like this secret. My gut flexes, and I watch as she peers down the corridor, her hands eager to respond when I reply.

You're not being funny

As if she anticipates my response, hers comes through almost immediately.

I'm not joking.

I missed you last night. Don't taunt me.

I'm scowling down at my phone when Justine knocks and walks in, and I hold my hand up, stopping her from talking. She takes a seat on the sofa and checks her iPad as I wait for my girl to respond.

I'm bare and so wet.

Groaning, I drop my feet and twist the screen of my computer away from my PA. Lauren crosses her ankles, and I know she is telling the truth. Fuck. I need to see her.

. . .

You're playing with fire, Lauren.

Her head tips back, and I can practically hear her husky laugh.

Burns unit, here we come!

She even goes as far as to send a fire emoji, the little minx. I laugh shortly. This woman has got me by the balls. I'm infatuated with her.

"Justine, cancel any meetings for the next hour," I instruct, my voice tight.

"But we're meeting wi—"

"Rearrange. Leave me, please." I don't look up, but I know she is staring at me, confused. I've never dismissed her like this. "Justine," I warn.

"Of course."

Get up here now!

After twenty minutes, I grow impatient and check the cameras again, only to find Lauren working behind the main desk as though she hasn't given me the most painful erection of my life. Adjusting my cock, I pick up the phone and dial the front desk. She answers, welcoming me with a sweet greeting.

"I swear to god, if you do not get that little ass up here, I will bend you over that desk in front of all my guests." Sweat beads my upper lip as I picture just that.

Her light gasp goes straight to my dick. "I'm afraid we have no available dates for the presidential suite that weekend. The following weekend might be more viable?" Her tone is weak and raspy. Not for me, you little prick tease!

"I'm going to give you the most presidential fuck of your life. So much so that you'll beg me to stop."

"Of course, sir, we have other rooms available."

I make a low and frustrated sound in the back of my throat. "GET. UPSTAIRS. NOW."

I watch as she presses her lips together to stop herself laughing, and I almost snap my phone in two.

"*Lauren*, don't. I'm aching for you."

She scans the people around her, ensuring no one is paying attention. "I know," her voice dips, and the same pained huff I hear in mine laces hers, too. She's struggling with the distance, despite the close proximity. It's torture, being so close and not being able to touch. It's worse now that I know everything there is to know about her body.

"Make your excuses and get up here."

"I can't." Her eyes flick to the main camera. "We agreed," she says softly and puts the phone down.

Fuck!

I swipe up my jacket and pull it on, buttoning to disguise the added pressure against my trousers. I don't recall the journey down, and my face is set in a hard scowl when I storm out of the elevator and stride towards the main desk. Lauren is tapping away, and Felicity, her line manager, is double-checking over some paperwork. "Miss Lindel, we've had a complaint. Come with me." Lauren gapes at me, horrified. I angle my head and fix her with my most intimidating stare.

You're in big trouble, pretty girl.

"Oh, I can't see why." She swallows nervously.

"That's not for you to decide. My office now." I don't even glance at her manager but turn and stalk back to the elevators. Lauren's heels click steadily behind me. We enter the lift, and a couple enters with us. My girl twitches beside me, her hands smoothing down her skirt and her lips parting in anticipation.

We exit on my floor, and I lengthen my strides, forcing her to hurry up and follow me inside. Her face lifts, her eyes wide, and no sooner is she in the safety of my office, I slam the door and pounce, planting my mouth to hers and hoisting up her skirt. She's bare and freshly shaved, and my balls burn with the need to fuck her. "I'm not happy about this," I growl angrily. Why the fuck isn't she wearing any underwear?

"I'm behind on my laundry," she pants as I devour her mouth. I bolt the door and lift her, walking us to my desk. "You've only got yourself to blame," she squeaks.

"Nice try," I scoff, not fooled by her cute face and false excuse. I perch her on the edge and balance her heels on the wood. "You smell real fucking good, Lauren." I'm already unzipping my trousers and pulling my cock out. Lauren whimpers needily. I roll the head of my cock over her clit, and her head drops back. "Have you touched yourself since we've been apart?"

"Yes." Her thighs tense as I tap my cock when she desperately wants it.

"Did you come, pretty girl?"

"Yes."

I part her like a flower, my dick gliding down the seam of her glistening cunt. "Do you know what I love about your pussy?"

Lauren's head drops forward, and she deadpans me.

"That it's attached to me?" Her brow lifts, and I can't help but laugh.

"That too," I assure, and drop a quick kiss on her mouth. "Look how tiny you are," I groan, running my cock back and forth. My dick is a dark, angry fucking red, swollen, and desperate to be inside her.

Lauren peers down between us, her moan huffing out softly as she watches me play with her.

"I can feel the resistance, sense how small you are." I apply a little pressure, pushing the head of my cock against her hole, and it fights back. "But you always take it all. You eat it up like it's your last meal." I groan and then drive upwards, seating myself deep inside.

Lauren's head snaps back—her face a picture of pleasured shock. "Cain." She grips my tie, and I thrust, enjoying the feel and sound of her wet pussy.

The door jangles, and we snap apart.

"Shit," Lauren squeaks.

"It's locked." I drop my forehead to hers and line myself up, sliding back in. "Shush," I warn, easing in and out at a ridiculously slow pace.

"Cain, the police are here," Justine announces, knocking on the door.

Groaning, I ram myself to the hilt and hold myself deep for a second, enjoying the feel of my girl wrapped so snuggly around me. I issue Lauren with an apologetic smile, slowly easing out and standing, helping to sort her skirt out before zipping my trousers. I walk to the door, but Lauren grabs my hand and shakes her head. "Cain?" she pleads.

"It's fine. I was planning to tell her, anyway."

With a grimace, Lauren stands off to the side, shifting awkwardly as I unlock the door and let my PA in. "What's going on?" She strides straight in. "You never lock the do—" Her eyes meet Lauren's and widen. "Shit," she blurts.

"Justine, this is Lauren, my girlfriend." Holding out my

hand to Lauren, I wait for her to take it and pull her to me. "This is Justine, my PA."

"Hello," Lauren whispers, then clears her throat. "It's nice to meet you." She holds out her hand, but Justine looks at it like she might pick up an incurable disease. Laughing awkwardly, Lauren drops it, and I kiss her shoulder.

"How long?" Justine asks.

"A little while."

Nodding, she comes to terms with what she has walked in on. No doubt going over the series of events of the past few weeks. "Well, Lauren, it's nice to officially meet you."

"Likewise. I'll speak to you later." Lauren attempts to dash away, but I snag her back and kiss her softly. "Stop it." She blushes.

My grin is lopsided. "Do your laundry," I admonish.

I wait for Lauren to leave until I turn to face Justine. "Until today, I never crossed the line," I mutter when I find her glowering at me.

"We have enough to deal with. I can't be fending off more drama if this comes out. Keep that in your pants." She points to my trousers with her pen.

"Yes, Ma'am."

She makes a sound in the back of her throat. "And don't call me that. You make me feel old. The police are in meeting room three."

"Have you called Danvers?"

"He's on the way."

CHAPTER 28

Lauren

It's been several days since Cain called me up to his office, and our contact has been short and sweet. What with Royce and Kat, he is snowed under, and any contact is strictly kept to facetime and the odd text. I miss him, despite seeing him every day. I crave his presence, but mostly, I hate that I can't be there for him when everything is so chaotic around us. I worry if he is sleeping, although his nightmare seems to have bothered me more than him.

The hotel has hit an all-new record since his step-father's arrest. Everyone wants to stay at The Carson-Ivory. We've been vetting guests due to the influx of bookings, and I've noticed more than one socialite has been loitering in the foyer, dolled up to the nines. I've never been insecure or overly untrustworthy, and I vowed not to let Martin's or Kristy's betrayal alter that, but seeing the preened women vying for a certain man's attention has me making an extra effort in the mornings. I had left his office with an ache in my chest after he referred to me as his girlfriend.

I watch as one woman with a willowy figure and long silky blonde hair keeps checking the elevator every time it opens. She's beautiful, classically so, with delicate features and golden skin. I can imagine Cain with someone like her. They would look phenomenal together, a real powerhouse.

My phone pings, disrupting my thoughts. Slipping it out of my pocket, I find a text from Cain.

What's got you frowning so hard, pretty girl?

Smirking, I stare at the central camera and roll my eyes.

Haven't you got any work to do?

Yes, I'm a very busy and important man. In fact, after your little stunt the other day, I've been working tirelessly on a new deal. I've decided I'm holding your underwear hostage…all of it. X

Scoffing loudly, I tap a quick reply whilst Beryl is busy arranging a taxi for a guest.

You expect me to work without any underwear on?

Yes, in fact, I could do with some paperwork. Be a good girl and bring it up to me.

. . .

I scan the reception to ensure no one is watching and send a quick reply.

We agreed to be careful.

After being caught by his PA, there is no way I am going back upstairs. Felicity has already tried to grill me about this supposed complaint. I fobbed her off with a lie about not checking someone in quick enough. I'm placing my phone away when another text comes through.

I'm not in the mood for careful. I want to bury myself so deep you ache for days. Knickers off. Paperwork. Now!

"Lauren, phone away, please, unless you wish to obtain another complaint," Felicity says from behind me. Jumping, I stash my phone away and apologise. I side-step around her, but her hand reaches out to stop me, and my brows shoot up. "Just because the boss played nice when you had your accident doesn't give you the right to take advantage of his goodwill. Return your mobile to your locker, and do what you're paid to do," she snaps icily.

I crook my neck, staring at her head-on. "Thank you, Felicity. Having met Mr Carson-Ivory on several occasions, I can assure you I'm not that stupid. Excuse me." I expect her to call me back, to put me in my place, but she lets me walk away. My phone rings, and I slip it free to find Cain calling me.

"What the fuck was that about?"

"What do you mean?" I give a half-shrug, knowing he can see me.

"Does she always treat you like that?" Cain growls down the phone.

"You're in a bad mood." I pout.

"I wonder why," he huffs. "I want to see you."

I keep my voice low and walk down the hall towards the staff room. It's quiet there, and I can talk to Cain without fear of being overheard. "Give me a second." I pop my head around the door. It's empty, so I perch on one of the comfy chairs. "Hopefully, by the weekend, things will have died down a bit."

"Is Felicity always like that?" Cain reiterates, expecting an answer.

"She's harmless."

"That's not what I asked."

"I can handle a woman on a power trip," I mutter. "I need to get back. We'll arrange to see each other this weekend."

"You look really fucking pretty in those heels."

"Does security know you have a new obsession with the cameras?" Laughing, I ring off and pocket my phone, returning to the front desk. I don't hear from Cain for the rest of the day, and Felicity gives me a wide berth, too. With it being busy, I don't check my phone, but I'm glad that I returned to my locker because there is an envelope waiting for me—the thick black scrawl and tiny cactus tells me it's from Cain. I'm tempted to open it, but several employees enter the staff room, so I collect up my things and meet Oliver and Amberley out the back.

"You're joining us then. We thought you'd already gone?" Amberley smirks. They managed to coax me to join them for a drink. She's asked me daily about what's been going on with Cain, but until he releases a statement, I've kept quiet. I only know the little he has told me, but it's nothing like what the papers are detailing. I wonder if it was as fabricated when his father committed suicide. It's not something I want to remind him of, so I haven't pushed the issue.

"No chance. I need it after today," I tell them about Felicity, and Oliver grumbles about how much of a bitch she is.

"We're going to have to double security if we get many more guests," he continues, moaning as we enter the bar. It's a small place with ample lighting and dark wood, giving it a moody atmosphere. It's perfect for Oliver and his grim disposition.

"I know. God, my feet are killing me." We get seated at the bar and order a round.

"Have you thought about complaining?" he asks, checking his phone.

"No, she is more annoying than anything." I sip my wine and sigh. "I've never known the hotel so packed."

"Business is booming for our boss. I bet he is raking it in. Did you read the papers? That bloke stole all that money and his father's company. No wonder his dad killed himself." Amberley's head snaps to mine, and I give my head a little shake. I'm not discussing it now. I'm surprised she isn't up to date on the information the press is releasing.

"I don't want to speculate. If it's true, this will only dredge up the past, and I can't imagine that's nice." I clear my throat and avoid her gaze.

"If he accumulates Ivory Corp, he is going to be one rich bastard. It's not like he needs it. He's already loaded. It's a bit greedy, isn't it?" Oliver harrumphs, cracking pistachio nuts and nibbling them as he contemplates Cain's motives.

I want to come to Cain's defence and demand he apologise, but instead, I frown into my own glass, feeling out of sorts and missing my man. Uncomfortable around Oliver, I decide to leave. Jumping down from my seat, I flick my fringe out of the way, saying, "I've got a bit of a headache. I'll see you both tomorrow."

"I'll come with you." Amberley hops off her stool and gives Oliver a quick hug. "See you tomorrow,"

"Night."

My friend hooks her arm with mine and gives me a sympathetic smile. "It's all a bit shit, isn't it?" We cross out into the cool evening air.

"Everyone has an opinion, but I doubt they know the half of it."

"How is he?"

Shrugging, I hold my hand out, seeing a taxi heading our way. "I've not seen him since it happened. It's not any of my business. He'll talk to me if he wants."

"You can talk to me, Lauren. I won't abuse your trust."

I falter, shocked at her soft admission. Of course, I trust her. "I know. I'm just a bit wary of what I say when he and I shouldn't even be dating. His life is a crazy mess at the moment, and I don't want to add to it." We share a tense but short silence before she holds her own hand out to make sure the taxi sees us.

"Did you get your envelope?" Amberley's animated smile drives any tension away.

"How do you know about that?" I step back to face her as the vehicle pulls up.

"Who do you think put it in your locker?"

"I did. Thank you. I'll open it when I get home." I give her a quick squeeze.

"Text me!" she demands.

"I will."

—

My apartment is a sanctuary I can't offer to Cain. Sitting here in the peace and quiet leaves a lingering sense of hopelessness. Waiting on the sidelines as this unravels around us feels close to emotional torture. I'm yet to hear from him, but I figure that's because he is waiting for me to open the envelope and call him. I wanted to rip it open when I walked through the door, but instead, I forced myself to have a shower and get something to eat. Now I'm sitting cross-legged on my bed, the weighted item in between my fingers as I wonder what's inside. The thick paper tears loudly, and inside is a brightly coloured package. I slip it free and turn it over, looking at the image of crystal waters, palm trees, and idyllic beach huts. I flip the card, and my eyes fill with unshed tears. It's for a luxury stay at the award-winning private villa and pool resort on Koh Samui. My stomach swoops, butterflies rupture in my chest, and I blink furiously to stop myself from crying.

I trace a thumb over the pretty lettering of Cain's surname. It's his resort.

I can't believe he has done this. I'm not sure what to say or how to thank him. I dial his number, and it connects instantly. "Number one prick," he murmurs, amused.

I can't accept this. "Cain," I groan out his name, flummoxed by his generosity.

"Don't *Cain* me. We're going." Direct, unmoving, and full of confidence. I find myself smiling, despite most of me repelling the kindness of this gift.

I make a noise of protest. "It's too much. You didn't need to do this." My eyes are glued to the picturesque tropical escape.

"You wouldn't come swimming with me. It's not too cold in Thailand." My shocked laugh huffs out of me.

"Cain, you can't book a holiday because I said I was cold!"

"I can." I hear him clattering about at the other end, then the whoosh of wind down the line as he walks to wherever it is he is going. "The hotel will manage."

"I've not been at the hotel long enough to accrue holiday for a week," I tell him. "Plus, I was off with a concussion. I probably owe hours," I grumble awkwardly.

"I'm not taking no as an answer. Pack a bag. Get your passport and come and hide across the ocean with me."

"I don't know." I'm anxious, terrified to get caught, scared

to let myself be dragged away on this crazy, beautiful ride with
him. It's not for another three weeks, but nothing is easy about
any of this.

"You do have a passport, don't you?"

Laughing, I drop the card. "Yes."

"Then it's sorted." I can hear the smile in his voice and
match it with my own. "I can't wait to get you to myself, pretty
girl. I've missed you."

"We see each other every day," I muse.

"From a distance—it doesn't count." His sigh is heavy. I
can sense the strain this investigation is having on him. "I need
this time to regroup, and I want you with me."

I drop back on my bed and slam my eyes shut, forcing the
reservations aside and opening myself up to this world and the
reality of living in it with Cain.

"Okay."

"Good. Open the door. I'm on my way up." I spring up
from the bed and rush down the hall, leaning to peer out of
the peephole as a hooded figure walks towards me.

"Cain?" I double-check he's still on the line.

"It's me. Open up."

Yanking the door open wide, I laugh in surprise when I
take in his dark attire: baggy joggers and a hooded jumper. He
looks so far removed from the suited man I love to watch that
I begin to giggle. "How did you get here?"

"Deeks."

Swooping down and swinging me over his shoulder, he
kicks my door shut and propels us towards my bedroom, flop-
ping me down and grinning wickedly. He reaches back to pull
his jumper off in one sexy movement, throwing it away care-
lessly and advancing on me.

"That was hot." I grin as he crawls over me and slants his
mouth across mine in a greedy, deep moan.

CHAPTER 29

Cain

I'm floating in the pool when Lauren steps out of the villa —a pale pink bikini on and her endless legs on show. She's carrying a book and a large sun hat. She drops her things on a lounger, walks to sit on the side of the pool, and dips her feet in, toes swishing below the surface as she picks at the platter. "This is something else." Resting back on her forearms, she tilts her face to the afternoon sun, her lips teasing a smile.

Large leafy trees cast dappling shade over one end of the decking, but the infinity pool is bathed in sun. I swim over, hooking my elbows on the edge and leaning to kiss her thigh. "Beats a boardroom," I comment.

"I bet." Her smile is wide, lips stained from the berries. "Did you really just buy a place in Aspen? I always wanted to go there," she muses, reaching for another strawberry and biting into it. Her comment reveals some of the idiocy in the article she's read.

"No." I bite at her skin.

"Oh."

"I already have one." I grin, and she laughs throatily. "We should go."

Her laughter tapers off, and she eyes me before she licks the juice from her finger. "That's not why I'm with you. This is all really beautiful, and I'm so grateful you asked me to come, but I can't just drop everything." Her lips twist wryly. She was reluctant to come away with me, scared to get caught, and worried about how she would be perceived if our relationship came out into the open. "People are already suspicious of me suddenly going on holiday. I agreed to this for you."

"Just me?"

"And my own selfish reason."

I slide the tray out of the way and lean in at my full height, running my hands up her thighs and wetting them. "How selfish?"

"Sinful."

"As sinful as when I saw you on your knees in the lobby, and I wanted to tan your arse in front of all my guests," I confess.

Her eyes widen at that little revelation. "Thereabouts." Breathless, she stares at my lips.

"Something on your mind, pretty girl?"

"You know there is, Cain." She smirks as she leans closer, her eyes full of quiet heat, the kind that begs for attention. It sways in her gaze, anticipating my next move. Waiting. Wanting. She's such a good girl.

I keep her waiting, moving to close the gap at an agonising pace. Her breath catches, and my mouth pulls, satisfied. I'm torturing myself. Torturing us both towards something no amount of money could ever buy me. I have the entire week to keep us on the precipice.

"Cain," she rasps.

"Yes?" My eyes follow the line my thumb draws over her lower lip and the way she swallows her moan.

"Kiss me."

My lips quirk into a smile. A light breeze picks up and lifts her hair to trail over my arm. I twist to spiral it around and use it to pull her close. She gasps, and I inhale it like the only available air. Her kiss is soft—mine is not. I sweep my tongue in her mouth. There isn't an inch on this body that I've left untouched—there is no available skin for another man to try and claim as his own. I want my kisses to weld to her bones so that it's always my touch she feels. My name she aches to cry. My mark that carries her through the rest of her life because at this moment, I want to own her so completely. The truth of those feelings is an aching grip along my spine. I have no intention of letting this woman ever go. This island may be her safe place—away from London, away from prying eyes. But she is mine.

My wet torso drips water over her thighs, the beads trickling down and back into the pool. Cupping her breasts, I squeeze them hard, earning a pained hiss, but she moans sweetly when my thumbs brush her peaked nipples. Her hands come up to my face as she kisses me roughly. "Someone might see."

They might. It's mid-afternoon, and although the staff are in the adjacent hut, hidden behind the privacy screens, they are still in hearing distance. The thought makes me desperate to taste her. Lauren gasps as the cool water crests over the edge and washes between her legs. I knock her knees apart, pressing my way in, and I push her backwards. The water has made a mockery of her swimwear, and it has moulded to her pussy like a second skin. "These are a mess." I pluck the material and let it connect with her skin in a quiet splat.

"Useless," she whispers.

"Completely pointless."

"A waste of time." Her stomach hollows, and I thread my

fingers and tease at pulling them away, my mouth biting into the flesh of her creamy thighs. Lauren chokes out a plea, arching. Waiting but never taking—always waiting for me to give.

"They're in my fucking way."

"I don't need them," she garbles. My mouth moves upwards, and her legs flatten on the poolside.

"No, you don't," I muse. Her hands inch towards her breasts but stop, seeking instruction. I lick and nip, and I drag the bottoms away, throwing them over my shoulder. The water laps, the air kisses her pale skin, and her bare cunt glistens.

"You're so wet for me."

"Cain, please."

"How selfish are you feeling, Lauren?"

"The worst," she writhes.

"Take what you want." I dip into the water, my chin sliding under so I'm eye-level with her open legs. Gritting my teeth, I withhold from pouncing to tongue fuck her. "Touch yourself."

Go on, pretty girl. Let me see you like this.

Dainty fingers trace over her navel and farther still until they slide over her slick hole, and she moans, low and throaty. I grip her thighs, holding her legs apart, my fingers biting into her skin, marking her, and holding her down. "Until you come," I growl.

She dips her finger and drags it up to circle her clit. It's the sexiest fucking thing I've ever seen, and I don't care who tells me differently, but I will never cease to be amazed at how this woman gives herself so completely to me. She pleasures herself without restraint, massaging her clit and dipping her finger into her pussy, then two.

"You're weeping, pretty girl." I bite her thigh, and her answering moan tells me she's close. Her fingers disappear into her pink hole, and I groan at the wetness glistening on her hand. When she pinches her clit, her thighs tighten, her arse raises off the side, and my name on her lips has me surging forward in the water as her pussy pulses and throbs its release. "Fuck, Lauren." I drag her to my mouth and fuck her deeply, her creamy orgasm soaking into my tongue and sliding down my throat. "More, bite me," she begs, her nails sinking into my scalp. "Cain!" she chokes and sobs. I lick and suck until the last remnant of her orgasm eases away, and she is boneless, panting, and all fucking mine for the taking. I drag her to me, pulling her into the water. Her mouth crashes against mine, feverish and tasting like strawberries.

I kick my swim trunks away, wrapping her legs around my waist. Her breasts are heavy against my chest, her hands gliding to take handfuls of my hair. She tugs, and I bite her lip harder until she whines. My cock jolts, my balls feel heavy, and I thrust. Her head lolls back, her moan a sweet hiss of pain.

"Fuck, so tight." Massaging her ass, I allow her enough time to accommodate my size, and my cock twitches painfully, weeping deep inside. Her breasts are thrust high, tempting me to bite them. I suck a pink nipple into my mouth and graze my teeth over the sensitive pearl. I work it between my teeth until she cries out and grips my head to stall me. I let it go, but only so I can sink my teeth into the flesh beside it. I bite and suck, and eventually, she relaxes in my arms, and I fuck into her.

Her mouth opens, and her eyes glitter back into my own. "I feel so full," she whispers as I begin to thrust high, deep, and hard. Her hips rock and clash against my own. Her hand runs to pull my mouth open. "Harder, fuck me harder," she cries, her tongue delving to meet mine.

The water sloshes, her moans urge me on, and every thrust into her salves the ache in my body that I never seem to be able to calm. Pressing my forehead to hers, I rut upward as her mouth drops, and her pussy flutters and clamps down, sucking me in, and holding me deep. I pant as my own release erupts, and I push into her farther. She sobs into my neck, and

I hold her tightly. "I know." I wrap my arms around her back and drag my mouth to kiss her. "I lose myself, too."

Her breath stutters out—her face is tucked away as she comes back down from her high. "When you speak like that, I forget I didn't like you." She smiles sleepily.

"You never disliked me," I grin, pecking her swollen mouth. "You wanted me when you knew you shouldn't."

"Pale skin and all?" Her brow quips, and I throw my head back, laughing. She grunts as my cock flexes inside.

"Haven't you learnt anything in the short time we've indulged in one another?" I drop to kiss her shoulder, and it is pale, as pure as snow and petal-soft. I've made sure she is wearing plenty of sunscreen and is covering up. "It's one of the things that drew me to you," I admit and nip the skin, sucking the droplets of water away. I lift her arm, holding her wrist to show her the light blemish of my touch, the scrape of my beard imprinted into her skin.

"All the better to leave my mark." I kiss the blemish and enjoy how her head dips as she smiles, a smile she wanted to keep for herself, a smile I know will grace her face in the quiet of her mind when we are apart and she is thinking of me. I don't allow her that luxury. I pull her face up to mine. "You're fucking beautiful, Lauren." My chest rumbles with appreciation. Her hair is curling at the tips, and her skin is flushed. She's stunning. "I'm glad you came away with me."

Her face splits into a smile. "I love it here, and to think I was going to say no,"

"No chance," I drawl. "Ready to get out?"

She laughs lightly and nods against my shoulder. I ease free and wade through the water, taking the steps to get out. "Can we shower? I want to wash my hair." She sits back, relaxing in my hold as I carry her through the villa, my wet feet leaving a string of prints. Pulling a strand, she sniffs it, wrinkling her nose. "I need to rinse out the chlorine." I take her straight to the shower, lowering her and flicking it on. The heat pelts my skin, and I pull her back, dropping my head on her shoulder, securing my arms around her waist as she works around me, her small face twisted to the spray.

Her hands work through her hair, causing bubbles to foam and sluice between us. Gathering them, I take over and drive my own hands into her hair, massaging until she groans happily and melts into me. "I'm so tired." She yawns, laughing.

I soap her body and my own before stepping us forwards to wash it off. "Fancy a nap?"

Twisting, she runs her hands up my chest. "Just sleep though because I really am knackered," she blurts, red-faced.

I throw my head back, laughing loudly.

"It's jet lag," she says defensively when I laugh longer. I wrap her in a bath towel, pat her dry and do the same with me as she sorts her hair. "What have you done to my body?" She pouts as I lay us down, tucking the thin sheet under her neck and yanking her leg firmly in place over my thighs.

Laughing, I thread our fingers and sigh. "Owned it."

She goes quiet and thoughtful, and I close my eyes, knowing that my feelings for this woman transcend simple attraction. They've eclipsed any possibility of ever coming back from being only her boss. I click the switch for the blinds, and they whir shut, pulling darkness in from every corner of the room. Locking us away from the world.

Lauren presses her face into my chest and exhales.

~

"Show us the pool." Lauren spins her phone around so that Amberley can see the view, and she coos dramatically. "Lucky bitch. So, other than getting your rocks off, what have you done?" Lauren flicks an amused smile my way.

"Not much." Her cheeks turn light pink.

"You'll get a water infection!" Amberley warns, and I grin as I read through my emails. We're four days in, and we've barely left the poolside.

"You're on loudspeaker," Lauren chastises.

"Good. If she comes home bow-legged, I'm not covering any more of her shifts!" Amberley declares playfully. Shaking my head, I check the main news outlets back home for any updates. Danvers has been keeping me updated, but sometimes, the odd bit of info slips through, and it can be detrimental to us.

"Not even if I give you unlimited access to the wellbeing centre?" I muse loudly, clicking and scrolling.

Silence sits between us all, and I look over my laptop at Lauren biting her lip. "Well… I guess I could cover another," Amberley garbles.

"As I thought." That one is predictable, and she is growing on me.

"Wait, you don't actually want to be bow-legged, do you, Lauren?" she suddenly blurts, and Laurens groans, laughing.

"No, and you don't need to cover for me. I'll text you tomorrow—we're going snorkelling soon."

"I'm getting ready for work, anyway. Love you!" The phone bleeps and Lauren walks to sit next to me. I woke up gasping again last night, and she has been quieter than normal this morning.

"Everything okay?"

"Just keeping tabs on the case."

"I know we've not spoken about it much. I'm not sure how I can help, but I'm here, even if you want to vent." She searches my eyes, but I don't allow her to see the tension pulsating behind my eyes.

"I have a lawyer for that."

Her gaze is cautious—her hands cupped in her lap. "I know, but every now and again, you get this absent look, and I wa—" she voices softly, but I cut her off.

"I'm fine, Lauren," I impart calmly. She nods, but her mouth pinches. I lean in and kiss her. "I'm fine. It's fine." I address what she won't. My nightmares. I refuse to give them any power, so I don't want her to. "They happen, and then they go. It's fine." Her mouth twists sadly.

"Do you think Royce will try to get revenge?"

"Oh, I'm banking on it." I smile grimly. "When we return to London, it will be difficult for us to spend time together. That's why I wanted this time with you." I don't want her worrying about the case. Cautious, yes. Worried, no.

"And you needed a break." Her brow lifts, forcing me to step away from the laptop. I close the lid and rub my jaw.

"I do." She's in shorts, a t-shirt, and cute sandals. I've arranged for a boat trip to one of the islands, where we can snorkel and have lunch. It's been years since I enjoyed the islands. The last time I came here was with the guys to celebrate Matt's birthday. The island has grown so much since then, with more hotels and new staff. We've developed the resort, adding newer amenities and increasing the luxury villas.

"Are you sure no one will go to the press about us?" Her smile falters, and I hook my arm around her neck, tugging her to me and dotting a quick kiss on her mouth.

"A good portion of this island works for me in some capacity, and the other gets work from all the tourists," I inform her, but her bottom lip pouts, uncertainty clouding her big eyes. "I'm their boss—they know not to cross me." She pulls in a quick breath, ready to remind me I'm her boss too. "You're different," I deliver flatly, and her eyes roll. I peck her mouth again. "They won't go to the press."

"The staff in the villa seem to love you."

"I hand-picked those for our stay. Look, Perry won't want me to tell you this, but a couple of years ago, there was a groundskeeper who broke into one of the suites. This was before I had this villa built. It was in the hotel. Perry wasn't alone, and it made headlines."

Her face contorts in concern. "What did you do?"

"Nothing nice,"—my lips twist ruefully—"but those that I didn't punish, I gave a pay rise. The islanders are good people, hard workers, and the guy who took the footage was shunned by the community. Those who didn't question his whereabouts were let go, and anyone that profited from it was sued. I ruined the man's reputation, and so they know that if they look after me, I will look after them." I shrug lightly.

"So the person Perry was with, were they okay?"

"Persons." I laugh as her face gapes.

"Like a gang bang?" Her cute face wrinkles in disapproval.

"Sounds like hard work. I struggle with just you." Her face stretches into amused shock.

My laughter topples her perplexed face into a wide grin. "I'm a lot to handle."

CHAPTER 30

Lauren

C ain and I bob in the water. We've been here all afternoon, enjoying the peace of the island and swimming. We ate lunch on the beach and, after sunbathing, decided to head back in the water to snorkel again. Clear water laps at our shoulders, soaking our hair and dazzling under the blistering sun. I've got a healthy but light glow to my skin, and Cain is tanned and gorgeous. I worry that people will notice and put two and two together, but Cain shrugs, saying they have no proof.

Bright flicks of colour move around us, and I poke my face below the water, watching the fish go about their day. "I could watch them all day," I say, breathlessly wiping water from my chin. Our snorkels grip tightly, obscuring our faces. I smile at Cain and dip back below, going completely under. Fish dart away and vanish between the coral, and then Cain is there beside me, another vibrant force swimming through the water. He twists and grips my ankle, tugging me. The pressure of the water has my bikini bottoms sliding down my hip, and Cain pulls on the tie before I kick away and breach the surface, cursing him. He appears before me and yanks his mask away. Indents line his face, and I laugh as I remove my own. "I nearly lost my bikini!" I shriek, kicking to stay afloat as I try to retie the small strands.

Grinning, he wades towards me, and kisses me, his fingers tracing my shoulder. "You're starting to burn." He lifts his chin towards the beach, and we swim back in.

This holiday has been the highlight of our relationship. Here, away from London, removed from the chaos, we get to be Cain and Lauren, no more and nothing less. The stress of the investigation is still hanging heavily over him, but I'm glad that between those tense moments, when his face is plagued by emotions and the truth of the ugly situation is eating at him, I can be a place of solace. We've dined together each night and lazed by the pool, and when he has taken an hour or so a day to keep abreast of the situation, he has planned for a masseuse or left me with my book, sunbathing. If I had only just met Cain and this was a holiday fling, I would be halfway in love with him. But I already was before we left the UK, and now I'm drowning in his attentiveness and addicted to losing myself in him. I've not admitted my feelings, but I'm sure he knows. Last night, we walked the beach and then made out like horny teenagers—we'd been animalistic and desperate for one another.

This thing between us was, at times, too much for me to comprehend and yet more than enough for me to know that he was, without a doubt, *it* for me. It was fierce yet delicate, raw and unfiltered. It was so utterly consuming that it caught me off guard, stealing my breath and sending a heated wave of happiness to spread through me like untamed ivy, twining around any available surface and claiming it as its own.

He takes my hand and leads me up the sand to where our blankets and towels are. We pat ourselves dry and sit down, guzzling iced water from the cooler. "Pass the cream." He screws the cap back on, and we swap bottles. He shifts me back and lathers my skin in cream as I gulp my water down, thirsty from swimming.

"I can't believe this is our last day." We fly out in the early hours, and I'm not ready to go home and return to normality. I like Koh Samui Cain. I like who I get to be with him here. We've done the tourist bit and visited landmarks. We hired a moped and whipped around the streets. It's been such a refreshing change from playing it safe and waiting for the world not to be looking so we could snatch some time. I'm going to miss being able to walk over and kiss him, to hold his hand and talk freely without the fear of people pulling out the pitchforks and writing about it in some tabloid.

"We'll come back. Every year. It can be our thing."

"I thought cactus was our thing?"

"I want more than one thing with you." The lid clips shut, and Cain drops back, and I twist as he rests his head on his hands.

"Such as?" I manoeuvre to lay over his chest, my fingers tracing the few beads of water left on his neck.

"Lots of things, big and small."

"Cactus big?" I grin.

"Bigger," he muses thoughtfully. My smile is wistful, and my emotions come racing back, racing around my chest and forcing words I have swallowed back time and time again to hide in the safety of my mouth. But I want to voice them.

Cain rolls us and gives me a lazy grin. The kind that only encourages those words to find a stage to speak from—that smile gives those words hope. I suck in a breath and stare up at him. His weight presses me into the sand. His fingers drag up my thigh and pull it aside to gain access between my legs.

"What's going on in that head? You look like you might cry and laugh at the same time." He chuckles. I open my mouth but suck in a breath, internally at war with my emotions. "It can't be that bad, can it?"

"I'm not saying this to hear it back. In fact, I don't want you to say it at all." I laugh nervously. "Because if you did, say it, I mean… I would think you didn't mean it, but were trying to make me feel better. Because if you already felt it, you'd have said it by now…or maybe not," I ramble, then groan as Cain's forehead creases in confusion. "Promise me that you won't say it back?"

"How can I when I don't know what you're going to say," he counters, trapping me in the sand like last night, and lifting my hand, he drops a kiss on my fingers.

"Pinky swear." I hold my little finger up, and he wraps his larger one around it. I search his gaze, and when he doesn't speak up, I shake our joined hands, forcing a verbal response, my heart pumping erratically in my chest.

"I, Cain Cactus Carson-Ivory, pinky swear not to say it back."

Rolling my eyes, I laugh at his choice of phrasing. My lips go dry, and so I lick them. With my heart in my throat and my hands shaking, I voice the one thing I never found hard to say to anyone else, and I realise that it's because this time, it really means something—not a sweet endearment or a parting goodbye to a close friend. Not the kind of love I felt for Martin when our friendship grew more intimate and I fancied myself in love. This has ensnared me, and I'm intoxicated by how completely real it is. "I'm in love with you, and I know that might change things. I hope it doesn't, but I needed to say it so you know where I stand," I blurt, panic and sincerity crisp in my words.

There is a moment of surprise in Cain's eyes, but it is quickly softened when he smiles lazily at me. His gaze runs over my face, and his lips quip at the side. A big hand cups my chin and he leans in. "It won't change things. Being with you makes me happy, and I've not had much of that for a long while."

"Okay. Good." My breath fans his face, and then he is kissing me. Slow and sweet, and it makes my soul cry. He didn't say it back, as I asked, but there are times like now, when he is kissing me like he is in physical pain, that I wonder if those feelings aren't reciprocated. Times like the morning I left his penthouse after he imprinted our time onto his sofa and the way in which he says things that could make the hardest of hearts break.

We don't mention it again, not when we head back on the small boat, and I excuse myself to take a shower, and he works on his laptop, or over dinner, when we chat about a show we have both seen. It seems normal and, like he says, unchanged. I feel lighter for confessing but heavy with the thought of returning to our normal lives. The tension that has quietly radiated off Cain since we arrived is still present, and I know returning to deal with Royce is something he is both eager for and apprehensive about. Kat has been in daily contact, and although she is playing it cool, Perry has mentioned several times that she isn't dealing with it well.

That's where Cain is now, out talking to Perry as I sit up in bed reading my book. The door is open, but I can't hear what is being said, only the deep comforting rumble of his voice and how that small action alone makes my heart swell. I try to concentrate on the words, but they don't register. I just keep reading over the same sentence.

Cain steps through the door and drops his phone on the chair before tugging his shirt off and ridding himself of his shorts. He's not wearing boxers, and his cock hangs heavy and proud between his thick thighs. I get the silly girlish notion of being smug that he is mine. "What's that smirk for?" He sounds tired, and when I look up, he has circles under his eyes.

He's not sleeping. Not since everything with Royce happened. It's like he is on tenterhooks waiting for it to all blow up in his face. He tugs the sheet up and gets in, plucking my book from my hand and dropping it on the bedside table.

"Hey! I was reading that." I pout.

"You've not turned the page in ages," he drawls, hooking his arm to pull me beneath him and pressing my arms above my head. "What's it about?" he asks, casually tugging at my silk shorts and pushing them down my legs. I kick them the rest of the way off.

"It's a romance," I answer breathlessly.

"Oh, is it better than this one?" His tone is low and intimate. He's speaking about us. He moves to hold the top of the camisole in both hands. My eyes plead for him not to do what I think he is about to, but he grins, and with a steady jerk, he rips it right down the middle. I gape. "So, is it better?" he asks, cupping my breast and then leaning to drag his tongue up under the curve and flicking it against my peaking nipple.

"No," I whimper.

"Because you love me?" he questions quietly. Cobalt blue eyes lift from where his chin is now resting on my sternum, blowing a stream of air along my skin.

"I do."

Nodding, he drops his face, and I feel his lips widen against my skin. My confession may have been a surprise to him, but it's a small bud waiting to grow between us. I want to stretch my roots and tether them to him. When we walked along the beach tonight, I caught Cain staring at me a few times. Sometimes, he would pull me in and kiss me, and then others, he would simply look away. I know he is digging through his own feelings—trying to reconcile his feelings about us and his relationships with his parents—the pain of losing one and hating another. Loving Cain is easy, but I know for him, whatever this is, this is all he can give right now, and I'm okay with that. When he looks up, he is moving to capture my mouth, and I feed off of the sense of belonging he brings me. It's slow and sensual, and he kisses me as though he has all the time in the world and not enough hours, both at once.

My fingers delve into his hair, and he knots his own in my damp strands. I arch, anticipating his movements to become more dominating, more frenzied, but instead, his hand kneads my bottom and his cock presses at my entrance. "I've heard plenty of people say those words to me over the years." The rough confession wisps across my mouth. I hold his gaze. "Today was the first time I believed them." He sinks in slowly, the thick, smooth ridge of his erection filling me until his hips are flush against mine. My lips part, my eyes glitter, and he slowly pulls out and swallows, his eyes discerning as they pour heatedly into mine. His body sinks back in. Soft, slow and caring. I choke out a sweet moan.

"I believe them because you're the only woman I want to hear say them." His hips swivel, drag back and then return to send a wave of heat gliding through me. I hum as his cock hits deeply, and his mouth moves towards mine. "I don't deserve them, but I promise to keep making you feel like you can say them," he professes solemnly.

I nod, my lips twisting with emotion as my eyes pool with tears. I blink, and hot salty tracks run into my hair. It's not a confession of love, but his quiet acceptance to respect my feelings and not take advantage somehow means more. He kisses my tears, whispers how beautiful I am, and then spends the night giving me more than enough reasons to keep telling him.

～

When we hit the tarmac and wait for the pilot to announce we can disembark, Cain's phone starts pinging with multiple notifications. We kept our phones off, deciding to enjoy the quiet for one last stretch before we went back to pretending we weren't secretly dating. I switch my own on, and a string of notifications and missed calls pop up. Amberley's name bounces across my screen, along with my parents. "What's going on?"

"Fuck!" Cain snaps, scrolling through his phone. He answers his phone the second it begins ringing. "I want names, Justine!" he demands and rubs at his forehead. "I don't care! How the fuck did this go to print?"

"Cain, what's going on?" He's furious, and my stomach plummets when my phone pings again. My attention goes to my mobile, and I unlock it.

"NO!" Cain roars, jumping out of his seat and ripping it from my hand. "Don't look." Panicked eyes meet mine, and I jump in shock.

"Why?"

"Fuck, because it will break your heart, and I can't fix it. I'm sorry." His jaw sits taut, angry. His chest heaves, and I clutch at my throat, anxiety sending white spots behind my vision as my imagination runs wild. Fix what?

I try to snatch my phone back, but he holds it out of reach. "Cain!"

"They know, Lauren. It's everywhere. There are images of us all over the internet." His flat tone hits like a train going full speed.

I sag back in my chair. "What? But you said… What images?" My mouth goes dry, bitter with the burn of acid.

"Ones that no one has a right to ever see." Cain drops in front of my seat. The look of pity tells me that every possible outcome I had thought up would have been far kinder because he means images of us together intimately. The plane moves, but when Cain grips me and holds me still, I realise it's me moving. I'm shaking uncontrollably. The air around me closes in, and I suck in to stop from passing out.

I shake my head. "My parents…" Dread leeches the

colour from me, and he reaches to cup my face, but I scramble back and out of the seat, pulling at my jumper, feeling too constricted in it.

"Lauren." Cain follows me down the small plane, and I come face to face with an embarrassed-looking stewardess. Arms wrap around my waist, and he holds me against his chest as I gulp for air. "Some water, please," he says as my vision blots and tears take over. "I'll handle it all. Everything. I'm sorry."

"Not your fault." I sniff. The stewardess steps out the small door, and as she does, I see through the gap an image staring back at me from a screen.

It's the night on the beach. Cain has me pinned down, and my eyes are wide with pleasure. My skin is bright under the glow of the moon. We're both without a scrap of clothing and drenched in sweat. Sweat and sand, we're covered in it, and it's the sand alone that is concealing any lack of modesty we have left. A sob works up my throat, careening to tear through the plane like a guillotine as I let it free.

His hold tightens, promising safety when I feel at my most vulnerable. "FUCK! Get that off!" Cain bellows. I'm crying loudly. Humiliated and sick to my stomach by what the world is seeing. By what someone stole from us. Cain scoops me up and pulls me onto his lap as I hide my face and bawl into his neck for the longest time.

Finally, when I'm all out of tears, he says, "I don't know how to make this better, but let me try. Come back to mine, and we'll meet with Danvers, my lawyer." He kisses my hair, and I nod, sniffing unattractively.

"My parents will have seen that. They will thi—"

"That you had your privacy violated. That photo should never have been taken. Never shared. That moment was for us and us alone." He holds me to his chest, and I nod tearfully.

I tilt my head up at Cain, and he cups my face as a bottle

of water is placed beside us. "You're going to fire me for real this time, aren't you?" I hiccup, and he laughs humourlessly.

"Afraid so." My phone buzzes between us. It's my mum again. I stare at Cain in panic, and he takes the phone and answers it. "Hello. Cain, speaking."

I can hear the rushed tones of my mother's voice, and I cringe in my seat. "Yes, I'm her boss. Amongst other things." He clears his throat, and I bite my lip as my mother chirps down the line. I'm a coward. I should have answered. "I know. My team is working on it. She's in shock. Upset. I apologise for not taking better care of your daughter." My mouth turns down at his need to take the blame. I hold my hand out, and Cain drops down, giving me the phone.

"Hello, Mum."

"Oh gosh, Lauren. Are you okay, sweetie?"

"No." I begin to cry again, and she coos down the phone, her light, reassuring tone settling some of my anxiety.

"There are some rotten people in this world," she tells me. Cain cups my neck and massages as I sniffle into the phone. "So, is it serious?" my mother asks, and I force my eyes away from naturally flicking to Cain for reassurance.

I chew my lip, and he twists my head his way, fixing me with a genuine stare. "It is," he answers for me, gruff, honest, and still angry. My lip wobbles, and he uncaps the water and holds it to me as his own rings.

"I need to take this," he mouths.

I nod and let him walk away as I cry down the phone to my mum and even harder when my dad comes on the line.

When I think that's the end of my humiliation and I finally say goodbye, a message from Martin pings through.

I always wondered how you managed to secure a job there. Now I know.

· · ·

I'm blinking furiously at the screen when Cain reappears, and sensing the change in my mood, he plucks my phone from me, ignoring my protest, and reading the message. "Who is Martin?"

Dropping my head with a sigh, I hide my face and rub as lethargy seeps into my body. "My ex."

"I take it that it didn't end well?" Cain murmurs.

Shaking my head, I tip my chin and meet him head-on. "I caught him with my friend. They were having an affair." I should voice the truth about Henrik, but I've not heard from him, so I keep tight-lipped.

"So I should thank him?" Cain replies thoughtfully. "I mean, I'm assuming that is why you moved to London?"

"It is."

"I should definitely thank him," Cain concludes and taps the mobile. The line rings, and I shift uncomfortably in my seat, but Cain grips my hand tightly, offering reassurance, and then Martin's snide voice huffs down the line.

"I suppose you think you moved up in the world," he laughs dryly. "The infamous Carson-Ivory," he spits, "He's using you, Lauren. I thought you had more respect than to spread your legs for a guy like that."

"I hate to tear into your riveting monologue," Cain begins in an eloquent drawl. "However, I wanted to thank you."

Silence emanates for a few seconds. "Thank me, whatever for?" Martin bustles, taken aback by who he is conversing with.

"For fucking up so spectacularly and sending my girl this way. Don't contact Lauren again." The line cuts and Cain throws my phone down in the empty seat before lifting my chin. "I don't care about your past. He did us both a favour. Is there anything else?" he asks simply, and I hide my trembling hands and give my head a little shake.

CHAPTER 31

Cain

After a weekend of meetings and time with our friends, Lauren is slowly coming to terms with what has happened. I'm just glad the photos weren't any more intrusive, capturing more intimate parts of her. All I can do now is maintain damage control. Danvers believes it was the PI who followed us to Thailand. I'd have thought, with his dwindling cash flow, that Royce would have called his dog off. We're waiting for some more information, but it wouldn't surprise me if that was who took the images. It's the only power Royce has, and by using it, he just folded.

Not to mention, if we can prove it, the camera welding twat is about to lose his licence. Following me is one thing, but taking illicit photographs is a whole other ball game.

I demanded an emergency meeting with the managers and HR once Danvers arrived, informing them that our relationship had always been conducted outside of the office. However, as we were staying at one of the resorts, it was difficult to argue the non-fraternisation policy. Lauren would no longer be working for Carson-Ivory hotels and resorts, and the only statement we put out was that our personal lives would stay private, and that Lauren was no longer an employee. The story has been printed over multiple outlets, and I disabled all her social media to avoid her having to see it.

"You okay?" I thread my fingers with her as we drive to the hotel. She needs to clear out her locker, and Amberley could have done it for her, but we agreed to show a united front. Not to mention, with Royce being in the know, I didn't want to leave her alone. She was against the idea at first, not wanting to show her face, but I know the only way to fight fire is with fire, and so here we are, heading to face the press and leave with her head high.

"I feel sick with nerves," she scoffs, shifting in the seat beside me.

"Head high, Lauren. Remember what Amberley said? Under all that sand, you could have been wearing a bikini." I couldn't fake the illusion of clothing. My ass was all over the internet as bold as day. The angle, the sand, and the fading light did us a favour—her a favour. I would never be so insensitive to admit it to her, but I think she looked incredible in that photo. I've never been a smug man, but finally getting her out in the open, being able to say she is mine, does shit to me. I can't attach a label to it because it terrifies me.

"Sometimes, I feel like I'm watching it happen to someone else, and then the next minute, I want to hide under a rock. Too humiliated to even speak." Shy, watery eyes bounce to mine and away again.

"Give it time. They will write about someone else soon enough, and this will be like a bad dream."

"It is a bad dream. I don't know if I can do this." Her voice wavers. Violent anger churns in my stomach at whichever lowlife took those images and made her feel this way.

"You can. I'm here." I drop a kiss on the back of her

hand. "I'm here, Lauren." Big, wide eyes meet mine, but anxiety glistens back at me, and I drop our linked hand to my knee.

"I know, thank you. I'm grateful that Perry offered me a job, though," she sighs raggedly. Her fingers flex in mine as we near the hotel. I grunt. I'm not. His revenue will double, and every pumped-up jock in there will have seen my girl and want more when they find her pretty face behind the desk.

She looks like a powerhouse in her neat, knee-length dress and heels. Her face is set in a stony frown—her lips a cute but sexy pink.

We stop at a set of traffic lights, and like always, my head pulls to the left, seeking out the small window that is barely visible over the top of a wooden fence. "See that window?" I point over her shoulder, and she turns, nodding. "I drive past it every day. To most, it is just a solitary window." It will never be just a window to me—it was the beginning of the end. For years, I've driven past this window, entered that building, and stood on the threshold, unable to cross over in fear of reliving it all again. It's both a form of torture and all that keeps me going.

As though she can read my thoughts and is attuned to my mood, she squeezes my hand. "Is that?" Lauren peers back at me. "Where your father...died?"

Nodding, I change gear and pull away, the window disappearing behind buildings. "I drive by it every day to remind myself why I started this and that everything else is just noise." I pick her hand up and kiss her knuckles. "Sometimes, that noise can seem deafening. It's too loud, and you can't hear anything else—like your eardrums might rupture, but it's just noise, and you need to find a sound you like better. Don't let their noise get to you." I flick my gaze at her, and she bites her lip, nodding in agreement.

The press is scattered down the street, and as soon as my car pulls to a stop, flash bulbs attack us from all angles. "Head high. Don't acknowledge them. I'm here the whole fucking way," I say when her breath disappears into her throat in a pained gasp.

She nods, and then I'm out of the car, forcing my way through the throng. Camera flashes and voices erupt around me. Security arrives to assist, and I pull her door wide and take her hand in mine. She keeps her chin up, but her eyes avert as we walk to the hotel and inside. Several employees stare as we walk across the lobby, and I slip my hand to slide around her lower back as Amberley smiles in greeting. "Hi, I forgot to mention that Cameras Direct has a flash sale outside —one crappy camera lens for the price of two."

"How long did it take you to come up with that joke?" I muse, rubbing my lip as more staff peer to look at us standing at the main desk.

"Most of the morning." She blushes, and Lauren shifts beside me awkwardly. "Are you ready for your induction?" she asks Lauren.

"I guess. It's just a lot in one day," she replies softly.

"You'll do amazingly. Perry can't wait for you to start," her friend reassures. Lauren nods, and her small hands shake at her front.

"Shall we go and get your stuff?"

Lauren nods, and I feel her hand reach for mine. I grip it tightly and escort her down to the staff room, daring anyone to voice their opinion. She clears her throat and walks in with a timid smile affixed in place. Multiple sets of eyes swing our way, and Lauren says a quiet good morning and lets go of my hand, heading for her locker. An uncomfortable silence permits the air.

"Good morning." I force the attention back to myself, and a handful of surprised responses murmur in return. I walk to stand behind Lauren as she begins pulling all her things out of the locker. "Anything else—kitchen sink?" I drawl as I pull a coat and some spare shoes from her hands.

"No," she laughs softly.

"Is that a mouldy banana, shameful?" I tut.

"Cain," she groans, embarrassed, pressing onto her tiptoes only to find it empty, "you're not funny." She ducks her head to hide her pink cheeks.

I kiss her hair, smirking. "Pass me that bag," I load my arms up, take her hand, and then walk her back towards the door, not giving anyone else the time of day, not when some of them are scowling at my girl like she just fed their favourite pet to the wolves. "Anyone you want to say goodbye to?"

"Albert in maintenance and Beryl."

—

As soon as she's said goodbye, we head across town for Lauren's induction at Magnitude, Perry's gym. She swaps out her heels for some flat white pumps and pulls her hair into a long plait. I packed my gym bag because the thought of leaving her to the mercy of all those men has my hands gripping the steering wheel extra hard. I pull up in one of the private parking spots, and we head to the main reception. Lauren falters when a few members stop what they are doing to look our way. "Head high, pretty girl. They only wish they could land someone like you." I wink, straightening my jacket.

"Flattery will get you everywhere." She smirks.

"Alien!" Perry rounds the desk and scoops Lauren up. "Buzzing to have you as part of the team." As far as bosses go, Perry is going to be a breeze compared to me. Lauren flicks a pointed look my way, and we share a smile as he puts her down. "Here, this is your new uniform. Waist down, wear what you want." He hands her a stack of packaged polo shirts.

"Okay. I know I've already said it, but thank you. I really appreciate you doing this."

"I wanted you here weeks ago. I was already in two minds

about offering you a job when this idiot fired you the first time." He thumbs at me, and Lauren's throaty laugh radiates around the reception.

A beefed-up bloke saunters past, and he eyes my girl. "How's it going?" He gives her a flirty wink, and her cheeks heat for all the wrong reasons.

"Hello," she responds and then chuckles when she catches me glaring after him. "No cavemen allowed." She points at me.

"Not even big cactus ones?"

"What is it with you two and cactuses?" Perry shakes his head, then moves behind the reception. "I'll give you a tour, and then we can go over the basics with Faye when she comes back from the bank—she's running some errands."

"Okay, great," Lauren says breezily, slipping her bag off and moving to stand behind the desk.

"I thought you got rid of Faye?" I turn to Perry, suppressing a growl.

"I was going to, but Becky went on maternity," he says flippantly.

Lauren frowns, and I drop my bag, lift her onto the desk and edge between her thighs. "Faye can be a little handsy," I say, pinched. "But nothing happened," I assure her. Realisation dawns, and her mouth pops open. I dive in, taking advantage, and kiss her.

"Jesus, stop manhandling my staff," my friend snaps, moving some files out of the way. The woman in question bounces into the gym. Her eyes light up when they see me, but dim when I turn back to Lauren. I fist her plait and kiss her possessively, making a huge fucking point to anyone who is in viewing distance that Lauren is off limits. "Don't take any attitude," I plead to her, searching her eyes.

Nodding, she smiles and tugs at my suit. "Does that extend to you?"

I drop my mouth to her ear. "No, you love me and the attitude I give you." With that, I peck her pouty mouth, slide her off the desk, and grab my bag, leaving her with Perry to go and work out some of the tension threaded through my muscles.

Mikael is already set up at the far side of the weight room, so I stroll over and tape my hand. "Hey, man. How're things?" he greets.

"Well, my ass is all over the internet, so there's that." I grin. I've long since learnt how to set the tone for a conversation if I want the upper hand or when to sit back and observe if I need them to show theirs. Mikael is a decent guy, and making light of the situation will not only put him at ease but keep it on a foundation of my choosing. "Not too happy about my girl being photographed," I quip, pulling the tape taut and flexing my fingers to give it a little movement.

"Not too happy that you're going to pretend my face belongs to said photographer?" he jokes back.

"Just here to clear my head." I work my neck and close the distance.

"It's Lauren, right? Perry mentioned she's starting here today." He lifts his hands and moves his feet to try to throw me off guard.

"She's currently on the grand tour." I mimic his movements, circling the mat.

"So that's why you look like you want to crush a skull." He grins, and I snatch my fist out and clip his ear. "You know there are some real meatheads here who won't care about your big bank account," he taunts. Jabbing rapidly and catching my shoulder.

"I train here. I'm aware," I enunciate, rolling my neck.

"So if I tell you that your girl is getting hit on right now, you won't care?" He nods over my shoulder, and I whip around. His arm snags my waist, and he lifts me off the ground and throws me down with a *thunk*. The air huffs out of me, and he laughs. "You gonna invite me to the wedding, lover boy?"

I flip him and swing, connecting my fist with his jaw. "Best ask mummy if you can come out and play. I heard you moved back home," I grunt, rolling and securing him in a headlock.

"It's temporary, you dickhead," he wheezes as he hooks his legs and slams me down on the mat. "I'm going through a divorce."

"Cry me a river." I snap out of his touch, flip to my feet and roundhouse kick him in the chest. Mikael staggers back and jumps straight at me.

"No crying over here, my friend,"—he bounces on his heels—"in fact, I heard your sister is single." His arms hang by his side, leaving him exposed and vulnerable, but I know he is baiting me.

"I couldn't pay her to fuck you."

"Shit, she'll be pissed to know she did it for free." He shrugs, and I growl, charging at him. He clocks me in the face, and then we are swinging and ducking, fists pounding into sinewy muscle and bouncing off bone. "How're you gonna keep your cool in a courtroom if you can't even take a few digs?" He flicks his head to the side, ensuring that I miss him.

"That's a clear-cut case. That fucking arsehole will be wearing cuffs before he gets his next haircut." I jab in quick succession and catch him near the temple. He sways and then sets himself right before kicking high and slapping his foot against my ear, and I growl because that shit burns!

"Yeah, well, all I'm saying is make sure you don't join him," Mikael pants. He shakes his head and frowns over my shoulder. "Orton is, in fact, hitting on your missus." I run at Mikael and take him down, twisting to check the room and find Lauren looking pissed as one of the guys walks around her like she is a prime bit of meat. I jump up and stalk across the room like a crazed bull, disrupting workouts and invading everyone's personal space until I happen upon Orton eye-fucking my girl. Perry appears in my peripheral, but I ignore him striding this way. Too late, loser!

He reaches for her hair, but she moves out of the way. "Don't fret, angel. You had a little sand, is all—" His buddies chuckle, and I boulder my way in, hoist Lauren over my shoulder, clapping my hand over her arse to avoid anyone looking up her skirt.

His face drops as I raise my finger and point it in his face. "Hands off, asshole!"

Hands held high, Orton eyes me warily. "I was joking, sorry." Those same eyes flick over my shoulder.

"For heaven's sake. Put me down, Cain!" Her small fist digs into my back.

"No!" I bark. Perry steps in my place, levelling Orton with a hard scowl as I stalk off with her draped over my back. "I want to introduce you to someone," I say, slapping her bottom and grinning when she tries to pinch my arse.

CHAPTER 32

Lauren

I read over the message multiple times. It appeared in my inbox first thing this morning, and I've stared at the threat throughout the day.

Even now, sitting in this restaurant amongst the guests with my face aflame, knowing they have read the article, I can't stop thinking about Henrik's message. When Cain suggested we go out for lunch, I refused, but he is adamant we need to show we have moved past the image being leaked. I know he is right, but until this whole thing blows over, I am mentally stuck on that plane. Humiliated and exposed.

Nervously, I look up for Cain, feeling too vulnerable sitting alone at the table. Some of the faces I recognise, others I know have been victims of the same kind of scandal, but I still can't look them in the eye. Embarrassed, I read over the message again, avoiding the gazes of those around me.

. . .

You understand how this works. Your new beau doesn't scare me, Lauren.
I'd hate to have to hurt your brother's reputation, after all.

He's ensuring I keep quiet by playing on the threat he has
used to safeguard his name. A part of me wants to know what
information he has, but the other is too afraid to be privy to
something he deems damaging. I should tell Cain, come clean
and be damned of the consequences to James. Henrik
wouldn't be so stupid as to hurt me physically. He'd go after
James's business—it would be a form of entertainment to him.

Cain returns from the bathroom, and I slide my phone
back into my bag. "Are you ready to go?" he questions, taking
the seat opposite me as I finish my drink. "Stop overthinking,"
he chides softly when my eyes skirt around the room once
again.

"How are you so blasé?" I scoff. I want to be annoyed with
him for brushing it off, but I know that acting indifferently is
the only way to come out of this without giving the press more
ammunition. He's been my rock, shouldering any and all of
the burden. I know his lawyer has dealt with having the image
retracted, but it's too late. Too many eyes have seen everything
I only ever wished to give to the man opposite me.

"Because half of these people have had their life pulled
apart online. They can hardly judge us without holding themselves accountable for their own choices," he muses and places
a few notes down on the table. "Come on." He stands, and I
follow suit, slipping my hand in his and heading across the
restaurant and out into the street.

Across the street, a photographer raises his camera, and I
duck my head, but Cain lifts my chin and drops a kiss on my
mouth. "A kiss for every photographer—aren't you a lucky
girl?" He smirks.

"I love you," I mouth, and he hooks up my pinky with his
own and brings it to dot a kiss on our linked digits.

"Let me take you back to work. Perry will put out a missing persons' report if we're any later."

~

Faye walks towards reception, and I pocket my phone and finish up the email I'm sending for a late payment. She's nice enough, but after what Cain mentioned and the news article, I've tried to keep a polite and professional distance.

"Did you book in those two sessions?" she queries, stepping behind the desk and reaching for her coffee cup.

"Yes, I managed to get them to stay on for another class afterwards. Reena had some space left."

"Seriously? I feel tired just thinking about it." Faye's eyebrows shoot up, and she lowers into a seat beside me, sipping quietly.

"I know. This gym has some really dedicated members." I laugh lightly.

"What about you? You're petite. What do you do to work out?" she asks as Perry rounds the desk, grabbing his water.

"Cain. She does Cain." He laughs dirtily, and I go bright red.

"Perry!" I blurt, mortified. Faye laughs, and I grab his bottle, squirting water in his face.

"Hey!" He coughs, lifting his top to dry off. "It's the best kind of workout." He grins and rubs his wet hand down my cheek.

"Get off!"

He chuckles and drops down on the desk. "Do you need a lift home?"

"No. Deeks is picking me up." Cain had arranged that when we returned from Koh Samui. For the past four weeks, Kelvin has been driving me to and from work. It's nice, but I think Cain is being over-cautious.

"You need to get him and his little band of merry men to sign up." He winks.

"Could you imagine? He'd dwarf half the people here." I smirk.

"The bloke is scary," Perry replies and pushes off the desk. "If you're sorted for a lift, then I'm heading out. Catch up with you girls later."

The gym is open from six a.m. until ten at night, with four of us rotating the reception. Cain assured me I could work a standard shift, but I don't want my new colleagues to hate me, so I'm currently working until closing. We only have another hour left, and it goes by quickly. Classes end, and I do a sweep of the gym, ensuring no one is inside before hanging up a tracksuit top in the lost property.

Over the last month, I've started to work out a little, using the facilities before I clock in and once or twice, Cain has watched as I have had a PT session with Mikael. The first two weeks after we returned from our holiday were hard, the press was relentless, and when they weren't camped outside my flat, they were posting regular updates about our relationship, scrutinising what I wear or my looks. The latest was Lindel in Love and how I was setting myself up for heartache with a man out of my league. Being at the gym, working out, and focusing on getting fit have kept my mind occupied. It's been a small solace during the chaos.

I collect my belongings and help Faye lock up. Deeks is waiting in his car for me. It's a big blacked-out thing parked diagonally over several spaces. I hoist open the door and climb in. "Hey!"

"How was work?"

"Good, thanks, you?"

"You don't want to know about my work," he remarks, reversing out of the spot and driving us across the car park. We've never discussed his work. I decide to ask.

"I do. What is it you do when you're not ferrying me about?"

"Nothing good." He changes gear and checks the mirror, growling lightly. I check my own mirror but see nothing out of the ordinary.

"Oh, do you ever want to do something different, better?" I wonder, relaxing back in my seat.

Kelvin twists to look at me. His bald head shines under the streetlight, and although he views me with kindness, he's scary, like Perry said. "Feel like I already am." He winks. Taking on this role and looking out for me—that's his idea of better.

"Do you have any family?" I suddenly find myself asking.

"No, why? Are you in the market for an older brother?" He laughs. "Maybe I can be uncle Deeks." He regards me with a toothy grin.

"Might be."

"Then I have a family," he says soberly. I smile to myself as we drive back to the flats, him checking his mirror more than usual.

"What is it?"

"Nothing, just being over-cautious," he assures. Henrik's message is on my mind, and I contemplate mentioning it to him, but I know he would tell Cain, and I want to be the one to do that. I stay quiet, and when he walks me out of the lift and to my door, I thank him and keep my secret to myself.

"I'll see you in the morning." He yawns as he walks away.

"Night, Deeks!"

I call Cain with every intention of confessing the truth, but when it connects, he is fired up about the case. "You have a court date?" I exclaim. This is great news. Everything has moved at breakneck speed. That's good, he tells me. It means that the evidence he supplied is enough to imprison Royce for a long time. Even if he pleads guilty, he is looking at some serious jail time. Good behaviour won't have him leaving any time soon. Kat has mentioned that he has aged considerably

in the last two months, and whilst I feel bad for her, I want
Cain to have everything that was stolen from him. For the
most part, we don't discuss it. There are too many frayed
emotions and not enough answers, plus Kat and Cain are
trying to hold on to the relationship they are building. "That's
amazing!" Henrik slips to the back of my mind, and I decide
then and there it's best to let this all blow over with Royce
before I admit anything to Cain.

"Come over so I can celebrate. The guys are on their
way."

"It's getting late. I can come to you tomorrow?" I suggest.

"I want to see you, stay here for the night, and I will drop
you to work in the morning."

"Okay."

"Speak to Deeks. I'll see you soon, pretty girl."

I get changed out of my work clothes, find something to
slip on, and quickly pack a small bag. I debate calling Deeks,
but it's nearly eleven p.m., and he looked tired. I leave my
apartment to catch the tube.

It's dark, and even though I can hear some of his guys
laughing down the side of the building, I tug my hood up and
walk across the car park, trying to keep out of sight. "Lauren?" Kelvin's deep voice carries, and I grimace because he
will be annoyed at me. "Where are you going?" He sounds
pissed off. I turn to face him as someone starts their car, their
lights illuminating me. Lifting my arm, I shade my eyes as they
wheelspin in my direction. *"LAUREN!"*

―

The last person I expect to see when I open my eyes is my
brother, James. Frowning, I look around the room and try to
piece together what is happening. His suit jacket is slung over
his chair, and he is staring at the floor, bored stiff. I eye up the

machinery and lift my aching hand to find a cannula attached. "James?" He startles and turns my way.

"She's awake!" he announces, standing, but my dad barrels into view and gently folds me in his big arms.

"Oh, thank god. Lauren." He sniffs into my hair.

"Be careful, Robert!" my mum admonishes and shuffles to the other side, cupping my hand and holding it tightly, her eyes filled to the brim with tears.

"Mum?"

"James, go and get the nurse!" Mum pleads. "Do you remember anything? How are you feeling?"

Blinking, I try to find the information they want as they stroke my hair, and my dad looks at me worriedly. "I... I think." My head hurts, as do my leg and waist. "I was hit." I swallow emotionally as my brain finally begins to take stock of my injuries. Everything comes rushing back. The car lights. Deeks's panicked roar. The pain.

I begin to well up, emotion prickling my eyes, and my mum leans in and gives me a soft squeeze. "It's okay, love—the nurse is on their way."

Where's Cain?

My family crowd me as the nurse checks my vitals behind the curtain. I frown at my mum, but she is looking at my dad with concerned eyes. "All vitals are good," the male attendant states as he scribbles on his notes, "with your previous concussion, we were a little concerned, but you're doing okay."

"Seriously, Lauren, looking before you cross the road is simple road safety." James sighs, dropping back into his seat like a petulant child and not the grown man he appears to be.

Ignoring him, I peer around my parents, but it's just us in here. "My leg," I hiss, trying to shift.

"Yes, unfortunately, the impact resulted in a break. We've pinned your femur. You'll need some physio," the nurse states. "Rehabilitation is tough, but you seem like a tough cookie." He smiles encouragingly.

"Oh." I lift the sheet to find my leg secured in a cast. "How am I supposed to work?" I worry.

"Try not to panic. Let's just get you back home first." Dad gives my shoulder a light squeeze. Back home to theirs?

"Where's Cain?" I demand. Why isn't he here? My mum worries at her bottom lip. "Why are you looking at me like that?" When my dad sucks in a breath, I flick an anxious look between my parents. "Dad?" I press.

"He's… Your accident has been a shock to us all—" He pats my hand, and my mother offers a reassuring smile. Where is he? My stomach swoops, and I grapple with the possibility of Cain walking away from me.

"But he's coming later, right? Someone call him," I croak.

My mum opens her mouth to answer, but my father cups her wrist affectionately. "Jan, let me. Lauren, he's struggling with this." My father's low, coarse tone sends panic through me.

"No, call him." I grip my mum's hand tightly. "Mum, please?"

The nurse yanks the curtain apart as he leaves, and my eyes slam to Cain's as he sits just outside the cubicle, talking quietly on the phone. I sag in relief and give him a watery smile, but resigned grief stares back at me, and I begin to shake my head. He looks gaunt—traumatised by what's happened. "No." I choke when he stands. He slides his hands into his pockets and walks to me, face set in a stony frown. Eyes full of pain. "Don't you dare!" I whisper hotly. He's going to end this.

"Don't make it any harder for me, pretty girl." His gaze sweeps the machines and then me.

I choke out a shocked gasp of air, tears pooling to run down my cheeks. "You promised me." I shake in the bed. "You promised to keep giving me reasons!" I hiccup as he picks up my hand and kisses the back of my palm. "No!" I slap his hand away and silently beg for him not to do this.

"Lauren," he rasps, pulling to hold me to his chest, but I plant my palms to his wide torso and push him away. "It's not safe. I'm not losing you, too," he vows roughly.

"So don't!" I cry shortly.

"I underestimated him. I can't do this." He cups my face and leans to place a kiss on my lips, but I snap away, gasping sharply as pain ricochets through my thigh. I grip my cast, groaning as my stomach revolts at the sharp stab of pain throbbing through me. "Shit, Lauren. Try not to make any sudden movements. Let me call the nurse back."

"Get off me." I waft my hand, blinking through the tears.

"I'm doing this because I care about you." He more than cares about me. I've felt it for a while. He wanted serious, and that's what we are. I'm in his corner, and he's supposed to be in mine!

"You love me," I tell him tersely, "and that terrifies you." I shake my head as hot tears run into my hair. Pain takes over, and I writhe on the bed. "It's just noise." I suck in a shaky breath. "It's just noise," I beg softly.

Swallowing, he steps back and looks down when my hand grips his. He clears his throat and untangles himself, pressing the button to call a nurse.

"Lauren, be realistic. This hasn't been fun for you, sneaking about, lying to your family, people invading your privacy, and now this. You could have died."

The fear of losing him sinks heavily in my gut. I watch as he runs an agitated hand through his hair before frowning at me.

"You're a coward," I whisper. "You fucking coward." I can't believe he is doing this. Pushing me away. Playing the martyr.

My mum appears, and I shrug her away when she tries to comfort me. The nurse comes back in, and one look is enough for them to adjust my pain meds. It's an instant relief, and I let go of the tension in my shoulders.

"Royce is out for blood. You deserve more than this," he snaps, his hand motioning around the sterile room.

I flick a look at James, sitting with his fingers pressed to his temples, clearly unimpressed with the dramatics. "I lied," I admit. "Martin wasn't the only reason I left." The medication is coursing through my system, making me feel sluggish and dozy.

"Let's not worry about that now," Dad soothes.

Cain needs to know that Royce isn't the only threat. My fear of losing him eclipses that of James's safety. "His dad was blackmailing me. Martin's dad has been blackmailing me," I confess woodenly, my tongue thick, my limbs too heavy.

Cain's face narrows into a dark cloud. "What?" he growls. I ignore my parents' look of horror and meet James's shocked face between their bodies.

"I'm sorry, James," I slur apologetically and turn to Cain. "After the affair, Henrik threatened to hurt my family. He said he had information on James that could ruin him." Cain glares at my brother, sitting wide-eyed. "I was scared, and I didn't know what to do. He asked me to leave, and I was already looking for work in London, so when I was offered a job at the hotel, I left," I admit through my tears.

"What information?" my dad demands, twisting to glare at James, going ashen in his chair.

"He's having an affair with Henrik's wife," Cain delivers coolly. "Or is it that you're close to bankruptcy?" He flicks his brow up, and I gape at him and then at my brother. How the hell does he know all this?

"Now, wait a minute." My mum flusters, pursing her lips and standing tall, but she only manages to reach his chest. Cain grips my hand tightly when I try to shift in the bed. I sigh in relief. Grateful to have told him, everyone. Grateful that he is still here.

"James?" Dad presses.

"Is that true?" I whisper. James and Caroline?

"You had me investigated?" James snaps.

Why would Cain look into James? Cain laughs. "Your sister admits she covered for your sorry ass and left town, and all you care about is what I've done?" He rounds the bed and grips my brother's shirt. "She's being punished for your idiocy, and you haven't even asked if she's okay!" he roars.

The curtain is yanked back, and several nurses appear. "I think it best if you take this conversation outside," an older woman says sharply.

Cain grips harder and narrows his eyes at my brother. "How is she, James? Or are you as inconvenienced to be here as you look?"

My parents look at us both, confused. They have always been oblivious to James's behaviour. Even now, they only see him as their golden boy.

"She's alive," my brother drawls, giving a slight shrug of indifference.

"You piece of shit!" Cain roars, slamming James into the wall.

Several of the nurses intervene, breaking the men apart, and my mum holds my hand tightly in hers. "I'm sorry we're going to have to ask you to leave," a nurse demands, and Cain buttons his jacket. He works his neck and sucks in a deep breath.

"No, wait!"

"Henrik wouldn't harm Lauren—this is your doing!" James spits angrily and storms out.

My father rushes after him, demanding answers, and I reach to grip Cain's hand, scared he will leave. He flinches, and I stare hopefully at him. "Cain, don't do this," I beg shamelessly. "Please?"

He leans over the bed and cups my face, kissing me sweetly. "You're right, I do. I've been telling you for weeks," he admits softly. I nod and hold his face to mine.

"I know." I sniff. He loves me, but he can't bring himself

to say it. "It's okay. I'm okay," I promise him—searching his eyes and praying he doesn't let his fear of losing me outweigh what we have. It outshines simple lust and devours the ruse of needless attachment. I love this man with a ferocity that scares and excites me, and I know he shares those feelings. Behind that harsh exterior and the brutal and cold front he portrays to the world is another man, a more passionate, more loving man, and it's that man that I'm at risk of losing—because that man is in deep pain.

"My dad would have adored you, Lauren," he tells me, and I kiss him back, absorbing the warmth of his lips and holding him close as I pour my love into our kiss. He pulls his face away, devoid of almost all emotion. There is a flicker of remorse, a slash of agony staring back at me. He grips my pinky finger. "I'm keeping our pinky promise."

No!

"Please don't." I cup my mouth.

He looks grief stricken. He swallows dryly and pockets his hands. "Losing one person was bad enough. I'm sorry, Lauren." He excuses himself and walks away, heaving out a low and harsh sigh.

I call him back as he strides through the curtain, but he dips his head and walks with purpose through the ward without a backward glance. "You coward!" I hiccup as he disappears from view. "You damn coward," I splutter quietly, as tears fill my vision. It's not a quick blow, but one that builds and only becomes harder to bear. "Oh god." I sob, blinking furiously to clear my gaze. Pain pours like wet cement through me, settling heavy and solid in my gut. I sniffle and begin shaking my head in denial. I look at my mum in panic, a low wail of pain erupting from me. She hugs me flush to her chest as I sob loudly, gasping as the air in my lungs chases after a man who has no intention of returning it. He's sealed himself away. Pulled the harsher version around himself and cut me out.

"I'm here, love. I'm here," she soothes, but her soft loving words careen off the pain stabbing through me. It grips my throat and suffocates me slowly, teasing a long and difficult torture. The kind that takes time to break you.

"Go after him!" I beg, but she shakes her head and holds me harder as I choke and cry. "Mum!" I plead, unable to move.

"Oh, Lauren. I'm so sorry. I can't. You could have died. I just can't."

CHAPTER 33

Lauren

Three months later.

"How are you feeling?" Pollyanna, my physio, asks, inspecting my leg. "You're weight-bearing, and the movement is good. Are you still feeling resistance?" She peers up at me from where she is sitting.

"A little, but it feels good to walk on it," I admit.

"And *you*—how are you, Lauren—are you eating?" I eye the older woman with a closed expression. She is a long-term friend of my parents, so each session, I find her trying to dig a little, trying to push beyond being my physiotherapist. She means well, but nothing she or anyone else says will fill this ache I'm carrying. My leg has been the least of my worries.

"I'm good, thank you." The lie forms easily, too easily. It's the same one I have been spouting since Cain walked out of the hospital.

"You look like you've lost weight," she presses gently. A

few pounds—it's hardly a cause for concern! With my physio and Mum's cooking, if anything, I've toned up!

"Do I? Well, Mum is feeding me plenty," I reply woodenly and lean to pick up my handbag. "Thank you, Polly. See you next month. It's our last appointment, right?"

"It is." She stands and leads me to the door. "Lauren, it's okay to admit if you're struggling?"

My eyes slam shut, and I suck in a deep breath because I'm more than struggling. I've never known pain like it. It's not a small pinprick, but an avalanche of agony, and the weight forces you to endure it seeping into your pores. I can feel it multiplying and ripping through me like an ancient disease. "I appreciate your concern, but there's nothing anyone can say to me that I've not already been telling myself," I croak and ease open the door.

Her hand lands on my forearm. "If you don't want to talk to me, then I have a friend who's a therapist and lives a few miles away."

"I know my mum is concerned, but she shouldn't be talking to you." My smile is polite, but I hold her eyes a little bit longer than usual, silently reminding her about patient confidentiality. I don't want to talk about Cain. "I'm not the first woman to have her heart broken." With that, I turn and leave, edging down the corridor.

How many times have I said those words to myself? Over and over, forcing me to accept that heartbreak is a passage in life—that we all will have our hearts broken at least once. I never felt this way about Martin and Kristy, and they had both been lifelong friends. It had been painful—I was in shock and felt deeply betrayed—but this pain, it's so much more. Heavier, more lethal. It crawled inside and entwined itself to each bone, attached itself to each organ, and I can't shake it. Breathing hurts, smiling feels alien, and when I'm not dragging the weight of it with me, I'm lost in a void.

I pass Harold, the hardware store owner, who smiles

sympathetically at me, and unlike before where I withered inside and bravely smiled, faking my strength, I give him a non-committal hello and keep going.

Less than six months ago, I lived a different life—was a different woman. So much has happened in such a short space of time. I've done a complete 360 and found myself back at the beginning. Only this time, it all feels strange. This place was my home, where I envisioned having children, settling down, and building a life around my friends and family. Since then, I've had two relationships and three jobs. I feel like a failure. For every door that opens, another slams shut, and I'm reluctant to open any new ones at this point.

I know I won't stay in Henley-on-Thames forever. I've been looking for jobs in Manchester and Liverpool, needing a completely fresh start—somewhere away from here—away from the possibility of bumping into Cain. I want to peel myself away from anyone who knows me and build myself back up. Build a new me, someone stronger and wiser. I want to tear the ivy-like pain from deep within me and replace it with a strength that not even I can shake. I had called Cain a coward, but I'm no different, hiding behind the comfort of my parents, licking my wounds, and wallowing in heartache. I don't imagine I will feel all that much better if I move away, but I won't have to pretend to those closest to me that I'm okay when in truth, my world imploded, and it's been rotting inside me ever since.

Lifting my chin, I pick up my speed, and my mouth twists my face into a semblance of a smile. For the first time in a long while, I can see the light at the end of the tunnel. It's dim and lacking full connection, but I see it.

My phone rings, and I turn it over, expecting it to be my mother, but Perry's name flashes back at me. Sucking in a deep breath, I connect the call. "Hey, you!" I say chirpily.

"Alien! How're things? Physio going okay?"

"I've just left my appointment." I force a light laugh and

walk towards my mum's car in the small parking space at the back of the health centre. "It's healing well. I'll be running a marathon in no time."

"Bullshit, you hate exercise." He chortles.

"Eating ice cream seems so much more fun," I joke. The weekend after Cain left me, Perry turned up at my parents' house with a worried-looking Amberley. The following weekend, he was back, and it soon became clear that he was doing Cain's bidding. After that, I forced myself to act as though I wasn't crushed by his friend's dismissal of our relationship. I played the upset but understanding ex long enough for him to believe I wasn't struggling to get out of bed each day. My lies are as exhausting as the loss I'm lugging around.

"Did Kat reach out?" he suddenly asks. I've been in touch with everyone back in London. Amberley has visited when she isn't working, and twice, Deeks has been to check in on me. Kat and I have texted, but we've remained distant. She is building a relationship with Cain, and other than him, we haven't much in common. I never felt I got to know her well enough. Trying now seems like a lie, even if I seem to be good at telling them.

"No. why?"

"Oh, it's her birthday this weekend, and she's having a party at Carson Court. She mentioned inviting you, but I wasn't sure how you'd feel about coming to Cain's house?"

Carson Court? It's the first I've heard of it. I frown, feeling thoroughly cut off from everything going on back in London. I'd made solid friends and built a new life. I loved being in London, the city life, and being my own woman. Whilst I've been stuck in rehabilitation, it seems everyone else has been moving on without me. The notion presses on my solar plexus and robs me of any available air. It hurts to know the group is making plans without me—that Cain has a home. I'd felt so sure that he was it for me and that we'd move in together. How wrong I was.

The court case is gaining him more exposure than ever before. His life is progressing at light speed, and I've been left with nothing. No prospects. No apartment. My career has hit a stalemate, and the thought of entering into another relationship makes me feel physically sick. The only thing I've learnt from all this is I have a poor choice in men, and I'm far more naïve than I realised. Far more wistful than I dared admit. I'm embarrassed to think I believed I belonged with him. Shame trickles down my spine, an icy pain stiffening my back and making my breath catch sharply.

"I'm actually busy, so maybe another time," I say quietly.

"We miss you, alien." His voice takes on a sullen tone. "The group feels disjointed and…" He sighs heavily. "Did you hear that the photographer was located and confessed? He was on Royce's books—and the driver of the car that hit you. They are all going to pay for their part, Lauren."

I nod and unlock my mother's car, sliding in and massaging my leg when it twinges. "Yes." My tone is light, but I can't disguise the croak of humiliation I'm attacked with whenever I am reminded of that incident. "It'll help the case against Royce," I voice woodenly. That's all Cain cares about —ruining his stepfather. It was all he truly cared about. Royce was an addiction, a dark obsession that Cain couldn't walk away from.

"We don't need to talk about this if you don't want to?" I hear him swallow on the other end of the phone, and I close my eyes and try to be patient, to fold my feelings away and keep the upbeat lilt in my tone.

"It's not really any of my business, Perry. I'm glad Royce is finally having to face up to his actions."

"Are you about next weekend? I can come and visit— maybe we can make a weekend of it. Go to the seaside or something?" Excitement slides down the line, and I smile softly.

"I'm hoping to view some apartments," I lie. "I'll let you know."

"I can view them with you. Are they in London?" he questions.

"No. I was thinking of up north. It's still in the works so —" My voice trails off, uncomfortable with my half-truths.

"Oh, I thought you liked working at the cafe?"

My laugh is short and sarcastic. It costs me to utilise that emotion because I've been devoid of any for so long. "It's nice enough, but it's never been where my heart is, Perry," I chastise and feel guilty when he clears his throat uncomfortably.

"I know. I... I guess I'm just shocked. I hoped you'd move back. I really miss you, Lauren," he expresses quietly.

"I miss you too." I bite my lip to fight the tears building behind my eyes. "I need a change though, to start over. The last few months have been a lot to digest, you know." The confession is robbed from me. I regret saying it the second it's out there, but it's too late.

"Yeah, but you're doing okay though, right?" It's the first time he has questioned me since he first came to visit, and I can sense the doubt in his voice, feel it reach for me with concerned arms and grip onto my shoulders, weighing them down. "You kind of just bounced back. I got the impression you were fine. No offence, but you've dealt with the split far better than Cain has," he scoffs loosely.

It's like a shockwave has surged through me. I suck in a deep breath and swallow the bitter laugh bubbling in my stomach. Anger simmers, and I grit my teeth hard enough to break my own jaw. I did keep bouncing back. At first. That photographer had punctured my resolve, forcing a little of my fight to slowly leak out. Cain had been there to pump life back into me, to be the wall of comfort. He'd promised to keep me safe. To give me reason to allow myself to be vulnerable. However, the public humiliation and being hit by a car had been for nothing because he'd cast me aside like a spare piece of clothing, and I felt spare. Worthless. I hated that feeling—hated even more so that I felt it because of someone. My anger creeps its way to my mouth, and before I can stop myself, I snap.

"He'll get over it. I had to." I sound harsh, bitter even, and when Perry doesn't answer for a few seconds, I know he is starting to question everything I've falsely thrown his way over the past few months.

"He was trying to protect you," he replies, and my eyes close.

"I need to head home. I'll let you know if I'm free next weekend."

"Okay." Confusion tinges his voice. I debate whether to apologise for being so curt with him, but I'm still smarting from his comment about Cain. It's almost laughable. I *want* to laugh, but I worry I'll say something else I will further regret.

"Bye, Perry." I cut the call and draw in a deep breath. I want to scream until my lungs are coarse and broken. Scream until my voice breaks and I can no longer speak. Hearing how Cain has apparently suffered makes me furious. I almost start the car with the intention of driving to give him a piece of my mind. How dare he act the victim? He was the one who left me!

—

"So that's one Americano, two teas with extra milk, a cappuccino, and four scones with jam?" I recite from the till and look back up at the group of elderly ladies idling by the counter.

"Yes, dear."

"That'll be twenty-three pounds and forty-six pence, please."

"Table six—you will bring it over?" The lady closest to me hands me a note, and I cash it, pulling up her change.

I hand it over along with the table number as I smile. "Just pop this on your table, and I will find you. It will be a few minutes," I state, eyeing the small queue behind them.

I take several more orders and pass the receipts to Annabelle, who begins preparing the drinks. Barry dings the bell, and I swap with my colleague so I can load up a tray and head over to table six. The cups clink as I lower it to grip the tray in one hand and begin decanting it on their table. "You're Jan's daughter?" one of them asks. My cheeks flush, but I give a simple nod and carry on placing cups and plates down. "His loss." She leans to pat my hand, and I force a polite smile on my face. Her hand squeezes, and my eyes widen. I can feel the falseness seeping out of me. I dart a look around the table, and the array of pitying gazes makes me want to crawl under the nearest surface and disappear.

"That's what I keep saying," I quip and stand up straight, reinforcing my spine in the process. "Let me know if you need anything else." I twist and walk away, replacing the tray and heading straight to the front.

Martin is waiting impatiently, and as soon as he sees me, he lifts his hand in a half-wave. Annabelle rolls her eyes, but I breeze to the counter and smile brightly. "The usual?" I ask, already reaching to key it in on the till.

"Please. Your leg is healing nicely," he murmurs awkwardly. I can't see Kristy anywhere, but he never comes in with her. He is here like clockwork every Saturday lunch to pick up a latte macchiato and a blueberry muffin. I could never envision Cain ordering anything like that.

"The physio is working," I say casually as I ring up his order and hold out my hand for the money. I can hear jingling in his palm.

"I know it's not my place to say bu—"

"So don't," I cut him off and hold his surprised gaze with

a diamond-hard one of my own. I have no interest in what he thinks.

"You're not yourself." He swallows uncomfortably, shifting from foot to foot as he tries to keep his voice low.

"Apparently, it's normal for patients who face a near-death experience," I throw back under my breath. The lie forms slowly, a thick black lump of tar sticking to my tongue, and I can't swallow it back. Martin sees right through it, and his mouth twists sadly.

"Lauren. We're worried." He winces pityingly.

"Fuck you, Martin," I spit, throwing his change in the till and slamming his muffin on the side.

Annabelle's head shoots up, and she rushes to bring his drink over, swapping places with me. I mutter about taking my break and wander out to the back, pressing my way out of the door and slamming my eyes closed. It's a few moments later before the door opens, and I tilt my head as my boss, Barry, steps out gingerly. "I'm sorry." I shrug. Tears swim in my eyes, and I quickly wipe them away.

"He deserves far worse, but I honestly think his concern comes from a decent place. You're not yourself, Lauren."

"I'm fine." I pick at my sleeve, avoiding his gaze. I have lost a little weight. It's likely stress causing the weight loss. My usually bubbly persona is flat and stagnant. I'm not myself, and it shows.

He steps in my way and lifts my chin. "You need to talk to someone. You can talk to me? I won't run to the gossip mill," he accentuates when I suck in a breath to tell yet another lie.

"I know." I sniffle. "I can't sleep. Sometimes I think I'm losing my mind, and then the pain is back, and I wish I *could* lose it." I watch as his face falls in concern. He tugs me to his chest and I whimper. "I'm sorry. I don't know what's got into me."

"You've put on a brave face long enough. We can see

you're hurting—even when you smile, we can see it," he says, softly stroking my hair.

"I feel so weak," I confess.

"You've been through a lot. Most would have crumbled long ago, but you've got a fire in you that half this town has never seen the likes of."

"Well, it's burning out."

"It's still there. When my Darcey passed, I was a zombie. I can't remember anything but the pain."

"Now you're making me feel bad—no one died." I try to stand, but Barry squeezes my shoulders and wipes a fresh set of tears. His wide mouth and ridiculous moustache remind me of a cartoon character, and his loud personality adds to his animated features. Only now, they are twisted with a sadness that mirrors my own. He's hurting for me.

"Sometimes that's worse. When they are dead, you know that's it. There is finality about it. Everything you wanted to say; needed to hear. All those moments that you want to run over again live on in you, but die with them. It's done." His weary shoulders lift with a defeat that resonates through me. "It's a different kind of heartache. This kind, the one you're fighting,"—his fingers squeeze my shoulder—"it's eating away at you. The antidote is wandering around elsewhere, and you know you can't take it because it isn't for you anymore." My boss's words rupture the last shred of composure I have. I break down, sobbing into his chest, and he holds me tightly, rubbing my back. "Let it out. It feels better to let it out, love. It's time to get your fire back."

I cry for an age, allowing everything to unfurl like a turbulent wave crashing into the shore, drying me from the inside out. My shoulders shudder, and my lax body welcomes the physical contact. "This is really unprofessional of me. I'm so sorry, Barry." I mop up my tears, sniffling.

"I was expecting it at some point. Why don't you take the afternoon off?" Concerned eyes urge me to take the time.

"We're too busy. Saturdays are mayhem," I reason. I'm also better when I'm busy.

"We'll manage."

I shake my head and right myself. I do feel a little lighter, wrung out, but lighter. "Let me freshen up, and I'll be okay to carry on," I assure him, patting my swollen eyes dry.

My boss sighs and rubs my back. "Well, the offer stands if you need to call it a day." I follow Barry back inside and slip into the bathroom to wash my face. Annabelle and I have a few items of makeup stored in here, so I apply a little concealer and lip balm, pinching some colour back into my cheeks, but nothing can disguise the heartache I'm wrestling with. Sucking in a deep breath, I set my shoulders and search for the fire Barry was talking about. It's nothing but a flicker, but I smile when I feel it. Twisting my hair into a bun, I exit the bathroom, coming face to face with Cain's bright cobalt-blue eyes.

CHAPTER 34

Cain

"It's up here. Pull over!" Perry argues, pointing across my line of sight. I waft his arm away and indicate across the road as a bus sidles past and a small cafe appears down the road. His arm blocks my view once more when he points, thinking I'm going to miss it. "That's it!" he exclaims.

Amberley screams when I swerve, and I thrust him back into the seat, scowling. "Don't ever consider becoming an instructor. You'd cause more crashes than stop them," I mutter darkly.

"Sorry." He slumps. "I'm excited to see our girl," he professes, and my fingers grip the wheel with trepidation.

"Yes, well, she is likely to be happy to see you," I mutter.

"I don't know," he replies as I find a parking space. "She wasn't that chatty last time we spoke."

"She seemed okay when I spoke to her on Thursday," Amberley pipes up. "She usually finishes around four. Hopefully, Barry will let her have the afternoon off." I cannot remember a single moment when I was as terrified as I am now. Walking away from Lauren was, in some ways, as painful as losing my father. The possibility of losing her, no matter how small, had been enough to shake me into a frenzy of chaotic thoughts and irrational decision-making. I needed to protect her, and removing her from the equation entirely seemed like the best option. She'd never have agreed to it if I'd tried to send her away. It was the right decision. Royce backed away, the media had all but forgotten about her as the court case erupted, and my stepfather was charged on all accounts. Dragging him to a slow and long demise had suddenly felt unnecessary.

I just wanted my girl back.

Winning it all back and destroying him hadn't been a triumph because I'd lost something I truly didn't believe I could get back. I'd broken her heart.

Reputation, money, and property were easy to come by, but Lauren wasn't someone to be bought. I couldn't coerce or manipulate her—negotiation was futile. I'd seen the hurt on her face when I left—mirrored it as I staggered through the ward, anxiety crippling me. My own heart had shattered at seeing her injured, and it triggered a panicked response, reminding me of my father. The smell, her ashen face, and wide terror-filled eyes. It haunted me just as my father's suicide does. I'd never been prepared for the anguish and fear that would evoke.

I stare at the cafe a few feet away, and her animal-like wail as I'd left her with her mother rings through my ears, nailing me to the seat. No matter how much my friends reassure me that she will forgive me, no matter how tightly I grip onto the hope that she will, there is a small bead of doubt that has been eating at me all this time. She was wronged once, and I'd done so much worse. She'll be spitting fire. Poised but pissed. So fucking beautiful that I know I will want to kiss her on sight.

Perry's hand slaps my shoulder, and I shrug him off.

"She'll forgive you. In time, she will. You knew it wasn't going to be easy." He sighs as Amberley exits the car.

"Perry, I need her back."

"I know." He rubs my shoulder and pulls on the door handle, but I stop him and swallow roughly.

"You didn't hear how hurt she was. I really think I've fucked it up."

"She loves you."

"What if she hates me more?" I voice the one thing that has plagued me all this time.

Perry frowns and twists to face me, blocking out Amberley's worried face, peering through the window. "She hates what you did, not you. You chased her until you got her, so chase her until you get her back."

"Yeah," I reply, clearing my throat and shifting in the seat as anxiety ripples low in my stomach.

"Quit acting like a baby. It's freaking me out," he delivers coldly and exits the car. I scowl at his back as I watch them both smiling and chatting on the path, and I suck in a deep breath. Lauren's strong, but hearing the agony in her voice has troubled me—they didn't hear her. It made me sick to my stomach. I've never heard anything so raw leave another person before, and I hate myself for it. Hate that the one person I wish to cause no harm, I possibly hurt the most.

"Come on!" Amberley taps the window. I step out, smooth down my top, and adjust my watch. I catch sight of my reflection in the windowpane. I look tired. I've aged since I last got to look at my girl. She had tried to call me, and after the third attempt, I'd blocked all contact.

"Still hot," Amberley mutters impatiently, pushing me in the direction of the cafe Lauren's now working in. I grimace at the paint chipping from the signage and the red and white check tablecloths nearest to the front window. It's nice enough, but my girl deserves more.

The chatter inside slowly dies down as we enter, and Perry

strides straight for the counter. Amberley's beam falters, and she flicks a cautious look at me. Daggers are being glared my way by more than one person sitting at the over-waxed tables. My eyes scan the cafe for my girl, but she isn't here. Perry is leaning to chat with the younger woman serving, so I overtake Amberley, overhearing their conversation as I approach. "She's on her break."

"Where? Has she stepped out, or could you go and get her?" I interrupt.

"You can leave," an older man with wide but sagging shoulders huffs.

"We're paying customers," I throw back, unmoved by the hostility shining at me through dark brown eyes.

"They are." He uses his spatula to point at my friends. "You're not. Leave."

"Hello, Barry!" Amberley chirps. So this is Lauren's boss. I lift my eyebrow and glower at him.

He inspects me for a further second before he turns to look at Amberley. "Hello, love."

"I'm going nowhere," I declare quietly, drawing his attention back my way. I say it with as much force as necessary to ensure he isn't the only one that knows that I'm here for my girl and I'm not leaving until I have her.

"You could have done with adopting that viewpoint several months ago," someone snarks to my left. I snap around at a withered-looking old lady watching me. She stands shakily —her eyes narrowed in disgust. "You rich boys are all the same. *Boys.* She deserves a *man.*" She stabs her walking stick forcefully into my shoe.

I groan in pain as she bears all her weight, knocking me with her bag before slowly edging away. I wiggle my toes as they spasm painfully. Amberley giggles, and I scowl at them both as Perry grins childishly at me.

"Where is Lauren?" I mutter shortly, my toes pulsing in my shoe.

"If you don't leave, I'll call the police," Barry announces loudly.

"Okay, call them." I shrug, unfazed. Amberley grips my arm, I assume in warning, but I realise it's in shock when Lauren walks into view. Blotchy sunken eyes meet mine, flat and cold.

"You said she was doing okay," I seethe under my breath to Perry as he gawks at her, fixed to the spot.

"Oh god, Cain," Amberley chokes.

"I'm calling the police, love," Barry assures her, and Amberley rushes to pull her into a hug, her voice low and concerned. She looks as broken as I feel.

"She said she was. She always sounded so perky." I make to move towards her, and she holds her hand up.

"Lauren, I—"

She cuts us all off. "You need to leave. I'm working." Her voice is clipped as she heads behind the counter, putting a wide and secure barrier between us. My disbelief is written all over my face. Perry had mentioned she hadn't seemed herself on their last call, but I glare at him because he should have told me how badly she was doing.

"I'm not going," I tell her, moving to stand so I'm facing her. Her more angular face has my gut crippling in worry. Why the hell haven't her parents reached out to me? She's definitely lost a few pounds.

"Why are you here?" The curt tone she levels me with ensures I know she doesn't care for my answer. I rest my wrists on the counter. My father's watch digs into my skin, but it keeps me grounded. It reminds me to go slowly, even if I want to rip this counter away and swing her over my shoulder. "To break our pinky promise," I say softly, reaching for her finger on the countertop, but she moves it and tucks it beneath the surface, her hands shaking. I want to drag her into my chest and beg for forgiveness. Matteo needs to come and check her over.

"I'd rather you didn't." Her chin lifts, and cold eyes bite back at my guilt-ridden ones.

I search her face, and my mouth twists sadly as I look over her. There's a hardness that wasn't evident before. This is all my fault. Seeing her like this hurts as deeply as if someone was to slowly inch a knife into my gut. "I was trying to protect you." My words penetrate the silent room, and she laughs bitterly, her neck angled and her smooth jawline on show. "Lauren, can we talk out the back?"

"No." Her fringe looks too big for her small face, and with every passing second, I grow more concerned.

"When does your shift finish?" I ask when she lifts her chin, setting her shoulders in determination. I glance back at her eyes that at one point I had been so lost in, and something close to hatred glimmers back. Shifting uncomfortably, I hold her gaze and silently plead for her to see my regret.

"That's none of your business," she fires back. A customer at a nearby table chuckles, and I grit my teeth.

"I'm not leaving," I warn.

"Fine, what can I get you?" Her finger hovers over the till, and she flicks me an expectant look. I narrow my gaze, and her prim eyebrow swings upwards in challenge. My shoulders sag, and I look at Perry for help, but he is chewing his lip in worry.

"An espresso and whatever these two are having." I nod towards our friends, and Lauren clicks away on the till when they reel their order off. "Lauren, we need to talk," I say more firmly as she pulls saucers out from below the counter and loads up a tray.

"There is nothing you can say that I could possibly want to hear. That'll be eighteen pounds and ninety-two pence, please?" Her eyes avert as she holds the card machine out, but I reach into my jacket pocket and pull out a note. The second her hand reaches to take it, compulsion takes over. I take her hand, tug her forward, knocking the saucers sideways and slide my hand into her hair. Her eyes widen when realisation dawns.

"No," she gasps before I slam my mouth to hers. Her lips are dry and stiff, and when I peel my eyes open, she is glaring at me. I kiss her roughly, pouring all my love for her into it, and her jaw wobbles, but she doesn't kiss me back.

"Forgive me, pretty girl," I whisper. "I love you. You know I do," I confess roughly against her mouth. "I needed to keep you safe." Tears swim, her jaw locks, and she tugs herself free. "Lauren, ple—"

The slap is so unexpected that I suck in a surprised breath. My eyes snap to hers, and she dashes a tear away.

"You were protecting *you.*" Her voice is so quiet that if the entire cafe wasn't imitating fucking crickets and listening in on our conversation, I would have struggled to hear her. "You don't get to say those words. You don't get to show up here and play the fucking hero." She slams a spoon down.

"Walking away was the only way to keep you safe," I argue. Did nothing about our time together teach her anything about me? Annoyance burns through me—despite giving so much of myself to this woman, she barely seems to know me at all. I had to keep her safe!

"Bullshit!" Her small hand hits the surface with a slap that could rival the one she landed on my smarting cheek. "From who? Royce?" She looks me up and down in disgust, completely put off by my declaration. "He was already under investigation, and having me attacked put even more limelight on him. He knew that," she shouts, face turning red with fury. "He risked my life to hurt you, and it worked. He would hardly attempt it again because he would have been caught. *Was* caught," she spits scathingly. "You were protecting yourself, and just like him, you were willing to risk me for it. Turns out you have more in common with your stepfather than you realised." She scoffs.

Pain rattles through me as she logically brushes Royce's

threat aside and holds me accountable for why I really left her. I was terrified of loving someone, only to lose them again. I still am, but I miss her more. The atmosphere in the cafe becomes tangible and tense. I feel like I'm under a telescope with so many eyes and ears on us. I'm used to the constant attention, but having her liken me to that arsehole has my scalp prickling with animosity.

"And what's that?" I mutter darkly. I'm nothing like that man. Nothing.

"You're both selfish cowards." Our drinks are added to the tray, and she shunts it forward, sloshing liquid over the side of a cup. "Did you really think you could come back, and it'd be like nothing had happened?" She laughs scathingly.

Gritting my teeth, I swallow audibly. I had hoped she'd be more receptive to my appearance in her hometown. Difficult, yes. Full of such hatred, no. But then, I wasn't expecting to find her looking as hardened as she is now.

"No."

"Really?" she muses, not giving me an inch to make amends.

"I knew I'd have to win your trust and love back." I step up to the counter and slide my hand to hold hers, but she pulls away, shaking her head.

"You lost those things when you left me. You left *me*." Her voice catches, and I can tell she is close to tears, and her shoulders lift as she drags in a deep breath.

"Laure—"

"In a fucking hospital bed with a broken leg, Cain, just hours after I was hit by a car. If the pictures weren't bad enough, I then have an attempt on my life because of you,"— she points at me—"and you *leave!*" Her face contorts in anger, and I stand tall as she rips me a new one in front of all these people. "What was the point?" She laughs. Her tears slip free, but she looks calmer, resolute. "I trusted you. I supported you.

I *loved* you. I wanted to be with you. I sure hope it was all worth it."

"It wasn't."

"Too bad. Barry, I'm leaving." She unhooks her apron and walks away and towards the back.

I race after her, and Perry steps in my way and shakes his head. "Let her cool off, Cain." I push him away.

"Lauren!" The fire door clangs shut, and I storm through it. She is already halfway across the small car park, walking as quickly as her healing leg will allow. I cut her up, gripping her arms. "Just talk to me." Empty eyes meet mine. "Fuck, Lauren, you've lost weight." I open my mouth to say something else, and my own eyes sting. I've done this to her. I cup her face and wipe her tears away. "I'm so fucking sorry. Please, pretty girl. I fucked up. I was scared, and I didn't know just how scared until I saw you lying unconscious in that bed."

"Then I suggest you talk to someone about that," she says, low and devoid of emotion.

I rattle her head like it is the only way to get her to hear me. "You. I want to talk to you." She steps sideways, and I move with her, crowding her space. Pushing her back towards the building until we are against the wall, and I have her caged her in. I want to sink into her and wrap my arms around her at the same time. I've caused so much damage, and the evidence is in how withdrawn and heartbroken she is.

I grip her chin and lift her face to mine, but she tilts her face away, avoiding me. "God, Lauren. I feel sick seeing how much I've hurt you. Everyone kept telling me you were doing okay." My voice is thick, and I drop my forehead to hers.

"I'm fine." She tries to move out of my hold, but I pull her face back to mine.

"I love you, please. I'm sorry." I stare deeply at her, but she blinks blankly. "I knew if I could just get Royce locked away, I could come back and put things right. If I told you it was safe for you, you wouldn't have come home with your parents," I admonish softly, knowing how stubborn she is. I lean into her, and my body heats at being so close to her. She smells of grease and bacon, but I want to fuse myself to her and smell like it, too. I've missed her lilting voice and her wide, trusting eyes. The dark twinkle they get when she is aroused and how they lit up whenever she looked at me. Now they are empty. "You *know* me. I'm sorry I hurt you. I thought I was doing the right thing," my rough voice catches, and I suck in a helpless breath.

"Even if you did think that, you chose for me. I didn't get a choice." Her tiny shoulders shrug. "What's the point of being in a relationship if it's all one-sided?" Her eyes search mine, demanding I question myself and not answer her. "The truth is, it terrified you, and rather than buckle up and face this fear head-on, you cut and ran. You took the coward's way out. Did you really think, after Martin, I was ready for a relationship? I was terrified of what I was feeling. I knew it could blow up in my face, but you made me believe I could trust you. All I had to offer was myself, and I knew, deep down, it wouldn't be enough."

"It is. You are enough." I drop to kiss her, but she snaps away, warning me off of her.

"I was in agony, Cain. I had to have another surgery. Months of rehabilitation. I've lost my home and my job. You've gained everything. Just like you wanted. Congratulations." She tries to shrug me off, but I follow her. "I can't do this. Leave me alone."

"Lauren, I'm sorry. I want to make it right, fix what I've broken, and be with you. You're all I want, pretty girl. I miss you."

"I can't." She shrugs. "I just can't." She shoves me away and lifts her bag onto her shoulder.

"I was protecting you!" I cry, desperate to make her understand.

"I need some space. Time to think." Her face crumples, but she quickly sucks the emotions away.

"Lauren, wait!"

She spins around and levels me with a dark glare. "I said no, Cain. Don't follow me."

My hands grip my hair as she walks the short distance and around the corner. "FUCK!" I roar. I move to follow her, desperation clouding my judgement, but Perry appears at my side and slaps my back gently, holding me still. "Don't say anything. *Fuck*," I choke, shaking my head, my fingers ripping at my hair. I feel helpless and plagued with worry. "Get Matteo here. I want him to check her over," I say to both my friends as they stand bewildered in the car park. Amberley is chewing her lip sadly.

"Cain, I didn't know. I even joked with her that she was handling it better than you. She was always fine on the phone," he murmurs, rubbing his neck.

"Evidently, she isn't okay." I lift my head and look at him in complete defeat. "She's lost weight." I drag a hand down my face and stare across the car park, gripped with dread.

"Amberley said she had lost a bit of weight the last time she saw her, but she hadn't seen her look as upset as she did when we arrived. She's calling Matt now."

"Good." Sighing, I walk to a boulder, sit on it, and pull out my phone to unblock Lauren. I contemplate calling her, but I know she'd never answer. Leaving was the right thing for me, but seeing Lauren, I realise now how wrong it was for her. I underestimated her feelings.

"What about Kat?" Perry reminds me of my sister's party in a few hours.

"I'll be there, but then I'm coming back here first thing."

CHAPTER 35

Lauren

"Are you okay? You're a little quiet tonight?" my dad asks while sitting next to me in the garden. I came home and hid upstairs, too emotional to see my parents. James had been here with Caroline, and I didn't want them to see me, so I soaked in the bath, cried, and then concealed my red face with makeup before joining them all for a barbeque.

I turn my head to look at him and smile. "I'm okay."

"Do you want another burger? There are some left."

"No, I'm stuffed." I pat my rounded stomach. Mum is watering the plants, and James left not long ago with Caroline. Their relationship had been hot gossip, and I was grateful not to be the talk of the town for once when they admitted to their affair. In some ways, it was the perfect karma for Henrik. He'd threatened to ruin my family, but he'd only achieved in losing his own. He'd known about James's financial difficulties, but learning of his wife's infidelity had ruptured his plans to keep me quiet. There wasn't a person in this town who wasn't aware of his attempt to blackmail me—who didn't know the truth.

"What else have you eaten?" Dad absently scratches his brow, frowning heavily at me.

"I ate a banana for breakfast."

"Lauren," he chides.

"I know, but I wasn't hungry after serving all that greasy food." I pull a face, and he smiles softly at me. I don't tell him about my visitors and how unsettled I felt after seeing Cain. "It was nice of you to invite Caroline."

Dad scoffs. "It's the only reason James agreed to come over."

"He'll come around, Dad. He's proud, and he's embarrassed that you had to bail him out."

"Hope so." Dad slaps his knees and heaves up. "I'm getting another beer. Do you want anything?"

"I'll have a can of pop, please." I pull my legs up, tucking my knees underneath me, and watch as my mum potters in her garden. Before Cain, I had imagined Martin and me settling down and marrying, buying a house and turning it into a home. I pictured myself much like my mum, tending to a garden and making memories as a couple and then later as a family. I'd listened to the town talk, and it had fed this ideal. I'd been so closeted in this town. Conforming to what was expected of me.

Cain would never conform. He'd rebel and come back with a bang just to say, 'I told you so'. The possibility of building a life, a home, without him, is such a foreign concept. I can't see my future without him, but I cannot move beyond this pain, either. Lashing out and hurting him had been cathartic, if not a little petty. I wanted him to hurt like I had, but seeing him struggling only succeeded in making me feel guilty.

My dad reappears and passes me my drink. "If you don't

want to talk about it, then that's fine, but Gladys called and said you had some visitors at the cafe?"

I crack open my drink and take a long sip. I can't even be mad because Amberley told me Gladys had stabbed Cain in the foot with her walking stick. She's getting a free lunch when she next comes into the cafe.

"They've gone now," I reply. Amberley had text not long after I got out of the bath, saying they had returned to London for Kat's party, but Cain planned to come back tomorrow. I don't know how I feel about that—annoyed, anxious? I don't have the energy to fight with him.

My dad holds his beer up. "Here's to right hooks." He grins. The gossip mill has been hard at work. I knew this would happen—it was no different when Martin cheated on me. The town twisted the truth, and I'd been fed so many lies and bent truths.

"I didn't right hook him." I blush. "It was a slap, and I'm not sure if it shocked him or me more."

"I'm proud of you, honey." My dad sighs, twisting to face me in his chair. "I know this has been hard, but tonight is the first time I've seen some fire back in your eyes."

"You're proud of me for hitting someone?" I muse light-heartedly.

"He broke my little girl's heart—one of us had to give him what for." Dad winks, and I laugh, but my lips turn down slightly. "I'm proud of the woman you are and how strong you are. You're so bright and spirited, and when you moved to London, we knew you'd do well."

"Not that well. I'm living back at home," I joke.

"It's a pit stop." He smiles. "You'll get your swing back. Your apartment and job are waiting for you when you're ready to go back." He nods, lifting his beer and sipping loudly. Mum heads over and huffs, dropping into the chair beside my father.

"What?" I pull back, confused. "What do you mean?"

This is news to me. Perry never mentioned anything when I spoke to him.

"The flat, it's all paid for." Dad shrugs as Mum leans to grip his arm, flicking a worried glance my way.

"Why would you do that?" I splutter, shocked to find they have been so generous.

Mum shakes her head lovingly. "Not us, Lauren. Cain owns that building. He assured us the apartment wasn't a concern."

"But." I slump back in my chair, stunned. "Cain owns it?"

They nod, and I blink and give a broken laugh. I can't believe this. He had inserted himself in my life right from the start. "What about my job? Perry has never said anything."

"He told you your job was safe."

"He was being kind," I respond casually. "He's likely replaced my role with someone new by now."

"Even so, I think he'd find you something."

Shaking my head, I stand, still rattled at finding out Cain owns my apartment, the building I lived in. "I'm not sure I want to go back to London," I tell them truthfully. "I've been looking at apartments up north. I thought maybe I could find a front-of-house position in a hotel. There're some vacancies that I've been applying for." So far, I'm yet to hear back, and I worry my connection to Cain is to blame. His face is too well known, and mine is associated with him.

"Oh." My mum looks crestfallen. "That far? Lauren, honey, you can stay here until you're ready to go back to London. Your friends are there."

"So is Cain. I don't think I can face him again any time soon," I admit. Mum stands and gives me a hug. "He looked exhausted," I whisper into her neck.

"He's hurting too." I try to pull away, but she holds me in place. "He loves you, Lauren. Rose from the cafe told me he said he was trying to protect you." My mum stands back and cups my cheeks. I frown, not sure what to say because we've hardly discussed Cain.

I flick a look at my dad, and he shrugs. "We men do stupid things. He deserved that slap, though," my father adds quickly when I scowl at him.

"I'm not sure I can forgive him," I whisper. "Even if he was protecting me, he just cut me off. It was callous, and it hurt," I croak emotionally.

"We know. You'd have argued against his reasons, Lauren. You would never have agreed to go on a break whilst this all blew over. I honestly think he thought he was doing what was best. You've lost weight, and you barely socialise. You look lost, honey. We just want you better."

"How will he make it better?" I laugh. I can't believe I'm hearing this.

"You love him. We hoped you'd reconcile. You were glowing in London. Would it be so bad to forgive him?" Mum sighs.

"Mum! He broke my heart and left me drugged up in a hospital bed."

"With family," she chastises. "We all make mistakes. He probably thought he was doing you a favour."

Dad grumbles his agreement.

"I can't believe this—you're siding with him?" I demand quietly.

"No, we just want what's best for you," my dad says sternly, heaving to stand. "Lauren, love, he's an important man. I can't imagine the pressure that comes with that. He was under a great deal of stress with this court case and that poor excuse of a stepfather. If he did do this to protect you, then I'm glad to know he can put you before himself."

I stare at them, completely gobsmacked. "Really, because I can't help feeling like I was the last thing on his mind."

"Exactly," my mother says cryptically, and I frown. "He

was only thinking of you and your safety. His last thought was to protect you."

"I'm going to bed," I mutter before discarding the drink and leaving them outside.

Everyone and their dog will have fed their opinion back to my parents about our exchange in the cafe, and they'd made their minds up long before they planned to discuss it with me.

I get into bed but am unable to sleep—too worked up about the possibility of Cain returning tomorrow. I'm not sure I'm strong enough to face him again so soon. My father's words roll around in my mind.

If he did do this to protect you, then I'm glad to know he can put you before himself.

Ending things would have ensured my safety.

Cutting me off ensured he didn't falter from his decision.

All this pain was for the benefit of keeping me safe.

He treated me with the same level of harshness he did Royce. Tears pool in my eyes and roll down my cheeks in hot, salty beads.

It's warm outside, so I pick out a dress and straighten my hair. I don't bother too much with makeup and stick to concealer and lip balm. I'm digging under my bed for my other sandal when I hear the door knock. I snap up and race to check out my window, but I can't see any cars other than my parents in the drive. Frowning, I check the time and relax when I see it's only eight a.m. I manage to find my shoe and give myself a once over before deciding to grab a jumper to pull over the top and head downstairs. My parents are chatting quietly in the kitchen, and I hesitate at the door but decide to enter as another voice reaches my ears. "Matt?"

DeLuca stands and gives me a once over, his gaze critical and direct. "Hello, how is my favourite patient?"

I frown at him and notice his medical bag on the floor. "Confused. Why are you here?"

"Lauren, don't be rude," Mum prattles. "I am sorry," she apologises on my behalf. "Did you say one sugar or two?"

"Just one, please."

"He sent you, didn't he?" Crossing my arms, I lean my hip on the kitchen table. "I'm fine."

"Do you want my medical opinion or just that of your friend?" Matteo drawls.

"Knowing you, I will get both," I quip as my mum places our drinks down and pulls a chair out for Matteo.

"Are you happy for your parents to stay?" He holds my stare, and I nod. "Okay. I think, like usual, where you are concerned, Cain is overreacting. You've lost weight since I last saw you, but nothing to the degree Cain is stating. That said, you can't afford to lose any more. You're slight as it is." I open my mouth to defend myself, but Matt holds his hand up. "However, I hear you work full time and manage to do a fairly physical job. Waiting tables isn't easy." I relax and smile at him because he is the first person to consider all of this and not just that I've lost weight. "You still have colour in your face. That's good."

"I do eat," I affirm.

"Now, for my medical opinion." Matt walks to me and lifts my wrist, and I can only assume he is feeling for my pulse. "Chronic stress, even depression, can severely curb someone's appetite, resulting in them losing weight." I clear my throat as he sweeps his eyes over me. "Your hair has little shine, and your lips are dry. You're likely dehydrated and lacking nutrients. Are you taking any vitamins?" I flinch at his crass words and stare at the floor.

"No," I say quietly.

"What did you last eat?" He pulls my chin up.

"A burger and salad last night," I fire back as quickly. Hurt by his observation, I stroke a hand down my hair, self-conscious.

"Lauren, you're not taking care of yourself," he concludes softly. "Have you been to see a doctor?"

"No." I swallow, trying to batter down my emotions as his examination is met with concern by my parents. "I don't feel hungry." I shrug, welling up.

"Are you drinking plenty, passing urine—what about stools?" he asks in quick succession, and I snap back, embarrassed.

"I'm not talking to you about that!" I laugh, going red.

"Yes or no is fine, Lauren." He sighs, his eyes dancing with humour.

"Yes," I whisper.

"He's been beating himself up, you know," he says suddenly, so simply and quietly that I stare wordlessly at him. "It would've killed him if anything else happened to you." Matteo's accent thickens, and my heart twists in my chest like a wrung-out towel.

"I don't want to talk about Cain." I pull on my sleeves and cross my arms as Matt shines a light in my eyes and asks me to sit for my blood pressure.

"You left this town to keep James safe," Matteo reminds me, and I roll my lips together. "You put your brother first— you left to keep him safe. We do that for the people we love, Lauren. Cain did what he thought was best for you. You should hear him out. You're miserable apart."

"I don't want to talk about this," I whisper thickly, my throat closing with emotion.

"Lauren, you're being stubborn. Put yourself in his shoes. He witnessed his father die, and his mother is a waste of space. The only woman he has ever entertained longer than a night is you, and he put you right in the firing line. He was worried you'd get hurt, and when you did, Cain did the only thing he could do to keep functioning at a low level. He shut down."

"I don't want to talk about this," I cut in thickly.

"You've shut down," Matteo admonishes quietly, and I shake my head. Tears rush to pool in my eyes and slip down my cheeks. "I didn't give you up for you two to fuck it up," he drawls in jest, and I laugh, wiping my tears.

"You never stood a chance." Cain's low voice makes the hairs on my arms stand up.

I snap to look at Matt, and he leans down to peck my cheek. "Maybe you'll get your appetite back when you face the root of the problem," he says simply and stands, picking up his drink and suggesting he and my parents go into the living room. Cain steps into view and drops down to his haunches in front of me.

"What's the verdict?" he asks me softly.

"Still pale." I hum, drawing an invisible pattern on the tabletop, unable to meet his eye. His chuckle hits me right in the gut, and I bite down on the inside of my cheek.

"Lauren, look at me, please?" The soft rumble of his voice has my toes curling against the floor. I shake my head and wipe a stray tear. "I wanted so badly to come and see you. I was checking in with as many people as possible, and they all believed you were doing okay." He cups my face and twists my head to face him. "If I'd known you were struggling as much as this, I'd have dropped the case, picked you up and flown us to Koh Samui. That's all I want to do now. I'm worried about you. Worried you won't forgive me for—"

I tilt my head away, unable to hold his cobalt blue eyes radiating pure love and fear at me. He sighs, and I bite my lip, feeling a fresh wave of tears rise like a blocked pipe ready to spill over.

"Before I left the hospital, you said you knew I loved you." I drag in a shaky breath. "If you knew, why was it so hard to believe that I was trying to keep you safe? You know I value family over everything else. You're my family, Lauren. I want to build a life with you. I couldn't do that if Royce hurt you."

"Even if I try to reason it all away and make sense of why you chose to do it, I can't just shut off all this pain. Something happened to me when you walked out of that hospital. I don't even recognise myself anymore. I hate you for making me this weak." I swallow the ache in my throat and sniff as his face falls.

"Don't say that. I love you, pretty girl." He swipes his thumbs over my cheeks and closes the distance between us. "I'd never hurt you, not intentionally, never to this extent."

"But you have." My whisper-small voice has his fingers sliding into my hair. "I feel like I can't breathe. I just want it to stop."

"Then come home," he murmurs. His forehead rolls over mine, and then his lips brush against my mouth, cloud-soft and as light as a feather. "Please come home with me."

I shake my head. Too fearful, too untrusting.

"Lauren, please. I don't know what else to do. I'm scared that if I walk away and give you space, you'll disappear on me. I'm terrified to put too much pressure on you."

"Cain, you told me you couldn't lose another person. What happens two years down the line when someone else crawls out of the woodwork and threatens my safety? Are you going to drop me off at my parents' again?" I tug at my jumper and force myself to meet his gaze.

"No. Just for a second, think about how I felt losing my father—this grief you're experiencing is similar. Hospitals are a huge trigger for me, Lauren, the smell, the sounds. It all comes rushing back. I avoid them at all costs. I avoided them until you. I admit that, at first, I was in a high state of anxiety, and I made a rash decision. It was in the heat of the moment and irrational—fear-fuelled. But the more I thought about it, the more I felt it was the right thing to do. I knew I had to get rid of any threat from Royce before I could come back and win you over."

He has far more demons than he had previously let on. I knew they were lurking beneath all his bravado. "How's that working for you?" I ask directly, sadly.

"Honestly, pretty shit." He laughs shortly and then leans to press another kiss to my mouth, his lips moving with a gentleness I've missed. "Kiss me back, pretty girl."

My head rocks from side to side, and Cain's shoulder slumps heavily. His once bright blue eyes look hazy and dull. He runs his thumbs under my eyes and smiles sadly. "I've lost you, haven't I?"

I reach up and run my fingertip over his top lip. "You know you're a little rusty where relationships are concerned."

"I don't want relationships. I just want one. With you."

I begin to cry, and he hauls me to his chest. I drag in a deep breath, imprinting his earthy smell in my mind. I tuck my head into his neck and let the same rush of calm he always gave me wash over me. "Why did you buy my building?" I ask quietly.

"Because I wanted you to be safe, and you'd never have moved to another apartment block." He leans back and holds my face. "Even then, I wanted you safe, Lauren."

"Maybe you can give it to Deeks," I suggest.

"Do you really think after keeping my father's flat for all these years that I would be able to get rid of yours? You quickly became the sole purpose of my life. I thought you were the most beautiful woman, even with that big egg on your head," he confesses, and hopeful eyes latch to mine, desperate to find a connection again.

"Royce has been your purpose, Cain. Your hatred for him was so unhealthy."

"I know. I don't regret going after him. If I hadn't stood up to him, then he would have moved on to the next person and destroyed them. It ruled my life. It's over now."

I shrug, unsure what to say. It can't be undone. None of it can, and that's the hardest part for me because I can't forget this pain or the torment I've felt. At first, I would have given anything for him to come back, but the longer time went by, the more alone and lost I felt, and now I'm stuck in a void of fear. Too scared to hand myself over to him in the event that he decides to leave me again.

"Lauren, I—"

"I think you should go now, Cain." I flick a look up at him, and his face goes lax. "As soon as I secure a new place, I'll remove my things from 43B."

"You're accusing me of allowing my fears to overshadow our relationship, and you're doing the same!" He stands, frustrated, stabbing his fingers through his hair in agitation. "I'd never hurt you again. *Never*," he vows vehemently.

"You cut me off for three months, and after two days, you're expecting me to pretend it never happened."

"So, you're punishing me?" he demands, scowling down at me. "Lauren, leaving you wasn't easy for me!"

I stand slowly and walk towards the back door overlooking the garden. "No, I'm not punishing you. I'm too tired to punish you, Cain," I say wearily. "I just want to feel better." I open the door for him and stand partially behind it to put more distance between us.

"Then come home with me!" Frustration bends his features into a scowl.

"I need some space," I say slowly. "To think."

"About us?" He searches my eyes and grits his teeth, no doubt to stop himself from snapping at me. I'm not purposely making this hard for him, but a lot has happened.

"I'm coming back tomorrow," he declares, walking towards me. He cups my cheek and kisses me like he has the right to.

"Please don't." My voice catches, and Cain's jaw flexes. He ignores my plea and slants his mouth over mine again and holds me still, his lips moving softly, teasing, soft, and my own mouth moves against all sensibility. I find myself kissing him back. He chokes out a low huff and deepens the kiss. All the hurt and the pain subside, and I could cry with relief. There's no grief, only love, and I allow myself to be absorbed in its beauty for a moment longer.

"I'm sorry. So fucking sorry, Lauren."

I step away and avoid looking him in the eye. I'm not sure kissing him was a good idea—my thoughts are turbulent. My heart is rushing with too much blood.

"I give you my word, never again. I promise you, I won't ever hurt you like that again," Cain professes roughly. He dips to kiss me quickly before stepping back. "You look really beautiful, by the way."

"I need time."

"I'll see you tomorrow," he imparts gently and steps out of the door, striding across the garden and out of view with a determined pace in his step. I sag against the counter and put my face in my hands as my emotions hit like a tidal wave.

"You okay?" Matt's voice brings my head up, my lip wobbles, and he covers the short distance to sweep me into a hug. "I really hope you can learn to forgive him. We miss you."

"I miss you guys, too." I sniff as he drops a kiss on the top of my head.

"I know it hurts now, but just imagine how good it would feel if you came back. He loves you, Lauren, not just a little bit, but with all that he has. I've never seen him so low."

I pull back and give him a watery smile. "I'm scared," I admit feebly. "What about the next time something goes wrong?"

Matt leans against the counter. "I'm not going to say everything will be perfect. You might argue, and he might fuck up again. But not like this. Cain isn't the type of man to make the same mistake twice. He panicked. He suffered a trauma.

That doesn't just go away when you meet someone. He can't shut it off."

"I know," I say impatiently. Everyone around me is pushing me to forgive him, pushing his narrative, but no one seems to be fighting my corner, and it only acts to make my feelings seem inferior. "He really hurt me, Matt. I… I just don't know that we can work. We're so different."

"No." He shakes his head. "You're not. Strip the money away, the status, and deep down, to the bare roots, fundamentally, you are both very alike. Strong-willed and passionate. You both love hard and are career-minded. Your family means everything to you." He grips my hands and squeezes gently. "Look what you did for James and how you protected your parents. Cain is no different." He shrugs. "He'd do anything for you. And he did. Do you honestly think he found it easy to walk away from you? He was a mess. He drank himself stupid and lashed out at us all. He just wanted you safe." Matteo's eyes flare with distress. I step back and tuck my hair behind my ear. My mind is whirring into a chaotic storm. "You *are* punishing him for doing right by you," he delivers calmly, and my head snaps up.

"It's not right when it's this painful."

"I know. None of us expected you to take it so hard. Ask yourself why, Lauren?" He picks up his bag, seemingly irritated with me. I shift from one foot to the other, uncomfortable. "You love him." Exasperation quilts his voice. "And you're willing to throw it all away. Cain hurt you, but you're continuing to cause damage. It wouldn't be painful if you took him back," he says bluntly, and I flinch. My mouth turns down, and he sighs. "I'm sorry. That was cruel."

"It's fine," I whisper.

"I just don't see the point in all this pain when you both are happier together, and it was a mistake. One that was made with good intention." I chew my lip, unable to shift the growing belief that I'm being childish. "Look, I've got to go—

call me if you need anything," he says finally and walks towards the door.

Clearing my throat to keep the oncoming tears at bay, I swallow deeply and walk him out. "I will. Thanks for coming to check up on me."

"Don't be a stranger, okay?"

"Okay." I nod. Sighing, Matt hugs me again and walks away. It's another few seconds before I hear the throaty roar of a car, then silence settles.

CHAPTER 36

Cain

"Are you sure this is a good idea?" Perry asks me as we exit the property. I shove my hand in my trouser pocket and stop halfway down the drive, turning to look back at the empty farmhouse. It's quaint but extensive. There's room for expansion and enough land to turn this place into a spa and wedding retreat.

"Short of throwing her on a plane and refusing to let her come home, I don't know what else to do. This bides me time." I adjust my stance and slide my other hand into my other pocket.

"And it's not illegal?" Perry frowns at me in concern.

"I wasn't actually considering kidnapping her!" I scoff shortly.

He holds his hands up. "Hey, we all have our kinks." He hops back when I whip out a hand to slap him. "You think she'll go for it?" he finally asks when he stops grinning.

"I don't know. She loves working in hospitality. She's good

at it. She has the potential to be more than a warm welcome at the front desk. If she can't come to me, then I'll come to her."

"Your competition would piss themselves sodden if they could see what a soppy twat you are," Perry drawls, then jolts into a run as I turn to grab after him. He pelts across the grass verge, and I chase. "You're a big pussy, really!" He laughs, his feet crunching on the clean, white pebbled drive as he tries to dodge me.

He skids to a stop when I yank him into a headlock. "You love my girl." I laugh. "That's why you're going to help me get her here."

"If you choose Matteo to be your best man, I'll disown you." He struggles, wheezing in my gasp. I shove him away and stand back to appreciate the sandstone and crystal-clear bay windows.

"I can't believe you managed to snatch this place up so quickly." He moves to stand next to me. "You think this will work?"

"Just get Lauren here," I ask him quietly. He slaps my back and then heads towards the car, leaving me standing on the drive.

I'd never measured my life in hours, days, or even weeks —not until Lauren. I've spent most of our relationship counting down the hours to see her. The weeks to get her back. Those days had passed with a slowness that I felt drag over every part of me. Tearing up my skin and leaving me feeling raw and as broken as the woman I've travelled to see today.

I've spent my time between London and Lauren's home town. As promised, I was back the next day and then the next, settling into her place of work and quietly reinserting myself back into her life. I've worked out of her cafe for more hours than I've been at home.

I want to share so much with her: the new deal I'm

working on, Kat's new job, Carson Court. My father—I'm yet to take her to meet my father.

Those things feel so far out of reach, like a speck of light on the horizon, and if I blink, it will disappear. I want to give her so much. I've spent enough time talking to the cold stone plaque about Lauren—it seems ridiculous that she is yet to visit my father's resting place. It seems only fitting, given that his death was the catalyst for why our relationship broke down.

She's slowly forgiving me.

Cautious.

Quiet.

Slow.

She needs slow, and there's nothing I love more than indulging her with slow.

I wander around the farmhouse, checking every external window for a sign of Perry's car, but the rolling countryside sits unspoiled. A landscaped haven fit for my girl. The commute from London is minimal, and the location will put Henrik's country club to shame. Not everyone wants to put money in the pocket of a man capable of blackmail. Shoving my fisted hands into my own pockets, I rehearse what has been playing on my mind these past few days, but the subtle crunch of tires in the distance has me crossing the open landing and down one of the halls to look out over the winding drive as Perry's car churns up dust and kicks it into the air like a cloud of thick smoke.

A second silhouette sits in the passenger seat, and I suck in a relieved breath. I watch with a deep-rooted sense of unease as Perry chats with Lauren and urges her out of the car and across the driveway. She looks confused as she stares at the property—unsure why he has brought her here, that is, until Perry gets back in the car and drives off, leaving her staring after him. She wafts her hand at the dust cloud he leaves in his wake and, after a few beats, squints to stare back at the farm-house, looking for me.

It's a few more minutes before she ventures inside, and as soon as she does, I stand back from the main landing as her eyes widen at the interior of the main reception. It's light and airy with floor-to-ceiling panelling. A heavy wood and brass chandelier sends a shadow sprawling across the floor and wall, and then there is just my girl, twisting her hands nervously as she waits for me to show.

"Your eyes." My voice echoes, low and confident, even though I feel anything but. She's the only one capable of making me vulnerable, but I keep my tone steady for her.

She twists to search for me. "Cain?" Her softly spoken question caresses the walls and meets me up in the corridor of the property.

"They are the first thing I truly loved about you because no one has ever looked at me the way you do, Lauren. No one." She moves to follow my voice, and I move with her, step-ping out of sight but still keeping her in view.

Silence follows as she holds her breath, waiting. Curious. Her palm lifts to settle at the base of her neck, no doubt to calm her rapid heartbeat. My own drums heavily like a brass band delivering an intense percussion.

"Your integrity," I finally say, and she snorts to herself. It has my lips curling up at the sides. I know, pretty girl. She had none where I was concerned, but we had no hope against one another. It was inevitable. We'd orbited around our attraction until it had swallowed us whole and set us on fire. I'd burnt her more than she could handle. Martin and Kristy had already humiliated her. My actions magnified that pain and drowned Lauren. I don't want her to suffocate anymore. I don't want to face this pain any longer. I wanted to breathe in the calm she gave me.

"Your beautiful smile." I move nearer now. However,

Lauren steps farther away, so all I can see is the top of her head. I watch as she doubles back, a half smile visible on her lips. She looks sexy as hell in her jeans and simple shirt, baring her shoulders and collarbone. She's put on a little weight and seems back to her usual self. My initial shock at her weight loss was quickly rebuffed by Matteo, who had confirmed she was fit and well. Her features have always been angular and striking. The little weight she had lost had seemed worse than it was. Standing back, I watch as she looks around, searching the open landing for me. Drawing in a deep breath, I move towards her.

"Don't blame Perry for leaving you here." My shadow rolls along the wall, and then I step out from the far arch up on the landing and find my girl already watching the space. Her eyes sweep over my frame, her lip disappears behind her teeth, and I want to drag her up to one of the many bedrooms. I hold her stare, as quietly reserved as when we first met. "It was my idea," I confirm, jaw clenched as emotion bats my gut into a bruised organ. Stuffing my hand in my suit trousers, I take the stairs. Her breath catches, and the wall I expect to see around her has crumbled in the face of my own.

"Walking away was wrong of me," I acknowledge openly and fight the urge to eye-fuck her from across the room—she looks good—so damn good, and we are rarely alone, so having her here with me sends a stab of heat straight to my dick. "I'm sorry. It hurts me to know I hurt you like that. I never want to hurt you, pretty girl. Ever."

We are standing feet apart, and she shifts awkwardly, still unsure why she is here. She licks her lips and skates a guarded look around the room. Compelled to touch her, I twirl a lock of hair around my finger, then tuck it behind her ear, keeping us connected. "You look pretty." My eyes dance with heat as I sweep them over her full mouth and her pulse, fluttering like a caged bird at the base of her neck.

"I used to play here when I was a little girl," she surprises me by saying. Lauren looks around the open reception and up the grand staircase, taking the grandeur in with wide, curious eyes.

"I didn't know that." I match her tone, light and toeing along the line of desire. Her eyes snap to mine, and I smile. There is a moment when our desire is suspended in the air like the chandelier, and it tethers us. I want to wrap my hand around the cord and haul her to me, but I let it speak for itself. Allow her to feel the same undeniable tug that has drawn me to her since day one.

"There is a shallow pond down by the cornfield—we swam in it as children until the place was sold to a footballer."

Nodding, I twiddle with her hair. Her tone takes on a nostalgic lilt, and I follow her eye-line down to the water and through the main arch leading to the kitchen. It's overlooked by the farmhouse and is situated near the property line.

"Why are we here?" Lauren suddenly asks, her voice breathy and hesitant.

I give her my full attention. Pinching her hair between my fingers, I glide down until I'm skimming my fingertips along her collarbone. I need her to know I'm not leaving again, not indefinitely. "I'm not conceding defeat." Her eyes flick to mine, hold, and something close to fear shines back at me. "One of us was bound to mess up along the way. It's as inevitable as we are. I'm not perfect, Lauren. I don't want to be." I shrug, stepping to block her in and running my hand up her throat to cup her face. "I want to navigate the highs and lows with you, but until you're ready to enjoy the highs again, I'm giving you space, the time you need to think."

Her inaudible gasp spears my gut, and her small hand grips my forearm for support.

"This isn't goodbye. We don't say those words. They don't work for us. This is me saying, until next time," I vow quietly. Her eyes flare with so many different emotions that I get a front-row seat to the inner turmoil she is suffering.

"Cain." One painful swallow later, and she is blinking

back unshed tears. "I'm trying." Her shaken whisper has me hauling her into my chest.

"I know, Lauren. If you can't take me back now, then I've decided I'll let you come to me on your terms. When you're ready." I flick my eyes up to hers and lose myself in them for a second. "I don't want you moving away, stuck in some dead-end job, forced to make new friends when the ones you have already miss you."

"I miss them too." Her arms finally wrap to grip onto my suit jacket, and my stomach drops in relief.

"The farm is yours, or it will be in a few hours when my lawyer phones," I finally announce, locking my arms to stop her from stepping out of them in shock when she snaps back at my words.

Her head shakes, her eyes pinned into saucers of confusion. I watch her with a half-smile, cupping the petite curve of her jaw so I can stroke her cheeks. It's the easiest money I've ever spent. "Your family is here, you need their support, and I'll do whatever it takes to earn your trust again. I'm not buying you, Lauren. This isn't what this is about."

"So you're leaving again?" Hurt litters her wide gaze, but it softens when I shake my head. "No, not like that. I'm giving you space. I would never invest my time, money, and energy into you if I didn't think you had what it takes. I wouldn't be torturing myself by seeing you daily if I didn't believe we had a future."

"I torture you?" Her eyebrow pings up, but I know she is trying to skirt around the issue of the farm. It's thrown her completely. Even now, her eyes are flicking to take in the colossal entryway.

"Greatly." Smirking, I align our thighs, and her eyes widen in realisation. My cock burns into her stomach, and I tilt her face up to mine. "You know you do, pretty girl." Her breath catches, and I debate whether to kiss her or not. Instead, I step back and say, "Renovations start this week. Nothing drastic, but the barn needs some work."

"Renovations? Cain, wait." She attempts to pull my hands away, only her small fingers slide along mine and stay. "This is all very unexpected… you can't buy me a house!"

"Lauren, it's done."

"You can't just go around buying everything!" she accuses sharply.

My grin is arrogant. I'd buy her every damn star in the sky. Seeing my glee, she drops her arms in defeat.

"Lindel Farm: boutique weddings and spa, is yours. I don't want to lose you, Lauren, and if I have to buy you a property at every mile to get you to slowly come back to London, then I will. I'm starting with the farm."

"A venue. Cain! I don't know how——" She goes rigid and shrinks back as the size of the place finally dawns on her.

Her panic is adorable. She is a natural when it comes to dealing with people, and Perry has already agreed to set up a small gym for guests. She'll be a sought-out name in the wedding community. She bites her lip, and I want to drop forward and suck it into my mouth. My chest swells with emotion. She fell into my life and gave me true purpose—her sass and brightness chipped away at the hate. Leaving her this time scares me more—this time, the ball is in her court. I'm used to being in control. This puts me at a disadvantage.

"Promise you'll come back to me." I suck in a sharp breath, searching her eyes. "Promise me, pretty girl. Those few months couldn't have been it. I refuse to believe this is over." My shoulders inch upwards as my love for her overwhelms me in its intensity.

Her hand lifts to brush my hair off my forehead. Her smile is wistful, if not a little sad. "Until next time," she says, trying out the words. Her eyes roll over mine, and I see the promise there. The deliberation. She's struggling to comprehend what all of this means: the farm, me taking a step back to give her time to work through her emotions. This isn't over for her, either.

Two steps, a weak smile, and my mouth is on hers. Her breath catches, but her lips are soft under my own. I deepen the kiss, tracing my tongue across her lower lip and teasing for entry. She relents, and I sweep my tongue in, relieved when hers meets mine in a hot moan. Breaking the kiss, I lick my lips, enjoying how her eyes flare with need.

"I know, deep down behind the hurt, you feel the same." Leaning back, I peck her forehead, and her eyes slam shut. "So yes, until next time, Lauren." I drop a quick kiss on her lips and step away, but her arm reaches for mine.

The way she rushes to find a physical connection by gripping my suit jacket makes me feel guilty. "I don't need this farm. This is...it's a gesture too much. I don't even know how to run a business," she berates, throwing an arm out at the large building we are standing in.

My laugh makes her narrow her eyes. "Lauren, you can. You can read up on anything you need to know, or you can take a backseat role and oversee it under my support."

"You're doing it again, making decisions for me." She rubs at her temple, but I can tell she isn't mad—her eyes swim with tears of gratitude. "Cain, I can't ever repay something like this."

"I'm repaying you. I love you. It's me who owes you, pretty girl." My hands slide to run over the globes of her bottom as I pull her to me and lean down to drop a kiss on her nose. "I'm a phone call away, and Justine is currently hiring a team to manage the venue. I will help you get on your feet. Amberley can't wait to come and work for you," I finish and pull the keys from my pocket.

"My head is still struggling to cope with this," she scoffs, moving to peer down into a large reception room and formal living space. She finally twists, staring out of the large bay window.

I step in behind her and drop my head on her shoulder. "I know. I'm sorry."

"No. I meant coming here. I thought Perry and I were getting lunch, and now you're here, saying all this and,"—she gives a light, shocked laugh—"this is not lunch."

"No, it's not, but I can arrange that if you want?" Unable to stop myself, I wrap my arms around her waist and hold her flush to my chest.

Her head tilts back to look up at me. "With you?"

Surprise flickers in my gaze, and I lick my lips, uncertain how to respond. "If that's what you want?" I hedge softly, testing the waters with her. Lauren bites her lip when I hold her stare. "Or I can get Perry back here if you want to spend some time with him?" I've made some semblance of progress today. It's enough for me to know giving her the option to find her way back is what I needed to do.

Her heart pounds, attacking her ribs. I open my palm and flatten it beneath her breast. "Your heart is going crazy."

Lauren sucks in an uneven breath. "I feel like everything is centred on this moment. I'm scared that if you go, you won't be there when I come back." Her voice catches, and I turn her and wrap her up in my arms.

Tension ripples off her, but her face relaxes when she sees me shaking my head at her. "Lauren, I will be there when you are ready to come back, and I'll be there every morning and night after. I'm not going anywhere. I can't apologise any more than I already have."

"I know. I wasn't expecting you to."

"I can't prove you can trust me again if you don't give us another chance."

"I do forgive you, Cain. I believe you when you say you wanted to keep me safe. I just need to learn to trust that I'm making the right decision because I don't seem to be so good at that." She blushes, and I kiss her quickly.

"Don't hold me in regard to that fool." I mean Martin,

and her mouth twists with humour. "I'm the best decision you ever made," I declare teasingly.

"Even though it cost me my job, reputation, and nearly my——"

"Don't say life." I drop my head to hers and slam my eyes shut. "I still wake up sweating, thinking that you'd be gone when I arrived at the hospital."

"One day, we can laugh about it," Lauren murmurs.

"Not me, pretty girl," I vow softly. I clutch the keys in my palm, wrapping her own beneath to hand them over. Her eyes drop to my neck, and I'm certain she is watching how rapidly my pulse is beating. I swallow and clear my throat. "So, lunch?" I rush to change the subject, nauseous with the memory of her out cold in the hospital bed.

"I'd love to have lunch," she confirms, and I feel everything south of my neck sag in complete relief. I release her and nod, letting the keys transfer to her hands. She takes a moment to look at them and the open oak beams and the double-hung windows at the front of the house.

"Weddings?" Her nose wrinkles, unsure.

"Most hire a planner, or you can hire an events coordinator. Lauren, people warm to you. You're missed at the hotel. We don't need to open just yet. There's time," I reassure, threading our fingers together and walking us through to the kitchen, positioned to look out over the lake and countryside below.

"I don't know what to say."

"Say you'll come back to London with me?"

CHAPTER 37

Lauren

"Say you'll come back to London with me?" Cain's deep voice fans across the back of my neck, a teasing lilt disguising the desperation glowing from his eyes I witnessed just moments ago. He steps away and moves towards the industrial-style fridge. The physical distance only reinforces the bombshell he dropped when I arrived. He's going to leave. After all his efforts to close that distance between us, to break company policy and put us both at risk, he's taking a step back. Physically and mentally. Opening up the void to allow me to make the decision. This isn't a game of push and pull. There is a defined line that I've drawn, and he is crossing over to the other side and ensuring I do the work to pull us back in.

For all his reassurance, for the grandeur of his gesture, I can't shake the feeling that I'm about to let the best thing walk away from me.

I've known too much betrayal in the last few months, and rather than follow my gut instinct where this man was concerned, I allowed my fears and past traumas to manifest into punishment. I'm punishing us both. He hurt me, and I can't shy away from that. I don't think I will ever agree with how he decided to leave, but I understand why. I understand, and I accept we can't change it. It's a kind of pain I would accept to protect him, and I've spent many nights trawling through my thoughts and feelings to realise that his leaving hurt him too.

I've been so lost in my own pain that I didn't take the time to see that he is suffering greatly. He looks worn out, scared, and it's the same fear I saw in his eyes at the hospital. He's scared to lose me in a different way.

No one's ever looked at me that way, either. No man has loved me so passionately. So utterly devoted to my safety. My heart weeps for the hurt I've caused him—for pushing him away when he really did have my best interests at heart, even if it broke him to leave.

I watch his broad back as he fills out the fridge door and the slow, controlled breaths he takes, and I know I don't want another moment without him—another day apart. I don't want to roll over in my childhood bed, aching for the comfort of his arms or the solid wall of his chest to radiate heat into my back as he whispers gruffly in my ear. I want to come home from work and walk into a home that has him in it. To consider him when I'm out grocery shopping. I want the little things that no one cares about. The little moments that evoke those deep fuzzy feelings I only ever felt with Cain. I want to hear a stranger mention a word in passing and find myself drawn to a memory of this man because no matter who I'm with or where I am; he is always in the back of my mind. I want *that*. I want to be loved so irrevocably that he is willing to stab another knife into his own being to save it from happening to me.

"Okay," I say, rolling my lips as his back goes still, and he slowly slides a glass bottle back on the shelf before turning slowly to look at me.

"Okay?" His eyes bore into mine—asking more questions than his rough voice ever could. The fridge door clunks shut softly, and Cain makes a move towards me, then stops, waiting, needing clarification that I am, in fact, asking to go home with him.

I nod.

"Words, Lauren," he growls. Sucking in a small breath, I stare at his profile and feel the shift in him. That undeniable rush of dominance he exudes when he is determined to get his own way, the subtle lift of his chin, and the hard gleam in his eyes that refuses to accept anything less than what he desires. Me. His hand flexes, and I drop my gaze there, but he rams his hand in one pocket, and I can't help but ogle him and how sexy he looks in his suit.

"Oh, pretty girl, lift those eyes before I lose control." His voice wavers, and I lift my gaze and pin it to his as he grits his jaw tight enough to crack teeth. "Words. No noise. Just you and me. Say it."

"I want to come home, Cain," my voice trembles. Stored emotion overcomes me, and I lick my lips and swallow to stop from crying. Cain is at my front in record speed, tilting my face.

"Why are you crying?" He smoothes a tear into my skin, dragging his thumb down until he is running it along the plumb bow of my lip. I cup his hand, holding it still, and give him a watery smile. "Give me your pinky," he says, holding his own up in front of my face. I twist my hand so my finger is twined around his, and he grips our digits together tightly. His wide gaze is genuine and centred on me. "I'm breaking our promise. It's the only one I plan to break. We're making a new one," he delivers in a clipped and thoughtful manner.

"A new one?"

His lips quip at the edges, and he steps in to push me back

into the kitchen island. "I love you. I promise to say it to you every day, even on the days when we drive each other insane and we want to throttle each other."

"Even when you're being a prick?" I bite into my lower lip to suppress a smirk.

"That's when you like me the most, pretty girl." He flattens our thighs, and I feel the true meaning behind his words —his cock stabbing into my stomach signifies how much he likes that about me.

"I do." I hum as he pulls our fingers up to his lips and dots a little kiss on my pinky. "I'm sorry," I finally say, quietly and with complete conviction. I'm sorry for being so hard on him and degrading his character when I know he is better than Martin and Henrik—than Royce. He would never hurt me like they have.

"Lauren, we both fucked up. We hurt each other to protect ourselves. I'm glad I learned the lesson this early on. Never again," he vows and leans in to run his lips along mine. "You're my girl."

"You have a new home," I murmur into his mouth as he pecks my lips. I read that Carson Court had been returned to him. The penthouse isn't where he will be taking me. It will be like when I arrived in London months ago—foreign and all very new to me.

"*We*, pretty girl. *We* have a new home. It's waiting for you."

My lip trembles, and I nod. "I wish you'd have let me be there to support you, to be able to celebrate your win with you." Emotion clogs my throat.

"You did support me, but I never celebrated, Lauren. I've been clearing the path for you to come back. Let me take you home, and we can celebrate together."

"I missed you," I whisper as his hands cup my face and he kisses me sweetly. "Are we celebrating now?" I moan as he tilts my face away and runs his mouth along my jawline until he is nipping at the sensitive spot below my ear and sending a shockwave of shivers down my spine.

"We're celebrating," he confirms, delivering an open-mouthed kiss to my exposed neck. His teeth graze the skin, then sink in enough that I jolt and slam my palms to his chest, yelping softly. "I missed that sound." He chuckles, licking the sensitive spot until the angry throb is calmed.

"Ouch," I grumble, but my eyes are glowing with humour, and he soaks it up like a man starved, grinning wolfishly. "What happened to lunch?" I pout, knowing he has no intention of feeding me in the next hour.

He twists, pecks my lips, and then lowers to the floor on his knees and runs his hands up under the maxi dress I'm wearing until it's bunched around my waist so he can access my knickers and pull them down. He chews his lip, then drops his gaze to the apex of my thighs and smirks. "You smell fucking incredible, Lauren." Growling, he slides a palm between my legs so it is splayed over my bottom, and he can nudge me forward. I can feel the tickle of his breathing fanning over me.

"Cain." I gasp in need. He grins, swipes his tongue along my pussy and flicks at my clit. He repeats the same action over and over until my knees buckle, and he flattens the other hand over my stomach, holding me to the counter. He hums his approval, the vibration fluttering across my inner thigh. My head lolls back, and he begins again, one long lick followed by a precise flick that has my heart jerking in my chest. I anticipate the burst of pleasure to pop behind my breastbone when the hard flick comes, but instead, his teeth drag over my flesh, and I cry out, gripping his hair. He drives his tongue deep and fucks me with flat, wide strokes until I'm climaxing against his mouth. Cain laps it up, groaning and holding me still as he devours me with soft, open kisses.

"More," I whimper. It's something I have missed as much

as I have his presence. That tiny gap in time where he brings me so much pleasure I can't breathe for trying.

"Missed me?" He hums, his tone teasing. He licks and gently bites until I'm quivering and rocking my hips. He stands quickly, ignoring my whine, but instead slants his wet mouth over mine, forcing his tongue into my mouth, forcing me to taste what has kept him on his knees for this length of time. His eyes are alight with bright desire. "Words, Lauren."

He shakes his suit jacket off, leaving it to plop on the ground, and then he is yanking at his belt and hoisting my dress up and staring at my bare skin.

"Goddam, you're weeping. Lauren. Words," he demands, his movements jerky and rushed.

"Take me home. Take me."

"Yes, fuck." Cain shoves the material of my dress into my hands and grips my hips to lift me up, and then he is there, pressing the wide crown of his cock against my pussy. "Always resisting me," he huffs.

"It's because you're a big prick," I mewl as he applies pressure, and my body succumbs to the intrusion. Fire crackles, sparking and spreading over my skin, an intense swarm of emotion buzzing between us. Cain groans, dropping to watch as my body resists whilst pulling him in, slowly, inch by inch. His mouth drops open, and his eyes burn like a blue flame.

"I'm *your* prick. I love you," he sighs, sliding deeply and right to the hilt with a sharp twist of his hips. We moan in relief. The physical ache is soothed, and our lost hearts are reconnected.

I cup his face and urge his eyes up. "I love you," I gasp as he gently thrusts in and out. He leans to rest his forehead against mine.

"Welcome home, pretty girl."

"Don't ruin the moment." I fight a smile, and his full lips twist into an intimate smile, swivelling and sliding back in so my mouth pops open in a silent moan.

"This is home. You. Me. Us." Love radiates from his eyes —big hands hold me still, and the sense of calm and safety I feel only adds to the desire coursing through me. "I just need you."

Cain grunts, pumping in and out in languid strokes. Heavy but soft swirls of pleasure roll through my body, sliding like hot oil until all of my skin is coated in the sensation. "Me and you, pretty girl. I don't care where we are or who we are with. It's just me and you. It's home."

My eyes water and I drop to kiss his mouth, swirling my tongue in at the same pace he is setting between my thighs. "Home," I agree.

Cain wraps his arms around me, anchoring me to his chest, sliding to grip a handful of hair as he rocks us both to a long, slow orgasm. I cry out, holding him close, tilting my hips as he settles himself deeply, murmuring into my mouth, whispering at how good I feel. Our skin is damp, our eyes heavy, and his mouth latches to mine to kiss me into the most blissful comedown. He kisses me long after he has slipped out, long after I feel tears of joy slip free and coat my cheeks, tears he kisses away.

"Is there time to pull out of the sale?" I wonder. He doesn't need to do this for me. I'm coming home. The farm isn't necessary.

"I like the farm. Don't you want it?" He shifts to sort himself out, zipping his trousers and moving back in as he tugs my dress to cover me. I rest my arms on his shoulder and link my fingers behind his neck.

"It's stunning, but I'm coming home. I don't want it to be wasted money." I worry, but I will be sad to see it go. It's a gorgeous location, and the thought of bringing families together and being part of so many special moments in this picturesque setting gives me a warm, fuzzy feeling. A feeling Cain gives me.

Rural wedding venues are a dime a dozen, but I'd like to

think I could bring something new to the table. An intimate, luxury family wedding retreat. It's the kind of place I would want to secure myself to this man, to watch as he slides a thick band of love on my finger, with one of his devious and knowing grins I adore, before he loves me with a sweet kiss.

"You don't need to be based here. You can work from London and commute when needed. Lauren, this place will flourish under you. Let me do this for you. It's not wasted, not when it makes your eyes fire up with ideas like they are now."

"They are not." I pout, and Cain ducks to kiss me.

He laughs. "Oh, they are. You are already picturing how it will look." He turns me so we are staring out over the manicured lawns and the small fountain spraying water in the pond. "You can more than do this. It's a business, so delegate and give your unique touch to it. People love you, Lauren. *I* love you. Lindel Farm is the beginning of our new life."

When he puts it like that, it's hard not to be romanced by the beauty of the surroundings and the future we can build together.

"Can we look around properly?" I ask, resting my chin on his forearm.

"We can. Let's eat, then we can look around and collect some things from your parents before we head back to the city."

CHAPTER 38

Cain

Lauren relaxes in the seat as we cruise through London. She is smiling as she looks out of the window, and I can't pull my eyes away from the sense of peace she is radiating. I feel it too, pretty girl. Reaching for her hand, I secure it in mine and rest it on my thigh.

I fucking feel it too, right down to the dark corner of my heart that bled for so long.

She's a beacon of light—a blinding and unwavering force that I can call my own—call my home. I'm addicted to her calm and madly in love with the fire she brings. It has cauterised my internal wounds, healing me from the inside out until the only thing I can feel is her.

Her eyes swivel to meet mine, sensing I'm looking at her. Her cheeks flush, and her lips twist in a way that I only witness when she is looking my way. "Thank you for inviting my parents. It will be good to have them visit in a few weeks. I think they are happy to be shot of me," she drawls, amused, sliding sunglasses perched in her hair down onto her nose.

"They want you to be happy."

"They do." She sighs, rolling her neck to stare as the familiar streets rise above us. Perry should already be back in London by now, and I'm hoping he has picked up my message about dinner. I know Amberley and Matteo are free later. I want to surprise Lauren, bring us all back together, and make her first night extra special. I'm not the only person she has missed.

"And are you?" I find myself asking, even though I know the answer as surely as I know myself.

Lauren smiles warmly at me intimately. "I am. Very." I lift our threaded fingers and kiss hers. "Tell me about this house. You grew up there?" she asks, shifting to face me. My hair drops forward, and she leans to sweep it back. "How does it feel to have it back?" Her attentiveness never fails to make me feel centred. It's an unmatchable power when you've lived a life of hate and hurt.

I sigh deeply. How does it feel?

Until I get her there, I can't answer that.

"I did," I confirm. "My father bought the place when I was a small boy. Securing it feels good. But it's not home. Not yet." I wink at her, and she bites her lip. "I expected to feel elated when Royce was sentenced, to be calm, satisfied, smug even, when I won it all back." I shrug, changing gear and shaking my head. "I couldn't. I was hurting too damn much, and maybe, had we never met, I might have felt like that, but I just wanted you back. So, ask me again when you're waddling around with your belly swollen with our baby and a ring on that finger, and I'll tell you how I feel." I lay out my intentions as clear as day. My eyes convey my thoughts. I want it all, Lauren. Everything.

The proverbial picket fence, the big house, and family.

Happy kids and a beautiful wife. I want everything that was ripped from me.

Her breath catches, and she swallows slowly. "Those are some serious plans, Mr," she says softly, her eyes widening, but the twinkle of hope in them has me pulling her fingers back up for another kiss.

"Do you have a better one?" I muse, indicating down my street and rolling to a stop just before the high gates. "Because when I get you behind those gates, I plan to be either inside or next to you at all times. You're my end goal." My thumb runs over her ring finger, and she watches, fascinated and like me, picturing life past the pain.

"Your plan has potential," she teases, leaning to run her hand up my thigh, and I grip it as Kat pushes out the main gate. She stops short when she clocks us, and her face breaks into a surprised but tense smile.

"Lauren!" It's the first burst of emotion I've witnessed from my sister in some time. Lauren shoots me a concerned look. Kat is carrying a black cloud around with her, and, despite her cheerful manner, it shows in how she conducts herself and the vacant look in her eyes.

"She's struggling," I say subtly as Lauren reaches for the handle, but I lower the window because I want to drive her through the gates.

"Hi, Kat."

"So you're back?" The clipped tone has Lauren's shoulder dropping in hurt. I grip her thigh and narrow my eyes at my sister, who has spent most of her time glowering at us all. She's not been the same since our mother slapped her, but even more so since her father was arrested and their lies broke out into the world, disabling everything she once knew. She'd disappeared within herself. I don't know how to reach her because she now has her own demons to fight. I've eradicated mine and delivered them to her door.

I've broken a fundamental part of her, and I haven't a clue how to get it back.

"Yes," Lauren says slowly, clearly put out by Kat's rude welcome.

"Good." Kat nods and then steps back to allow me through as the gates finally open all the way, and Lauren can see Carson Court set back in the drive. "I've got work. See you later." Dropping her head, she walks down the street, and Lauren watches her go, confused.

"Don't take it personally. She is angry at everyone. She's hurting."

"She lives with you?"

"With us. I should have said. It's her home too. I couldn't ask her to leave."

Lauren nods, watching as my sister's hunched shoulders move away from us. "Do you think she's worried it will change now I'm here?" She twists to look back at me. Her lip is sucked into her mouth, where she chews it in worry.

"Hey," I tug her lip free. "No. She is out more than she is home. It's no longer the place we both grew up to love. It holds as many bad memories as it does good. For us both," I affirm as Lauren works her hands in her lap. "Nothing feels normal to her right now, and she despises the place as much as she needs the refuge. I'm hoping, in time, she finds herself again."

Lauren hums in agreement, clearly unsure and worried about Kat's mental state. I squeeze her hand, trying to pull her back to the now, to us, and her face twists until she is staring at the colonial mansion.

"It's stupidly big," she scoffs, caught off-guard by its size.

I can't help but laugh at her tone.

"So, this is home?" She is equally in awe as she is shocked. I nod, crunching over the drive and pulling up out front beside Deeks's car. "How do you even fill a place this big?" she asks, seemingly confused.

"You don't like it?" I laugh, uncertainty lacing my tone as she leans to peer up at the building. The white columns are as thick as trees. The colonial roof and wrap-around, a stark dark grey slate against the light wash walls.

"I... I was just expecting something smaller." Her laugh is light and stunned. "It's really beautiful, Cain. Not what I expected, but beautiful. More than beautiful," she murmurs as Deeks exits the side gate, accessing the security lounge. "Hey!" Lauren chirps happily, waving as the big, bald fucker heads our way.

"Hey, girl! Glad to have you back." He ambles over as I exit and walk around the bonnet to help Lauren. She flings her arms around the dodgy guy's neck and breathes in deeply. He folds her in a brotherly hug, lifting her off the ground. "Need help with your bags?"

"You work here?" My girl pulls back, looking between us both.

Deeks snorts, lowering her to my side. "Don't give the man ideas. I like my freedom." He grunts, moving to pop the boot and pull out the few bags Lauren packed. Deeks is far from a free man. You don't get as high in the food chain of crime as he is without making enemies or working for someone danger-ous. He is as cagey about his connections as he is devoted to looking out for Lauren.

"He's checking you're okay," I inform Lauren, and Deeks gives her a once over and levels me with a hard stare. We may not agree on much, but we have one thing in common, and it's enough mutuality to forget the rest.

"I'm okay," she assures him when he works his neck. "I needed a breather, Deeks. It got a bit too much, but I'm good, really good." Lauren steps back into my chest, and I drop my chin on top of her head.

"That's all I need to hear." He heaves her bags up and walks them towards the door.

"I'm sorry!" she shouts, and he stops and frowns back at

her, his eyes shielded from the sun. "For leaving that night and not telling you I was going." My hand flexes on her hip—she's talking about the accident. Her being wired up in hospital rips through my mind, and I shift uncomfortably at the reminder. He blames me for all her pain. I happen to agree with him, but it's no use telling him. It doesn't ease his anger. Kelvin Deeks is not the kind of man I wanted in my pocket, but where Lauren is concerned, he is the only man I need. He has loitered at Carson Court for her return, working to ensure no one was a threat to Lauren. I suspect he will keep tabs, even now she is home.

"*You* have nothing to be sorry about. I'll put these inside. Moneybags can take them upstairs." He juts his chin at me, and I snort.

"He'll warm to you." Lauren smiles apologetically, twisting to wrap her arms around my neck.

"He cares about you. That's all I give a shit about," I admit. "I don't need him to like me. He's not from good people, Lauren, but he's good to you and, in turn, me. It's enough." Her brows furrow and I run my finger across the line, smoothening it out. She knows just as well as I do that Kelvin Deeks is involved with the kind of people she would cross the road to avoid. She's damn lucky he took such a shine to her. Her good nature and air of innocence, despite being able to hold her own, has put her under the wing of a man who breaks bread with the worst of them. I narrow my gaze as I watch the big guy head inside with her bags. Lauren must sense the tension in me because she leans up and pecks my lips, pulling my attention back to her. I slide my palms over her bottom and tug her flush to me.

"Is it silly for me to ask to be carried over the threshold?" Her eyes twinkle, her cheeks heating a little. She feels silly, and I don't want that. Pecking her lips, I shake my head. No, it's not silly. It's what she deserves.

"It was what I planned until Kat and Deeks stomped all

over it with their sour moods." I swing her into my arms and make my way to the main doors. "Welcome home, pretty girl," I hum as I step inside. The two-storey foyer is gleaming, the handrails of the staircase glinting under the chandelier as it reflects light from the long windows. Justine has taken it upon herself to order flowers each week, and the light pink and white arrangement sits proudly on the centre table.

"Cain," she exclaims, whispering softly, her fingers rising to her lips as she looks around. "I can't believe you grew up here."

"Let me show you around." I hold out my hand, flexing my spread fingers, encouraging her to take it. She does, her smaller palms folding and linking us together. Her neck swings each way, peering through open doors and up at the second-floor landing.

Deeks appears as we move towards the room to our left. "I'll call you later. I have an errand to run." He passes us, dipping to peck Lauren's cheek, picking his jacket up on the way out and leaving us in peace. Alone. No noise. Just us.

"This is the formal living room," I announce, pushing the door wide for us to step in, and Lauren hums approvingly, taking in the ornate furnishing and looking down to my father's bar in the far corner.

"And what does one do in a formal living room?" She is terrible at disguising her humour, and I squeeze her ribs playfully.

"Quit being smart." I close the space between us and bite her shoulder softly. "One will be fucking in here lots," I inform in a rough murmur. Her gasp doesn't go unnoticed, no matter how quickly she tries to swallow it back.

She steps away, putting a little distance between us. "Just in here?" she wants to know, twisting to stare at me through her lashes, sultry and playful.

"No, not just in here," I respond. "*Everywhere.*"

"That's a lot of rooms," she ponders, running her fingers

back and forth over the sideboard. The cherry wood picks up her light skin and reflects it back at me. I can't wait to get my lips back on her and see the small pink blemishes that my stubble and teeth cause.

"Over eighteen thousand square feet." I grin.

"Minus Kat's space."

"Minus that."

"Are we just going to stay in here and talk about fucking, or are you going to keep showing me around?" Her brow quips, and my heart thuds with excitement. Adrenaline scatters along my spine and sends my dick into overdrive. I want her, and I drop my gaze and let her know it.

"Cain." She breathes lightly, her fingers shaking in their path across the glossy wood.

Clearing my throat, I nod her towards the door. "Follow me." I side-step, showing my intention, but I keep my gait small, allowing her to make the final move. Waiting for her to essentially decide our next move.

"Where?" She's breathless, and her cheeks are pink with desire.

"Master bedroom—the tour can wait."

She moves fast, pouncing on me and slamming her mouth against mine. "You're a terrible host," she punctuates between desperate kisses.

"And you're a fucking incredible one." I laugh, taking the stairs two at a time. We have all the time in the world to look around the house. The impact of her body thumping into my chest is cathartic. Like a wave crashing against the shore, only I soak it into my skin. Swallow her whole. Cupping her face, I hold her out of reach, separating our lips as I enter our room. My eyes hold, and I can see the same relief in hers.

We came out the other side, no matter the pain.

"I know." She smiles. "I know." My breath shudders out as I keep my emotions in check.

"Words, Lauren."

Soft lips sweep across mine. "I love you."

I want to pinch myself. All those nights, lost and angry. Days where I felt helpless and full of fucking rage, and she stepped into my life like a beam of light and cut right through me. Then it became about the hours—how many until I could see her, how few before we had to part ways and keep hiding —how many until she could forgive me.

Too many hours lost waiting to get her back and not nearly enough left to love her.

But she's here. My girl. Home.

"I love you too, pretty girl."

EPILOGUE

Lauren

"Have you seen my cream bikini, the one with the gold ties?" I call out to Cain as I pick up a towel and a pair of his shorts in search of it. He steps out of the bathroom, a towel wrapped around his waist, and holds it up for me. "Koh Samui me is messy." I grimace and cross the room to him.

"You're messy back home." He smirks, dipping to drop a kiss on my forehead. I pull back to disagree, but he pinches my chin lightly and lifts his brow. "No? There is foundation smudged on the carpet in several places, you leave sugar after making a drink, and if I find another hairpin, I could start selling them," he drawls when I pout.

"Okay, I'm messy," I concede, and his grin turns devious. He takes a step back and looks down at me, standing only in knickers, and runs a finger to trace along the seam resting against my stomach.

"Koh Samui you is fucking gorgeous."

"Stop. We're meeting everyone for breakfast. I can hear it

being set up on the decking." I lay a palm on his bare chest, but Cain pushes against it, challenging the resistance in my arm. My wrist folds back lightly, and he grunts under his breath, his eyes flickering with heat. "Cain," I warn.

"You'd better be quiet then," he counters, knocking his towel away and stepping out of the fluffy heap at his feet. "Better make sure you're a good girl for me and let me swallow those moans."

He's rock hard, and I don't mistake the way he flexes his fist to stop from reaching for me already.

"Perry will be here any second."

"He's learnt to knock," Cain muses, his lips twisting to fight a wolfish grin. He steps forward, so I take another back —forward, then back until my calves brush the bed, and I'm lowering to the mattress, Cain looming over me. His finger hooks under the front of my knickers, granting him space to slide his hand in and twist it, and he moves to massage my clit, causing me to grip his arms for support. "Shush."

"We both know I can't be quiet," I spit, darting a look towards the curtain-covered doors leading out onto the private decking by the pool.

"Then they'll definitely know to knock," he groans. He swoops down and kisses me hard and with purpose. His fingers dip between my legs and slip inside. My first moan is low and sweet, my face twisting in pleasure. "You look so good when you're aroused, pretty girl, half pain, half pleasure." He spanks my pussy and drives two fingers back in, and my second moan slips out in a surprised cry. My stomach flutters, and I know it's not just down to the man primed above me, hard and ready. I bite my lip and fight the urge to blurt out my little secret. He'll be mad as hell for not telling him. Mad and madly in love.

I reach to cup his cheek, and Cain frowns, taking my hand and holding it. "What?" He's worried. His frown line deepens, and I rock my hips, chasing the orgasm I can feel pebbling my skin from the inside out. A low thrumming ache that is rolling through me in deep, long, slow waves.

"Don't stop."

"You're worried. I can tell." He makes to move away, but I grip his hand and hold it still, riding his fingers.

"After, please," I beg him to continue, and he does until I'm wordlessly crying out and holding him to my chest.

"Lauren, what's wrong?"

"Nothing, it—"

A sharp bang at the window has us jumping to cover up. "Lovebirds, come on!" Perry calls as silhouettes move behind the curtain. Cain grumbles as our friends arrive for breakfast, their chatter filtering through the partially open door.

"I did warn you." I giggle, and Cain rises up and helps me to my feet.

"He's a pest."

"You invited them!" I laugh, slipping out of my knickers and pulling my bikini and a cover-up on.

"We're hungry!" Perry calls.

"Fuck off!" Cain snaps, walking to slam the door shut. Laughter sounds outside, and I grin as he pulls on some swim trunks and stands in front of me. "Tell me," he pleads, hands resting on my hips so he can stare down at me.

"After. It's nothing to worry about. You'll like it," I assure, knowing full well he will push until I unravel and share the news. News that will make this holiday all the more special.

"Okay." He nods, surprising me, so now I frown. What's he hiding?

"You tell me?" I demand, and he grins knowingly at me. It only adds to my curiosity. Shaking his head, he collects up his things and opens the door.

"Absolutely not. Let's get breakfast." Cain chuckles and walks out, leaving me scowling after him.

"Cain!" I shout him back, racing after him. He appears in the doorway, arms braced as he peeps through the curtain.

"You'll like it, pretty girl. Your heart is going to burst, and I can't wait to watch your gorgeous face when I tell you." I search his eyes, deep but bright blues, a perfect contradiction to the rolling sea in the backdrop. There is an odd energy about him, something ebbing below the surface. I hadn't noticed it early or had confused it with arousal, but it's there now. Fluctuating between us, a ball of electricity circling us both. I find my smile matching his own, and he shakes his head in happiness. "You're going to love it." He disappears, and I laugh, following him outside.

The table is full, and our friends are already filling their plates with fresh fruit and delicacies from the local market. I find a seat next to Amberley, across from Cain, who lounges back, smiling at me. I peek at Perry, whose eyes are alight with mischief.

"Am I missing something?" Amberley leans to whisper as she reaches for the plate of mango.

"You and me both," I muse, taking the plate off her. "Cain is acting weird."

"Perry and Matteo were being secretive on the way over. They're probably planning to dunk us in the pool or some-thing." She shrugs, scowling at the men who are watching us both.

"Kat not joining us?" I ask, wondering where she is. "Shall I go check on her?"

"Headache," Perry blurts quickly, his face showcasing a look of guilt. I tilt my head, and he clears his throat and rams a piece of orange in his mouth, refusing to meet my eye.

"Where's this island we're going to?" Matteo interrupts, reaching across to put watermelon on Amberley's plate. He's done it every day since we arrived, and when I questioned her about it, she played dumb, but I can feel the tension brewing between them—the whole group can. It's a heavy unspoken weight resting on all of our shoulders. Matt is in knots over her, and she has him at arm's length, has us all at arm's length, about it. For all my prying, she is tight-lipped. It's unlike her. She picks up the fruit and nibbles the end, resting back in her chair and staring out across the sea.

"It's a short boat ride over the bay and takes around ten minutes," Cain informs us all, his eyes on me. "Sunan will be loading the boat. Once we eat, we can head to the beach."

"Tell me," I mouth, and his lips sweep up in a playful quip. He shakes his head and bites into a croissant. Prick. I mouth that too, and he chuckles in his seat, leaning back to reach under the table and knock my foot with his own.

⁓

A little while later, we are set up on the beach. A cabana keeps us shaded, but I've moved to soak up the sun. Matt, Perry, and Kat are playing volleyball, and Amberley is reading a magazine. We spent the morning snorkelling and lounging on the private beach on an island close to the resort. It's the same beach Cain and I visited when we last came to Thailand. I run my fingers over my stomach as I watch Cain swimming a few yards out in the sea. His mind is as burdened as my own. I'm nervous and giddy with excitement, although since I've found out he has some news, I want to hold off telling him my own. He wades out of the water, dragging a hand through his hair and wiping his face free of water. "You're going to burn," he scolds, and I grin, holding my hand up to shade the light beaming down on us.

"Put cream on me?"

"Sure, let me get my towel." He flicks a nervous glance up the beach, and I frown, biting my lip as the guys begin to make their way back down the beach to us. Is he still nervous about the paparazzi? It was a big worry before we left London. Cain wanted complete privacy for our holiday. He drops his towel between our legs and straddles me, caking his hands in cream and begins gliding it up and down my limbs.

"Good swim?"

"It was."

"Are you okay?" Tilting my head, I watch him, wondering what's got under his skin.

"Pretty girl, I couldn't be better." I blink at him and the shadow forming on his sharp jawline. His eyes are eclectic in this light, and I smile at how handsome he is. How happy he is.

Maybe I'm worrying for no reason. Maybe my anxiety about the press is muddling my brain, or maybe it's hiding the truth from him that is making me imagine all sorts. "Okay. good."

"You?" He smiles, massaging my arms and rubbing the cream in. His chest is defined and wide, and I run a finger up the flat display of muscle.

"Hands to yourself." He tells me off, his lips widening when I chew my lip playfully. He moves his hands to my stomach, adding more cream. The cold liquid hits my waist, and I gasp in shock. "Cold?"

"Yes." I laugh, trying to look, but he is already smearing it in. It's thick and covers me like a second skin. "That will never soak in!" I'm laughing. My head tipped back as his fingers begin scrawling over my stomach.

"It's not supposed to," he replies softly. His finger shakes as he grips my hip—something about his tone is off. I frown, and he is watching me with wide and focused eyes.

"Oh my god!" Amberley gushes. I snap around, but she is looking at us, her hands grasped to her mouth. I spin to Cain and follow his eye-line to look down at my stomach.

The words *Marry me?* are etched into the cream, my bronzed skin rich against the white liquid. I gawp, my eyes fill, and then he is reaching below the towel and pulling out a ring box, popping the lid back and branding an emerald cut ring to me. I can't move, but somehow my hand reaches to touch my stomach. It feels like he is asking us both, unknowingly speaking to the little secret growing inside of me. "I loved you before I loved myself, Lauren. *You* loved me before I loved myself. I don't want another day where you're not my wife. I would marry you this afternoon if you'd allow it." Cain's voice breaks, and he clears it before reaching for my shaking hand, the ring poised.

"Be my wife?" he asks, waiting for my answer.

I nod, at first, too overcome with emotion.

"Words, Lauren." Cain swallows emotionally.

"Yes." I choke, tears slipping free. The cold band slides into place, heavy and smooth. "Yes!" I jump up and kiss him through my tears. "Yes." I nod against his grinning mouth.

Liquid rains down over us, and Perry stands to the side, spraying champagne.

"Finally, I thought you'd chickened out!" He chortles, shaking the bottle as bubbles spurt from the end. Cain cups my face and kisses me deeply. Amberley is crying and gushing behind me as Perry swings an arm around Kat's neck, tugging her to his side as they congratulate us.

"At least Lindel Farm can get some use." He pokes gently, and my mouth drops open. I swat his arm, and his cheeky laugh accompanies my own.

"I have bookings!" Pouting, I dip out of the way of his kiss, but he flattens me to the sand, kissing me roughly.

"One," he accuses jokingly. "Beryl and Albert don't count."

"They're the cutest couple."

"I beg to differ. I know a cuter pair." Cain pecks my mouth and shifts to rest on his knees.

I wriggle to balance on my arms, tilting my head to shade from the sun. "Anyway, how does it feel?" I whisper, blinking champagne from my lashes, my cheeks aching from smiling so widely.

"How does what feel?" He pouts, running a thumb along my lips.

I hold my hand up, giving it a little wiggle. "You told me to ask you again when I had a ring on this finger, and my stomach was swollen, so how does it feel?"

I'm smiling for a different reason now, and Cain's eyes pop wide, then drop to my stomach. He flattens a palm to my cream-covered skin.

"You're sure?"

Nodding, I confirm. "Yes, ten weeks." I wrap my arms around his neck. "I wanted to tell you so badly, but I wasn't sure until we arrived. I had an inkling."

"I feel like I've won the life lottery," he murmurs throatily.

"You're pregnant!" Matteo gasps, surprised, and I nod. "Congratulations." He rips the champagne free from Perry, shaking it to cover us as more whoops of joy fill the air.

"I love you." My voice catches, and Cain topples us back.

"I love you both, pretty girl. I love you both."

The End.

ALSO BY A. R. THOMAS

Stolen Hours (Coming 2023)

Escape The Light

The Whiskey Promises Series

The Panel Novella

Join My Reader Group!

Confessions Of A Smut Addict - A. R. Thomas' Reader Group

Want to be kept up to date with upcoming releases then subscribe to my newsletter.

https://dashboard.mailerlite.com/forms/436452/87905851521632159/share

Acknowledgments

If you've continued reading this far, then, well... Thank you!

If you know me by now, then you know I love angsty, messy romance. I want flawed characters who don't always do the right thing or make the right decision. I want three-dimensional characters that are packed with more than perfection. I want their faults. Enter Cain because we all know he messes up more than once and acts without thought. He is heart heavy, and I loved writing his and Lauren's story, but mostly, I love that you want to read them!

So, thank you!

Thank you to Jessica Grace for being my go-to girl on the days I'm not feeling like myself and for reading whatever drivel I send your way.

To my betas for helping sharpen After Hours into the story it is!

The biggest and most deserved thank you to Jasmine, my PA (I feel odd saying that... You're my friend first. How dare you live across the ocean!) I know you love Cain as much as I do, and I appreciate your time and support. God knows I bloody need it! LOL.

To ForgetYouNot.Designs for my gorgeous graphics! You are so talented, and I hope you know that.

Thank you to Claire Allmendinger, my editor. This is the third book you have worked on with me, and I still get nervous sending my manuscript across, but you're the sweetest soul, and I appreciate all your help.

Katie Lowrie, you are more than just a proofreader. You're an encyclopaedia... I have no idea where you store all that knowledge! Thank you for being there for all my silly questions.

And lastly, to everyone in between who has helped make this book happen!

ABOUT THE AUTHOR

A. R. Thomas is an indie author from England. She lives with her son, and when she's not screaming from the sidelines at his latest sporting event, she is usually lost to the thought of a book. She manages to make the most innocent of things sound dirty; it's both a gift and a curse, but thankfully her friends encourage her.

Connect with A. R. Thomas on social media

Printed in Great Britain
by Amazon

32915024R00231